ENJOY
THE
VIEW

SARAH
MORGENTHALER

D0089484

sourcebooks
casablanca

Published by Sourcebooks Casablanca, an imprint of Sourcebooks
P.O. Box 4410, Naperville, Illinois 60567-4410
(630) 961-3900
sourcebooks.com

Library of Congress Cataloging-in-Publication Data

Names: Morgenthaler, Sarah, author.
Title: Enjoy the view / Sarah Morgenthaler.
Description: Naperville, Illinois : Sourcebooks Casablanca, [2021] |
   Series: Moose Springs, Alaska ; book 3
Identifiers: LCCN 2020035778 | (paperback}
Subjects: GSAFD: Love stories.
Classification: LCC PS3613.O74878 E55 2021 | DDC 813/.6--dc23

LC record available at https://lccn.loc.gov/2020035778

Printed and bound in the United States of America.
SB 10 9 8 7 6 5 4 3 2 1

For Kyle. The mountains I climb will always be for you.

CHAPTER 1

PICKING UP HITCHHIKERS NEVER WORKED out for Easton Lockett. It would start fine, but then things always got really weird, really fast.

There'd been the guy who peed in his truck. And the teenage kid who barfed in it. The worst had been the old lady who kept hitting him with her cane until he gave her his phone. You'd think being robbed at cane-point would have been a lesson learned, but here he was, slowing down…again.

The problem was, when a man like Easton saw a woman walking along the road outside the city limits of Moose Springs, Alaska, with suitcase in hand, he couldn't keep on driving past. Especially when the closest phone was a ten-mile hike through curving mountain roads, and she was going the wrong direction.

Easton pulled his old, faded red truck up next to her and hit the hazard lights. Stretching across the front bench seat to crank a manual window handle was easier for Easton than most. At six foot six, there was little the professional mountaineer couldn't reach. He didn't want to frighten her—a strange man arriving unannounced on the side of the road when she was all alone—so he tried for a pleasant smile. The beard would hide it, but the effort was there.

"Do you need any help, ma'am?"

The instant Easton opened his mouth, she wheeled on him. Tilted sideways from the weight of her suitcase, she threw her free hand up in apparent disgust.

"You've *got* to be kidding me."

Now, for the record, he'd had a very pleasant morning. Pleasant wake up, pleasant breakfast, pleasant trip into town to see his friends. Pleasant drive down the Turnagain Arm, a few miles below the speed limit. The kind of morning that made a guy relax in his seat and think, *Yep, got life handled.*

The fist on her hip as she glared at him said *Nope, not handled at all.*

Easton rubbed his neck awkwardly below the bun he'd twisted his hair into. "You looked like you might need a ride," he hedged.

Her eyes narrowed at him suspiciously. "Don't think I'm oblivious, buddy. I know what you and your lackeys are up to. You're messing with us on purpose."

Easton had absolutely no idea what to say to that. He couldn't tell much about her from the way she was bundled up, except no one he knew would be wearing a jacket in early July. This woman was dressed as if it were winter, wrapped in layers from head to toe with only her nose and glacier-blue eyes poking out above her scarf.

"My lackeys?"

"Minions, flunkies, those with whom you're in cahoots. Trust me, I *know.*"

Easton's response was squeakier than what he'd hoped for when opening his mouth. "There's no cahoots."

"Sure." She obviously didn't believe him one bit. "You know, out here on this road, everyone is *so* helpful and wonderful and keeps stopping." She gestured in the direction of Moose Springs. "Which would be great back there, where everyone has been awful. I've found the nexus of evil in the nicest state in the country."

"I wouldn't call us a nexus," Easton defended. "Maybe more of a node."

"Great, the last one was a creep, and this one is a thesaurus. Jessie, what is wrong with this place?"

The woman dropped her suitcase to the ground. She pushed back the hood of her jacket, revealing sweat-dampened auburn hair tucked beneath a white winter-appropriate headband. If he'd been wrapped up like a burrito in seventy-degree heat, Easton would have been sweating too. Doubtful he'd look as striking as this stranger did though.

"Sorry to correct you, ma'am, but my name isn't Jessie."

"I never said it was." She gave him a frustrated look. "What can I do for you, now that my shot is ruined? *Again.*"

Never a big talker, Easton wasn't used to explaining himself. But he hadn't gotten a look like this one since he'd used his twin sister's favorite Cabbage Patch Kid as a way to teach himself physics.

What came up was bound to come down, no matter how high he catapulted the sucker with a rubber hose and two pine trees.

Easton cleared his throat, concentrating on speaking with his normal, deeper tone. No more squeaking. "I saw you on the side of the road. I thought you might need a ride or a phone to make a call for one."

"Right, I'm sure." Her voice dripped with sarcasm. "It's not going to work. The road is state property, and no one can kick us out of here."

Oh yes, she was ready to fight. Both hands on her hips now, the stunning redhead glared at him as if she could make him talk through force of eyeball violence alone. Which she probably could if he'd been up to no good. But he wasn't, so he didn't. Staring right back, Easton wondered how he had gotten himself in trouble so fast. Normally, it took a few months of a woman getting to know him before he had her so riled up.

"I really don't understand what you mean, ma'am."

Those ice-blue eyes narrowed at him, as if she were trying to see right through him. Then finally she sighed, shaking her head.

"No, you probably don't. You're probably the one guy all morning who wasn't an evil minion. The light was perfect, you know," she lamented, quicksilver emotions going from angry to disappointed. "The road was gorgeous, except everyone keeps *stopping*."

Aware he'd lost control of the situation here, Easton chose his words carefully. "I could always back up a few, if that helps?"

A slender hand flapped dismissively at him. "No, it's fine. It's already ruined."

Easton prided himself on being a relatively intelligent individual, but he had absolutely no idea what she was talking about.

She tilted her head to the side. "What? Jessie, I can't hear you. Reception is awful up here."

And she thought she was talking to someone. Great.

"Jessie. Jessie, I can't—and he's gone." A curse escaped her lips, and the frustrated stamp of her foot was dangerously close to being cute.

"I'm going to call someone to help you."

Easton kept one eye on her as he picked up the handheld CB radio in his truck, flipping over to the channel he knew the local police monitored. There were limits on the range of his CB, but Jonah—the head officer of Moose Springs' two-person police force—was known to drive the highway outside town to get a change of scenery. It was worth the effort to try.

"Hey, Jonah? I've got a lady out here on the highway just past Hunt Road who could use your help."

A crackle, then the officer's voice came on. "Is it an emergency? I've got a moose stuck in a swing set I'm dealing with."

"Not an emergency." Easton eyed the woman, who eyed him back. "I might need someone more official than myself for this one though."

"Let me try to—" Jonah broke off, then he muttered, "And there goes the teeter-totter. East, I'll call you back."

"Who are you talking to?" She looked at him suspiciously.

"A nice man who'll come give you a ride to Anchorage," Easton told her. "He'll take you somewhere with people who'll help you better than I can."

"Are you crazy?"

"Ma'am, I'm not the one talking to invisible people and ranting about minions."

"I'm not talking to invisible people. I'm *arguing* with invisible people who should have switched phone providers like I told them before we left." She turned toward the hill ahead of them, yelling, "Like I told you, Jessie."

Easton shook his head, amazed at his own bad luck. "Listen, I can't leave you out here."

"Fine." With a disgusted snort, she grabbed her suitcase and swung it over the side of the truck bed. It landed with a heavy, uneven thump.

"What's in there?" he asked.

"Rocks." Climbing into the passenger side of his truck, the woman pulled her scarf free from her mouth. At his dubious look, she frowned back. "What?"

"You've been walking down the side of the road carrying a suitcase full of rocks, and you think I'm the crazy one?"

A smirk was her only reply to his question. Instead, she pointed ahead of them. "You see that access road higher up the mountain? Can you give me a ride up there?"

Technically, he could. But it was a small winding mountain road, and he couldn't think of a reason why a stranger to town would be headed that direction.

"Are you sure you wouldn't rather go to Moose Springs?"

"My film crew is up there, and I can't hear them on the ear mic anymore. Since you and the last four you's that stopped to give me a ride have ruined this shot all morning, I need to talk to my coproducer. Is it me, or is it a thousand degrees in here?"

At which point she began to strip.

Easton usually didn't have a huge issue with attractive women who wanted to take their clothes off in his presence, but this one was making him nervous. As she shed layer after layer, the woman craned her head to evaluate his vehicle.

"Nice truck. I'm a Dodge girl myself, but there's something about these old Fords that I always liked."

Yes. Trucks. Easton could talk trucks. Trucks were a much easier topic of conversation than why she had a suitcase of rocks. "It used to be my dad's."

"1982?" she asked.

"'83."

His passenger shrugged out of her sweatshirt, revealing her tank top beneath. For some reason, she kept the scarf on. "Dual gas tanks really make a truck a truck, huh? And it helps with the crappy gas mileage."

Who was this woman? She was simultaneously insulting his baby while giving him an unwanted strip show. "The gas mileage isn't crappy." He'd just not look her way. Yep, staring at the road.

"It's not *not* crappy." She waved a hand over her overheated, flushed cheeks. "Can you turn the air conditioner on? I'm melting over here."

"Why would you wear so many layers in the middle of summer?"

"Because my outfit was fine for this morning, when the windchill was fifty degrees and Bree mic'd me. But now it's boiling hot, and we should have been done hours ago."

"The air conditioner doesn't work."

Closing her eyes in frustration, his passenger dropped her head back on the seat. "Of course it doesn't. This *is* a Ford."

"I'll try to bring a better truck next time," he murmured.

One eye opened, and the prettiest grin he'd ever seen on a woman flashed at him.

"If there is a next time," she told him archly. "I am luring you into the woods, you know."

See? Right there. It always had to get weird.

In hindsight, River Lane probably should have kept her temper better. If she had, she might have thought twice before stuffing herself in the passenger seat next to a man whose head nearly touched the ceiling of his truck.

Growing up on a cattle ranch in Wyoming, the actress-turned-director was used to impressively sized men. Everywhere she'd turned, there'd been one more tall, muscled cowboy trying not to step on her feet. But she'd never seen a man *this* tall or this built. Muscle roped along biceps thicker than the thickest part of her thighs, and his shoulders took up the room of a regular man and half of another one. A thick inch-and-a-half-long beard covered his face, a shade darker than his brown hair. Hair that was smooth and shiny and long enough to be all wrapped up in a man bun so sexy, it would make the guys back in LA green with envy.

His dark blue T-shirt and worn, faded jeans wouldn't have looked better on a fashion model. But really, it came down to the scuffed workboots. This guy was the real deal.

"You're looking at my feet."

River nodded. "Anything you need to know about a person, you can tell by their boots."

An eyebrow rose over one skeptical eye. The other eye

kept watch on her hands, like he thought she might pull out a weapon on him.

"I'm not going to rob you," she sighed, exasperated as he pulled onto the road, driving far too slowly.

"You're wearing tennis shoes," he said.

"So?"

"What's that say about your feet?"

"That they're tired of everyone being a pain in my ass. Jessie? Hey, can you hear me?"

He kept glancing at her out of the corner of his eye and not in an appreciative way.

She pulled her scarf away from her neck and waggled it at him. "The microphone is in the scarf. It's small so no one sees it, including looky-loos."

"Looky-loos?"

"One who slows down to see whatever's happening on the side of the road," River explained.

"Ma'am—"

"I left Wyoming a long time ago, and the ma'ams along with it. My name's River. Turn right up here."

"I wasn't being a looky-loo. I was being a neighborly, concerned individual." His low rumble sounded like rocks rolling down a roadcut. "Which I'm regretting more and more every minute. Let me see the scarf."

"No, I have it in perfect position."

"I'm not going in the woods with you unless I see it."

After her morning from hell, seeing him squirm made River finally laugh. "You're actually scared of me. You? Of me?"

His beard twitched. "I'm not one to discount a woman's ability to kick my butt. Not with a sister who's done so more times than I can count."

River tried to imagine what a female version of this man would look like. "Your family tree frightens me."

"It frightens me too, ma'am. About that earpiece…"

He had to be ma'aming her on purpose because otherwise, he was the densest person on the planet. Rolling her eyes, River pulled her carefully placed headset out of the scarf and waggled it at him. "See?"

Warm, brown eyes looked at her, not the blacktop in front of them. And it didn't matter if they were the prettiest eyes she'd ever seen on a man, River wasn't about to die on the side of the road because he drove them both into a tree.

"Focus, big guy. Eyes on the road. Hands at ten and two."

Exhaling a low chuckle, he did as he was told. For a moment. "You're not shy, are you?"

"Why would I be? And turn right."

He turned right, although not with as much enthusiasm as she would have hoped.

"You could have made me ride in the truck bed," she said, unable to keep from teasing him. River waggled her fingers. "I can't get you if I'm back there."

"It's still a possibility," he muttered.

Bumping along the rough gravel road, River slumped back in her seat. A headache was forming between her temples, and it wasn't the first one she'd had since coming to Moose Springs. She could only imagine how exasperated her film crew was with their lack of progress today. This was the first time River had been behind the camera too, not only in front of it, and she was so frustrated, she couldn't see straight.

Without the experience to pad her résumé, no one had wanted to take a chance on her directing/producing abilities. So when her agent had passed along that the Alaskan Tourism Board—a nonprofit organization working hand in hand with the Alaskan state government—was looking to have a documentary made about the tiny town of Moose Springs, River had jumped at the chance. She'd fought hard to get this job, and she'd called in every favor she had to get two of the best crew members in the industry to help her make this a documentary that knocked everyone's socks off.

The only problem? Moose Springs was about as welcoming to them as a grizzly bear with a face full of porcupine needles.

Small town hospitality her ass.

They were on a razor-thin budget, and River had yet to film anything in town legally. None of the permits she'd applied for had been emailed to them as promised by the city website, and they couldn't film in town without permits or permission from each local business owner. No one had agreed.

"Are you okay?"

River looked over at the man taking up the driver's side. Just when she thought she was immune to the male form—too many years with attractive costars of the opposite sex—a flannel-wrapped hottie like him dropped into her lap. Not that he was wearing flannel, but River would bet money his closet was full of the stuff. The fact that he was driving with one massive shoulder wedged against the window, like he was ready to bail out of the moving vehicle if she looked at him wrong, made her fight down a laugh.

It was possible River hadn't made the best first impression on him.

"I'm fine. Turn left over there."

Her crew was waiting for her when they crested the hill. They'd found a perfect location to shoot from, their rental SUV wedged dangerously close to a drop-off, leaving the road mostly free from vehicular hazards. Still, a few hard looks had been sent their way by locals forced to edge around their car as they passed on the tight winding road.

The man driving her was no different. With a wordless growl of annoyance, he slowed to a crawl and hit his hazard lights.

"They need to move," he told her in that low, rumbling voice. "A school bus will be coming through soon."

"It's impossible to find a good place to park around here."

"That's because it's not supposed to be for people parking. It's for people driving."

"It'll take more than a few growls to run us off," River replied as he pulled in behind the SUV.

With a snort, he killed the engine and got out of the truck. "I've got a chain and the number to a tow truck if that helps," he said before closing the door.

River followed suit, then she looked at the stranger who had driven her to her crew. River was average height, so she had to tilt her head back to meet his gaze. Yes, the man was huge, but no, he didn't intimidate her. Very little intimidated her. Growing up in the country might not have prepared her for surviving Los Angeles, but surviving Los Angeles had prepared her to survive anything.

Lean hard muscles from hiking and rock wall climbing defined her natural curves, and she hadn't felt so healthy and strong since leaving Wyoming—nineteen and naive. Who knew ten years was enough time to make it in Hollywood and then start a downward slide into ambiguity, threatening to lose it all? She refused to age out gracefully.

Screw that. If they were done with her, River was going out with a scream of defiance, not a whimper of defeat.

"Are you kidding me?" Jessie, her director of photography and coproducer, stomped over to her, sounding as disgusted as River felt. "All of these shots are ruined."

"I know, I know. It's not like I was flagging them down, Jessie."

"Well, you could've waved them past." Jessie, being the odd man out of their group of three, was one of few in the male-dominated industry who was more than happy to share a producer's spot with a woman. He was also a grumpy ninety-year-old woman stuck in a tightly muscled thirtysomething's body.

Being nagged by Jessie took up the bulk of River's days.

"Actually, I couldn't. Every single person was determined to convince me I needed help. This is what you get. We're filming somewhere people are nice. Nice people make sure someone isn't stuck on the side of the road. I told you this was a bad idea."

"It would have been a great idea if you'd—"

"What? Kicked their tires and told them to scoot along?"

Realizing she was twanging, River took a deep breath, then

another. After years of schooling away her natural accent, she rarely heard her redneck mountain roots in her voice anymore.

"I'm the producer. I know when the scene is getting screwed up."

"Coproducer, unless I end up quitting," Jessie countered. She was so used to his dramatics, River didn't even blink at the threat. "While you tried and failed to walk down a road, I tried and failed to get someone from city hall to answer the phone about our nonexistent permits. I gave up. No one is going to answer. If I can't get copies through email, we'll have to go down there."

"Fine, Jessie. I'll add it to the list."

"Top of the list." Bree, her audio specialist, jumped out of the SUV, laptop in hand. "I can't film in town without them."

"*We* can't film." Jessie sighed. "Really, ladies, I'm more than happy to be outnumbered, but I do exist."

"Do you though?" Bree arched an eyebrow at Jessie, then snickered at the annoyed expression on his face.

Jessie's hair was always messy, and he was very pale, as if he'd rolled off the couch in his grandmother's basement to emerge in the actual sunlight, when in actuality, he preferred to spend all his spare time outdoors like Bree and River did. Their mutual love of hiking and rock climbing had bonded the three beyond the usual professional camaraderie in their industry. Fair skinned to an extreme, even a little sun left Jessie sunburned and peeling. That fair skin had been an issue on every single movie they'd worked on together, to the point that River knew more about Jessie's skin care regimen than her own.

But man…was he talented. River couldn't have asked for a better cameraman and coproducer, even if he was difficult to work with sometimes. Jessie's attitude had gotten him on the wrong side of the wrong director, and like River, his job options were quickly shrinking. And as good as Jessie was, Bree was absolutely invaluable to River.

South Asian with a degree in film studies, Bree was beautiful enough to be on the opposite end of the camera she was so good at using, but she was also one of the best in the business at sound. The only reason River had managed to steal her from a big budget job was Bree's love of being outdoors. The call of Alaska had been enough to get her to come along. For River, this documentary was the most important thing to happen to her career-wise since she'd landed her first acting role. For Bree, it was a paid vacation.

A car edged around their vehicles, the driver giving everyone a dirty look. River's impromptu chauffeur frowned. The beard hid a lot of his facial expressions, but his voice was clearly unhappy with the parking situation.

"Where are we on moving your vehicle?"

Bree gave him a considering look before turning to River. "I know you're juggling a lot of jobs right now, but we can't get a good take if you get yourself kidnapped. A true crime documentary wasn't the plan."

The man with the truck raised his hand. "Technically, I think she kidnapped me."

"Who is that?" Jessie asked, pointing at her new bearded acquaintance. "He looks like an ax murderer."

The pair looked at River expectantly. River shrugged. "I literally have no idea."

They all turned to him, the massive stranger standing there, looking more awkward than she'd ever seen anyone appear in her life.

"Easton Lockett," he grunted by way of introduction.

"You got in a car with him and you didn't know who he was?" Jessie groaned. "People die that way."

Bree snickered. "Why are we so concerned about her? He's the one who looks like he needs a stiff drink."

"My morning has been more interesting than I expected," Easton told them.

Jessie nodded in understanding. "Actresses, right? Total drama queens."

"Excuse me?" River turned on Jessie. "I'm not the one causing the drama."

"No, you're just picking up strays on the highway like puppies."

They started arguing about who was the bigger pain in the ass, and River would have won if not for Easton interrupting by clearing his throat.

"I'd like to help get you out of here. Any way we could move this along?"

They all stared at him—understandably. The man was a mountain. Bree's head tilted to the side. "You look like Hagrid. A sexy, muscly Hagrid."

The poor man actually cringed. "Okay, on that note, I'm going to leave."

"No, wait a minute." River rubbed the bridge of her nose to ease the stress headache headed her way. "Listen, we need to get this footage for the intro to our documentary. I didn't waste half the day for nothing. Here's what we're going to do. We're going to make a sign that says we're filming, and someone's going to hold it."

"We don't have any extra hands, River," Jessie started to protest. "And it's way too windy to lean a sign against something."

"Oh, we have extra hands." She didn't fight the curve on her lips. "Easton, did you still want to help? Because I have the perfect job for you."

CHAPTER 2

SOMETIMES RIVER LANE FELT AS fake as her name.

She'd changed her given name to River the day she'd signed with her talent agency, and in the ten years since then, she'd never regretted it. The girl she'd once been had kicked the mud off her cowboy boots every evening. The woman she was now still wore boots, but the mud was more often slathered on her face than the backside of a barrel racer tossed on the first barrel.

You'd think at some point she'd be used to ending up on the ground.

The call came in as River started her first trek down the stretch of highway they were filming on. Easton was a few miles down the road, and whatever he was doing back there was working. Two cars had gone past already, and other than slowing down for safety—and to gawk—no one had stopped.

"This is River," she answered through her headset, glancing at the Anchorage number on her phone.

"River, it's Mischa. We need to talk."

"Usually that means someone's about to break up with me." River hoped her pleasant, joking tone would carry over to the woman on the other end of the line. Mischa was their contact for the Alaskan Tourism Board.

The job had seemed so cut and dried over the phone. But in the last couple of days, more doors had literally been shut in her face than River had ever experienced in her life. She had a mark on her nose to prove it.

"I've gotten a few complaint calls from the hotel manager at Moose Springs Resort." Mischa sighed, sounding tired. "They said you've been filming there without permission?"

"It's not exactly what happened..." River hesitated.

"They said you frightened a guest."

"No, the *black bear* we were filming frightened the guest. We accidentally scared it, which in turn almost got the guest trampled. It was kind of a domino effect."

The silence on the other end of the phone wasn't encouraging.

"Everyone was okay," River added, trying to downplay the incident. "And we're getting some fabulous shots off the highway as we speak. Legal shots too. They can't keep us from filming on the road."

The other woman sighed. "Moose Springs folk were never ones to let a camera crew in town. The resort doesn't even want you on the property anymore, and they were always the most laid-back about this kind of thing. Listen, I'm sorry, River. If this isn't working, we need to cut our losses and move on."

A fake expression of contented determination stayed on River's face because that was what the camera above her on the hill required. She was a professional. She would not rip her mic out and start screaming from sheer frustration.

"No, Mischa. Please don't do this. We've only gotten started. I have permits," River insisted. "I just don't *have* them. I'm working on it."

Another car went past, the driver and her passenger cracking up. That was the third vehicle in a row with visibly amused occupants. Focused on her phone call, River ignored them.

Through the crackle of bad reception, Mischa sounded dubious. "If you get the film made, then the board will be happy to compensate you for the project. But honestly, River, I'm not holding my breath. We've all enjoyed working with you, and we're excited to have a woman of your acting credentials supporting the state. Maybe we can work out something involving a commercial endorsement at a later time?"

It took everything she had not to tell Mischa where to tuck that suggestion. River finally had a project worth doing, something that was hers and hers alone, and they were ripping it away. She wouldn't let this happen.

Another car came by, this one barely slowing. For some reason, the lack of interest gave her hope.

"River?"

"Yes, I'm here. Sorry, there was traffic. Don't give the contract to anyone else. Let me and my people get the job done. I'll front the rest of the bill, and if we don't deliver, I'll eat the costs of filming and rework the project into something else. An indie film or something. Deal?"

Mischa agreed—albeit with audible reluctance—and ended the call, leaving River to stare at the background on her phone. It was a picture of her father and herself taken from a Christmas years ago. A man who had hated seeing her leave but had never once stopped supporting and encouraging her.

River refused to call him and tell him another career was over. She would make this documentary, no matter what.

The headset beeped, Jessie's voice coming over. "Hey, turn around and do a second loop. This time without the suitcase. You can leave it where you're at, tucked behind that boulder just off the road. It's out of the shot."

"Thank goodness. My arm is killing me."

"Think of it as weight training," he teased. "I didn't realize we were doing a reaction shot."

River grimaced. "Did I fall out of character?"

"Only for a moment. I'd hate to be whoever was on the other end of that call. Please tell me it was Sweeny. Watching you eat him alive has been the highlight of my career."

Sweeny had been the director on one of River's films, the one she'd met Jessie on. Brilliant, but a total pain to work for. Unlike her counterparts, River had gone head-to-head with him more than once. Somehow that turned into a brief, ill-advised, and excessively frustrating relationship that River was more than happy to be done with. Sweeny and Jessie had butted heads almost as much as River had, and he was a big part of why Jessie had lost his most recent project.

"I wish," she said. "I stopped taking his calls. Sweeny's still trying to 'fix' me."

Jessie snorted. "How's that working out for him?"

"About as well as it worked for him on set." Shrugging, River added, "I am who I am."

"And that's why we love you. So, who was the call?"

"Mischa. It's not good news. Let's get this last pass, and then I'll tell you both."

Without the constant interruption of stopping cars and the suitcase slowing her steps, River made quick work of the last pass along the highway. Plopping down on the rock she had tucked the suitcase behind, she waited for Bree and Jessie to pack up and meet her.

Rubbing the pressure points in her scalp to relieve tension, she glanced down the curving, mountainside highway. Somewhere down the road, a very attractive, very bearded man didn't know they were done. River would have called Easton, but she hadn't thought to get his number.

"Sorry, Easton," she murmured. "You'll have to wait until I get a ride."

Now that the filming was done, River could finally take a moment and enjoy being there. The Turnagain Arm flowed past on the other side of the road, the rough waters breaking and crashing. They'd picked this stretch of highway for a reason. The next turn was more picturesque but had so much wind, it had been difficult to walk without leaning over. Here everything but the waters were calmer. She spied three mountain goats on the cliff above her head, and at least one fish gave up the ghost when a hungry eagle dove into the water.

Poor sucker never saw it coming.

Moose Springs, Alaska, was the farthest from home she'd ever been. The jet-setting lifestyle River had dreamed of as a child never quite panned out. She hadn't seen the world. She'd seen the inside of a studio, then another, then more. She filmed on location, but most of those locations were in Los Angeles or Vancouver, and only once had her film career taken her to the East Coast. When people met her, they always assumed she had the world at her fingertips.

But River wasn't a classic. She was a cliché.

Thinking about Easton was much more pleasant than worrying about the current state of her career. When the crew's Subaru SUV pulled off the road across from her, River was deep in daydreams about scuffed boots and calloused hands. She joined her people, trying to decide the best way to break this to them.

"What's the news?" Bree asked, leaning a hip against the car.

"The tourism board got wind of our incident with the bear yesterday. They're dissolving the contract. Technically, they're still willing to buy the documentary, but they don't think we can pull it off."

Bree and Jess shared looks. These two were her people, and River wasn't going to railroad either of them into staying on the project if they weren't interested.

Jessie cleared his throat. "So are we packing this up?"

"I guess that's up to you two." River hated admitting to these professionals that her first film was already skidding off the tracks, but they were her friends too. Which only made it slightly less embarrassing. "This is paying you next to nothing, and without the board's backing, I'll have to cover all of postproduction myself. I'm not sure this is worth your time."

"We still *are* getting paid, right?" he asked. "Only on the back end, not up front?"

"Right," River said. "But if they don't end up buying the documentary, I'm not sure I can pay you as well as they would have."

"Well, there's no way I'm turning down a paid vacation in Alaska." Bree lifted her face to the sky as a pleasant breeze brought the scent of saltwater to their nostrils, inhaling deeply.

"You're not the only one who doesn't want the shame of getting kicked off a small-town documentary." Jessie grimaced at the very thought. "We'll make short work of this, get you the production cred you need, and we'll all go see some whales or something. Whatever it is people do around here."

"It is a working vacation," she reminded her friends. "And since I don't have the extra money, you'll have to whale watch on your own dime."

"We'll make it work," Bree promised.

River hugged her friends, even though Jessie allowed the hug grudgingly. "Oh. Apparently we're not welcome back at the hotel. Don't you love how the resort is the only place in town that rents a room? Not even one bed-and-breakfast."

Too bad the condominiums being built next to the resort weren't finished yet. They seemed to be halted midconstruction.

Nothing ever seemed to throw Bree, who simply shrugged. "We can sleep in the car."

Glancing at the already-stuffed vehicle, full of snacks and gear and one really big fluffy moose-themed blanket, River cringed. "I'm terrible. This whole thing is terrible. I'm standing here, seriously considering making the best crew in the industry share the back seat of our car."

"Some of my best memories are in the back seat of a Subaru," Jessie murmured.

Barking out a laugh, Bree said, "I doubt it. Your best memories are eating your grandmother's pot roast while playing video games."

"Why do you always have to bring Nana into it? You know it's a mutually beneficial arrangement—"

The two began to argue good-naturedly, as if River hadn't already proven herself to be the worst boss ever. And as good of friends as they were, neither Bree nor Jessie would put their professional reputations at risk for her. The industry was too cutthroat.

Their faith in her filled River's heart with warmth.

"It'll make a fun story, sleeping in our SUV." Now Bree seemed excited. Between their matching enthusiasm, River couldn't help but join in.

"Okay, fine. We're still making a documentary, folks. Let's go find a safe place for you two to get some more B-roll. I'll get to the bottom of this permit thing."

They piled into the car, then pulled back onto the road. They were halfway to their next filming site when suddenly River gasped. Bree braked, looking for whatever made River so horrified. "What is it?"

"Oh *crap*. We forgot Easton."

He'd just been trying to be nice. In the future, Easton was going to stick with aloof, unapproachable, and downright surly.

Nice was a pain in the ass. Nice earned him a redhead with a permanent marker and a mischievous look on her face.

Don't stop, River had written on her makeshift sign. *Filming movie.*

Which was how Easton Lockett, one of the most respected men in Moose Springs, found himself standing on the side of the road with a pizza box sign, telling everyone not to stop for the woman walking down the road.

If only he'd made the same choice for himself.

The absolute last person Easton wanted to see coming down the road at this moment turned around the bend, the heavy off-road tires of her sleek black Jeep slapping the pavement. There was nowhere to hide. And knowing his sister, there was nowhere he *could* hide to keep her from finding him in a pride-compromising position.

With a groan of dismay, Easton waggled the sign at her as she slowed down, then pulled off the side of the road behind his truck.

"You've got to be kidding me."

"I've been thinking the same thing for the last hour," Easton replied, bemused.

Ashtyn Lockett had been a thorn in Easton's side since the day she was born fifteen seconds before him. At some point since he'd seen her yesterday, she'd decided to dye her pixie cut a vibrant aquamarine with pink tips. Next week, it would be something different but equally bold.

She must've been taking the day off by the water, because only half of the piercings she normally sported jewelry in were filled. Her nose piercing and eyebrow were adorned, but the multiple holes in her ears were piercing free. Unlike River, his twin was dressed for the weather. A ribbed tank top showing the extensive and expensive tattoos on her arms. Shorts and sandals with bright nail polish from her morning pedicure. Even brighter colors on her fingernails.

Easton had spent a lot of his life glaring over his sister's head at the guys who were interested in her, but there really was no need. Ash had never needed anyone to protect her. She was perfectly capable of handling her business all on her own.

"What the hell are you doing?" Brown eyes the exact same color as Easton's eyes widened.

Sighing, Easton lifted his pizza box up in the air, turning it toward the oncoming traffic.

"I'm being a Good Samaritan."

"Are you? Because it kind of looks like you're making an idiot out of yourself for some tourists."

"They're not tourists." Deep denial was as good a coping mechanism as any. "They're filming some sort of movie around the bend. And before you grill me, I don't know anything about it. I saw a woman walking down the road, and I stopped to see if she needed help. She nearly skinned me alive for interrupting her shot."

Ash rolled her eyes. "Why would they pick here to film? Don't they know everyone's going to slow down and see what's wrong?"

"That's what I said, but she's...well...determined."

Gorgeous. Fiery. Way more trouble than he needed on any given day.

"How long are you planning on standing here?"

Easton didn't know, but he'd been out there for long enough; even his arms were starting to get sore. Finally, a familiar SUV drove past and performed a highly illegal U-turn, pulling right next to Easton. River stuck her head out from the passenger seat, her face lighting up as she took in him and his sign.

"No wonder no one stopped," she said. "You look like you want to kill someone."

"That's resting Easton face." Ash smirked at him. "He's normally worse."

He wasn't speaking to either of them. Nope. Not a word.

"Hey, thanks for the help. Sorry we forgot to tell you we got the shot. Here, dinner is on us." Leaning out the window, River tucked a twenty-dollar bill in his shirt collar, not giving Easton a chance to refuse before Bree, the driver, pulled away.

Ash lost it, leaning back against her Jeep, laughing so hard, her mascara started to run.

"If you could see your face," she all but cried.

"I feel dirty," he murmured, taking the twenty and stuffing it into his pocket.

"You *are* dirty." Gasping for breath, she wiped her eyes. "I think I love her, whoever she is."

The feeling wasn't mutual.

With an annoyed grunt, Easton tossed the pizza box in the back of Ash's Jeep. "Compost this, please."

Since his services were no longer needed, Easton decided there was no reason to stand there any longer, giving his sister ammunition.

"You never saw this," he warned her.

"Oh, everyone saw this."

Which was so true. In a place like Moose Springs, memories were long. The town would never—ever—let Easton live this down.

"Destroy the evidence, Ash. If you love me, destroy the evidence."

"Don't get your hopes up," his twin teased. As he headed for his truck, she called after him. "I might frame it instead!"

———————

River had to give them credit. Moose Springs was really good at being a total pain in the ass.

She'd been professional. She'd been nice. She'd even been accommodating. But what she refused to be was railroaded by a man and a sandwich.

It was time to play hardball with Officer Jonah.

"As I said before, I'm here to pick up my filming permits. And I'm not leaving until someone in this town can actually help me." She was guessing he hadn't heard her the first few times over the sound of mayo dripping down his chin.

Officer Jonah chewed on his hoagie for a while, chewed on it some more, and made a few thinking noises that left her wanting to stuff what was left of the sandwich in his face. Then he scratched the back of his head.

"I'm sorry, ma'am. I'm pretty sure you have to go to the city hall for that."

River braced her hands on her hips. "The city hall, huh?"

"Yep."

"So you're assuming I'm stupid."

Intelligent eyes glanced at her, a man caught in the act of being sneaky.

"Go ahead," she encouraged him. "Mansplain it for me. I couldn't possibly have known that was the place to go to get a permit, but I'm sure glad you're helpful enough to set me straight."

River could hear her drawl coming out, dripping with sarcasm, and she didn't bother to try to hide it. "Or I could save you some time and tell you that so far, myself and my people have spent countless hours on hold with a city hall that doesn't actually exist."

River continued in a firm voice. "Did you know that the address for the Moose Springs City Hall is very hard to find? Hard enough that I had to call the state government and stay on hold with *them* before somebody finally came up with the address to a barn on the far side of town, with weeds literally as tall as I am. But if you fight through the weeds, you find a sign on the door that says *Be Back in Ten.* Do you want to hazard a guess as to who came back in ten?"

The deputy policewoman one desk over shared an amused look with Officer Jonah. He wiped a thumb to the corner of his mouth. "No one?"

"No one, Officer Jonah. No one at all."

Maybe—just maybe—River had made a career in acting because she had a flare for the dramatic. She let that hang between them, holding the policeman's eyes.

"So I went to the DMV, who told me to go *back* to the city hall, because permits were only processed through the city hall. At which point I told the clerk I would immortalize them in film as the least helpful human being on the planet if they didn't tell me *something*. So it was suggested I find a woman named Ashtyn Lockett, the keeper of all the permits."

The deputy tried and failed to cover her laugh.

"Assuming I would get nothing but more runaround from the lovely locals in this town, I came here. Because who would know more than the local police about government type matters? Only there was a sign on *your* door saying you were getting a sandwich at Frankie's. From what I can tell, there is no place called Frankie's."

"It's a real nice restaurant." He hefted what was left of his sandwich to show her. "Pastrami and provolone."

"I'm sure it is. It's also not listed on the internet, in the yellow pages, or on any of the buildings in Moose Springs. And everyone I asked either hadn't heard of it or pretended they hadn't heard me. Again, I was referred to Ashtyn Lockett. I assume she's used to scare people."

"Upon occasion," he admitted.

Watching him chewing on his sandwich like a cow chewing its cud, River had to contain her natural inclination to rip the thing out of his mouth and cram it up his nostrils, one slice of pastrami at a time.

Instead, River drew herself up, steeled her spine, and said, "Officer Jonah. I *am* filming a documentary in the town of Moose Springs. I *will* be doing this whether or not I have the proper permits filed with the proper authorities. Because unlike the last film crews that tried to complete this assignment, I *cannot* be run off. So *where is my permit?*"

And that should have been that.

Only...well...it wasn't.

"I'd check with city hall, ma'am. They're in charge of all the permit type things."

River wasn't too dignified to scream.

Which of course was the exact moment Easton—in all his

bearded, rugged glory—had to duck his head through the door. Her scream had been mighty, and his eyes widened. Easton looked back and forth between them, a familiar take-out container in his hand.

He had his own sandwich. Son of a bitch.

"Is everything okay?" Easton asked cautiously, pausing inside the front door.

He was asking her, but Officer Mayoface decided to answer. "We're all good, Easton. Miss Lane—"

"Ms. Lane is fine, Easton, thank you," River cut off the policeman. She twisted back on him. "And I didn't tell you my name."

"Nope. But I've had half a dozen calls from concerned citizens this morning involving you harassing them." Jonah took another bite, mumbling around his pastrami, "To be honest, that's not the best way to start out in this town."

Taking a calming breath, River centered herself. She would not suffer any further indignity of letting him get to her. Before River accepted this job, she hadn't understood why no one had been here to document the town already. Moose Springs was gorgeous, the mountainscape stunning, and the sheer volume of wildlife any filmmaker's dream. Now she got it.

They had no intention of giving her—or anyone—filming permits.

"Let's start this over again. I have been hired by the Alaskan Tourism Board—"

"Which is run by a nonprofit organization and not a state body of government," Jonah said, interrupting her. "Meaning you don't have a pot to piss in, legally speaking. If the mayor doesn't want to grant you the right to film in town, he has the power to decline the request."

Okay. A mayor. She could work with that. "Who's the mayor?"

Jonah scratched his chin. "Well, to be honest, he's kind of taking a break."

"I'm sorry, he's what?"

"It's been a busy year, what with fighting to keep the town from being overrun by tourists and condos and Santa mooses..."

Did he say Santa mooses?

"Anyway, whenever he gets around to it, the mayor will be in charge of staffing city hall. They're the ones who run the website with your permits. But no one wants much to do with those kinds of jobs, and the mayor's been awfully busy. Plus, he's getting married soon."

River took a deep steadying breath. "So you're telling me, if I want to cash my paycheck and make my film, I have to wait for a town that doesn't have a governing body and a mayor on an undetermined hiatus to appoint a city hall employee to retrieve an email that says I have a permit?"

"Yes, ma'am."

"Or it'll stay in some email black hole of nothingness, unrecognized and irretrievable."

"That's right."

Which meant never. She was never getting her permit.

"Do you know what happens to good towns when documentary makers go rogue?" River said ominously. "It's not pretty, Jonah. It's not pretty at all."

"I'd strongly encourage you not to film guerrilla style, ma'am. The town is very serious about that."

"Who? Who is really serious about it? The empty barn of people?"

"I suppose the one who'll have to write you the tickets. Or put you in holding for disturbing the peace." Officer Jonah would have seemed a lot more official without a bit of lettuce stuck in his teeth, but River had the feeling he was completely serious.

"We'd rather not have any more tourists," the policewoman said cheerfully, sounding less than apologetic. "They tend to make a mess of things around here."

River didn't have a good answer for that, and Officer Jonah had already turned his full attention to the bag of chips accompanying his sandwich.

"Carbs kill," she told him with a snarl, turning on her heel. Easton moved to the side of the doorway, out of her way, which was smart because River was ready to walk right through him.

"Your town sucks," she told Easton as she stomped past him. Since he'd been nice enough to hold a sign for her, she didn't stick her tongue out at the giant of a man when he stretched out an arm to hold the door open for her.

"Only sometimes," he replied with a wink.

Easton always had questionable taste in women. Which was why he found himself ignoring his original task and following her outside.

He had to give River credit. She was ballsy. Most people wouldn't have been so willing to attack Easton's truck in front of a police station, with him standing there, watching her in bemusement. Technically, River was only kicking at the tire with her foot, but still. Property destruction was property destruction. At least she was smart enough not to kick the squad car.

"Stupid...piece of...son of a...sandwich eater..."

Each kick was punctuated by an insult until she finally stood back and riffled through her purse.

"If you're thinking of keying it, you might want to reconsider." Easton leaned against the passenger side door, arms folded loosely over his chest. "I draw the line at actual damage."

"I'm looking for my phone so I can report him. There has to be a jackass cop hotline for this county."

With a chuckle, he shook his head. "I hate to break it to you, but they don't tend to staff that too."

"I hate your sandwich."

Never had anyone said anything that random to him, and Easton had been on the top of Denali with people suffering from high altitude cerebral edemas.

"This one?"

"Yes."

In that moment, Easton could have done a lot of things. Run screaming was one. Pump up his tire was another. Instead, he unwrapped the paper from his sandwich and offered half to her.

"Don't hate the sandwich, hate the poor schmuck who had to be on the receiving end of your bad day."

River sighed and gave up, slouching against the truck next to him. She accepted the sandwich.

"Bologna on wheat?" She peered down at the offering critically before taking a bite. "Dry? What kind of a monster are you?"

"Never really cared much for mustard."

For some reason, that bit of information made her whole face shift away from frustration. And damn if she wasn't even more beautiful when she smiled. "So why are you here? Did Mayoface ruin your day too?"

"There's a poker game tonight. I was going to invite him. And I wanted to see how he got the moose out of the swing set."

River swallowed her bite, then took another. "Isn't that something you could have done through a text or a phone call?" she said between mouthfuls.

"Yeah, but I knew he'd be here. Not hard to find someone in a town this small."

Okay, so maybe he was teasing her. It was kind of hard not to. Easton deserved the eye roll she aimed at him. "Har har."

He took another bite. "They won't let you film in town, River. It's kind of our policy."

"Whose policy? From what I can tell, no one is actually in charge around here."

"Oh, Graham's in charge. He's just really good at pretending otherwise."

"Any idea where I can find this Graham?" He wasn't going to answer, and she must have known, because River snorted. "Of course not. He's in hiding. Well, they can't stop me if they don't see me. What will they do? Have someone follow us around to tattle?"

When he didn't immediately answer, those stunning blue eyes turned to him, narrowing. Easton held a hand up innocently. "Nope, not me. Do I look like the kind of guy who can sneak around?"

"You could be sneakier than you appear." River finished her half of the sandwich. "Well, I'm not giving up. Sorry, Moose Springs."

"Feel free to try, but you won't get anything for your trouble other than escorted to the county line. By the way, I said they wouldn't let you film *in* town," Easton told her. "But there's a lot out there worth filming."

When Easton jutted his chin toward the mountains surrounding them, she looked, then kept looking. A speculative expression crossed her features.

She turned, taking in the mountains around them. "Most of the people who come here do so for the skiing, right?"

He nodded.

"You know what, Easton Lockett? You might have earned yourself another twenty bucks."

Easton barked out a laugh. He pulled a piece of paper out of his pocket, scratching a number on it. "Here. Call this number. This expedition company is based out of Anchorage. They'll take you and your people around to the spots worth seeing."

She pocketed the number with a murmured thanks. "Hey, Easton? Sorry I accused you of being an evil mastermind and for kicking your tire. And thanks for the awful sandwich. I was getting hungry."

He winked at her in reply. "No worries. And, River?"

"Yeah?"

"Don't bother with Moose Springs. We're really not worth the trouble."

So far, he'd doubled the money he'd made that day by playing poker that night. Which meant Easton's sister felt obliged to take it all in one fell swoop.

It wasn't ideal to play with only the three of them—Easton, Ash, and Rick Harding—but Graham was having a hard time making it to game nights lately. The "break" he was on wasn't so much of a break as Jonah had implied. Easton had seen the amount of paperwork stacked in Graham's place.

"Bring Zoey next time," Easton suggested to his sister as Rick dealt out the next hand. "We could use some fresh blood."

They'd gathered at one of the tables near the bar, in case Rick needed to help a customer. Currently, the pool hall was empty, even though it was open. If someone wanted to come in, no one was stopping them, least of all Rick. But in the meantime, there were cards to play. Money to lose. And in Ash's case, money to take.

"If I bring Zoey," Ash said, "she and Graham will spend the whole time making googly eyes at each other. At least Rick and Lana can maintain a semblance of decorum. Usually."

Rick chuckled at her comment. "Lana's been gone for almost two weeks. My decorum was officially shot days ago."

"Eww." Ash made a face. "I didn't need to know that."

Rick had been dating the socialite turned Moose Springs property owner since Christmas, and from what Easton could tell, the two were getting serious, fast. Rick had an almost constant smile on his face these days, especially since Lana had agreed to pack up her longtime suite at the resort and move in with him.

The massive condominiums next to the resort were Lana's...or technically, they belonged to the company her family owned. No one really wanted the condos there, bringing in a more permanent type of tourism, but Easton understood Lana's reasoning behind them. Both Lana and Graham wanted the best for Moose Springs, even if they were at odds as to what that meant. Trying to enforce restrictions on Lana's condos took up the bulk of Graham's focus these days...and the bulk of all that paperwork.

Even though Lana had set up her permanent office out of Moose Springs, she still traveled a lot for work. Rick was a homebody, although he'd accompanied her a few times overseas. Easton didn't know how they managed to make the separation work, but every time they were together, it was clear both were incredibly happy.

Happy was good. Not being lonely was even better. Easton wasn't lonely. But he wasn't sure he was all that happy either. Lately, he'd felt like something was missing. Something more than a game of cards with friends could fix.

"Why isn't Jonah here?" Ash nodded her chin to Rick. "Two cards."

She was as easy to read as a book...at least to Easton anyway. Ash loved to win, and her entire body showed her hand, from the upright posture to the tiny smirk that tugged the corner of her lips.

"Something made his day worse for the wear." Easton couldn't help the humor in his voice.

"Sounds like the men in town met their match today, pizza boy."

Easton rolled his eyes at the newest nickname she'd found for him that evening. Ash had tried several on for size. "I liked 'traffic cone' better," he said.

Unlike his sister, Easton's cards were crap, but he didn't fold.

Rick's eye kept drifting down to his hand, then sliding away, a tell—if a subtle one. Easton wasn't going to give his money away, but it was hard not to stay in an extra round for the guy. Just because Rick was in a relationship with Lana didn't mean he was well-off. The pool hall wasn't making ends meet and hadn't for a long time now. One day, Rick would open to tourists, but that day wasn't there yet. He was pretty certain Rick lived off cereal and sheer grit.

"Two pairs." Rick laid down his cards.

"I've got nothing." Dropping his hand on the table, Easton leaned backward with a grunt.

"Three aces. Read 'em and weep, boys." Sweeping the chips over to her side of the table, Ash gloated, "One of these days, you'll learn not to play with the master."

"One of these days, you'll learn to win without rubbing it in."

She made a face at him, the same face she'd been making behind their parents' backs since they were toddlers. Since no one was looking, Easton indulged himself in the same, adding a tongue sticking out. Hearing his twin's peal of laughter was totally worth whatever lack of dignity his already-bruised pride had suffered today at the hands of a stranger.

"Hey, Easton," Rick said in his quiet voice. "You know anything about this film crew that's running around up here?"

"Not as much as he's about to." Ash was almost singsonging.

She looked so happy, Easton was immediately suspicious. "What's that supposed to mean?"

Ash smirked at him, pulling a file folder out of her bag. "Dad wanted me to give you this. A job came through, passed on to us by referral. They didn't want to step on your turf. Here's the paperwork. Three climbers want you to take them up Mount Veil. They don't have a lot of experience, but Dad accepted the job. You know how he is when people want to see his baby."

Mount Veil. At just over fifteen thousand feet, it wasn't the tallest or the most popular climb in Alaska. But the "fourteener"— any mountain over fourteen thousand feet—was worthy of any peak bagger's list, especially those with the guts to go into the Veil. No camera crew had ever gone up Mount Veil. It would be worth seeing...and worth filming.

A chill of dread ran down his spine, the kind that only happened when a redhead was involved. He knew who he'd see before even opening the folder. Sure enough, a familiar face peered up at him, in the most professional headshot any of his clients had ever sent before a climb.

Son of a...sandwich eater.

Of course, it was River Lane.

CHAPTER 3

IF JESSIE DIDN'T STOP SNORING, River was going to throttle him with his seat belt.

She'd do it nice and slow too.

River wasn't above sleeping in a car. She'd spent six months living in hers after the money she'd taken to LA had run out. Back then, she'd been too ashamed to tell her family how broke she'd become. There was something circuitous about ending up back in a car tonight, at the start of a new career that so far was not going to plan.

Parked in an employee overflow parking lot on the far end of the Moose Springs Resort's property, River figured they'd have to move the next night. Someone would eventually notice they were parked out there instead of in the main lot with the rest of the guests, even if the closely encroaching forest made them harder to see from the road. The benefit was the sheer amount of wildlife moving around the parking lot, as if it weren't a big deal for deer to nibble grasses a few feet away from their vehicle or a raccoon to spend all night trying to get into the bear-proof trash bin across the lot.

Their B-roll was getting better by the minute.

As uncomfortable as the car was, at least it was a roof over their heads. They'd moved the bulk of the equipment to the floorboards and strapped the suitcases to the top of the vehicle, giving Bree and Jessie each a seat to stretch out on to sleep. Since River had gotten them into this mess, she'd offered to sleep in the back, wedged between a tripod and the rear door.

River had grown up sleeping on a bedroll beneath the stars, three days' ride from home and surrounded by cowboys. She was no stranger to annoying nocturnal guttural noises: snores, snorts, or worse. But there was something particularly awful about the combination of Jessie's ear-shattering version of sleep apnea and Bree changing positions with a car-wobbling dramatic flop. Every. Single. Minute.

"I'm going to kill them," she whispered to the Subaru, which must have been in as much pain as she was.

A wet guttural rattle from Jessie reminded her the seat belt wasn't that far out of reach.

River was used to being in close quarters with the pair. Still, the SUV reminded her of a coffin, squeezing the life out of her with every snort and whack of Bree's elbow into the seat back. Yep, lack of sleep or not, she was done.

Escaping the vehicle through the back hatch door, River resisted letting the door close with a loud thump.

Freed of her confines, River could finally take a deep breath, relaxing and appreciating the scenery around her. The sun never set this time of year, but within the shadow of the mountain range, they'd managed to sleep in a semblance of darkness. Now, as dawn approached, the dark grays and hazy blues of night had lightened, the sun rising higher in the sky. She had plenty of natural light to make her way across the parking lot and down to the road.

Yesterday had been tough, but things were looking better. They'd regrouped and decided to take Easton's advice to film outside town. The guide service he'd suggested had been booked, but they'd been referred to someone else closer to Moose Springs. A local.

She really hoped this one was more welcoming then the ones they'd encountered so far.

After some research, they'd learned that Mount Veil was the most impressive and exciting geological location near Moose Springs. Something worth making a documentary about, something that could bring more attention to the town. Few people climbed it, but those who did all came down saying the experience had been amazing. And it was either that or film River walking along the road some more. Since River loved to climb, this documentary was exactly up her alley. Bree was instantly on board, but it had taken some convincing to get Jessie to agree to filming on a mountain.

He liked climbing, but he'd never summited a fourteener before.

"Not like we have a choice," River said to herself, rolling her shoulders to try to ease the strain of the last few days.

She was standing on the precipice of one more failed project, and River wasn't sure her career could survive much more. Standing there, worrying herself into a stomach ulcer wasn't going to help anything. Muscles aching to be used, River considered going for a run. But with Mount Veil fresh in her mind, what she really wanted to do was climb. Climbing had always been a source of stress release for her. When things got too tough, River would head for the hills...literally. She'd always been able to find a calmness when climbing that no other form of exercise could match.

Maybe it was the fact that with each grip, each movement, she knew that some progress had been made. A set goal was clearly achieved. Unless she fell. And even falling—as much as it hurt— was better than standing still, doing nothing.

At least River would know she'd tried.

The parking lot turnoff was still in sight, if barely, by the time River found what she was looking for. It was only a roadcut, but the rock face was smooth and slick, a challenge worth tackling. The cold, hard granite beneath her fingertips had yet to weather into the soft, crumbling surface that left so many roadcuts too dangerous for climbing. This road was new, probably cut into the mountainside to build a backroad access to the resort during construction. River had done her research and knew the Moose Springs Resort had been around for almost twenty-five years.

Twenty-five years young...younger than her.

"Hollywood is the only place where almost thirty makes someone feel old," River grumbled to herself, kicking off her shoes and socks. "And I am so *over* it."

Ever since River had started actively climbing—about the time she realized that calming activities like yoga or meditation were *not* her thing—she'd started carrying a pair of tight climbing shoes and a bag of chalk with her when she went places.

She never knew when a chance to climb would come up, even if it was only pulling off the side of the road or playing around on some boulders between film shoots. Unfortunately, she'd left both shoes and chalk with the rest of her gear, and there was no way she was returning and risking waking her crew. Early morning or not, if they knew what River had planned, they'd insist on filming her. But right now, there was no one watching. No cameras turned on her, no expression forced on her face. Just the rock.

A challenge, only for her.

Free-climbing wasn't as safe as climbing with a harness and ropes, and she was taking a risk by not using chalk for her hands. It was the chalk more than the shoes that made her pause.

"You have no business on Mount Veil if you can't handle a twenty-foot roadcut," River reminded herself, setting her fingers into the first hold.

There had been a moment on her first solo climb when every muscle in her body had reacted in fear, freezing up. The result was her instructor having to talk her down and a solid twenty minutes of shaking like a leaf when her feet finally found the ground. River never forgot that feeling. Each time she started a climb, easy or tough, she remembered that fear, embracing it and using it to drive her upward.

The roadcut was more challenging than River had expected, nearly vertical with fewer holds the higher she went. Pausing to think about where she was going next, River considered two paths, one angling to the right and one nearly straight up to the top. The straight to the top route would be quicker, but River wasn't looking for quick. She wanted to feel the strain in her arms and shoulders, to tax her back, thighs, and calves.

They had a long day of filming ahead of them, and River refused to cheat herself out of a moment of relaxation now.

A tiny breath of surprise escaped her lips as River's hand slipped. For a moment, she hung there, two stories off the ground, by the fingertips of her left hand. Years ago, it would have scared her, but today, she simply enjoyed the stretch on her arm, loosening the tension in her shoulders as she dangled. Then River hauled herself upward with the strength of her bicep, her free hand and toes finding purchase in the rock. Resting her weight on her toes took the strain off her arms as she peered up. The top of the rock face was within sight, but the holds were harder to find, and the next one would require a dyno to reach.

"Sorry, Jessie." She inhaled a deep breath, then let it out slowly. "I know you would have loved to film this. But I'm allowed a me moment."

Then she let go and jumped.

The first time River had tried a dynamic move, she'd landed flat on her butt. Now, they were her favorite. There was a moment during a dyno, when a climber let go of the safety of their hold, trusting that the momentum of their jump would take them to the next hold beyond their reach. To dyno was to trust oneself. Otherwise, flying became falling. River had learned young that when you fall off a horse, get right back on. A rock was no different, even if the fall hurt worse.

"Gotcha," she breathed, fingers finding their grip, legs dangling. Her right foot found a second grip parallel to her shoulder, her left hand crossed over her head to a hold above her right shoulder.

Okay, maybe it was more like yoga than River wanted to admit.

A few more feet and River hoisted herself over the top of the roadcut, where a natural shelf cut horizontal into the mountain. The result was the perfect ledge for her to stand on, one arm looped around a pine tree growing at an angle out of the cliffside. On a branch somewhere behind her, a pair of songbirds chirped and flirted with each other, ignoring the crunching of the red squirrel eating pine seeds a few trees away. She swore she could smell the distant ocean on the breeze.

The sun never set at the top of the world. At least not in July. But as she stood on the shelf, sweat trickling between her shoulder blades and blood pumping, River raised her eyes higher in the sky. This was a new day, a new chance to find the elusive thing beyond her fingertips that chasing her dreams had never discovered. That single, integral part of herself that had always been missing.

Taking her crew up Mount Veil was a risk, but like a dyno, when you jumped, you had to trust yourself. Every instinct in River's body told her what she was looking for was there, up in those mountains. She didn't want to climb Mount Veil; she *had* to. To prove to herself she could do this. To prove to herself that she didn't stop being worthwhile because a bunch of Hollywood executives thought she was too old. The part of her soul that was drawn to climbing was calling her to Mount Veil, to find what she'd always been looking for. Whatever that was going to be… River knew it would be her missing piece.

As the peaks in the distance slipped behind the morning's

cloud cover, it didn't matter one bit that River couldn't see her goal. She didn't have to see it.

Hope already burned through her veins.

———————————

One of these days, Easton was going to learn to knock before walking through Graham's front door.

"Oops, sorry," he mumbled, sharing in the mutual embarrassment of the kitchen's two occupants. "I brought breakfast."

It was a good breakfast too. Homemade breakfast burritos, the kind his father only made on special occasions. Or when Easton booked a well-paying climb up his favorite mountain.

The Locketts were creatures of habit, and Easton was no exception. His natural inclination to do things the same way, the same speed, at the same time had served him well in his chosen profession. Alpine climbing wasn't free soloing in Yosemite: dramatic and pulse racing as a climber clung to the side of a sheer drop-off hundreds of feet above the ground. No, to get to the top of a monster like Mount Veil, slow and steady won the race every time. Following good habits that kept him and his clients safe.

But being a creature of habit sometimes meant walking into your friend's kitchen first thing in the morning and accidentally interrupting. Good thing Graham always had a sense of humor about it, but this was starting to become routine. The house, the diner, behind Easton's truck. At this point, he'd have to walk around with his hand over his eyes to preserve everyone's dignity.

The couple couldn't keep their hands off each other.

It would be annoying if Graham hadn't been so stupidly happy with his fiancée. But Easton could have easily lived without walking in on the two of them going at it like teenagers *again*.

"Am I going to have to start hanging a sock on the front door?" Graham joked while a flushed Zoey tried to rearrange her shirt in a semblance of order.

"You knew I was coming by." Easton had agreed to give Zoey a ride to work that morning. Her car needed new brake pads, and Graham was trying to get them installed before he opened his popular one-man diner, the Tourist Trap, for lunch. "At least put up a warning sign."

"Nah, it's more fun when we might get caught." Graham winked at his fiancée.

Easton chuckled at the rueful expression on Zoey's face. "If he bothers you too much, let me know."

Zoey flashed Graham a fond look. "He always bothers me, but I've learned to live with it."

"My best friend and my girl, ladies and gentlemen. I deserve better."

Actually, Graham was beyond lucky and he knew it. Easton had been present the night Zoey Caldwell walked into Graham's diner a year ago. All it had taken was one shy hello, and Graham had been glued to her heels like a man in love ever since. The fact that she had decided to stay had been as unsurprising as it was relieving. Neither Easton nor Ash wanted to deal with a broken-hearted Graham. If he was a pain in the ass when happy, it was nothing compared to when he got his heart crushed.

Graham was many things. Low maintenance wasn't one of them.

"What's that expression for?" Graham asked, not bothering to adjust...or find...his own shirt.

"How can you see an expression?" Zoey tilted her head. "All I see is beard."

"You watch the beard movement," Graham explained. "It's subtle, but it's there. I'll teach you Easton beard talk. It's part of your coursework for becoming a full member of Moose Springs. You've been here a year, so you're officially out of the probationary period."

"There are classes?" Zoey knelt, scratching Graham's blind border collie, Jake, behind his floppy ears.

"Oh yeah," Graham continued cheerfully. "Tourist dodging, moose impersonating, the annual running of the naked bearded men..."

"That's a class?" She seemed horrified.

"Ask Easton. I majored in tourist dodging, with a minor in telling them like it is. But you'll have to pass your final in beard talk. Men have to keep their faces warm in Alaska, and if you can't understand beard talk, you're going to spend a lot of time confused. What if I grow one?"

She arched an eyebrow. "Are you planning on growing one?"

"Depends if I feel like running naked."

They could go back and forth for hours, some bizarre aspect of their relationship both found utterly appealing. In their banter, it was entirely possible the two had completely forgotten his presence.

Setting the bag of breakfast burritos on the table, Easton nodded at the woman who had made his friend so happy. "Good luck today. You still have that big group scheduled?"

"Yep! Biggest so far. I can't wait."

There wasn't an ounce of sarcasm in her enthusiastic statement. Zoey loved her job up at the resort. A former waitress, Zoey could have worked with Graham at his diner. But the sheer amount of joy she took from careening around in her tour bus, telling visitors all about the local flora and fauna was hard to resist. In her year in Moose Springs, she'd quickly become a favorite with the tourists.

"Do I look okay?" she asked, nervousness clear. "The new summer shirts fit more snug than the winter ones."

A flash of consternation crossed Graham's features, but he smoothed it away when Zoey turned to face him.

Zoey Caldwell was a short, slender woman with eyeglasses sliding down her nose and bangs falling across her pretty face. Her monogrammed shirt was the same provided by Moose Springs Resort for all their staff, including their tour guides: a professional-looking collared button-down in royal blue.

Going blue shirt in Moose Springs was a sign of shame. No one wanted to be reliant on the monstrosity clinging to their mountain. Easton was surprised that Zoey didn't know most of the residents who worked at the hotel kept their shirts tucked out of sight until right before their shifts.

Zoey always sported hers proudly.

"You look perfect." Wrapping his arms around her waist, Graham added, "I'd vote for adding a sweatshirt. It might get chilly out there this morning. You can steal that gray college one of mine if you want. I know you like it."

Beaming at him, Zoey hustled off, disappearing into Graham's bedroom. Maybe Graham *was* capable of some form of emotional growth.

"Subtle," Easton said, because it wasn't any chillier than it ever was in an Alaskan summer.

"I'll explain it to her eventually." Graham sighed. "I haven't had the heart to tell her."

"Are you sure she wouldn't rather work with you at the Tourist Trap? You're the mayor now. You have enough on your plate without running your diner alone."

Being forced to become the main political figurehead in Moose Springs hadn't been Graham's idea, and he'd sure whined enough since being railroaded into the job. But he was a natural leader and cared about his town, and they had been the better under Graham's guidance.

A broad grin spread across Graham's face. "Buddy, the more you push me to hire help, the less inclined I am to do it. You know this, but still, you push."

"You're going to have a heart attack from exhaustion before you turn thirty-five."

"Nag, nag, nag. Really, we need to find you something else to focus on." Graham handed Easton a cup of coffee.

"Did you make this or Zoey?" Easton asked warily.

"Zoey. Yeah, yeah, I know. She's better at everything than me, coffee included." He took a sip from his mug, then sighed with contentment. "Life's looking good from where I'm standing, East, old buddy."

"You're annoying when you're happy."

"That's what Ash told me. Speaking of, I talked to her last night. She said you're taking that film crew up Mount Veil?"

He wasn't surprised Ash had already spilled the beans. "Better than letting them poke around town much longer."

"Ash is worried." Easton started to shrug, but Graham's expression tightened. "Yeah, I know how she is about that mountain, but she may have a point on this one. Do they have the experience to get up there?"

"Are you asking me if I know how to do my job?"

Graham clapped a hand on his shoulder. "Nah, never that. I'm just saying this sounds like more of a pain than normal. Someone else's pocketbook doesn't sound like a good enough cause to risk your neck."

Easton didn't love being on the side of out-of-towners, but he found himself defending River anyway.

"Wouldn't you rather them be out there, where most people wouldn't want to come visit anyway? Peak baggers already know about Mount Veil. This is the least amount of damage. We'll go up the mountain, take some nature shots, and come back down again. Then no one has to worry about it anymore."

Graham's raised eyebrow was more than a little skeptical.

"Dad gave his word that I'd guide the climb. I'm not embarrassing him by backing out now. Besides, after meeting her, she's liable to head up there by herself, camera crew in tow."

They both shared a grimace. Graham wasn't a mountaineer, but they both knew exactly how bad of an idea *that* was.

Easton hadn't been able to resist an internet search of his newest clients. He'd told himself it was for informational purposes only, but he'd found himself lingering on pictures of River taken by fans. Going into restaurants, making funny faces at her coworkers, even a few of her climbing indoor rock walls.

Her technique was good if nothing else.

Zoey returned to the kitchen, ready to go. Easton set his empty mug aside, then he tossed his keys to her.

Tilting her head to the side in confusion, Zoey lifted the truck's keys. "I'm driving?"

"I'll take you the long way, past some places you might want to take your tours." Easton couldn't resist adding, "Better to learn the backroads now. In a few months, there's going to be several feet of snow and a lot of naked, bearded men on them."

The top of the roadcut made a perfect place to relax for a while, taking in the town from a new point of view. Wiggling her toes in the cool morning air and munching the remains of a baggie of trail mix in her back pocket, River watched the employees of Moose Springs Resort driving to their workplace. In the distance, a partially finished luxury condominium project sat abandoned. The couple of condos that had been completed so far were as visually stunning as the Moose Springs Resort, with rich earth-toned paint palettes, lots of river rock stonework, and expensive log cabin siding. Considering the mountainside view those condos must have, River could imagine them selling easily…especially to some of the wealthier people she knew from the industry. A permanent vacation home in Moose Springs was perfect for those who loved to ski and fish or just be in this beautiful corner of the world.

Unfortunately, the project must be on a hiatus. If she squinted, River could see piles of construction material just inside the gated entry.

A familiar old truck went past with two figures inside, then a few minutes later returned, minus one occupant. The driver had good eyes. She was tucked out of the way up on her perch, but he still pulled over, walking to the base of the roadcut and peering up at her. One eyebrow rose, as if it were strange to find someone in her position.

"Why am I not surprised the person dangling dangerously over the edge is you?" Easton's rumble sounded amused.

"I could claim that I walk on the wild side, but I really don't want to hear Jessie snore anymore. Bree's the dangerous one though. She almost took my eye out with her elbow."

The eyebrow rose further. "You're sleeping in your rental car?"

"Not that it's any of your business, nosy, but *we're* sleeping in *our* rental car. Haven't you heard of the concept of a starving artist?"

"I didn't realize film stars made a habit of going hungry," he replied with a low chuckle. At her own raised eyebrow, Easton added, "I figured it out after I learned your name."

River breathed out a laugh, relaxing back. "Well, I'm behind the camera now. Mostly. We'll see if the dining options become fewer and further in between."

Easton wasn't the worst thing she'd ever seen in the morning. In fact, he was pretty high up on the list of the best. He'd traded the dark T-shirt of yesterday with a white cotton one stretching across his chest, snug on his forearms and loose around his muscled waist. Another pair of worn jeans and those boots that told everyone he met he worked physically for a living.

The man bun was nice and tidy. The beard made her want to run her fingers through it. But they'd only met, and, well...

beard stroking seemed like the kind of thing two people did when they were better acquainted. And maybe had candles lit for beard-stroking ambiance.

"Want to join me? There's room for two." River patted the rock beside her.

"You make a habit of climbing roadcuts?" he asked her.

"Nope." She shook her head. "But it was either this or commit unspeakable crimes to my DP."

"DP?"

"Jessie. Director of photography. He who snores to the point that relatively sane women want to murder him."

It was hard to see from way up there, but River was fairly certain one corner of the beard twitched. Kicking off his boots and peeling off his socks, Easton glanced at the roadcut above him, then chose his own handhold. She hadn't expected him to *actually* join her, invitation or not.

When it came to climbing, River knew her own skills. Still... watching Easton free solo was akin to watching a Kentucky Derby winner walking through a miniature horse pen at a petting zoo.

Easton didn't climb the rock. He flowed over it.

"Someone's a stud," River teased as she watched him climb, popping a peanut in her mouth. "You should charge people to watch you do that."

Okay, so maybe she was flirting. River couldn't help it. When his forehead turned all flushed in embarrassment and surprise, he was kind of adorable.

"I almost didn't recognize you without a pizza box in your hand."

"Thanks for that." Could his rumbling voice be any sexier?

Easton hoisted himself over the ledge with one hand, where River had needed two.

Settling in next to her required his hip to brush against hers, his torso angled so his broad shoulders didn't force her into a dangerous sideways tilt. His hand was braced behind her hip, so close, all she had to do was lean a little.

Funny. She'd always liked a man with a handsome face. This man's face was covered with at least an inch and a half of thick dark-brown beard, so there was no way to know what he looked like beneath it all.

Easton had really pretty eyes though, and when she offered him access to her trail mix bag, he accepted as if they were old friends.

As nice as his eyes were, his voice was even better.

"My sister wants to have that pizza box framed. She's the one I was with when you paid me for my goods and services. Speaking of which…" He dug into his back pocket. "Here."

When Easton flapped the twenty-dollar bill at her, River shook her head. "You earned that fair and square. And your sister is gorgeous."

"She's a brat. We're twins."

"You're kidding." River couldn't believe it.

"Nope. Take the money back. I don't want it."

"Sorry, I'm busy enjoying my morning. More trail mix?"

This time, she poured some in his palm. Easton dumped the whole handful in his mouth and swallowed without choking, the second impressive thing he'd done that morning.

Eyeing her powder-free hands and bare toes, Easton shook his head. "I'd have gone with shoes. The last thing you want is a sliced heel right now."

"Not worth the trade-off." River wiggled her toes at him. They sat in comfortable silence until she added, "Seriously though, thanks for the help yesterday. Your pizza box holding skills are commendable. Almost as good as your climbing skills."

"I suppose I don't need to check *your* climbing skills if you're already up here. That surface was slick, with not a lot of holds. I'm tempted to be impressed."

Flashing him a grin, River popped another peanut in her mouth. "I'm tempted to take that as a compliment."

"Not a lot of free soloing up on the Old Man though."

River hadn't heard that one before. "The Old Man?"

"It's what we call Mount Veil."

"Gotcha." She tilted her head. "I love a compliment as much as the next girl, but why do my climbing skills matter to you?"

"Because it'll be a lot easier getting you and your people up the mountain if I don't have to carry you on my back."

River blinked. "What's that?"

"You didn't know?" Easton asked, sounding as confused as she was. "I learned last night that you three are my clients for the expedition up Mount Veil."

"All I knew was that after being given the runaround by that number you gave me, Jessie made arrangements with a local climb-ing company to take us out there." River indicated the mountain range rising higher behind them. "You're our guide?"

"So I've been informed."

Pausing midchew, River considered that. "Hmm. Well, that makes things super awkward."

"Does it?"

"No, not really, but I may have to reconsider asking you for a drink now since you're officially on the payroll."

Easton shook his head with a chuckle. "Are you sure you want to do this? Veil's no joke. I can just as easily take you out to—"

To his credit, Easton didn't finish that sentence.

"On a nature walk?" River looked at him challengingly.

"Someplace less difficult to access," Easton countered. "Our nature isn't a cakewalk. Plenty of wildlife and lots of chances to get into trouble."

"That doesn't sound like me at all." River laughed softly, then leaned back on her palms. "Don't worry. I've been climbing in the Rockies since I was a child, although nothing too technical. Bree and Jessie have some experience too. I've been training in earnest the last several years. I made a run at El Cap last spring."

"You free soloed El Capitan?"

"That's the goal, but no. I was part of a three-man team. We climbed the Nose with equipment."

"There's enough free-climbing on that route to make most pass. I *am* impressed."

For some reason, the good opinion of this stranger on her climbing skills was a hundred times better than a stranger's opinion of her acting skills. Maybe because acting was what she did. But climbing was who River was.

"Alpine climbing up here is different," Easton warned her. "The windchill can be brutal, and most of Mount Veil is glaciated. Crevasses kill in these mountains faster than you can blink. You're using a whole different set of skills to summit than in the lower forty-eight."

"Yes, but since Moose Springs wants nothing to do with us, Mount Veil is the best option I've got. My movie is up there." Twisting so she could face him, River took in Easton from head to toe. "You know, this might work."

Instant suspicion filled his eyes. "What?"

"It's nothing to worry about."

"And yet I find myself worried."

"Can the beard be trimmed a little?"

A flat look was his only answer. River bumped his shoulder companionably. "Easton Lockett. I would have connected the dots sooner, but all the emails have been from a Joshua L."

"Dad's my camp manager. He doesn't go on climbs with us, but he puts together the client lists and arranges the supplies. Dad's an old pro at all this." Easton glanced at her. "I have some paperwork I need you to sign."

"Umm...technically, I have paperwork for you."

"Do I even want to ask?" Easton sighed.

"You're going to need to sign a nondisclosure agreement, a medical directive in case something happens on the mountain, and a form that states you refuse to hold anyone associated with the film liable for any damage or death that may occur during filming." River winked at him and added, "If Bree bops you over the head with a baseball, you're welcome to press charges, but we try to limit that as much as possible. But the big one is the nondisclosure agreement."

He wasn't only hot and skilled and...well...hot. Easton was smart too. Smart enough to narrow his eyes.

"River. Why am I signing paperwork for you?"

Biting her lip to keep from giggling, River decided the look of slowly dawning horror on his face was better than beard stroking, tight shirts, or man buns could ever be. Leaning in, River whispered in his ear.

"Because you, handsome, are going to star in a documentary."

CHAPTER 4

"YOUR GIRLFRIEND MADE THE FRONT page."

From across their breakfast table, Ash tossed the local newspaper at him. On the front was a picture of a very familiar redhead and her team of hooligans, all three trying and failing miserably to hide the film equipment in their hands. Even in newspaper ink, River was gorgeous. Especially when facing down the newspaper photographer with a defiant glare that would make the bravest of men shrink back a few feet.

She looked even better climbing down a rock face, not that Easton had snuck a peek.

"'World famous actress films documentary about Moose Springs,'" he read aloud. "Why am I looking at this?"

"Because you're on page two. Tasha from the *Moose Springs Daily Register* had so many interesting things to say about you."

A smirk crossed his twin's face, making Easton internally groan.

"Great. Do I want to know?"

"Probably not, but I'm going to tell you anyway. I'm a good sister like that."

Elbows on the table, Ash leaned in, holding her coffee mug

cradled between her hands as the smirk widened. This same table had sat in their family's kitchen for three generations. The house had been updated over those years; the table had not. Three generations of cereal bowls, glass rings, and pot roast dinners. Three lifetimes of memories.

Easton had moved to a small house on the far side of the two-hundred-acre Lockett homestead after high school, needing his own space. And their family land certainly had that. Theirs was one of the largest personal properties within the town of Moose Springs, with some of the prettiest views of the surrounding countryside.

Unlike Easton, Ash had never moved out, and he doubted she ever would. Come hell or high water, there was nothing strong enough to make her leave her home. Which meant Easton was stuck drinking her sludge-like coffee in the mornings when he came to check on his family.

Usually a sleepy grunt was all Easton got from his sister or father, but this morning, his twin sister was beaming like the cat that got in the cream.

"Tasha wrote the truth. She says the town's most skilled outdoorsman sold out and is showcasing our town in a tourism film. A film you also...and here's where Tasha went for blood. You agreed to be a part of too."

Sighing audibly this time, Easton reached for his coffee. "It wasn't like that, Ash."

"Oh, it gets better. Listen to this."

Stealing the paper back from him despite his grab to keep it from her, Ash cleared her throat with dramatic exuberance.

"Tasha says, and I quote: 'Along with hauling them up our hidden gem of a mountain, one of the best for climbing in the nation, Mr. Lockett is risking further commercialization of the oversaturated Moose Springs at a time when residents are still deeply concerned about the luxury condominiums project spear-headed by socialite Lana Montgomery and the Montgomery Group. Rumors of subsequent plans for additional residential buildings adjacent to Moose Springs Resort...blah blah blah...'"

Ash took a long sip of her coffee. "She goes on for a while about how awful Lana is."

"Again, we like Lana," Easton felt compelled to remind his sister for the hundredth time.

"I can like her and still acknowledge the evil music that plays every time she enters the room. Appreciating the overthrow of our world by powerful women and leading the resistance to that particular overthrowing of my hometown aren't mutually exclusive. Oh, here we go." She lifted the paper higher. "'With our own residents helping to assist people like Ms. Montgomery and the invading film crew, it is logical to extrapolate that Easton Lockett is personally responsible for the single-handed destruction of Moose Springs, and we all need to attack him with a pitchfork.'"

Leveling a look at her, Easton said, "It does not say that."

"Okay, maybe not," she conceded. "Tasha does talk about you though. Local mountaineering legend, which is total overselling, by the way. Yada yada going up Mount Veil. Then some climate change stuff and talking about the climbing season becoming less predictable."

"She's not wrong."

"Tasha also quotes you as not being available for comment."

"I didn't know she was calling for that." Shifting in discomfort beneath his sister's knowing stare would only make him lose whatever ground he had to stand on.

He'd never successfully gotten anything past Ash in his life, so he didn't know why he was bothering now.

"Are you and Tasha still a thing?"

"We were never a thing. Just a…"

"Thing." Ash eyed him knowingly. "The other thing."

Nope, he was not talking about that. Easton decided on deflection. "How was your date? The guy from Seward."

"About what you'd expect. Almost everyone in Seward lives in the same apartment building. The vibe over there is too close for my comfort. I'm not sure it'll last."

"What was his name?"

With a shrug, she said, "I'll tell you if it lasts. The article did add in a theory about temperature fluctuations increasing the risk of avalanches."

Eyeing her at the random comment, this time it was Ash's turn to shift uncomfortably.

"I'm only mentioning it," she murmured, voice defensive.

They'd had more than one throwdown over the safety of his choice in occupation. This from a woman who happily flew helicopters in the worst weather imaginable and saw no issues with her own safety.

"I'm keeping my eye out for signs of trouble," Easton said. "You need to stop worrying about this one."

When Ash didn't reply, Easton leaned back in his chair,

balancing on the back two legs as he tossed a piece of elk sausage in his mouth. The Locketts lived off the land as much as possible, although Easton had gotten in a bad habit of showing up at the Tourist Trap most days for lunch. If he had a heart attack from the delicious but greasy fare Graham was slinging, it would be Easton's own fault.

"You break that chair, you're making me a new one."

Their father, Joshua Lockett, limped past to the coffeepot. Widowed two years earlier after Easton's mother finally lost her battle with cancer, Joshua was the remaining parent in their lives. One whose presence registered like the force of nature he'd always been. There was nothing Joshua couldn't do, build, or fix. When a man made a living from conquering mountains, it was hard to best him.

Joshua had taught Easton and Ash everything they knew about mountaineering, but Ash was happier in her helicopter, and after a bad leg injury, Joshua couldn't keep the kind of pace required on a professional climb. If he resented a life of helping his daughter load and unload food and supply shipments for deliveries to more remote locations, he never said anything.

Locketts didn't complain. They got the job done, whatever needed doing.

"No cane today, Dad?" Ash joined their father at the coffee-pot. He paused midpour on his own cup, topping off the mug in Ash's hand before adding what was left to his.

His sister could get away with things Easton never could. Asking their father about his cane was one of those things.

In the privacy of their own home, Joshua would use his cane

on bad leg days. When winter came, most days were bad leg days. But in town or in front of others, he refused to let it show. Talking about the cane earned the kind of look that made most men—including Easton—want to disappear into the floor. But when Ash asked, she got a smile from their father.

"Feeling pretty good today, honey. Thanks."

Serving himself up a plate of the eggs and sausage Easton had made for breakfast, Joshua joined them at the table.

He eyed the chair, then Easton. The critical look wasn't what made Easton nervous. That was normal. It was the mischief in Joshua's eye that Easton didn't trust.

"What's this I heard about you being in some movie?"

Easton dropped his head back. "I'm not in a movie. I'll be standing next to some people taking footage of the mountains. At most, they might get a shot of my feet."

Ash snorted. "You're totally getting a major role. Dad, do you think he'll remember us when he's famous?"

Joshua took a bite of eggs. "Probably not."

"Do you have to tell him everything?" Easton asked his twin. "Just once, it would be nice if you two weren't in cahoots."

"Makes up for all those years when you two kids were the ones in cahoots." With a playful wink at Ash, Joshua took a sip of coffee. "So what role are you playing? First man to fall off a mountain on film?"

"He might be playing sexy mountaineer number two," she added helpfully. "How have your ab workouts been?"

Ignoring their comments, Easton rose to his feet and went to the sink, washing off his plate before sticking it in the dishwasher.

To take away their ammunition, he rolled up the newspaper and stuffed it into his back pocket. "This is me leaving to go to work."

"Tell Spielberg we said hi, Son."

Ash was still snickering as the door closed behind him.

The old Ford truck started when he turned the key. Not every day was he lucky enough to experience that pleasure. Equipment check day was sometimes a long and frustrating process, and showing up late never helped get things off to a good start.

Equipment check day was all about going through River and her crew's equipment with a fine-tooth comb. Assuming even an experienced alpine climber had the right gear for a climb was risky. All it took was one thing to derail a trip. Mount Veil might not be a monster like Denali, but fifteen thousand feet was plenty tall enough to run into trouble.

Providing his clients with a detailed packing list was part of his guide service and the one they tended to go off course on the easiest. He hoped she'd had time to get together everything they needed. Easton had long since learned that a well-packed crew made a happy guide, and a happy guide got his clients to summit on time.

He had an hour before he was supposed to meet River and her team. Which meant he might have time to get a real, palatable cup of coffee before the equipment check.

As he turned off the single lane gravel access road leading from their property and onto the main highway into Moose Springs, Easton's phone rang. This time, he didn't ignore it.

"Easton, it's Tasha."

"Yep."

Yep, meaning she totally screwed him. Dad and Ash might

give him a ribbing, but there were plenty in Moose Springs who would take the article seriously. Increased tourism was a bane to everyone's existence. This was the first time Easton had ever been accused of aiding and abetting, which stuck in his craw something fierce.

Easton had spent his life protecting this town, and he didn't like being on the defensive about his decisions.

As always, Tasha cheerfully ignored his flat tone. "Hey, if you're not too busy, I was wondering if we could get together. I'd love a few comments about the climb you're about to take."

The woman was ballsy, which he'd always liked. Well, until her enjoyment of a takedown had left him at her mercy in front of the entire town. "Really, Tash? After gutting me like a fish on the front page?"

With a cluck of her tongue, she corrected him, "Technically, the gutting was on page two. And I did try to contact you. Not my fault you stopped taking my calls."

Easton grunted. He'd stopped taking her calls because those calls were only for one thing. Call him old-fashioned, but Easton preferred an actual relationship with his...relationships.

"Come on. I'll buy you a drink, and we can talk about it."

Tasha was complicated. To say they'd dated would have been an overstatement. To say they didn't was to leave out some very important details. But he liked her enough to keep getting tugged into her vicinity.

"I'm busy now," he told her, annoyed at his own lingering regret. "I have a gear check with my team."

"I'd love to see what—"

"Nope."

"What about one question on—"

Easton barked out a laugh. The woman was relentless in the pursuit of a story, and he had to respect her ability to get the information she wanted. Which made it even more fun to tell her that he legally couldn't say squat.

"I'll meet you for coffee at Dirty Joe's, but it'll have to be quick. The climb is off the record because I signed an NDA yesterday."

The silence over the phone told him she was spinning that bit of information over in her mind.

"What are they doing that requires an NDA?"

"It's par for the course. There's no story here, only some people taking photos of animals on Mount Veil because they can't film in town. That's it, Natasha."

"Okay, fine. We'll figure out a way to get around the NDA." A pause, then she added in a low purr, "You know I love it when you say my full name."

Yep. Which was why he always told himself not to say it.

Coffee with Tasha wasn't safe. Neither was the location where she wanted to meet, but Dirty Joe's Coffee Woes was adjacent to the park where he'd scheduled River and her team to meet him. Easton didn't have a home office. A website—grudgingly done by Ash—was the limit to his advertising. He wasn't interested in expanding, and he received far more requests for climbs than he could ever accommodate.

Most of his climbs were Denali, but Easton was one of only a couple of guides in the state who would take clients up Mount Veil. And if he could, Easton always accepted the climbs for Mount Veil every time.

He loved that mountain. Tasha knew it too.

The coffee shop was a tiny place, constantly busy with only a few bistro tables and mismatched chairs to share between the customers. Usually Easton got his coffee and drank it in the park, but Tasha had either the luck to get the table in the corner or had bribed—or driven—someone to vacate their seat. Normally, he would have offered to buy her a coffee, because coffee generally turned into lunch, then dinner, then his place. This time, he bought his own coffee, only felt a little guilty about not offering to buy hers, and then sat down with her.

Tasha took a sip, eyes locked on him. "So you're heading up the Old Man again. Are you excited? This is the second time this season, right?"

He nodded, remaining silent.

She knew fully well Easton had done a run at Mount Veil at the start of the summer, escorting a small group of hikers out of Anchorage up the mountain before taking a group up Denali at the end of May and then another in June. The Denali trek was three weeks long, and most guides didn't take a second trip up there like Easton had. The Denali money was good, and no one had expected him to go for a fourth summit that summer.

Easton hadn't planned on it either, but River Lane had a way of messing with his plans.

Tapping her fingernails against the handle of her coffee cup,

Tasha pursed her lips. "Aren't you worried you're pushing it? That's a lot of high-altitude climbing in one season."

"I'll manage."

Tasha chuckled. "Short, succinct answers. I really got you on the piece, huh? It wasn't personal, Easton. You know we're always good."

Even as she sat across from him, a table safely between them, Easton could see the way Tasha was fidgeting in her seat. She had two modes: a hundred miles an hour or sleeping. At one point, it had seemed cute. Now, he recognized it for what it was. She was ready to pounce.

He just didn't know if it was the verbal pouncing or the other kind.

"I'm trying to keep myself out of more trouble," Easton replied. "And the Old Man isn't the tallest peak in the state. I'll be fine."

"Do you ever get tired of taking peak baggers up there? Because if this documentary is at all successful, you're going to get overrun with groups wanting to add our mountain to their list of conquests. Isn't part of being a hidden gem staying hidden?"

"You think I'm trying to make an extra buck at the town's expense." It wasn't a question. Tasha leaned in, voice lowered. "I think you have a family that relies on your income."

"Ash and Dad are doing fine." Easton frowned at her. "Tash, do you actually believe what you put in that article?"

For once, she hesitated, glancing away. "I think social outrage sells stories."

"At my expense? At my clients' expenses?" He wasn't hurt.

Tasha wasn't someone Easton had let close enough to hurt him, but he was wary.

"Like I said, it's nothing personal." Taking his hand, Tasha squeezed his fingers. "But if I upset you, I'm sorry."

Easton didn't have the willpower to be mad at many people. Grumpy, yes. Mad, no. Squeezing back, he removed his hand from hers. Fingers were much safer when wrapped around a coffee cup.

"It's fine. You're doing your job."

The defensiveness in her shoulders softened. "Thanks, Easton. You know how I get when I'm onto something good. And your client is the hot button story in this town right now. Famous actress on a career slide—"

At his confused look, Tasha leaned in again. "Didn't you know? You probably didn't watch her films, did you? The last few have been flops. Now River's behind the camera, here. Do you think she's trying to make a name for herself as a filmmaker? The entertainment industry is notorious for keeping women and marginalized groups from behind the camera. Is that why she took this job?"

Just because she wasn't trying to trick him—he hoped— didn't mean Tasha wouldn't print anything he accidentally let slip. Easton didn't know a thing about his client other than her name and someone in her crew liked pineapple on their pepperoni pizza. He'd been forced to smell that particular combination in the pizza box sign long enough. But Tasha would never believe that.

Taking refuge behind the NDA was the safest bet. "Nondisclosure agreement, remember?"

Tasha snickered. "You're immovable, aren't you? That's why

I like you. You've always been a challenge. Why didn't we ever work out?"

"We weren't that compatible."

That was a softer version of the truth. The thing was, Tasha wasn't loyal. She wasn't disloyal per se, but Easton was going to die with the name of every person he'd ever cared about etched onto his heart. The names weren't many, but they ran deep. Not falling for Tasha was the best thing Easton had ever done for himself.

"We weren't that *incompatible*," Tasha reminded him.

Well…that was true too.

Easton was saved from having to reply by the bell jingling as a new customer hustled through the door, auburn hair loose around her shoulders.

River was either oblivious to or didn't care how many eyes drifted her way, including Easton's own. Busy scrolling through her phone as she stood in line, River was halfway to the counter before she noticed Easton noticing her. River hopped out of line and met him at the table.

"Hey, I didn't realize you'd be here." The stunning redhead gave them both a warm greeting as she checked the smartwatch on her wrist. "I was going to grab something before we met up."

Easton raised his own cup in salute. "Great minds think alike."

"Or redundantly," she countered playfully. Rolling her eyes, she added, "Did you see that article today in the local paper? Someone is getting a strongly worded letter. We haven't even started to film yet, and apparently we're the scourge of the town—"

"River." Cutting her off midsentence, Easton looked toward his companion. "This is Tasha."

"Oh, sorry." River offered a hand to the other woman. "It's nice to meet you."

Tasha perked up immediately. "Come join us. I'd love to buy you a cup of coffee."

Even as she scooted her chair over to make room, River's blue eyes were narrowing. "Wait, what was your name again?"

"Be careful what you say around her," Easton warned, only half playfully. "She's a reporter."

Tasha gave him a horrified look. "Tattle much?"

Easton rose and put a few dollars on the table. "You can handle yourself." When he glanced at River, he saw her staring at Tasha with flat dislike. He hid his mirth behind his coffee cup. "You both can. A smart man leaves at this point."

Heading for the door, Easton could hear his client's voice, volume and tone flexing around her words as if they were living beings.

"You know what, Tasha? I'm actually really glad to run into you this morning. And yes, I'd love to chat. Number one, and this is absolutely on the record: Don't you dare think for one second you can come after a member of my team and get away with it. Easton is officially on the payroll, so back off my people. Number two—"

As the door shut behind him, Easton couldn't help a slight smile. One of her people, huh? He'd been called worse things.

CHAPTER 5

RIVER WOULDN'T LIE. SHE'D ENJOYED every second of letting the reporter have it.

One of the things she'd been warned of early in her career was that above all else, she needed to be pleasant. Don't make waves. Don't push back. And maybe at first, she'd gone along with it because she was new to LA, broke and scared. Hungry for more than only her dream of being an actress, River had been living off discount peanut butter and stale bread, sleeping in her car, and praying she didn't have to tuck tail and crawl back home defeated. She'd needed the work, so she'd followed that advice.

One of the things she had finally learned in the industry was her most important lesson yet. Pleasant was code for pushover.

Screw. That.

She'd had her fair share of battles with the press, and while some reporter with an agenda to push was not even on her radar of what affected her, Tasha crossed the line when she went after Easton. He was the only one in this town who'd tried to help them, and trying to make him feel bad for taking her and the crew to Mount Veil was the straw that broke the camel's back.

And boy, taking the reporter to task had been exactly what she needed.

Two coffees in hand, River nearly bounced as she crossed the street to the park where she'd left the rental SUV. A familiar faded red truck was parked next to her. Leaning against the tailgate, Easton Lockett was a sight for sore eyes.

"Should I make sure Tasha still has a pulse?" he asked.

"I probably shouldn't have been so tough on her," River said. "But she was mean to you, and you're very good-looking."

The beard twitched. If he was smiling under there, it was impossible to tell, but her gut said his lips were doing something.

"Do I need to call for Jonah again?"

River laughed, leaning back against the tailgate next to him. "You realize you've been threatening me with the cops since the minute we met. I'm starting to think you don't trust me."

"I'm going into the bush with you." Arms folded loose across his chest, it was hard not to notice biceps the size of his, right at her eye level. "If I didn't trust you, I'd never step foot above ten thousand feet with you."

"What about below ten thousand feet?" she asked.

"I can hold my own closer to sea level." He gazed down at her, adding mischievously, "But canceling on you might be even scarier."

"Oh, trust me, it would be." River handed him the second coffee. "Here, I brought you a refill. Least I can do for making you the talk of the town."

"Not a big deal." Even with the beard, River could see him choke on his first sip of coffee. "Damn, woman. What did you put in here?"

"Hey, I never claimed to know how you like your coffee. I just brought you one. I call that the River Lane special. Half hot chocolate, half coffee, and enough espresso to raise your heart rate."

"You're worse than Ash." The man was brave enough to take another sip, grimace, then keep on drinking.

River gestured toward the SUV. "Okay, how do we do this?"

"We need to do an equipment check. And then afterward, I need to evaluate everyone's skill levels. Where's the rest of the crew?"

"Shooting B-roll."

"Shooting who?"

Upon seeing the confused expression on his face, River had to hide her smile behind her cup. "B-roll is extra footage that can be used to fill in gaps in the documentary. We're trying to get everything we can before we leave town. Don't worry. I have everyone's packs in the car."

"Are you sure that's a good idea? You're going to get caught. There's an official watch out on you right now."

River almost spit her coffee. "I'm sorry, what was that?"

"The town has a message board, and everyone posts the newest film crew sighting. They have you on high alert."

"Show me."

After some serious pressure, Easton finally caved and took out his phone. Sure enough, the website he pulled up showed a running list of—

"Wait. Are they calling this alien invader sightings?"

"They think Jessie kind of looks like E.T."

"I mean...they're not wrong." River slumped against the truck. "Is this why Jonah shows up everywhere we are?"

"Probably." His expression shifted from amusement to a frown. "If I'm taking everyone up, I need an accurate skill assessment of all of them."

"We're a skeleton crew, big guy. We all split the tasks, or we'd never get anything done. Don't worry. They'll get here eventually."

Easton wasn't happy with her answer. "Then this will have to wait."

When River opened her mouth, Easton cut her off before she dug her heels in and forced the issue. "I understand the conflict, and I'm not disagreeing with your need for splitting tasks. I just can't responsibly take you three up a mountain like Veil and not have an idea of your competency levels. I've had clients who'd never used crampons. I've had clients who didn't even know how to put them on or had the wrong size for their boots. Now's the time to be figuring this out, not after the helicopter has dropped us off on the slope."

River perked up. "Oooh, we're taking a helicopter?"

"Unless you want to hike miles of tundra and destroy your feet before we get there." Easton gave her a sexy smile. "Have at it, but I'm taking the helicopter."

That smile was far more dangerous than even the broad shoulders or tightly muscled arms only inches away from her. To distract herself, River changed the subject. "Do you think we'll need the crampons? We got them because they were on the list, but I've never needed them before." River pulled a receipt out of her pocket, waving it at him. "I kept thinking you were going to add a kitchen sink. And then you did."

"It's not a sink. It's a lightweight collapsible bowl for washing dishes when we're lower on the mountain. Believe it or not, fish don't love soap bubbles in their rivers."

"And Rivers can read. The label says camping sink. See? Right here. *Sink.*"

Chuckling, he finished his coffee and folded the paper cup, tucking it in his pocket. "Trust me, you'll want it. And we won't need the crampons at first, but we'll be climbing a glacier once we get above the tree line. You'll be glad when the mountain turns into one massive Slip 'N Slide."

"Is it bad I might enjoy that?"

"Yes, because it's my job to dive after you."

River gave a playful sigh. "And we were never heard from again. At least it was good while it lasted."

"We'll always have the police station," he agreed placidly.

"And the weird bucket sink that's not a sink but is totally a sink."

Silence, then Easton looked over at her. "They aren't coming, are they?"

"They're probably running from Officer Jonah as we speak."

Easton checked the website on his phone. "They were last seen in—" He paused midsentence, scanning the thread. "The resort lobby."

"That's not creepy at all. Where am I?"

A flush reddened his forehead. "Flirting with me in the park across from Dirty Joe's Coffee Woes."

She twisted the cup in her hand. "Is that what DJCW stands for?"

"He's not that dirty," Easton assured her.

"But he is or at some point *has* been dirty. Enough to have earned the nickname Dirty Joe."

His mouth twitched upward again.

Suddenly, the coffee in her cup was far less appealing. "Your town is the weirdest town, you know that, right?"

"We do our best. You need to call your people, but you and I can go over most of this together now. That'll cut the least into their filming time. And running from Jonah time."

There really was no arguing with his logic. She had no choice but to agree.

When River made the call, at first she only got hard pushback. They'd found the perfect place to hide on the resort grounds and had set up the tripod. Tearing down now would only cause more work than they'd scheduled time for that day. Bree, carefree as always, was more than willing to adjust plans, but Jessie made his normal fuss. Finally, River managed to lure Jessie in with agreeing to buy everyone dinner afterward but not without a few well-honed barbs on his end about River's pain in the ass new boyfriend.

"Well, that was unpleasant." She hung up the phone, joining Easton at the pile of gear they'd pulled from her vehicle and spread on the ground.

"I could hear him from all the way over here." Easton picked up one of their tents. "That guy's got a pair of lungs on him."

"And I was accused of being dramatic. Speaking of, you have the face."

"What face?"

"The face you had when I asked you to agree to be filmed. What's wrong?"

He lifted up the lightweight tent in one hand. "This is a single-walled tent."

Easton frowned at the matching tents in her crew's equipment piles. She didn't know why. Of all their gear, the brand-new tents were the best part.

"Yeah, we got a great price on them too. I haggled."

"Successfully?"

"Oh definitely. They never saw us coming. I haggled them down and then hit them with a group coupon. Not only was the price fabulous, they're four-season tents and weigh under two pounds." River mimicked an explosion with her hand, then wriggled her fingertips at Easton. "Boom."

He smacked an open palm down on the tent fabric. "I hate to break it to you, but a single-walled tent up there is going to turn into a condensation factory. The moisture will coat the inside of your tent, refreeze, and fall on your head. You don't want to sleep in that; it'll be a nightmare."

"They were the best tents that didn't require a small mortgage to buy," River countered.

Easton shook his head. "You want to cut corners, do it somewhere else. Not in your gear, and not on a climb like this."

"I could always pay you less and get the better tents." The option had appeal, but Easton only stared at her. She stared back. His eyes narrowed. Hers narrowed a lot more. The beard took on a stubborn set, bristling out. River didn't have a beard, so she pushed out her chin and pretended.

"What are you doing?" he asked, sounding concerned.

"Intimidating you."

"Are you sure that's what you're doing?"

"Definitely."

Unlike most, he didn't even flinch under her stare. The man was immovable, and the sparkle in his eyes only grew the farther she lifted her chin.

"I'm not letting my clients turn into Popsicles. Get better tents," he told her.

"Fine," River sighed. "I'll figure it out."

If looks could kill, Easton would be bleeding out with an ice pick wedged into his own crevasse.

Compromise didn't seem like her forte, and Easton knew a determined woman when he saw one. When faced with someone who didn't play well with others, the best thing to do was know what motivated them. As Easton and River continued to sort through their gear, Easton decided to pry a little.

"Why the shift from acting to filming?" he asked her.

"Do you want the on the record answer or the off the record answer? Because one is a whole lot sweeter than the other."

"I never needed much sugarcoating. Tell me the real reason."

"Men suck. I'm planning on destroying them all."

At her dead serious tone, Easton found himself smiling. "See? My first instincts were right about you. You're a threat."

"And don't you forget it." River flashed him a quick grin. Just like that, she wasn't ready to kill him anymore. The woman was quicksilver, and normally, that wasn't his thing.

But, man. He liked how she kept him on his toes.

"I'm not one for standing around and watching things go to crap." River's voice firmed. "It was time to find something new.

Being in front of the camera hasn't been working out too well lately, so it's time to try being behind it."

After a moment, she arched an eyebrow at him. "What about you?"

"What about me?"

"Are you a threat?"

By the humorous look on her face, he could tell she wasn't talking about a threat to herself. With a low chuckle, Easton said, "Only to the fish I catch for dinner or the mountains I try to summit."

"Do you normally climb Mount Veil? Denali's the tallest on the continent."

She'd done her homework. Easton nodded. "Most of my climbs are on Denali. I'd rather go up the Old Man, but most people don't come all this way to climb a fourteener."

"You don't do this year-round, right? Taking people out climbing is seasonal, isn't it?"

"Unfortunately." Easton shrugged. "I teach indoor climbing when the weather turns colder. Plus, my sister runs supplies in the area in her helicopter. She's busier in winter, so Dad and I help. Ash is the one flying us to the mountain. "

"In her helicopter. Your sister is so cool."

"My sister is terrifying."

"You don't look like the type to be frightened of much. Only women, huh?"

Easton caught her eye. "You'd have loved my mother. She was almost as tough as you. I'd rather climb Everest naked than tick her off."

"That's an image," River murmured, her eyes flickering

across his shoulders. "Have you ever been to Everest? With your clothes on?"

"Nope." He let that hang between them to make her grin, then he added, "But damn, do I want to go."

"Maybe that's what I'll do." River tilted her head in consideration. "Go around the world and film mountain climbs."

"I hope you've got some money put away," Easton said. "I've been saving for years to get to Nepal by myself. Taking three people up there, plus the cost of getting the equipment up—" Midsentence, Easton stopped. "Hey, speaking of, I need to see the film equipment."

A hand flap was all he received. "It's fine. We've been hauling it everywhere. You don't have to worry. It's not very much weight."

"You're paying me to worry, River," he reminded her. For some reason, he liked the way her name felt on his tongue. Clearing his throat, Easton turned back to his inspections.

Easton already knew River was a competent climber based on how she had organized her pack. She had no issues with her gear, and she seemed in good enough shape for the climb.

"How many fourteeners have you done?"

"Only Rainier." Upon seeing his frown, River frowned in return. "Why? Is that a problem?"

"The Old Man might not be as tall as Everest or the rest of those monsters, but he's got more than a few tricks up his sleeve. If you don't respect him, he's not going to give you a pass."

"Isn't that why we hired you? Aren't you supposed to be the best?"

The challenge in her question pricked at his pride, and Easton raised his eyes to hers. She wasn't wrong. If anyone knew these mountains, it was Easton. Mountaineering had been in his family for multiple generations. Mount Veil wasn't only his paycheck. It was his way of life.

"I'll do my job up there," Easton told her, holding River's gaze. "But I can't carry three climbers on my back if things go wrong."

"Things won't go wrong." River's confident smile could take down anyone within a five-mile radius.

"So why are you making the documentary? Other than the tourism board asking you to do it?"

"Two years ago, the best part I've ever seen in my life was dropped in my lap. The script was terrible, but the part..." Expression dreamy, River settled down on the grass next to him. "The part was amazing. It was a historical film, set in the early 1900s. It was about early women mountaineers. I already liked to climb, so I fought for the part."

"What movie is it?" Easton was deeply attracted to strong women, and the idea of a movie about a group of them doing something he loved was right up his alley.

River's dreamy expression turned fierce. "It's not. The project got axed before the first scene was filmed. Back to a stack of terrible roles that want all my clothes off. I don't mind a love scene, but what's been offered has been gratuitous garbage or a joke. I didn't work this hard to learn my craft to go down like that."

"So you decided to...I don't know the right word for it. Be the film person?"

"Directing," River supplied for him. "Producing. And don't get me started on that. The industry is terrible about letting women behind the camera. After two years of fighting, the Moose Springs documentary was the first job I've been offered."

"So now you're here."

"I'm here, and with your help, we're going to make the most amazing documentary about the most amazing place, Easton. And it will matter. What we're doing now *matters*. My time and talent will not be wasted on shower scenes in bad horror movies."

Something told him that was what River was chasing, as much as the summit.

"To be honest, I can't imagine you not getting the parts you want. When I was looking up everyone last night, I kept running into phrases like 'magnetic' and 'America's sweetheart.'" Her snort was so indelicate, Easton couldn't help but chuckle. "Not your choice of words?"

"My publicist's choice of words. She gets paid very well."

Easton glanced toward the direction of the mountain in question, hidden behind the closer peaks in the range. "Are you sure you want to do this, River? Veil's a hard climb. People have died up there."

"I'm not afraid."

He shifted on the grass, resting his arms on his knees. "I am. You should always be a little afraid of what the mountains are capable of doing. We're nothing to them, a speck on the ground. A flea trying to hop to the top of a man's head."

"Some men are taller than others, cowboy. Harder to hop up." River shot him a grin, and Easton found himself returning it.

"What?" she asked.

"I like your accent," he told her. "It only comes out when you feel strongly about something."

They fell quiet, the silence between them awkward. But when Easton looked over, River was gazing at him, her expression unreadable.

"Hey, Easton? Did you want to...I don't know...do something after this? Get a drink?"

He hesitated, not sure what he wanted to say. Yes, because... well...yes. And no, because...definitely no. But probably yes.

"I'm not trying to get you drunk," she said, rolling her eyes in playful exasperation. "Can you even get drunk?"

"Not that I've noticed so far."

"Is that a no?"

"No. If you get your friends here before the day runs out, I might even give you a yes."

Had he agreed to a date? Or drinks between two traveling companions? Easton didn't know, and the proximity to her wasn't helping clear his head. Putting distance between them was probably a good idea.

Moving on to the next pile, Easton had started to make mental note of what extra rope he needed to bring when an unknown vehicle pulled into the park beside them. He frowned until he recognized the driver, Dillon, and the two people climbing out of the back seat. Dillon rolled down the window.

"Hey, East."

"New car?" he asked Dillon, the town's most infamous rideshare driver.

"Yep, she's a beauty all right."

She was a Ford, so he was betting River wouldn't agree. Sure enough, a quick glance to his client showed her hiding her smirk behind her coffee cup.

Several years earlier, a failed career in stock car racing had sent Dillon home to Moose Springs with his tail between his legs. Scruffy, young, and hungry, Dillon hadn't found his way yet, but he had found an excuse to stay behind the wheel, even if not at the speed he was accustomed. Not all the resort guests zipped around in Ferraris or were driven in high-dollar coaches. Some rented normal cars or took rideshares around town and to their sightseeing destinations.

Dillon was nice, but you couldn't pay Easton enough money to climb in a vehicle with him.

"I hope you people know how expensive rideshares are in this town." Jessie paused for effect as he and Bree hauled their equipment out of the car's back seat. "And there was a *moose*. I was filming a moose, River, and this one didn't spook and try to trample anyone." He hefted his camera. "If you want more than thirty seconds of wildlife on this thing, you have to let me film them."

"There are a lot of moose," Easton whispered to her out of the corner of his mouth. "Named the town after them."

River coughed to hide her laugh.

"Is she the actress everyone is talking about?" Dillon asked.

"Director and producer," Easton corrected the kid. For some reason, it annoyed him a little that Dillon seemed interested in River. Not that everyone didn't already stare at her, and the younger man wasn't a bad guy. It was just...annoying.

Easton stood and moved to the window, bracing a hand on the hood of Dillion's sedan.

"They're with me."

Three words spoken pleasantly, but the right three words for this town. Dillon shrugged, shooting Easton an amused look. "Well, you all have a nice day. Remember my number if you want a ride again. I'll be here all week."

"What number was it again?" Bree started to ask, amenable to the suggestion, but Jessie started making cutting gestures across his throat. "I mean...no. We're...no."

Disappointed, Dillon drove away.

"A moose, River." Jessie turned back to her, petulant and grumpy.

"I'll find you another one." Easton gave Jessie a companionable thump on the shoulder.

"Stop whining," Bree told him, walking over to River. "We got plenty on the handheld alone. After we add in your footage, we'll have more than enough. River, look at this."

When she opened a handheld video camera, playing back the film, both women's heads turned to the screen, utterly focused on what they were looking at.

Which left no one to care how bad Jessie felt. Except for Easton.

Jessie sucked in a deep breath, as if put upon terribly. "The *only* thing worth shutting down for was getting to eat something. Is there food here? No? Exactly."

"Are you going to complain this much on the mountain?" Easton asked.

"Depends on them." Jessie frowned, then he sighed again. "And my blood sugar."

Checking the time on his phone, Easton said, "We'll run

through this and then get some dinner. My treat. The company can pay for all of us tonight. And you can park the car at my place. I don't have extra rooms, but there's a couch and you have your sleeping bags. Plus, there's a shower."

Normally, Easton would never have made the offer, but...well... he didn't care for the idea of River sleeping in a car in the middle of a parking lot somewhere, even if it had been their own faults.

Jessie opened his mouth, then closed it again, unable to find anything in the offer to complain about. "Okay, that's a good deal."

Feeling her watching him, Easton glanced at River. When she winked at him, his hands stopped working. There was no other reason for the rope to slip out of his fingers.

A smirk touched Jessie's lips. "Don't do it, buddy. She's chewed up and spit out tougher than you."

Easton didn't need the warning. He wasn't surprised one bit by that piece of information.

"Oh!" Bree held up her phone, perking up. "How about this?"

"Looks good." River took the phone and tilted it his way. "Hey, Easton?"

Her voice calling his name did something to him. Something Easton couldn't begin to understand and didn't want to...not yet. But when she said his name, he couldn't help but look into her eyes. He'd drunk from glacier pools and never seen anything as blue. There were worse things than being chewed on for a while.

"Have you ever heard of the Tourist Trap?"

Worse things like taking them there.

As tiny diners went, this one smelled better than most.

"Nope. Nope nope nope. Out."

River blinked, utterly unprepared for the reaction of the Tourist Trap's cook when she and her crew walked in the door. Handsome enough to attract his own level of attention and large enough not to look diminutive next Easton—who was leaning against the bar to talk to him. The cook's vigorous head shake took River aback.

"Excuse me?" she asked, looking between him and Easton.

Their guide had left the park before they had, the gear check completed and everyone signed off as safe to climb. The restaurant was packed, and finding parking had been a nightmare. The only reason they weren't still outside circling the lot was she had noticed Easton's truck behind the building in the employees-only section and parked next to him.

"It's on the sign," the cook said, pointing to the dry erase board behind him. Sure enough, it read 'No film crews allowed.' "I have the right to refuse service to anyone I deem a threat to my other customers."

"Graham, don't be a bully."

Graham the mayor? No, it couldn't be.

A short, slender woman with delicate glasses perched on her nose was seated on a stool at Easton's side. She leaned over and said something to Graham, earning a loud and long-suffering sigh from the cook. Everyone was watching, making River's blood boil.

"I'm not a bully, Zoey Bear. I'm protecting my establishment and my employees from being harassed by a media outlet."

Zoey aimed a firm look at him. "You're the only employee. And you're the only one harassing people."

"Okay, fine," Graham said, king of his tiny domain of processed meats. "But don't blame me if their food is lukewarm and barely edible."

"I was under the assumption it always is," River shot back. "Are you usually this rude to your customers?"

An amused look was his only response. "Only the ones I don't want."

Before River could reply, Bree grabbed her arm, looking around excitedly. "This is how it's supposed to be here. Didn't you read the reviews? It's one of those places where they deliberately insult the customers."

"Can we hasten along the hazing of the new people and get to the fries?" Jessie's voice had taken on a whine. "I'm starving."

"I want a Growly Bear." Bree held up her phone. "The review site says we can't leave without one."

"It's a bad idea." Shaking her head at a picture of a very inebriated individual holding up a bright blue drink, River added, "We have work to do. We can celebrate after the shoot is over."

Graham winked at River, as if she and he weren't becoming mortal enemies then and there. "You run a tight ship, Captain. Come on. A Growly Bear makes everyone feel better."

Bree and Jessie looked so disappointed, River caved and turned to Graham. "Fine, whatever. One Growly Bear each, but that's it. Plus all the things on the grill for all of us."

"I don't know," he murmured. "It feels like we're running low. This big ass guy walked in here first and he cleaned us out."

"Graham." Easton's growl was menacing enough, it made the person on his other side jump. "Feed her."

"Only her?"

Easton aimed a flat stare at Graham, who grinned and didn't even flinch. The man must have had nerves of steel, because everyone else around them—her crew included—shifted out of Easton's proximity. Finally, he held up his hands in supplication. "Hey, hey, no need to yell, buddy. I didn't know you were so sweet on her."

If there hadn't been so much hair on Easton's face, River might have been able to tell if the comment made Easton flush with embarrassment.

Token protest to their existence made, Graham took their orders and payment with the quick, professional actions of someone who had to move a lot of patrons through his door. Except the man had never met Bree. Bree, who could spend an hour staring at a menu in a restaurant. Give her more than three options, and they would be stuck for an hour.

To his credit, Graham tried to be patient. He waited. And waited. And waited some more. Eventually, he leaned on the counter.

"Darlin', I hate to break it to you, but the options aren't going to get any better the longer you think about it. I can put the meat on the fries or the fries on the meat. Or get you really drunk. But that's it."

As usual, Jessie—impatient as ever—was going insane. "Hey there, SH. Help a lady out. What's good here?"

"SH?" Zoey asked.

"Sexy Hagrid," they replied in unison.

The look that crossed Graham's face was akin to a small child at Christmas. "Everyone's eating for free."

"He's not like Hagrid," Zoey protested. "Your muscles are

much more muscly and less ogre-ish. And the beard is sexy, not off-putting."

"Far sexier than Hagrid." River winked at him while Jessie sized up his arms.

"Hagrid after a *lot* of cardio."

Bree chimed in. "Maybe if Hagrid and a wood nymph had a slightly less Hagrid-esque child."

When Easton stood, River hooked his arm and pulled him back down, snickering. "Come on. You're one of the crew now. You're going to get some ribbing. It's part of the whole 'we're isolated on location, so we annoy each other as much as possible' theory of surviving film shoots."

"No cameras," Graham warned them as he dropped a fresh basket of fries into the fryer. "I will deep-fry your equipment."

"He actually will," Zoey said. She flashed a pretty smile at Graham, then turned shy eyes to River. "You're River Lane, aren't you?"

"Most days." River turned to Zoey with the friendly pleasantness she always took when meeting fans. "It's nice to meet you, Zoey."

Unlike with Easton, it was more than easy to see the flush of embarrassment on the other woman's face. Zoey opened her mouth, then closed it again. She mumbled something close to *it's nice to meet you*, then sat back down on her seat.

"Hey, East, I think my fiancée got starstruck," Graham said, not unkindly. "Help a lady out? Anything embarrassing you could share about your companion over there?"

Oh, they were doing *this* now?

"Graham, don't tease her," Zoey immediately said. "I mean it, mister."

"Can Easton tease her?" he countered. "They're teammates. She said the ribbing was mutual."

"Your ribbing gets mean."

"Easton can tease me all he wants," River told the other woman reassuringly. "Bring it on. When your life is regularly plastered over entertainment news, and rarely with stories that are true, you build up a thick skin."

When Easton's mouth twitched a little on one side, River knew he was willing to play the game.

"She did kidnap me," Easton said.

"No, I didn't." River shook her head. "You offered me the ride. If anyone was kidnapped, it was me. You'll have to do better than that."

"She tried to poison me with the worst coffee I've ever had."

"There's no accounting for taste." River stole one of his fries. "Come on. Hit me where I live."

"She told me I had to go on a date with her tonight."

Despite herself, River couldn't keep the offense out of her voice. "I did *not*. I never once pressured you—and this is not a date."

"Food, alcohol, your being mad at me. Feels like most of my dates. If you order a salad and steal all my fries, I might as well call it what it is."

Graham leaned on the counter, stealing Zoey's hand. "Sounds rough, man. I'd try to save you from her, but I'm a little busy at the moment."

Busy not helping his customers, not flipping the delicious-smelling burgers on the grill, and not even considering the french fries that currently had River drooling.

"You're not the mayor, are you?" she asked suspiciously.

"Of course not. That's way too much work for a guy like me."

River felt her eyes narrow. That had rolled off his tongue far too easily. "So...if I were to say I was going to film wherever I wanted, that wouldn't be your problem, right?"

A flinch. Ha! She had him.

"You owe me a permit."

"Sorry, darlin'. I'm fresh out." He gave her a charming smile. "You should ask Ashtyn Lockett. She might be able to help."

Right. River snorted as she watched Graham completely ignoring the next person in line. "How do you even stay in business?" This man's customer service skills were the absolute worst.

"Not without a lack of trying for the opposite. Your food's there on the counter."

Jessie looked horrified. "That's ours? Dude, why didn't you say anything?" He grabbed the tray and hustled off to the table Bree had saved for them.

Food served, Graham turned his full attention back to Zoey. The pair were adorable in their inability to focus on anything but each other. Which gave Easton a clear third wheel type of presence.

Drinking his beer with the occasional measured swig, Easton was studiously avoiding interrupting the love story happening three feet away. River was still starving, and her burger was calling her from the table, but she lingered.

"So, that reporter…"

"I'll make a call," Easton offered. "But my gut says Tasha's not going to write a very nice article about you."

"Yeah, well, she wrote a not-very-nice article about you. I couldn't give two craps about what she says about me. So, the reporter. Tasha. How long were you two together?"

Easton raised one eyebrow of his own.

"You're a really tall, very strong man. Men like you do this thing with their shoulders when they talk to someone they're attracted to. They kind of drop them, a subconscious effort to make themselves less large, less intimidating."

The eyebrows furrowed together, giving him a confused, cuddly bearlike appearance. "I'm not seeing her," he finally said.

"I wasn't worried," River replied. "You were only dropping one shoulder. You didn't go both shoulders, so I figured you weren't totally on board."

Easton's voice was a warm, low rumble, like rocks snuggling up to each other. "No, both feet are firmly in the ocean and swimming for shore."

"To smoother waters." River tilted her glass to him. Easton clinked his beer to her Growly Bear, then they both took a sip. "Yikes. What does he put in these?"

"Enough sugar to mask the consequences."

"Don't worry. I can hold my liquor." Licking the sweetness off her lips, River added, "This isn't actually a date, you know. I hate to disappoint you, but I don't date people who might leave me on a mountain summit if they get their feelings hurt."

"Are my feelings going to get hurt?" His eyes crinkled.

That voice. She could wrap herself up in that voice and cuddle on the couch all day in it.

"Let's say that I don't have a track record of happy exes in my past. They always expect one thing, and when they realize I'm nothing like what they imagined, it always goes downhill. Really, really fast."

Now, why did she say that? Talking about her exes was not the best way to...whatever it was they were doing right now.

Easton leaned into the counter, taking a fry and popping it into his mouth. "I have a hard time seeing that."

"You can take the girl out of Wyoming, but you can't take the Wyoming out of the girl. If I can outdrink you, outride you, and outshoot you, that's fine. But if I can change a tire faster than you without calling roadside assistance, then you and I aren't going to last long."

Easton took a sip of his beer, then asked, "Is this you trying to warn me or warn me off?"

"I suppose that's up to you."

He gazed at her.

"What?"

"I was thinking I'm not sure I want to go up a mountain with you."

"Oh really? Why's that?"

Leaning in, he let his eyes drop to her lips, but only for the briefest moment. "Because I'm not sure I could leave you up there."

Damn, that man could heat up a room with a single sentence. The tension between them wasn't thick enough to cut with a knife....it was melted chocolate. Warm and gooey and impossible to get off her skin. Dragging her closer as it threatened to solidify into something as sweet but dangerously real.

A little too real. River inhaled a deep, steadying breath.

"I should probably go eat my food," she murmured.

The low, deep rumble was even better when his voice softened. "I should stay right here."

River lifted her drink, trying not to look as giddy as she felt. It was the drink. Graham had poisoned her and made her flirt to the point of giddiness. Definitely the diner owner's fault.

As she walked away, River could hear Graham mutter to Easton, "Hey, buddy. You were going both shoulders there. Just sayin'."

"Shut up."

Unable to keep her lips from curving, River stole one more appreciative look at Easton as she joined her crew.

Yeah. She'd noticed the shoulder thing too.

CHAPTER 6

THE EVENING HAD BEEN FUN—AS fun as it could be listening to people screeching into the karaoke machine. By the time they left, Graham's expression had turned pained. River might've felt bad for him if he hadn't been such a brat.

"It won't last forever," Easton promised, clapping a sympathetic hand on Graham's shoulder.

Groaning into his hands, Graham wasn't convinced. "Yeah, buddy. I think it will."

When they left the diner, River drove, having been careful to set her drink aside after a couple of sips. Bree had drunk deep on her Growly Bear, and Jessie had been talking to the gummy bears at the bottom of his glass by the time they left for Easton's place.

She'd expected a cabin in the woods, with a borderline serial killer vibe. Following Easton along a narrow gravel lane through his family's property had done nothing to dissuade her of the notion. But when they arrived, she'd found a nice—okay, adorable—house, complete with flower boxes on the windows and a rocking chair on the porch. Inside, everything was clean and organized, from the books in alphabetical order on hand-carved cedar bookshelves to the dishes angled perfectly so on the drying rack.

It wasn't even extra weirdly overorganized. He'd left a sweat-shirt draped on the back of a chair, and he had a loose change jar next to his keys, with several pens and a couple of wadded up receipts along with the quarters and dimes.

"You're disappointingly normal." Bree sighed. "I was hoping for the heads of baby dolls lining the walls."

"I was thinking the same thing." River shared a grin with her friend. "Not even a meat hook in sight."

"The meat hooks are in the barn."

They both went still, heads swiveling to the man closing the door behind them. Easton winked at them.

Jessie flopped down on the closest recliner. "Well, meat hooks or not, I'm glad we're not sleeping in the car again. I'm too old for that. I should've stopped at half the Growly Bear like you did. The ceiling is spinning. What was in that thing?"

"Graham's sense of humor," Easton informed them.

While Jessie made himself comfortable and Bree began fiddling with the handheld camera, Easton gave River a tour of the place. Fridge, check. Living room complete with spare pillows and blankets, check. Tiny bathroom with the white fluffy towels. Yep. Check, check, check.

Unfortunately, the towel situation was going to be a problem.

Not the number of towels available for use in Easton's home or the quality of said towels. They were nice, bright white, and very fluffy. The problem was River kept imagining those towels wrapped around him, her mind nosediving straight to the gutter.

Standing in Easton's bathroom, River tried not to look directly at the towels in his muscled arms, all fluffy and soft and contrasting to his warm, tan skin.

"Here," Easton told her, offering one. "There's more in the cabinet for the others."

"I don't want it." The words slipped out before River could keep them in. "I mean, it's a towel. Nothing to see here. Move along."

"How many of those Growly Bears did you drink again?" Easton's eyes sparkled in the bathroom's low lighting.

Sparkly eyes weren't fair either. Neither was the proximity of this tiny bathroom, where a good breath could have her parts accidentally squished into his. And after watching him out of the corner of her eye all night at the Tourist Trap, squishing and squashing weren't too far from her mind.

Especially if towels were involved.

"I'm going to shower." River flapped her hand at him. "Shoo."

"You can't shoo me out of my own bathroom." One side of his mouth twitched upward.

"Did you plan on staying?" River raised an eyebrow. The result was his neck flushing red as he muttered something inaudible, the door clicking shut behind him as he made his getaway.

After kicking Easton out of the bathroom, River took a quick shower. The water was hot and relaxing, even if her mind kept trying to cover Easton with chocolate sauce. The man had crawled into her head and was making a home there, a distraction to her even when he wasn't present.

His shower curtain had cartoon rubber ducks on it. River thought that was funny for a mountaineer living in Alaska.

A knock on the door startled her out of her thoughts.

"It's me," Bree said through the door. "Can I brush my teeth? There's a line forming out here."

"Yeah, I'll hurry it up."

At the start of her career, River had done a handful of commercials and a couple of low-paying modeling gigs. Enough to be used to small spaces with multiple people getting ready. While Bree went about her flossing routine, River sadly ended her shower. Sneaking her hand outside the curtain to grab a towel, River wrapped herself up and sat on the edge of the tub.

"He's awfully good-looking." Bree glanced at River in the mirror, words muffled by her fingers and the floss. "I'm starting to think you like him."

"If I did, it doesn't matter." With a sigh, River shook her head. "Besides, you know me. Tall and rugged always distracts me, but it's the endgame I'm focused on."

"Right." Bree smirked at her.

River chewed her lower lip to keep from laughing. "Okay, I will admit that he's gorgeous. And I kind of want to steal his hair tie and watch his hair flowing in the wind."

Bree tossed her floss away, then flashed her teeth at the mirror to check her handiwork. "I want to steal his hair tie to see what's under there. He might have a bald spot or a really big mole. Just saying. Now out. It's my turn for a shower."

River dressed quickly in soft yoga pants and a comfortable sweater, then padded through the unfamiliar house. She found Easton at the kitchen table, feet kicked up on a second chair as he combed through a stack of maps.

"There's water in the fridge." Easton indicated the counter behind him with a tilt of his head. "Glasses in the cupboard above the sink."

Murmuring thanks, she poured herself a glass and sat in the chair next to him. Peering at his papers, she tried to understand what she was looking at.

"What is that?" River leaned closer in inspection.

"A topographic map."

"I know what a topographic map is. What's this overlay?" She pointed to a feature on the map unlike any she was used to seeing, with several teardrop-shaped demarcations.

Easton dropped one foot down to the floor, turning so River could access the materials in front of him more readily. "It's an avalanche map of the region." With his index finger, he traced two of the shapes. "These are from last year. The third is from this spring."

It was one thing to know these mountains had the risk of avalanches. It was another to have that risk right there in front of her. Maybe he caught on to the sudden increase in her heart rate, because Easton patted his hand down on the map, covering the forms from view.

"There's not a mountain out there with snowpack that doesn't have the potential of avalanches. Some mountain towns have controlled avalanches to keep the danger of a natural slide down. The resort does it."

"Isn't that dangerous for the town if something goes wrong?"

Easton shrugged. "I suppose they think it's better to risk the townsfolk than risk losing a batch of tourists. Don't know why. The tourists keep coming back."

Not teasing him was impossible. "Ooh, harsh. Tourist party of three over here."

"Yeah, but you're not as annoying as most," Easton said before adding, "You're worse, actually."

"You love us. We're like cheap take-out food. Once you get used to us, you'll always want us around."

He chuckled, a lower, deeper rumble than his normal voice. "I'll take your word for it."

They shared an almost comfortable moment of silence. Almost. Easton cleared his throat.

"I checked the weather report. Winds are gusting on the mountain until noon tomorrow. It isn't safe for Ash to fly in there to drop off the supplies until later, and we're too much weight to all go at the same time. We'll get a start first thing the day after. You have some time tomorrow if you need to shoot anything else."

"I think the guys are pretty set," River admitted. "But I'll ask them. We would have loved to get some more interviews about the area, but no one wants to talk to us."

"It's not personal. When you have so many people rotating in and out of your town, you start to avoid the faces you don't recognize. We're nice, but a lot of the resort's clientele are…"

Easton hesitated.

"Rich, entitled, won't lift a finger for themselves?" River shrugged. "Yeah, I know the type. I know lots of great people in LA, but once in a while, someone is a real stinker."

He grimaced. "The first few years after the resort was built, we all tried to embrace the visitors. Welcome them, be helpful. Alaska is a friendly state. But at some point, the town ran out of patience."

"Aren't you dependent on tourism? That's why I'm here, remember? To help increase the amount of tourism in the area."

"Those are fighting words around here," he told her, not unkindly but definitely not joking. "Do you know how many times I was asked for directions last year? Four hundred and thirty-two. The town had a contest, and I came in second."

"I can't believe people were brave enough to approach you that many times." After some quick math in her head, River's jaw dropped. "That's one point two times a day all year long. Who won?"

"Jonah, poor guy."

"I'm having a hard time feeling too sorry for him."

Easton's low laugh was comfortable as it filled the air around her. Scooting her chair closer to him was too easy. River leaned in to look at the notebook next to his maps. He'd marked down a list of the days they would be gone, with some numbers next to it.

"Negative *forty*?" she asked. "In July?"

"That's the range, but most days won't get that cold. A lot depends on the windchill." Easton tapped a thumb against the notebook. "The sooner we start up, the more days we have in case something goes wrong."

Glancing at him, River asked, "Do you expect there to be problems?"

"No, but I try to prepare for them if I can."

That would have to be good enough. River had never been on a guided climb before, only outings with friends or alone, so she had to trust he knew what he was doing. Still, her need to understand everything made her steal the next in his pile of maps.

"Okay, so what am I looking at here?" Waggling her eyebrows at him, River added, "An X usually marks the treasure."

"In this case, X marks where Ash is kicking us all out of her helicopter. You want to film the best parts of Mount Veil, right? We need to start here, low of the south face of the mountain. We'll be below ten thousand feet here, but don't be fooled. That's some rough country."

"Grizzly country?"

His eyes met hers. "We're in Alaska. You're going to have a hard time staying away from the wildlife. But I'd worry more about the moose. They kill more people here than bears or wolves ever do."

"Wolves." River took a deep breath. "Okay, I can handle this."

"I'm not planning on letting anything eat you," Easton said. "It's harder to get paid that way."

She flashed him a quick grin. "Half up front, half when I don't die?"

"All up front, but I get my gratuity if you don't die."

"Deal."

River held out her fist to bump his without considering the effect it would have on them when his skin touched hers. Their eyes met again, and this time, River looked away first in an attempt to cover her reaction to the contact.

Clearing his throat gruffly, Easton ran his finger along the topographic map of Mount Veil. "We'll climb along this path until we reach the tree line. Once we're above that, the climb gets tougher. We'll pass through the Veil—"

"What's the Veil?"

"You'll see," he told her. "It's not worth ruining the surprise of seeing it for the first time. Descriptions never do it justice anyway. And that's as far as I can promise to take you. Going through the Veil requires skill, and mistakes there can kill. If all of you are okay through the Veil, then we'll reevaluate whether we're going to summit."

"What do you mean, whether?" River immediately forgot all about sexy rough knuckles and biceps the size of her head. She bristled. "I'm not going on a nature walk here, Easton. I have a job to do, and we're already pushing things by going outside city limits."

"River, is there a clause in your contract about payment upon delivery of the film?"

"How do you know that?"

"Because we've successfully run out every single film crew that's ever come here. I understand you have a job to do, but so do I. I'll help you get your movie made, but not at the expense of your safety."

"How about this: we'll summit unless the risk of death or near dismemberment looms above us. If it does, then you'll turn your head and pretend not to notice me summiting."

"We'll figure it out when we get up there," Easton said firmly. "I'll try my best."

"It's not Denali," she reminded him.

"This mountain has taken over a dozen lives in the last twenty years. I'd rather not have you and yours on my conscience."

As he talked, Easton leaned his head to the side, cracking his neck. The action distracted her, pulling her attention to his hair. The man bun taunted her with its very presence. What was under there? More glorious hair? Or something thin, wispy, and frightening to behold?

"The Old Man is isolated. Almost no one climbs it, so there isn't a tent city, like with Denali. Getting the camps set at higher altitude will be a lot of work." Easton gave her a suspicious look. "What are you doing?"

"Nothing." Innocence. Maintain the innocence.

He wasn't buying it. "You're craning your head and staring at me, River."

"I'm just...thinking," she murmured.

"About my head?"

"Something like that."

The kitchen was cooler than River was used to, or maybe the excitement and nerves of the climb were starting to hit her. Either way, he noticed the tiny shiver that went through her.

"You want some coffee?"

River always wanted some coffee. That was a given. She also wanted a blanket, so she went into the living room closet where Easton had told her extra blankets were available. She could hear Easton tinkering with the coffeepot in the kitchen as she checked on her friends.

Jessie had passed out in the recliner, out like a light. Cuddled up on the couch, Bree was almost there herself. Taking a moment to tuck a blanket around each of them, River took the last blanket—a well-loved and well-worn quilt—and returned to the kitchen. Easton had started a pot of coffee and set two mugs on the counter.

"Caffeine at night? You live a risky life, Easton Lockett."

His warm, deep chuckle was even better than the blanket she'd pulled around her shoulders. "It's decaf," he said. "Either way, that doesn't hit me as hard as it does some people."

"High tolerance?"

"I think there's more of me to caffeinate than most." The pot finished dripping, so Easton handed her a cup. "Creamer and sweetener are on the counter."

River fixed her coffee, then settled back down at the kitchen table. "You used a real coffeepot. I haven't seen one of those in years. No coffee pods for you?"

"Nope. Those things are wasteful. Bad for the environment. That sort of thing bothers us up here."

Sighing in contentment at her drink, River tucked her legs beneath her, curling up as much as she could on a hard kitchen chair. "Thanks for the coffee. And for taking us in. We're a motley crew, aren't we?"

"It's fine. Though I'm kind of surprised I *have* to take you in." After adding creamer to his own mug, he joined her at the table. "Are you going to tell me why you were sleeping in your car instead of staying in the resort?"

"We...sort of got kicked out." At the growing smirk on his face, River pushed on defensively. "Hey, it wasn't my fault. There was a black bear right outside the lobby. Do you know how often you get something like that? Of course, we had to film it. That's a given."

"Which makes the resort look like they aren't safe." Easton smiled so wide, she could finally see his white teeth. "Literally the one place in this whole town that would have welcomed you, and you turn them against you."

"You're enjoying this far too much."

"Seems risky though, knowing you didn't have permits. There's some heavy fines for those kinds of shenanigans."

"Don't worry. Your guide check won't bounce, but don't expect more than the standard gratuity for your efforts. It's okay to be subpar."

Easton exhaled a small laugh. "Sorry, sweetheart, I don't have it in me."

"Sweetheart?"

Flushing, he actually scooted back in his chair as if to give her more room. "Sorry, that slipped out."

Truly sounding apologetic—and a bit embarrassed—Easton glanced down at the papers on the tabletop without meeting her gaze.

Touching her fingertips to his arm to pull his attention back to her, River winked at him. "I like it better when you say it instead of the tabloids. I might actually believe you. And yes, I took the risk. I have a bad habit of leaping before I look." Sipping her coffee, she hummed in contentment at the warmth going down her throat. "Everything in life is a gamble, Mr. Lockett. You might have a barn full of meat hooks after all. But you never win unless you try."

A sheepish expression crossed his face. "Will you be super freaked out if I tell you I really do have a barn full of meat hooks?"

"No."

"Yes."

She pushed his arm with the flat of her hand. "Shut up. You don't."

"Five bucks, you won't even step foot in there. My great-aunt and great-uncle used to live here. Fishing and hunting wild game were how they survived through the winter. I used to be scared to death of their barn when I was a little kid."

"How about now?" she pressed.

Easton's beard twitched. "Now, I don't go in there."

River could feel her eyes widen. "You're too chicken to take them down."

"I'm not chicken. I just don't..." Easton trailed off. "Yeah, it's pretty much the worst. I'm too chicken."

"Show me."

"You'll run screaming," he warned her.

"Oh no, there's no backing out," River breathed. "You *have* to show me."

"When you start screaming, Jessie and Bree will start screaming."

"We're going outside right now."

Rising to his feet, Easton offered her his hand. "Don't say I didn't warn you."

As dates went, it was good they weren't on one. Taking a woman to a barn full of sharp, pointy objects was not a great way to be romantic. Especially when Easton was struggling to keep his eyes on her face and not the curve of her hips wrapped up in his favorite blanket.

The hand-stitched quilt his grandmother had given him never looked so good.

Technically, he was showing her the barn, but River was three steps ahead of him, her hands finding the side door and tugging. Her enthusiasm would have been endearing if he didn't think they were a few precious moments from her calling the cops on him.

"Why do you keep the door locked?" River tried to peer in a cobweb-covered window. "Are there people in there? Animals? *People-animals?*"

This was already a bad idea. "I have cousins with small children," Easton told her. "I don't want anyone getting hurt."

She watched with eagerness as he unlocked the door and twisted the handle. The stupid thing always got stuck. "You're totally going to take me captive, aren't you?"

Did she have to sound so happy about the prospect?

"Remember, this was your idea, not mine," Easton said. "I was fine drinking coffee at the kitchen table." Setting his shoulder to the door, he gave enough of a shove to force the creaky thing open.

When she started to step inside, Easton grabbed for her hand. "Hold on. Let me find a light. It's dangerous in here."

"How dangerous? I'll accidentally step in the pit you've dug to keep innocent, naïve film crews in type of dangerous?"

"Sue me and take my business and all my family's property type of dangerous."

"You're not supporting the narrative I built up in my head about this, Easton. You're being a party pooper."

Wiping the cobwebs off his other hand, he found the light switch. "Yeah. That's what people keep saying."

The small wooden barn was flooded with light, albeit the

muted light of bulbs covered in dust. There were very legitimate reasons why this barn had terrified him as a child.

River turned a circle, staring up at the ceiling and walls, where every farming utensil known to modern man was either hung or suspended. A table in the corner, stained with years of cleaning game, was particularly horrific to behold. Chains hung from beams for reasons still unknown to his adult mind.

And the scythe collection. Who kept a scythe collection?

"This. Is. Insane." River's eyes looked about to pop out of her head, they were so wide. "No, really, Easton. Your great-uncle was a nut job. Is that a headless mannequin?"

"There are more in the next room. Want to see?"

Of course she wanted to see. There wasn't one or two. The barn was full of so many headless mannequins.

"What did he do with the heads?" River asked. "Do you think he kept them?"

"I always assumed they came without the heads."

"No way. Not with that many scythes."

Scratching the back of his neck, Easton felt obligated to defend his kin. "He was a nice man. Always helped out around the community."

"As a cover for his evening exploits?" A gasp of utter delight came from her mouth. "This is so macabre. Let me film this. Please, pretty please, I have to film this."

"No way. Okay, you've had your peek." He started to gently herd her back into the main part of the barn and toward the door, but River ducked beneath his arm, sneaking past him.

"No, Easton, it's so awful, no one would ever believe me if I don't have proof." Grabbing a chain hanging from the rafters, she wiggled it. "You have to let me film this. You could sell tickets to this place. Is that *blood*?"

"It's probably rust."

"But you don't *know*."

Extracting her from the barn was going to require more effort. "I have ice cream in the house." Sweets always lured people, didn't they?

"I don't eat sugar late at night."

Except for her. Easton grabbed the chain above her hand, giving it a test tug, since she seemed determined to hang off it.

"Who doesn't eat sugar at night?" he asked.

"People who are supposed to be a size zero for the camera but are stuck at normal human being sizes."

Smiling down at the stunning redhead, Easton decided he liked her just as she was. "It's a tough life being famous."

"It had its perks."

"Had?" Standing so near hadn't been the plan, especially since he couldn't take his eyes off her.

"Some of the perks are still currently being appreciated." When River's gaze lingered at his bicep, Easton wondered if maybe this steadily growing attraction wasn't all one-sided.

He really hoped it wasn't.

"I prefer a life of constant motion," River added. "Work has become stagnant of late, so I'm carving my own path, making the most of the opportunities out there."

"I keep noticing." Watching her lick her lower lip was killing him. His voice lowered. "You're hard to miss."

"Be careful, Easton," River warned him. "Keep going both shoulders on me, and I might like it."

Easton wasn't sure who had closed the distance between them, him or her. Either way, neither was backing down. The only thing stranger than standing in this barn was standing in it smelling the shampoo from her still-wet hair, wondering what it might be like to wrap his arm around her, to draw her in close and see if this was more than some good-natured teasing.

Suddenly, she giggled. "You are not flirting with me surrounded by what is definitely not rust."

"You started it."

Winking, River said, "I'll kiss you right now if you admit your great-uncle chopped the mannequin heads off with the scythes."

Again, Easton's bone-deep loyalty reared its ugly head, when other options seemed much more enticing. "I think the mannequin heads were used as part of a health class thing for the local high school. Some body part identification project."

"That is so, so disappointing."

Sighing, River leaned too heavily on her definitely-not-rust chain. Years of neglect and a loose bolt resulted in the entire thing giving way. She shrieked as the chain fell over her shoulders and feet with an excessive amount of clanging and clattering, dust and cobwebs and a few spiders along with it.

"It's in my mouth. The blood dust is *in my mouth*," River wailed as she spat and flailed at her face, not that her actions were doing much to save herself. "I'm eating someone. I've been in the mountains of Alaska for less than a week, and I'm already eating someone."

Picking a few spiderwebs out of her hair for her, Easton watched as she dusted herself off. "I told you it's not safe in here. But no. You had to come see."

"The allure was too great." Her sigh was one of deep contentment, even as he kicked the chain aside and started herding her back toward the door.

"But..."

"Nope."

River walked backward on her toes, still trying to peer over his shoulder. "The jars. I didn't even see what's in all the glass jars."

"Trust me, you don't want to know." Easton and Graham had learned that particular lesson a long time ago. When the door was safely shut behind them, River fell back against the wood siding of the barn, dissolving into giggles.

"I ate person dust."

"It really is rust." Probably. He hoped.

Clearly, she wasn't buying into his far less interesting narrative. "I'll get a DNA test when we come back. Easton, that was the best thing I've ever seen. You're cruel for not letting me film it, but it was awesome."

Bracing a hand against the barn siding above her head, Easton smiled down at her. "Nothing scares you, does it?"

"Lots of things scare me." Inhaling a deep breath, she reached above her head, looping her slender fingers around his wrist. "Going somewhere with you isn't one of them."

It had been a long time since he had wanted to kiss a woman this badly. Eyes flickering down to her mouth, he tried to tell himself this was a bad idea. Maybe it hadn't been rust...

"You're going up a mountain with me," he reminded her, hating his own words. "We should probably keep this professional."

"Agreed. You're filming a movie with me."

"I'm not—" he started to protest, but River's eyes sparkled with mischief.

"Technically, you're the male lead."

Easton grimaced. "You promised it would only be my feet."

"We'll start with the feet and move up."

Easton shifted closer, not because he wanted to but because he had to. Resisting her arm slipping around his waist wasn't in the realm of possibilities.

"Thank you for showing me your torture barn," she whispered.

"Thanks for not running screaming."

When her fingers hooked into his, still above her head, and her other arm tightened around his waist, Easton took that as permission. The curve of her hip felt good beneath his palm, and when he tugged her closer, she came willingly. When she licked her lower lip, he started to dip his head down.

"River? Are you okay?" Bree's voice calling from the house couldn't have come at a worse time. "Easton, I know Krav Maga."

Easton dropped his forehead to the barn wood above her head. "Everyone knows Krav Maga."

"Bree's actually good at it," River said into his chest. When he pulled back, her hair gleamed like burning embers in the low light from the house windows. Never had Easton wanted to thread his fingers through something more.

"River?" Bree called again.

Stepping back to give her space, Easton sighed when River yelled back. "Bree, you have to see this."

Abandoning him for Bree, River dragged her over to the barn. A couple of startled curses later, Bree let out an ooh of sheer pleasure. She stuck her head out the door, mirroring the mischief on River's face.

"Easton," Bree breathed. "You *have* to let us film this."

———————————

In the end, the answer stayed a no, and Easton's hands stayed to himself. It was probably better that way, especially considering how important it was they would be able to work with each other on the climb.

Bree and River played rock, paper, scissors for the couch after it had been determined no one was killing anyone or filming anything in the barn. They were still rechallenging each other when he went to bed, feeling guilty that one of the two women was going to end up sleeping in a nonreclining chair, and both were subjected to Jessie's crescendo of nasal noises.

"Deviated septums don't make friends, buddy," Easton muttered to himself, listening to the other man's snores.

Sleep didn't come easily. Knowing she was sleeping in his living room made it hard to rest, and Easton's brain kept rolling over the plans he had made. The supply list, the weather reports, the best places to take them to film, and the planned ascent. Details that were always important loomed larger in his mind.

Normally, Easton had a maximum of an afternoon of

interaction with his clients before a climb. He'd never almost kissed one by his barn or had her crashed out on his couch.

An early riser, Easton maybe got an hour or two at most of rest before his eyes opened of their own accord. His house guests were dead to the world, never stirring even when Easton ate his breakfast and made a couple of calls. And when Ash's Jeep pulled into the drive, he met her on the porch.

Sharper than the rest of them on her worst day, Ash immediately recognized the SUV in the drive.

"You brought them here?" she asked, stepping through the front door.

Following her inside, Easton shrugged. "I suffered a momentary lack of clarity."

"I'll say." Ash snorted. "What if they try to murder you in your sleep? I don't trust the actress. She looks like she's one good sneeze away from a mental break."

Opening one eye, the woman in question made a sleepy noise. "Hey. It's at least two sneezes." River yawned, pulled the blanket higher up her neck, then rolled over.

"She was sleeping in her car, Ash."

"So? How is that your problem?"

"It wasn't my *problem*." Easton's eyes flickered over to the red hair on his couch pillow. "These are my clients. I might as well start things off with them right. Did you get ahold of Ruby?"

"Yes, and I think you're drinking the Kool-Aid. She's willing to meet everyone. But seriously, don't drag it out. Ruby Lou's not as young as she used to be."

"None of us are," Easton said. "Is everything ready for tomorrow?"

"It will be." Ash crossed her arms over her chest. "I'll fly up there and drop off the supplies, but don't expect me to do anything but drop it."

He hadn't expected her to. Wrapping his sister in a hug—and earning a gagging noise from her in response—Easton smirked as she fought her way free.

"Gross. Take a shower." As she left, Ash pointed a warning finger at him. "Stress out my grandma, and I'm kicking your ass."

"Yup."

On the off chance he actually smelled as bad as his sister inferred, Easton took his shower. Having so many people in his house wasn't uncomfortable or abnormal; they'd been having parties here for a lot of years now. More than once, his friends or family had slept on his couch, floor, or even porch. What Easton *wasn't* used to was having strangers in his home.

He almost ran into River as he left the bathroom, still rubbing the towel over his hair to dry it.

"Whoa." River took a step back, eyes widening. Thinking he'd startled her off-balance, Easton reached for her arm to steady her.

"Dude," Jessie murmured to Bree at the end of the hall. "Did he move in slow motion for anyone else? Like, step, step, towel, wet hair flip, sexy naked rescue."

"He didn't rescue me." River's eyes narrowed. "He grabbed on."

Well, that wasn't fair.

"River bobbled. And I didn't flip my hair."

"You kind of flipped your hair," River told him. "There was a motion."

Easton frowned. "There wasn't."

"Nope," she insisted, her hand flapping in his head's direction. "There was definitely a motion."

Across the living room, Bree edged toward Jessie. "Where's the handheld?"

"Why are you whispering?" he asked her.

Bree pointed a finger Easton's way. "Because he might move if I speak too loud."

Maybe Easton should have dressed more, but they were lucky he'd remembered to bring pants along with him to the shower. He could have emerged in a pair of socks and a toothbrush. Wishing he could extract himself from the situation, Easton tried skirting River, only to find Bree standing there, handheld video camera at the ready.

"Bree, you can't film him coming out of the shower." River went up on her tiptoes, shielding Easton's chest from view of the lens.

"But…"

"No, Bree." River exhaled a sigh. "Those white fluffy towels. It's so wrong."

Glancing at the towel, then back at River, Easton couldn't remember a point since they'd met where he wasn't utterly confused. "I have no idea what that means," he told her.

"It's probably for the best." River patted his shoulder. "Hey, since you let us crash here, breakfast is on me. I don't cook, but I'm happy to buy you breakfast in town."

"There's cereal in the cupboard. Milk in the fridge." Easton looked longingly at the bedroom door, wondering if he could get through the two women in the hall or if he should give up. "Use it up. It'll go bad when we're out there."

"Don't shipping costs make this like liquid gold or something?" Jessie asked, already digging into the refrigerator. He jiggled the milk carton at them.

Easton didn't dignify that with an answer. Yes, it was more expensive to get certain things shipped to them from the lower forty-eight, but he'd had to listen to tourists poking and prodding at everyone for years now. The fascination over his milk costs to strangers never ceased to annoy him.

Distracting them with free food seemed to be the trick, because Easton was able to finally escape the trio and get himself a shirt. He returned to find them making short work of a massive box of cereal. As he stuck with toast and coffee, Easton glanced at River. She was watching him out of the corner of her eye, and when they locked gazes, she managed to look guilty.

Huh. That was new.

Suspicious, Easton narrowed his eyes at River. "What did you do?"

The woman was good. He almost believed her when she blinked innocently at him. "Nothing."

"Why don't I believe you?"

River would make an excellent poker player, but Bree's face split in a massive grin. She must have known they were outed, because River sighed. "Well...okay. You see, we kind of decided to add a bit more to the roll."

Easton rolled his eyes. "You didn't."

"We had to." River and Bree nodded in agreement. "The barn was too torture-y to resist."

"My property, ladies. That film belongs to me without my permission."

"Do you have any idea the kind of money we could get selling that footage for stock film?" Bree added. "We'll cut you in, I promise."

Groaning in exasperation, Easton closed his eyes.

"Are you counting to ten?" River sounded as suspicious as he had been. "You are not counting to ten, because I'm a grown-ass woman, dammit. You don't get to count to ten when dealing with me."

Easton opened one eye, then smirked at the flush of heat on her cheeks. "You're cute when you're riled up," he told her in front of them because he could.

River's jaw dropped open, then clamped shut.

Before she could decide what to say, Easton continued, "I have someone you might want to talk to. For your documentary." Maybe this wasn't the right thing, but as the trio turned their heads his way, Easton pushed on. "My grandma Ruby always loved this town, and she's been here her whole life. She agreed to tell you stories, the kind of stuff most people don't even know about. Dad was bringing her by his house for a visit today anyway. She gets bored in the nursing home."

They all stared at him, silent.

Easton cleared his throat. "Only if you want. She agreed to talk to you, but you'll have to ask her if she's willing to be filmed. She'll be at my dad's place later."

He'd thought maybe he'd offended them until he realized they were stunned into silence.

River's eyes had widened. "You're *kidding* me. No one will talk to us. I called around for months trying to get people to agree to interviews, and we got nowhere."

"Yeah, everyone's been jerks that way."

At Jessie's drawled comment, the two women murmured agreement. Easton leveled a flat look them. "Those jerks are my friends and family," he reminded them.

River's hand touched his arm. "Sorry, Easton," she said. "That came out wrong. It's been tough here."

"Yeah," Bree echoed. "I'm sorry too."

With a snort, Jessie sat back in his chair. "Well, I'm not sorry."

"Really, Jessie?" Bree rolled her eyes.

"I'm *not*. A kid threw his gum at me yesterday. Locks like mine and gum do not mix."

Bree kicked him in the leg, ignoring Jessie's yelp of pain. "He let us stay in his house last night, and we're getting an interview. Maybe even on camera, so try not to be an ass."

"It's part of my charm," he assured her.

"Is it though?"

The pair began bickering, which seemed to be part of a pattern for them. Maybe River was used to it, because she seemed to tune them out completely. Instead, she squeezed his hand.

"We'll take your lead on this, Easton. I promise."

River looked so sweet and innocent and completely capable of not causing utter chaos in his life. Easton drained his coffee.

He'd believe that when he saw it.

CHAPTER 7

SEEING EASTON SOAKING WET HAD officially destroyed River's calm. All that long brown hair falling over his shoulder...all damp and Easton-y.

So Easton-y.

Even as she sat in an armchair across from his grandmother, River had to fight to keep her focus on Ruby Lou and not Easton, who was standing guard over her wheelchair, arms crossed and beard bristly. River didn't think they'd done anything to put his back up, but it was hard to tell with him. He might have been standing there, thinking about cabbage rolls, for all she knew. Or maybe he thought they were being offensively invasive with his grandmother.

Ruby Lou was fascinating. She might have been in her nineties, but her eyes were bright and her enthusiasm contagious. And her stories hysterical. They had to take several breaks in between filming to let Ruby Lou rest her voice and to allow her to gather her thoughts. But they now had more information on the inner workings of Moose Springs than ever. The interview had gone far better than River could have hoped for. She'd never been on that side of things, having always been the one being interviewed, but the pleasure on Ruby Lou's face at each question had been worth every second.

River definitely owed Easton big time.

Every so often, Ruby Lou would turn in her wheelchair and take Easton's hand. Each time, he allowed himself to be patted, nudged, or moved wherever Ruby Lou decided. Stoic affection for grandmothers might be River's new favorite thing ever.

"He's a handsome boy, isn't he?" Ruby Lou said, smiling at her grandson proudly.

Yes. Absolutely. The sanctity and innocence of white towels had forever been ruined.

"Ruby, would you be willing to tell us more of how the town reacted to the resort being built?" Jessie asked. "And, Easton, stop looking like a Dothraki. You're ruining the shot."

"A what?"

Jessie was not impressed. "Dude, if you didn't watch *Game of Thrones*, you and I are never going to be soul mates."

"Guess I'll have to manage," Easton said.

The two shared a smile. Why hadn't she kissed him last night? Oh, that's right. Because it was wrong. Wrong and...torture-y. So torture-y.

Fingers snapped to get her attention. "River?" Bree murmured.

"Hmm?"

"You're drifting, River."

"Sorry, Ruby Lou. I was thinking that yes, your grandson is very handsome." Leaning in, River added conspiratorially, "He's refusing to let us put him on film, except for his legs."

"Feet," Easton rumbled.

"We're up to his knees at the very least. Maybe you could convince him?"

Ruby Lou's eyes lit up, catching on to River's joke. "Of course I could. I'd love to see my flesh and blood in a real movie."

"It's a documentary, Grandma—"

"It's a real movie," Ruby Lou said firmly. "Don't you put down the hard work of these nice people. It's better than playing around on rocks for a living. And you do look like a Dothraki, child. Try not to stand so straight."

"*Burn.*" Jessie made a noise of sheer bliss from behind his camera. "Ruby Lou, you are my absolute favorite person alive."

Ruby continued to talk, but when her stories started to blend with each other, River knew it was time to wrap things up. River took her hands, squeezing them gently in gratitude. "Thank you so much. You were wonderful."

"Do you think I could see the movie when you're done with it?" Ruby Lou asked.

"Of course. I'll mail a copy right to you as soon as it gets out of postproduction."

"Easton, are you taking this sweet girl up through the Veil?"

Kneeling next to her wheelchair, Easton rested his arm behind her frail shoulders. "I'm taking her to the Veil, Grandma. I haven't decided if we're trying to summit yet."

"In July?"

Consternation crossed his features, and he sighed. "Have you been listening to Ash?"

"Maybe Ashtyn has been listening to me." She leaned over and patted Easton's arm. "You'll be careful."

"I always am."

Ruby Lou placed her fingers against Easton's bearded jaw. "Your grandfather would tell you that you need a haircut."

With a low chuckle, Easton kissed her cheek fondly. "I'll think about it."

She turned to River. "You take care of my grandson, dear. He's a good boy, but he doesn't always listen to reason. The mountain is in his blood, and that kind of love can poison you."

"Grandma—" Easton started, but she held up a hand, cutting him off.

"No, you listen. Both of you. It's one thing to go up there to see if you can. But it becomes an obsession. Your daddy had the poison, Easton, and you're getting it too. There's more to life than how high you can stand on a piece of rock."

She turned back to River. "If he takes you up there, you make sure you bring him back down. One of these days, the Old Man's going to be tired of being beaten. He's a patient one, more patient than the rest of us."

"We'll take care of each other," River promised.

As grandmother and grandson started for the front door, Jessie turned to Bree, who was still fiddling with the handheld. "What do you think? How was the audio?"

"Great." Bree glanced over at Ruby Lou. "If I didn't think it would be too tough on her, I'd ask her to do the voiceover for all of the historical background. She has the soul of a born storyteller."

Right as Easton opened the door for her wheelchair, Ruby Lou sat straighter, turning those bright eyes their way. "I'm not so weak as you think. I could still dance circles around everyone here."

"The soul of a storyteller and the ears of an elephant." Easton said. "Grandma, what do *you* think?"

"Would I get to go to Hollywood?"

"Do you want to go to Hollywood, Mrs. Lockett?" Bree asked.

"I always did want to see that big sign. And put my hand on one of the stars."

Jessie looked up from where he was breaking down the equipment. "On the walk of fame?"

"No, child, one of the stars. Robert Redford, maybe."

Easton cringed. "Okay, and that's my cue to wrap this thing up. Come on, Grandma. Dad just pulled up to give you a ride back home."

Easton wheeled his grandmother to the door to a chorus of thank-yous from River's crew, then disappeared outside.

Bree looked askance at River. "Wow, you could not stay focused."

"It's Easton's fault. Did you *see* him this morning?"

"That man should wear nothing but jeans and water all the time." Eyeing her speculatively, Bree said, "When I went to check on you last night, I had the feeling I was walking into something."

"Nothing happened. I was...it was the Growly Bear. I drank more than you did."

Snickering, Bree shook her head. "Liar."

"Or maybe he's superhot," River joked. "And I can't keep from throwing myself at him when everyone's back is turned."

"That sounds a lot more realistic."

Growing serious, River started to help take down the

equipment. "Listen, it really isn't anything. Don't worry. My focus is completely on the film."

"Are we ignoring the mountain-sized elephant in the room?" Jessie took the tripod out of River's hands. He had never trusted her to mess with the gear. "I researched the stats last night. People have to be rescued off Denali all the time, but Mount Veil is something else. Are we sure we're ready for this?"

"I'm ready for it." Rising to her feet, Bree pushed a case at him. "And if you're going to panic up there, you'd better say something now."

"I'm not panicking. I'm saying it's a scary climb. Climber for climber, the mortality rate for the Old Man—" Jessie stopped, making a face. "He's got me saying it now. The mortality rate for *Mount Veil* is the worst in the state. It's not dangerous. It's stupid dangerous."

"What else can we do? We're basically banished from town," River reminded them. "We can't have a whole movie with Ruby Lou talking to the camera. I'm willing to listen if you have any better ideas, but I'm all out."

Silence met her comment. None of them had any better ideas. She didn't want Jessie to be worried, so she patted him on the shoulder. "We have Easton. He's been up there plenty of times."

"Do you think he's as good as the online reviews say?"

River looked through the window where the mountaineer in question was helping his grandmother into the back seat of a car. Looking good in jeans and a towel was nice, but what she needed from him was a lot more important. Her career depended on it.

"I sure hope so."

————

As she waited for her crew to pack up, River headed out to the porch, taking in the homestead.

The word didn't accurately describe how immaculate the grounds were, with every stack of firewood and piece of equipment carefully organized and set in its designated space. Next to an old but meticulously maintained hay shed was a small horse paddock. Behind it was a modest livestock barn with a low-hanging metal roof. Nothing like the thirty-stall stables back at the ranch, but the three animals grazing in the paddock were as close to home as River had been in a long time.

Too long.

Since no one seemed to be needing her, River slipped off the porch and across the drive. Of the three horses searching through the dirt for the last remaining bits of hay, a gray gelding was feeling friendlier than the others, coming over to say hello.

"Hey there, handsome." Scratching the gelding beneath the chin earned him leaning into the fence, looking for more.

"He likes you."

The man was quiet for having so much weight on those two feet. When Easton joined her at the fence, leaning on his elbows, it occurred to River that the top of her head barely came to his shoulder. She wasn't used to feeling short around anyone and certainly not around someone who had an annoying ability to not let her take charge of things.

"Your grandmother is incredible," River told him.

He nodded in agreement. "Yep. You wouldn't believe how good her pot roast is."

River glanced over at the house where Bree and Jessie were in deep discussion on the porch. "Easton, thank you again. This is going to be amazing footage. Are you *sure* you don't mind?"

He was quiet for long enough, River wasn't sure he was going to answer. Finally, he spoke, his voice pitched quiet. "When you live in a place like this, you get a lot of strangers showing up, putting their handprints on everything. Family is one thing you don't let anyone put their hands on."

"When you have a daughter, she's never going to get a date, is she?"

"Probably not." Resting a loose fist on the porch railing, Easton added fondly, "Grandma says she's going to tell everyone about the documentary and have the whole nursing home watch it when it comes out." Warm brown eyes found hers. "Be kind to her when you edit it. This means more than you realize."

"I will."

Overly aware of his arm near hers, the gum he was chewing, and the light tapping of his thumb against the wood rail, River forced her focus on the short red gelding who'd joined his pasture mate, curious to see what was happening.

"He's gorgeous." Stroking his mane, River watched the two geldings eyeing each other.

"That's Sonny. He's pretty, but he's a troublemaker." Easton reached over to scratch beneath the gray's chin, like River had. "Chance is more my style. He's friendly and smart and would rather hang out with you than get one over on you."

Nodding toward the palomino mare in the corner, River asked, "How about her?"

"Old Skip?" Affection filled Easton's voice. "She still runs these two boys ragged. But we've retired her. Unless my cousins come over and want to ride, she gets a free pass. She's earned it. Dad took her all over these hills, then Ash all but rode the feet off her." Easton glanced at her. "Do you ride?"

Once, River had spent every day on a horse. Now, the only horsepower in her life was the car she drove on LA highways. Ten years, and she still hadn't gotten used to the loss of these animals in her life.

"I haven't in a while," River admitted. "But I used to live in a saddle."

After a moment's pause, Easton asked quietly, "Do you want to ride with me?"

There was something in the way he said it that sent a thrill of anticipation up her spine. When she was fifteen, she remembered one of the handsome young ranch hands riding up to her older sister, holding the reins of a second saddled horse jogging along with his own. That soft question of "Do you want to ride with me?" had left her beyond jealous of her sister.

Tall, gangly, and fiercely independent, River was the first one the boys picked to rope with them, to brand cattle with them, and to ride broncs with them. But no one—boy or man—had ever asked her to ride with him. Not the way Easton was asking her.

They weren't even on the mountain yet, and River could already tell this was going to be a problem.

"Yeah." Feeling abnormally shy, she nodded. "I'd like that."

Easton pushed off the fence. "I'll get them ready."

When River informed her crew she wouldn't be accompanying them back to Easton's place to go over the footage, Jessie looked skeptical and murmured something about Easton murdering her in the woods. Bree's eyes brightened.

"Can I follow and film it?" she asked.

Jessie snorted. "The murder or the sexy stuff right beforehand?"

"There's not going to be either," River told him, knowing she should say yes to the filming. But really, this time, she kind of wanted to say no.

"We have to go through this footage," Jessie decided. He pressed the handheld at her. "Here. Get everything you can."

River shook her head. "I'm only going for a ride. This doesn't have anything to do with the movie."

"The *documentary*." Enunciating the word, Jessie rolled his eyes at her. "First rule of a documentary: you document."

"Fine." River accepted the camera. "But if I drop it, that's on you."

"If you drop it, the bill's on you."

When River returned to the paddock, Easton had pulled two saddles out of wherever they stored their tack, with worn leather bridles hanging ready on a nearby fence post. Chance, the handsome gray, was already saddled, and the second saddle was sitting on the fence rail next to the aging palomino.

"You're putting me on Skip?"

"She's a good horse," Easton said. "Heck of an endurance mare back in her day."

"I'd like to ride Sonny." When Easton hesitated, River patted his arm. "Don't worry. I can ride anything that moves."

With a shrug, Easton did as she asked, saddling up the little bay instead. He looked even more handsome with his tack on, but River was an experienced enough hand to know a gleam in a horse's eye when she saw it.

Easton frowned at the horse. "You might want to let me lunge him out a few circles before we go."

"Nope, we're good."

And they were. At least they were for the first two steps around the yard while Sonny decided what he wanted to do about her being on his back.

"Don't even think about it, buster," River warned him.

Sonny snorted, decision made.

Boy, that guy could buck. There was no viciousness to his antics, more feeling his oats than anything particularly dangerous, and River was laughing breathlessly by the time the horse came to a stop.

"Are you all done?" she asked him. Sonny snorted again, stamping a rear hoof. Twisting around to grin at Easton, River called over, "I think that means he's done."

Standing there, Chance's reins in his hand, Easton stared at her. "What?"

"Nothing." Easton shook his head. "Just never seen anyone enjoy a horse trying to pitch them off."

"I like him. There's nothing wrong with a little spunk."

River wasn't certain, but she could have sworn she heard Easton murmur something about redheads.

Once Sonny got all the extra energy out of his system, Easton swung up into the saddle and turned his far more laid-back mount toward a trailhead on the far side of the homestead. River squeezed her knees, encouraging Sonny to lengthen his stride and catch up with the pair. She expected the overcorrect as her mount happily broke into a faster gait.

"We're going this way," she told Easton as they trotted past, laughing at her gelding's enthusiasm.

Leaning forward, Easton and Chance lunged ahead as if River and Sonny were standing still.

"Are you going to let them do that to you?" River asked as Sonny's hindquarters skated to the right, his energy uncontainable.

The second she loosened the reins, her gelding was off like a shot. The pounding of hooves, real grass beneath her...how long had it been since the wind whistled through her ears until all she could hear was her horse's snorts and her own racing heart? Sonny was a speedster, but Chance wasn't a slowpoke by any means. By the time they caught up, the gray's stride had lengthened out.

For several breathless seconds, the pair ran side by side until Easton signaled her to slow up. Rougher ground ahead would have been bad to race over, although River was surprised he'd indulged the run at all. Easton angled his gelding over, riding so close their stirrups bumped.

"You can ride." He sounded impressed.

River patted Sonny's neck. "Back home, they put you up on a horse before you can even walk."

"How'd you end up...you know."

"Acting?" She shrugged. "Same old story we've all heard a thousand times. Rancher's daughter wants more than the country life and leaves home. Stuffs all her things in an old car, drives to Hollywood, and tries to make it big."

"Did you?" he asked.

River winked at him. "You've never heard of me, so I must not have."

Easton shot her an amused look.

"It took me a couple of years. I worked as an extra on set during the day, took acting classes and waited tables at night, and kept showing up for auditions. Then I got my break. Ten years, six movies, and one really bad miniseries later, I've finally improved in my craft enough to handle the parts I couldn't handle eight years ago. Only no one wants to give them to an actress turning thirty. So here I am, about to climb Mount Veil to start all over again on the production side."

His expression was one of disbelief and confusion. "I can't image aging out of a career that young."

"Trust me, I never imagined it either."

They turned a corner, and River's breath caught. Easton stopped, letting the reins lie loose on Chance's neck.

In front of them, miles to the north, a pinnacle of rock and snow jutted into the sky. The numerous other mountains in the Chugach range had obscured the bulk of this peak from view, but from where they stood, on a rocky outcropping, they had an almost unfettered view of the mountain.

It rose so high above them, River had to crane her head back to take it all in. "That's Mount Veil?"

"That's Mount Veil."

"Why do they call it that?"

"You'll see when we get up there." Easton glanced at her, watching River up at their destination. "You ready? It's not too late to change mountains."

"Are you trying to talk me out of going?"

"If I can talk you out of going, you shouldn't be going in the first place."

River looked over at him. There was a looseness in Easton's shoulders, a calmness in his face as he gazed up at the mountain. She'd seen a man in love before. A hundred dollars down, she'd be willing to bet the love of Easton Lockett's life was the majestic peak rising in front of them.

"I've climbed a lot, but Veil...there's something about it. When you get up there, it's like the rest of the world disappears. No one's looking at you, expecting anything. It's you and the mountain range. No one and nothing else matters. There's not a lot of oxygen at that elevation, but when I'm up there, I can finally breathe. I can be who I really am. I'm not..."

"Trapped."

Their eyes met, and River couldn't help the shiver that rolled through her. Her horse shifted beneath her in response to the tightening of her limbs.

"Are we doing this?" Easton asked quietly.

Four words that shouldn't have felt so loaded lay between them. Then she reached out her hand, trusting without even looking that he'd take it in his own. Lifting her eyes to Mount Veil, River squeezed Easton's fingers. If there was freedom at the peak, there was no stopping her. She'd been trapped her whole life too.

"When do we leave?"

Easton was a man of routine. And when it came to saying goodbye to his friends and family before an expedition, he always did so the same way: a game of pool at Rick's place with Graham after the Tourist Trap closed. Dropping by the house afterward to see Ash.

That was it. Anything else would be making too big of a deal about it all.

These days, where Graham went, Zoey was dragged along. So Easton appreciated it when Graham came alone, the time-honored tradition of a beer and a game standing strong. And if Graham gave him a hug and an admonishment to be careful before hustling out the door to be with Zoey, that was fine too.

When he left Rick's and drove to his family's home, Easton made sure to take his time, to appreciate this town he loved so much. Roads he knew by memory because they were the same roads he'd traveled every day of his life. The same gravel lane leading to the same house.

The same people who'd been there from day one.

Ash was an exercise junkie, focused on putting only the best things inside her body. So it always struck him as wrong when he found her out on the front porch with a cigarette in her mouth. His twin only smoked when she was worried or when she was sad. Lately, she'd been trying to hide it from him, but she was his twin. He always knew.

Easton didn't say anything as he sat next to her. They'd sat on this same porch for a long time now, and he never needed to say anything. Eventually, Ash leaned her shoulder into his.

"I hate this part," she whispered.

"I know."

"You can't work taking people on nature walks up at the big house?" Ash glanced up at him. "Hold their hands as they frolic through the flowers?"

Teasing her for her worry would have been easy. Theirs was a relationship built on mutual good-natured mockery to hide affection far deeper than most would ever know. But some things he would never tease her for, and admitting she was scared was one of those things.

"I could, but I'd hate it."

Having a twin wasn't as easy as an adult as it was when they were younger. Being tied so tightly together was harder when real life got in the way. On some level, they both knew they were drifting apart compared to when they were kids, and neither wanted that. But he knew what she needed from him to be happy: to give up the way of life that made him happy. And as much as he loved her, Easton wasn't willing to change who he was for someone else.

Not even Ash.

"It's going to be okay," he told her. "I know you don't believe me, but it will."

"Maybe." Taking a long drag on the cigarette in her mouth, she shook her head. "Probably. But one day, it won't. Are you ready for that? Because I'm sure not."

There was nothing he could say to that. Nothing to make her feel better anyway, so Easton simply sat with her. And when she sighed and rested her head on his shoulder, he knew she'd given up the fight.

The next trip, it would start all over again, because Ash didn't know how to stop caring so deeply.

"These things will kill you." He flicked the end of her cigarette. "And they smell awful."

"Then it's a good thing you're out of here. Go whine to someone else."

Smiling a little, he added, "Dad will be ticked if he catches you smoking."

She flashed him a quick smirk. "Then I'd better smoke another so he doesn't miss it."

Falling silent, she finished her cigarette, then pinched the end out with her bare fingertips.

"You need anything before I leave?" he asked her.

"Nah, I'm good." Ash stood, then nudged his leg with her foot. "Hey, East? Be careful up there."

Mountaineering was dangerous, and they both knew it. So Easton rose to his feet and wrapped her up in the kind of hug he knew his twin needed. Dropping a kiss to the top of her head, he whispered the same promise he'd made every time he left.

"I always am."

CHAPTER 8

THE MAN WAS HOT, BUT damn, Easton was boring.

River was trying, she really was. The beard and the bun made trying less difficult than it otherwise would have been, but the reality was they could only be lectured about caching equipment, acclimatization strategies, and avalanche safety for so long before they wanted to flop on the floor and cry mercy.

Easton had gathered everyone at the tiny airstrip on the outskirts of town, holding court out of the bed of his truck as they waited for Ash and her helicopter to return from a morning supply run two towns over. No one had minded the idea of a quick safety briefing, but that had been well over an hour ago. Easton kept droning on and on.

Being hot would only get him so far. There was no fixing boring.

"Can you go over it one more time for me?" Bree asked, blinking innocently. "I always have the receiver *on*, right?"

With inhuman patience, Easton nodded, holding up a bright yellow avalanche transceiver. "No, not at camp. We only turn these on when we're climbing."

"She's screwing with you, man," Jessie said. "You've gone

over this four times already. We know, okay? Besides, all of us have RECCO reflectors imbedded in our jackets. See?"

Jessie flipped open the jacket next to his hip, showing a leather tab protecting the radio signal boosting reflector from the elements.

Looking less than impressed, Easton handed a receiver to each of them. "Those help but aren't a replacement for a transceiver in the kind of terrain we're going into. This isn't a ski slope, kid."

"Did he call me a *kid*?" Jessie sounded affronted.

Bree eyed Jessie critically. "I mean, standing next to him, you do kind of look like you should be eating pizza and playing Unicorns and Magpies at the high school lunch table."

Wounded to the core, Jessie drew himself up with righteous indignation. "You did *not* go there. UniMagP is a deeply philosophical representation of the sexism in the current gaming culture—"

"I didn't criticize it. I'm saying that's what you used to do—"

The pair launched into a verbal brawl over whether Bree had insulted Jessie's beloved pastime. Easton watched the exchange with absolutely no expression on his face. "Unicorns and Magpies?"

"It's a new card game," Bree explained while Jessie sputtered in indignation. "Think Magic meets *World of Warcraft* meets evil unicorns and plucky magpies determined to save the world."

"Hey, Bree? Jessie? I think we're on a schedule here." River tapped her smartwatch. "Plus, I have the feeling we're driving our guide nuts."

"The way this works will feel counterintuitive," Easton continued.

Oh, the poor man had brought visual aids. Didn't he understand that made him a target?

"Here's the mountain. We're going to be flying here, the drop-off site. We'll hike to our first camp, set up, and spend the night there…what are you doing?"

Jessie zoomed in on Easton's narrowed eyes. "I'm filming the lesson plan," he replied. "You never know what the most important aspect of the lecture might be."

"How about focusing on the lesson plan so you don't get in trouble up there?"

Humming, Jessie continued to film. Easton took a deep breath, as if doing a mental yoga pose. Bree pulled the handheld out, filming Easton from a second angle to mess with him. Leaving River as the only one actually listening. Dutifully playing the role of "hiker paying attention number three," River crossed her legs and stuck the end of her pen in her mouth, fluttering her eyelids at Easton.

"Could you explain the visual aids to me one more time, teach?" she asked. Flutter flutter flutter. Legs recrossing, pen nibble.

"It's fine," he grumbled. "You all are going to fall off the mountain, but I already got paid."

River stood, joining Easton and patting him on the shoulder.

"We've got this. Start at the bottom, head to the top, filming the wildlife is good, getting eaten or trampled is bad. Once we get high enough, we'll need to acclimate to the lower oxygen levels. If we do feel sick, say something to you immediately. Is that about right?"

"What about the tents?" he asked.

"What about the tents?" River replied, fluttering her eyelashes at him again.

A flat look met her question, and River had to bite her lower lip to cover her laugh. Riling him up was too much fun. Every time she was successful at it, his eyebrows would knit together. The more riled, the closer the eyebrows were to touching.

"The tents are with the rest of our gear. And I get points for finding three brand-new four-season double-walled tents on such short notice. Your dad helped hook me up."

"When did you talk to my father?"

"He came by the house while you were on your farewell tour last night. We all drove to Anchorage and got what we needed. He's a nice guy. Told me all the stories."

Easton went still.

"And I'm talking *all* the stories. He showed me pictures too. We dug deep. There was bathtub stuff." She'd never seen a man so horrified in her life. Dissolving into helpless giggles, River took mercy on him. "Okay, it wasn't bathtub stuff, but now that I know bathtub stuff exists, don't think I won't get my hands on it. He just showed me lots of climbing pictures. I didn't know he went to Everest."

"Yeah, in '88. It wasn't a good year for it. Not many people from his expedition summited."

"Great pictures though. Hey, Easton? Has anyone ever successfully made you go full unibrow?"

Bree and Jessie made their escape while River took one for the team, letting him focus his annoyance down at her. Although, in hindsight, he didn't seem all that annoyed. Instead, all six and a half glorious feet of him shifted closer until he was standing as near to her as he had the night at the torture barn.

And okay, so maybe she deserved some teasing in return, but did he have to do so with his broad chest mere inches from her nose?

"Has anyone ever told you that you can be a very aggravating woman?" Easton rumbled sexily.

"It's been brought up a few times."

"And half the things that come out of your mouth make absolutely no sense?"

River beamed up at him. "I mean, they make sense to me, but I can understand the confusion."

Tugging at the collar of her shirt, River wondered why the temperature had suddenly gotten so stuffy. Was anyone else light-headed?

"You're gorgeous," he told her, that low rumble deepening even further.

"I'm sorry?"

"If we're doing this, don't think I won't go on the offensive. When you brought up the bathtub pictures, you dropped the gauntlet."

River arched an eyebrow. "Meaning?"

"Meaning this is going to be a really, really interesting climb up the Old Man."

"I'm not climbing any men. So you can...and the chest...with the thoughts..." Stepping away from him, River looked up at Easton in horror. "How do you do that?"

"I don't know what you mean."

Oh, he so completely knew what she meant. Otherwise, he wouldn't be watching her like this, like she was an ice cream cone and he was...

"I'm not finishing my thought," River told him. "It's a bad thought. You're technically an employee. This is bad. And..."

"Complicated?" he murmured, lips near her ear.

Oh, screw it. No one was looking, and he was right there. Half an inch at most between his body and hers, and they had a long trip ahead of them where no showering would be had. She wasn't going to smell any better than she did right then.

When he took her fingers, entwining them before resting them on his chest, River was pretty sure her ovaries flinched in warning.

"We're not having Alaskan mountain babies," she warned him, breathless. Seriously, how hot had it gotten? Menopause hit in late twenties sometimes. This was definitely not because of him.

A warm laugh filled the air between them. "I'm just trying to keep up."

Too many abdominal muscles beneath her fingertip, each one flexing in response to her fingernails lightly scratching down them.

"Do you want to do this?" he asked her, the softest of pressure of his hands wrapping around her waist.

"I think I'm going to be really, really disappointed if we don't," she breathed.

"Then, River, you are about to be really, really disappointed." Easton winked at her. "Try not to go full unibrow."

He left her standing there, her nonmenopausal parts wailing in protest.

"That was so mean, Easton," River called after him.

"Yep."

"And I'm really not liking you right now!"

"Ten four."

Leaning back against nothing, River stayed at an uncomfortable angle, trying not to fall flat on her back or face or any important parts in between. Only when her team came over did River sigh lustily.

"Bree? I might like him."

She nudged River upright. "You think?"

It didn't take long before Ash's badass dragon of the sky came thumping into view. After his attempt at teaching his clients the proper safety protocol, Easton was ready for some backup, even in the form of his twin.

From their place on the tarmac, the crew had a view of the talons painted on the underside of Ash's Robinson helicopter.

"I think I want to be your sister when I grow up." River sighed. "And now I totally understand your respect for powerful women."

"Scary women."

"Strong, smart, powerful women."

Easton tilted his head in acknowledgment. "All that too. But scary is on the list."

The film crew greeted her and promptly asked Ash to sign a waiver and let them film her. Ash never let anyone run roughshod over her, but Easton had gained an increasing respect for River. It was possible the two were evenly matched.

"No filming," Ash declared, as if that would be the end of it.

"We won't film you," River promised. "Only the helicopter."

"I said no filming."

Bree piped up. "It's an awesome helicopter."

"Yes, but you're not filming it."

"How about out the windows while we're flying?" Jessie countered, making the request sound entirely reasonable.

"You sure about this?" Ash asked Easton. "I'm exhausted, and I've been around them for less than fifteen seconds."

"I don't know. They're growing on me."

"Fine, they can film out the window. And that's it." Ash frowned at him. "I'm not a human scale, but that doesn't look like the agreed upon gear weight."

Confused, Easton turned around to find their gear pile had grown while his back was turned. Not a little. A *lot*.

River followed his gaze. "From the expression I think is on your face beneath all the bristly parts, I feel like you're not happy."

No, he definitely wasn't. Easton couldn't remember the last time he'd been this ticked off at a client.

"We did a gear check, River." He glared down at the offending pile. "This wasn't part of it."

"You didn't expect a camera crew filming an ascent of a mountain not to bring their filming equipment, did you?"

"You didn't expect to sneak all this filming equipment into your packs without my knowing, did *you*?"

Easton never had to close his eyes and count to ten twice in one day. So far, it hadn't worked for him, and he was rather disillusioned with the whole process. When his eyes opened again, he was as frustrated as he'd been before he'd counted, only now he had a pair of bright blue eyes narrowed at him.

"You did not take another time out."

Teeth grinding, Easton heard his jaw creak.

"Listen here, big guy. These are my people, and I'm not going to let you belittle them. We might not look like much, but we are more than capable of accomplishing this. Including carrying our equipment."

Inhaling a deep breath, Easton didn't take a third time out. However, he did look this woman in the eyes, holding her gaze and refusing to back down.

Whisky. She reminded him of Fireball whisky...sweet and smooth but spicy and strong as hell. Trouble bottled up and far too tempting to reach for. Liable to burn him up from the inside out.

River planted her hands on her hips, considering her equipment. "We'll leave the booms behind. And some of the lighting. The rest we can split up among us."

"Even doing that, it's too much weight. I can't back down on this one, River. You have to lighten the load."

"I can't afford to. If we can't film, there's no point in going up there."

With a curse, Easton stomped away from her. River stood her ground, waiting until he turned and came back.

"Fine. I'll call in an extra guide to help share the load."

When River opened her mouth to protest, Easton cut her off. "Extra guide or we're going home. And you're paying for him, not me. Am I making the call or not?"

Ash watched the exchange, asking, "Are they still growing on you?"

Easton didn't dignify that with an answer. River finally nodded, so he walked away to make his call. When he returned, he met her stubborn gaze with one of his own.

"I'm this close to grounding the entire climb," Easton told her. "If I can't trust you, then I have no interest in going up there with you. It's my life on the line, River. I'm not interested in throwing it away."

"You can trust me. I just knew what you'd say about the gear."

"Yeah, for good reason. There's a limit to how much we all can carry, because that's what's safe. You're underestimating what this mountain will throw at you. Not your fault, because you've never been up there. I have." Easton added, "I found a second guide. He's on his way, but he has to get someone to watch his dog."

Ash looked skeptical. "You're taking Ben?"

"Ben's good. I trained him."

"Ben's mediocre, probably because you trained him." Ash headed back to her helicopter, leaving Easton to face the redhead alone. Watching the exchange seemed to have shifted River's mood for the better, if the growing smirk on her face was any indicator.

"Adding Ben to the climb will cost you an extra twenty percent," he told his client, because it was more mature than tugging her braid or chasing her around the tarmac. The noise that escaped River's throat was close to a growl. It was cute, even though she had been driving him crazy all morning.

"You're running fast and loose with my credit score, Easton." She narrowed her eyes at him.

"You'll live. I'm planning on bringing you back down here in one piece."

Moving closer, Easton dipped his head to catch her eye. She frowned, a frown that probably convinced most people to do what she wanted. Easton needed more than a frown from a pretty woman to make a bad decision.

No, when it came to River, it was when she was smiling at him that he started making all the wrong choices.

"Stop that."

"Stop what?"

A fingernail poked him in the chest. "If you want to sexy loom, bring it on. Sexy loom to your heart's content. You see this?" She gestured to herself, neck to knees. "Unaffected. Un...a...ffected."

"You're wasting a lot of effort trying to convince me of a lot of things today."

"And you're going to see what happens when you try to force a cowgirl into a corner. We don't wait patiently for someone to save us. Or dance with us. Or do that *Dirty Dancing* lifting move. We are not doing any lifting moves, Easton."

Barking out a laugh, he stepped back. "I have literally no idea what to say to that."

River exhaled a hard breath, eyes lingering on his shoulders, then sliding down to his chest and abdomen. "You realize it's only seven in the morning, and you've got me ready to start some hard drinking."

"It's nine. You spent two hours not listening to the safety talk."

"It's still day drinking."

An old, life-weary Jeep pulled up to the parking lot, looking like it could use a drink or two as well. The driver, a fit climber in his early twenties, popped out with an enthusiastic wave.

"Hey, man," Ben greeted Easton, a hand clasp turning into a hug. "Boy, you surprised me this morning. Can't say I mind though. You know I love taking a run at the Old Man anytime I can."

"Congratulations, folks," Jessie murmured into his camera. "We've found another overly developed male specimen. This one had daddy issues and is two feet shorter than our monotone leader, which will help tell them apart."

Easton gave River a pained look, but she shrugged. "Hey, I only pay him. I don't control him. Your climb, right? Us peons have to do as we're told."

Turning to the entire group, Easton made introductions. "Ben, these are the three stooges. Get ready to sign a ridiculous amount of paperwork to be in their company. Three stooges, this is Ben. He's coming with us. Congratulations, you have yourself better than a two to one client-guide ratio."

"Almost a private tour," Ben added cheerfully, reaching over to shake everyone's hands. The poor guy almost swallowed his tongue when he set eyes on Bree. Ben mumbled under his breath to Easton. "Damn, that woman is beautiful. How do you work with her without going all tongue-tied?"

Bree raised an eyebrow. It wasn't her "love at first sight" eyebrow.

"Don't hit on my crew, Ben," River said firmly. "Especially if they're not interested."

Jessie peered over the top of his camera. "I think she put you in your place."

Ben seemed crestfallen, but only for a moment. Then he grinned at them. "A trip up the Old Man is always better than staying at home. I'll take it."

"Hey," Ash yelled. "I've got more jobs to do today than hauling you lot around. Stop flirting and start grabbing your crap."

Throwing him a smirk, River looked at Easton. "She's talking to you."

"She's talking to you."

"She's talking to all of you," Jessie decided, stealing the copilot seat. "All right, people. Tuck your sex drives in your back pockets. Let's make a documentary."

If looks could kill, Ash would have flown them right into the mountainside. Instead, she started the rotor, checking her instruments one last time.

"If anyone asks, I was not party to any of this," his sister muttered under her breath.

River waggled her eyebrows at him as she followed Bree into the helicopter. "Welcome to the dark side, Easton."

Considering the view as he climbed in after her, Easton figured this once, the dark side was worth it.

CHAPTER 9

RIVER HAD FLOWN BEFORE, AND she'd even been in a helicopter. But nothing had prepared her for the reality of flying to Mount Veil.

The heavy whip of the rotor blades above her head drowned out everything but the rapid beating of her heart. Below her feet, the flat, sparsely vegetated tundra gave way to huge slabs of rock thrusting into the sky, peaks speckled white with snow despite the summer warmth. In the distance, growing closer by the second, was a mountain rising higher than the rest. A beautiful behemoth of ice and snow, darkened below the tree line with thick evergreen cover.

River had never seen anything so exciting—and so frightening—in her life.

"That's Mount Veil," Easton informed them, speaking louder to be heard over the rotor blades as they approached.

That was her film. That was what she would climb. Without thinking, River reached over and gripped Easton's hand. She couldn't remember the last time she had wanted to do something as much as she wanted to climb the mountain before them. The challenge was intense, and that was what she loved about it.

"You ready?" He gave her fingers a light squeeze.

"So ready," River replied.

The helicopter was strong, but it wasn't big enough to carry all of them and their gear. This first trip was River, her team, and Easton, and then Ben and the supplies would follow. So far, the flight out had consisted of listening to Bree and Jessie argue about light reflection in the aircraft's windows while River stared in wonder through the lens of her own eyes.

Wedged in between River and the door, Easton didn't look very comfortable. Every so often, she would glance over at him, and more than once, his eyes had been on her instead of looking at the insane view around them.

Maybe he was used to this place, but still...she couldn't help her racing heartbeat from being the center of his attention.

"You might want to look out the window," Easton suggested. "You'll be too tired to care about a pretty view when we're on the way back home."

"Some views are better than others," River said teasingly. Because, well, she'd been doing some looking too.

Instead of flushing or turning away, he held her eyes. Overly aware of the pressure of his hip against her own and her hand still gripping his, River inhaled a deep breath. The motion caused his gaze to flicker down, and she snickered at the expression on his face when Easton realized he was totally busted checking her out.

"You're determined to get me in trouble out here, aren't you?" he murmured ruefully.

River released his hand. "Hey, what happens on the mountain stays on the mountain."

"Unless we film everything," Bree piped up, changing the

angle of the camera braced against her shoulder. "Then whatever happens on the mountain will be up for mass consumption."

"Am I going to have to call a hand check on you two?" Ash asked. "Hold on, kids. This part always gets rough."

The closer they got to Mount Veil, the bumpier the ride became. They angled upward instead of setting down at the base, flying higher on the heavily forested mountainside than River would have expected.

"Why aren't we starting down on the tundra?" River asked as the trees started to thin with the higher elevation. "Aren't we climbing the entire thing?"

"We're starting below the tree line so I can get a grasp of your skill levels," he explained. "No point heading up there unless you can handle it down here."

"Aren't we missing all the wildlife down there?"

"That's some of the most heavily populated grizzly country in these parts. Do you want to climb, or do you want to be eaten for dinner?"

Even though his voice was teasing, River cringed. "Good point. Keep flying, Ash."

The landing was smoother than the approach, despite setting down on an open slab of what looked to be granite. At their pilot's direction, they hopped out with their filming gear, then waited for Ash to go back for Ben and the rest of their supplies.

The view from the mountainside wasn't as grand in scale as it had been in the air, but it was equally impressive in its own right. Everywhere they turned, mountains rose around them. The thick, heady scent of evergreen overwhelmed her senses. They'd dressed for the weather, but the lower temperature at this elevation caused her lungs to inhale cold, fresh air with every breath.

She *loved* it.

"Is that really necessary?" River turned to see Easton grimacing at Jessie and the camera pointed his direction. "I thought you wouldn't be filming me."

Undeterred, Jessie continued filming. "We agreed to only minimally film you. It's a small mountain and you're a huge guy. At some point, the cameras will have no choice. Sorry, it's part of the deal. What's the point of having a documentary if we're not going to document any of it?"

"I thought the rule was knees only."

"You can go thigh level, Jessie," River said, having sympathy for their guide.

Yes, he'd signed the paperwork. Yes, he knew he would be on film, but they'd assured Easton the camera would only turn his way when necessary. But it was clear he was far from comfortable being filmed, and there was no reason to make him twitchy now, when technically, Ash was coming back with an escape route. It wasn't beyond the realm of possibility that Easton could jump ship and leave them there.

The crisp, clean air wiped free the lingering worries and doubts River hadn't realized she still felt about this project. Gazing up at the mountain above them, River couldn't help but turn a circle, arms outstretched as she soaked it all in.

"Ignore her," Bree suggested to Easton as she passed by, camera panning their surroundings. "She gets like this every time we're away from civilization."

"Yeah." Easton nodded at River. "Me too."

Then he was forced to sidestep, because Bree was going to film where he was standing, and it was either move out of her way or get stepped on.

"So what's the plan?" River asked, hoping to distract him away from the crew.

"We wait for Ben, gear up, and start for that ridge." He pointed up the mountain a solid thousand feet above their heads. "There's a few stops along the way that might make for a good shot for you." One wide shoulder shrugged. "I'm guessing on that. Not quite sure what you're looking for up here. I usually take people up and get them back down again."

"If there's anything cool you can think of," River said, "I'd love to film it. Otherwise, we'll grab what we can get along the way."

She craned her neck, trying and failing to see the summit above them. The cloud cover was too low, blocking their goal from view. "I can't imagine having a lack of amazing footage from here."

River's theory wasn't wrong. In the time it took for Ash and Ben to return, both her camera crew had wandered off in opposite directions, filming everything around them. Easton led the way as Ben trailed behind, making sure no one got lost. Ben was a fun, likable presence as they hiked. Unlike Easton, he was happy being on camera, sharing tales of Moose Springs as they headed for the ridge Easton had indicated.

The day's climb wasn't easy, but River loved every minute of it. Stuck on a climbing wall in LA was nothing compared to being out here, the wind in her hair and real rock beneath her gloved fingertips. A sea of mountains in every direction, with Veil itself rising above her, taunting her with its elusive summit.

But, man, it was cold. And as the sun drifted lower on the horizon, the cold only increased.

"You can almost forget it's summer, huh?" she murmured as they set up camp beneath an alcove of overhanging rock.

The new tents she'd purchased for the climb were tricky. Like the rest of her crew, River was struggling to put up her tent, and it didn't miss her attention that Easton was watching them all with a critical eye.

"I could put up my other tent while blindfolded in a blizzard," she told him. "Keep your judgy looks to yourself."

She knew when he was standing over her because the guy was massive, and the shadow on the ground was massive too.

"If you're going to lurk, please do so out of my light." River nodded her head toward her crew. "If you're bored, Jessie could use some more stock footage right now."

The beard twitched, giving him away. "You really want to be caught on film putting this up wrong?"

"It's not wrong, it's…" Breathing a soft curse, River realized he was right. "I would have noticed that. Trust me, I can stand over you and find lots of things to point out you're doing wrong too, buddy."

Dropping down to his heels didn't make him seem much shorter, not with those broad shoulders and muscled chest. But his normally deadpanned face was creased with humor.

"You aren't intimidated by me at all, are you?"

"Is there any reason I should be?" River arched an eyebrow at him.

Chuckling, Easton shook his head. "Not that I can think of. I already set up my tent, and we don't need the dining tent until we get to the snow. Want some help?"

"Nope, but I appreciate the offer." River's name might have been fake, but her spine was strong as steel and true. She could, and would, set up her own tent.

"You remind me of whisky," Easton murmured.

"Is that a good thing or a bad thing?"

"Depends on how long I stay within arm's reach."

River wasn't sure what to say about that, but if she was whisky, he was the biggest, most decadent brownie. And chocolate sauce.

Easton was all the chocolate sauce.

"Why do I have a feeling I don't want to know what you're thinking?"

"My mind's a wild, sticky, confusing place," River admitted. "Trust me, I don't want to think what I'm thinking either."

This time, he didn't ask. Easton simply took the piece of her tent frame she couldn't figure out and locked it into place, a casual action by someone who actually could do this with his eyes closed.

"You're my kind of confusing." His eyes sparkled with humor. "And you might want to film that."

"Film what?"

"The grizzly watching us right now."

He nodded toward the edge of the ridge, some twenty feet away. Sure enough, a grizzly bear was standing there, watching them curiously. At which point River learned something very important about herself. She wasn't the best at putting up a tent, but at least she didn't run screaming when a four-hundred-pound grizzly with allergies sneezed.

Jessie would never be able to say the same. Never had River seen anyone panic to the extent Jessie panicked upon realizing there was a bear in their camp.

"Stop, drop, and roll!" Bree kept yelling to Jessie as he shrieked and panicked...doing all the things one was not supposed to do in the presence of an apex predator. "Don't climb the tree! People, Jessie climbed the tree."

Ben stood there, fingers wrapped around the bear spray in his hand, looking concerned for the first time that day. "Dude. That's a great way to get eaten."

"No one will eat Jessie," Bree decided as the bear gave them some serious side-eye before lumbering away. "There's not enough to eat."

As Jessie and Bree immediately started arguing about who had the better survival instincts, River glanced at their guide.

"We're not making it off the mountain alive, are we?" River asked him as Jessie started to climb down from his tree.

"You will," Easton said as he rose to his feet. "No promises on the rest of them."

Easton didn't know when the marmot started following them.

Marmots tended to be shy creatures, similar in appearance to beavers and cute as could be with their tiny faces and mass of fluffy fur. The movement of this one caught his eye as they hiked, but Easton was used to seeing marmots in the bush. They tended to live at or below the tree line, but sometimes they lived higher. He doubted one would be camped out on the summit waiting for them, but they were as likely to hang out at high elevations as Dall sheep.

He figured it would disappear at some point, but for some reason, it paralleled their path as they passed through the tree line at eleven thousand feet. Here the world was ice and snow. Still, it hung close, at first staying even with Ben, then moving up to Bree. It tried Jessie, then River, but like Goldilocks and the three bears, apparently Easton was just right.

The marmot stayed with him.

Easton tried to ignore it when the thing started making chittering noises at him. Because, well, it kind of sounded like the marmot was talking to him. Which was weird. What was weirder was when it decided to walk closer, keeping up the running commentary.

"What's with the furball?" Ben called up. "I've never seen a marmot this friendly."

"Yeah, Easton," Bree said. "I think someone has a crush on you."

"Don't tease him." River pointed at the marmot. "Tease him and film it. Come on, people. This is gold."

Easton stopped in his tracks, well aware of the camera on him as he turned to look down at the animal at his feet.

"What?" he asked the marmot. "Did you need something?"

Apparently, it needed to be acknowledged and maybe a hug, because it scooted nearer and all but stood on his foot, gazing up at him with beady, soulful eyes.

"Do you think it's all the hair?" Bree asked softly. "Maybe the marmot thinks Easton's a really big, grumpier marmot. Are you getting this, Jessie?"

"I'm already on it." With a purr of satisfaction, Jessie knelt at marmot level. "Easton, what's its name?"

"How should I know?" Easton said, knowing they were making fun of him. But when he saw the huge grin on River's face, the part of him that became stupider in her presence grudgingly played along. "The idiot with the camera wants to know what your name is."

The marmot chirped.

"It said it refuses to be defined by the confines of a name. It's far too cosmopolitan for that." Okay, that was worth the soft peal of delight he pulled from River. "Come on, people. We have a schedule here."

No one moved except to cluster closer. The marmot chirped in alarm, scuttling behind Easton's feet. Then it proceeded to scold him for allowing such a thing to occur.

Easton refused to have any feelings on the matter. Nope. No feelings at all.

It took him a while to get them all going, and it really didn't help when the marmot of dubious nomenclature decided to continue along, as if it were a given that it was now part of the group. Easton tried a few times to spook it away, thinking maybe the animal was sick and that was why it was acting strangely. But every attempt was met with a chittering lecture from the furball, so eventually Easton gave up and continued on his hike.

They filmed as they walked, and as he watched them work,

Easton could tell that River was good at her job. She left her people alone to do what they were best at, but she was always watching who was filming what, and every so often, she'd redirect their attentions to a different, better shot.

At first, he was impressed. That feeling quickly changed as Easton realized the only one in this group he could depend on to think rationally was the marmot. The rest of them were determined to poke and prod into every single dangerous place they could find, hauling their cameras along with them. Ben should have helped, but the poor guy was utterly infatuated with Bree. Where she filmed, he followed.

"So, if I asked—" Ben tried as they took a break to rehydrate and grab a quick lunch.

"Nope." Bree didn't even look at him as she scrolled through the film on the handheld.

"Not even a—"

"Still a no."

River said firmly, "Tough break, but this is a professional worksite. Let's keep it that way, okay?"

Catching his eye, River had the audacity to wink at Easton. Whatever this was, he knew flirtation when it smacked him in the face. And like a marmot with a thus far undiagnosed emotional disorder, Easton had been on River's heels since they met.

"I think she's being a bit hypocritical," he muttered to the marmot. It stared at him, beady black eyes unblinking in its rapt attention, until Easton was successfully weirded out. "Never mind."

He'd set a route that would take them past one of his favorite places on this part of the mountain: a waterfall that rarely warmed up enough to do more than drip fresh water to the existing layer of ice. The result was a sheet of gleaming water frozen in place, and definitely worth the time and effort of reaching it.

"What do you think?" Easton asked River as they turned a bend in the rock.

"What do I think of—*oh*." Jaw dropping, River stared in shock. He hadn't told anyone where they were headed, and Ben was astute enough not to give the surprise away.

"Easton, this is gorgeous."

Even the marmot seemed impressed. Easton was starting to feel good about his choices, up until the moment River breathed, "I'm going to climb it."

"No." No way. Bad idea.

"Is it frozen enough to be stable?"

"Define stable," Easton hedged. "Technically, yes. But that's not an easy climb, River."

"I never assumed it was. That's the fun. Why am I lugging around two ice axes if I'm not going to use them?"

Easton knew he was fighting a losing battle. Moving to the base of the ice waterfall, River never bothered to look at him as she argued her case. Instead, she stared up at the sheet of solid water, as if something had made the water freeze in midmotion.

"Don't you ever get tired of saying no?" River asked.

Placing a hand against the ice, he could practically see her mind racing at all the different possibilities of ascent. Her team had already started shooting the waterfall from every angle, leaving Ben to try to follow both as they found new and interesting ways to almost lose their balance on the icy rocks.

"This was supposed to be for your shoot only," Easton told her. "Do you have any idea the kind of skill it takes to do this?"

The expression of excitement on her face only grew.

No way. Out of the freaking question. Over Easton's dead body.

"You don't get to tell me no," River told him as if reading his mind. "I'm aware of the dangers. But isn't part of this documentary to show what's really out here worth seeing? The things worth doing besides getting drunk at the Tourist Trap or snowboarding at the resort? Easton, look at this. Have you ever seen anything so beautiful?"

Actually, he was looking at something even more beautiful than the ice waterfall, which was why every single part of him was recoiling from the risk.

"Have you ever climbed ice like this?" he finally asked.

River shook her head.

"This isn't like rock. The ice feels solid, but it's like a piece of cold glass. Tap it too hard and it'll shatter. The last thing you want is to be thirty feet up and the whole sheet goes."

His warning was intended to dissuade her, but instead, River's eyes brightened even more. For a long moment, Easton considered whether he wanted to throw down over an ice climb. Then with a sigh, he pulled out his ropes to start a belay system. "Fine, but if it goes, don't blame me. I'm officially and legally warning you that you should not do this."

"And I'm officially and legally telling you that I *so* don't care. When am I ever going to have this chance again?" After double-checking their equipment, River turned to Easton. "Ready?"

He should have wrapped an arm around her waist, pulled her

close, and done anything else to convince her there were a lot of other ways to have fun than to do this.

Instead, Easton grunted, "Climb on."

When she'd first seen the waterfall, all River could think about was how badly she wanted to climb it. And yes, it was dangerous. She hadn't cared.

She also hadn't thought through the realities of having Easton on the ground beneath her.

River was enough of an adrenaline junkie to enjoy the thrill of her racing heart. What she didn't like was the understanding that if she messed up—or if the falls simply shattered there was no way Easton would be able to get out of the way.

With every placement of her axes, she couldn't shake the image of razor-sharp shards of ice dropping down on him while he was tied to her.

"I never should have agreed to the belay," River muttered.

Even as the words left her mouth, River's ax slipped from the ice. She tried to catch herself with the other one, but she was already falling.

There was something about having an expert on the ground beneath her. Easton had known exactly how much line to feed out as she climbed that she'd never felt the pull of the rope connecting them. He weighed enough that she didn't even pull him off his feet with the fall. At least, she didn't think she had by how short her drop was before the rope caught her. Still, a fall was a fall, even when safely secured, and it stole her breath.

Body reacting on instinct, River's legs came up, her feet bracing hard against the waterfall for balance.

This time, she froze, realizing what she'd done.

"River?" Easton called up to her. "You good?"

"I'm hoping I didn't bring all this down on our heads. Remind me not to kick the super deadly sheet of ice again."

"It wasn't that hard. You've got this. Keep climbing."

She started to go up again, doing her best not to repeat her mistake. Easton's confidence in her had been reassuring, but River's heart continued to race until she reached the top of the falls. Hauling herself over the edge, she turned and waved down to her crew where they filmed below.

Then, to her absolute horror, Easton unclipped from the belay rope and started to climb after her. Unlike River, there was no one to catch him if Easton fell. But he'd already committed to the climb, and yelling at him wasn't going to help anything.

River had no choice but to watch him, every swing of his ice axes as fluid and effortless as the last, until he was below her on the falls.

"You're trying to give me a heart attack," River accused him when he was close enough to hear her.

Easton flashed her a grin so broad, even the beard couldn't cover how much he was enjoying himself. Then, because he actually must be trying to make her keel over, he let go of one of his axes and twisted, dangling above the ground as he took in the view around them.

"Easton, I'm not above spanking you."

"And here I thought you wanted to keep this professional."

Easton pulled his cell phone out of his pocket and snapped a picture while still dangling. Taking one more of her peering down at him, Easton then tucked his phone away and crested the falls like it was nothing. She was impressed—more than impressed—but somewhat annoyed too.

"You free-climbed that," she growled at him.

"Yep."

"After all the crap you gave me for wanting to climb this, you head on up like it's nothing."

Easton shrugged, then unexpectedly draped a heavy arm over her shoulders, pulling her tight to his side. Below them, the marmot scuttled around in a circle, frantic at being left behind.

"Hey, Easton?"

"Yeah?"

"Does the marmot seem off to you?"

"It's totally bonkers." They sat in silence for a moment, then he spoke. "Hey, River?"

"Hmm?"

"I like climbing with you."

Resting her head on his shoulder, River was unable to help her smile. "Yeah. Me too."

The day's climb had taken the energy out of her.

Across the campfire from the rest of her party, River stayed seated cross-legged on the thin layer of snow, her weatherproof snow pants softening the chill. She could only imagine how cold it would be in the dead of winter, when this mountain would be untouchable. Her fingernails idly scratched at the ground next to her hip, an unconscious tic as she stared into the flames.

After the waterfall climb, they'd spent a significant amount of time interviewing River about what experiencing that climb had been like. Deciding to use her in the film hadn't been River's first choice, but they were limited with how many interviews they had. When it came to the experience of being on Mount Veil so far, River would have to do.

They'd made camp, this time setting up the dining tent so they would have a place to prep their food and eat it away from the snow. The scent of their campfire mingled in her nostrils with the heavy aroma of pine. She could have joined the three card players in the dining tent, but River was enjoying sitting beside the fire, relaxing and taking it all in.

"You realize what it says about you that you always choose to play the unicorn, right?" Jessie told Bree. "The unicorns are inevitably evil, no matter what you draw for abilities."

With a snort, Bree laid down a card. "I'm increasing my light-footedness. And your insistence on only playing the magpies clearly delineates your need to prove your heroic qualities in a fake world, to counterbalance your less than heroic qualities in the real one."

"I wasn't skipping out on washing dishes," Jessie burst out. "I wanted noodle cups for dinner. People eat noodle cups."

"People who don't want to take their turns cooking and cleaning up eat noodle cups."

Easton interrupted them with a growl. "Hey, can you two cram it for a minute? I still don't understand where my fluffy bunny comes in."

The pair stopped arguing long enough to eyeball Easton. His cards were wedged in the fingers of one hand while he skimmed the worn sheet of rules held in the other. "Fluffy bunny is the warrior class, right?"

"You're killing me here, man." Jessie sighed with quickly lowering patience as Bree flipped the rule sheet over.

"You're an assassin class," Bree explained. "It's totally different. Warrior classes don't exist in this game."

"Why not?"

"Because not every game should require the hero and heroine to smash the bad guys to bits." Jessie sniffed. "UniMagP is all about finesse."

"I'm a *bunny*."

"You're an assassin bunny," he countered. "Which is the ultimate unknown. You can never trust a bunny."

"Nope," Bree agreed. "Try to draw a gravity card. Increased gravity increases weight, and you can squash what you hop on—"

River shared an amused look with Ben, who had taken a seat across the fire from her. "Do you think Easton's going to get it?" she asked.

"I think he's trying much harder than he normally would." At her curious expression, Ben chuckled. "I've been with him on climbs where he didn't say two words the whole trip, other than 'clip on' or 'we're stopping.' He's trying to get along with them."

"Why's that?"

Ben smiled at her. "Why do you think? I'm going to call it a night."

Since everyone was busy, River decided it was a good time

to sneak away from the campfire and get some time to herself. Taking the handheld with her, she slipped outside the circle of firelight. Since they were still in grizzly country, River didn't go too far. When the camp's fire had softened to a small orangey glow a hundred feet away, River found herself a smooth boulder to stretch out on. On her back, she held the camera above her face, pointed at the colors playing across the sky.

"Incredible," she said softly to the viewers she hoped would one day see what she was seeing now. "The way the sky changes to these pinks and reds behind the cloud cover. As if an artist had painted a sunset, but a storm is rolling in, determined to drive that sunset away. Only it won't, because up here, nothing can take this away. The beauty is too powerful."

A noise pulled her attention, the quiet clearing of a throat to warn her of another human's presence. Several feet away, Easton had paused beside a smaller boulder, waiting for her to notice him. His choice of leaning post was sturdy and strong, like he was.

"I thought you were scared to be alone in the woods with me." River stayed on her back but twisted so the handheld was turned his way.

"I didn't want to startle you." Easton pushed off the boulder and crossed the rocky, snowy ground between them.

"You walk quiet, mountain man."

Under the lower light, it was harder to make out his expression, but the warmth in his voice was familiar, matching the sparkle in his eyes.

"Nah, you're so used to stomping around, you don't know the difference."

"Uh-oh, people," River told her camera. "Easton's teasing me. I might actually like it, but don't tell him."

"Do you have to film everything?"

"It is part of the process. We tried Claymation, but your beard kept falling off the miniature clay Easton." She kept the camera on him as she patted the rock surface beside her. "Want to join me? I've got a boulder for two over here."

He tapped a playful finger twice to the side of the camera, so River regretfully turned back to the sky above her.

"Back home, when the sky turned bright colors like this, it was usually after bad weather. Everything would turn this bruised yellowish-green color, then get really dark. We'd all take cover because it meant a tornado was coming through. A few got really close. Then afterward, the sky would look like this."

Maybe the memories had taken her too deeply, because large, callused fingers slipped through her slimmer, softer ones. Once, she'd had calluses like those too, from long days and longer nights working horses and cattle with her family.

"How is it that I had to travel thousands of miles from home to find a place that reminds me so much of being back there?"

"Maybe you miss it," Easton said. "When I miss home, seems like everything reminds me of where I wish I was."

"Do you travel much?"

"Some. I'd like to travel more. Nepal, India, Tibet."

"All places with the highest mountains in the world." River turned to look at him and realized their faces were only inches apart. Suddenly, the sky above wasn't nearly as interesting. "You should go."

The way his expression changed, she knew he misunderstood her. Tightening her hold on his hand, River shook her head. "I meant to Nepal and everywhere else. To the tallest mountains. Don't let anything stop you. There's a big world out there. We shouldn't have to stay locked in a box and only see part of it. Besides, after watching you climb that waterfall today, I couldn't imagine anyone better for it."

For a moment, she thought he was going to kiss her. The look in his eyes when he gazed at her certainly said he was considering it. Tugging on his hand to indicate she was more than okay with any decision he might be struggling with, River wiggled closer. He shifted up to brace his weight on one elbow, their threaded fingers between their chests.

"Hey, Easton! Adventuring biscuits have been consumed, man. Time to get UniMagP'ed *up*."

"And that's how you ruin a perfectly good moment." River sighed, dropping her head back on the rock. "Thank you, Jessie."

Easton sat up. "Don't worry. Whatever this is, we have time to figure it out." Leaning in, Easton added quietly, "It's a long trip to the top."

As he rose and disappeared toward the campfire, River turned back to the sky above her. She'd always lived her life for the endgame. The job, the career, the summit. But as she considered his words, River couldn't help the curving of her lips.

Maybe this time, the best part would be getting there.

CHAPTER 10

RIVER WAS BORN TO BE in front of a camera.

He'd never seen her in one of her roles, but Easton had a good idea of how much of a professional River was. When it was time for her shots at the end of the day's climb, no matter how tired she was, she always helped her crew set up the equipment, find the right spot to film, and would only disappear in her tent for the briefest time to fix her hair for the scene. Then she would emerge with her acting face on, a calm and relaxed set to her features that could shift into whatever was required of her.

They even had a script for her, although Easton had no idea who had put it together or when. He would have noticed if one of his clients had been trying to hike with pen and paper in hand.

"We're finished with today's climb," River told the camera, glancing at the mountainscape around them. The day's journey had taken them higher above the tree line, and all around was snow and ice, dotted with the occasional dark boulder or the snow-free underside of an outcropping.

More than once over the last couple of days, Easton had found himself watching her drink in the scenery instead of paying attention to where he was stepping. Not the wisest choice, but his eyes kept drifting back despite his efforts to keep them on the path he led them on. Now that they were at a higher elevation, being distracted was even more dangerous. The marmot had stuck close, taking up residence outside Easton's tent and insisting on watching him with the same intentness Easton had been watching River with.

All in all, it was one of the more uncomfortable unrequited love triangles Easton had been involved in.

"It's stunningly beautiful up here above the tree line," River continued. "I've been on top of a mountain before, but nothing like this. Nothing like Mount Veil. I can't wait to get higher and see what it has to offer."

She paused as if to gather her thoughts.

"Our guide calls it the Old Man. When you're down in Moose Springs, the mountain kind of looks like a hunched-over man with his head bowed. Almost like he's bearing the weight of the world on his shoulders. But up here, the Old Man—"

River drifted off, and unlike the last pause, this one wasn't scripted.

"You can hear him creaking and groaning beneath you. Easton, is that the glacier beneath us we're hearing?"

Not used to being addressed when she was filming her interviews, Easton nodded. Immediately, the second camera was turned his way.

"Say it out loud," Jessie stage-whispered.

Glaring at him didn't do a thing, so Easton gave in. "It's the movement of the glacier. We're climbing a river of ice, one that moves slowly."

"A river of ice that moves slowly." River seemed amused. "That sounds familiar. This River is iced up and moving slowly, and we're only a little higher than eleven thousand feet. I feel like the air in my lungs isn't a full breath."

"High altitude sickness is real, River," Easton told her, folding his arms across his chest. "If you start feeling bad, you tell me."

River winked at him then turned back to the camera. "Our guide, Easton. He looks like the scariest guy in these mountains, but he's a big marshmallow."

"Oh, he's the scariest thing in these mountains by far." Jessie's quip was met by laughter throughout the crew. From across the campsite, Ben had stopped working to watch their filming. He shot Easton a smirk.

"You all have never gone through the Veil," Ben told them. "You'll think East is all peaches and cream when that happens."

They turned the cameras off, although Jessie still had the handheld tucked under his arm instead of putting it away.

"So, what do you think?" River rose to her feet and joined Easton where he was standing.

"I think we need to take it easy, maybe stay here an extra day. You're not the only one having trouble catching your breath. Jessie was looking winded too."

When she didn't argue with him, Easton gave her a searching once-over.

"I'm pretty sure my eyes are up here." Despite the humor in her tone, Easton could hear an underlying grumpiness.

"Your eyes are gorgeous," Easton told her, willing to flirt a little to see the resulting smile on her face. When she swayed on her feet, he put a hand on her hip. "The rest of you is starting to drag. Why don't you take a nap while the others finish setting up camp? I'll have Ben wake you when dinner is ready."

"Is it that obvious I'm beat?"

"Only because I pay attention." When she waggled her eyebrows at him, Easton added, "You pay me to pay attention."

"And here I thought I paid you to be a large human-shaped resting spot." She leaned into his shoulder, giving Easton an excuse to wrap his arm around her waist. River turned to gaze out at the mountain range rising like jagged teeth from the earth thousands of feet below. "I can't get over how gorgeous it is up here. If this view doesn't convince people to come to Moose Springs, nothing will."

Easton was fine with no one else ever coming to Moose Springs, but he was invested enough in his clients to want River's documentary to turn out well. Sometimes Easton felt torn in what they were doing here. He'd always fallen hard on the side of "no tourists," but Moose Springs was changing, slowly but surely. Lana and Graham had worked hard to try to balance the fiscal needs of the town versus the needs of the people to be left in peace.

Lana single-handedly getting the bulk of the town's commercial property out of corporate hands and into the hands of the residents had done a lot to smooth ruffled feathers. But even though Lana had become much more accepted in Moose Springs, no one loved her condo project next to the resort. If Graham managed to keep them from being completed, tying Lana up in red tape for the next century, no one would protest. Except for maybe Rick.

And yes, he didn't want strangers overrunning his town. But

tourism had brought Zoey and Lana into his friends' lives. Glancing over, Easton watched River drink in the mountain that was so important to him, relishing the weight of her form pressed against his side.

See? Tourism wasn't *that* bad.

The marmot chirped, an unhappy sound, then wiggled between their legs so it could lean against Easton too.

He could have stood there with her for as long as she wanted, enjoying her while she enjoyed the view. The marmot...he could have gone without it snuggling in closer. But Easton knew the safe hours for traveling were ticking down while he lingered. Finally, he stepped away. "I'm going to scout ahead. Let Ben know if you need anything." She didn't answer, not until he murmured her name. "River?"

"Hmm?"

"You sure you're okay?"

Maybe it was just him, but her color was a touch off, too pale for the blustering wind chilling their skin. Her eyes were still on the world around them, and for a moment, he thought she hadn't even heard him. Finally, she turned back to Easton, eyes bright.

"I'm amazing."

When Easton suggested she take a nap, River was grateful. She'd tried her best all day to ignore her growing headache. The pressure in her head had been steadily building, like a headband squeezing too tightly around her temples. Every hour of climbing had felt like four, and setting up camp was even worse.

Sadly, as good as that nap sounded, she couldn't take him up on it.

They all shared the tasks around camp, and asking someone to pick up the slack so she could rest wasn't okay. Instead, she helped finish setting up camp while Easton left them to check the route ahead, the marmot at his heels.

River was daydreaming about that nap Easton had recommended when the real headache hit, fast and with no further warning. The steady pressure abruptly turned into a sledgehammer, like someone striking her between the eyes. Midstep between her tent and the dining tent, River gasped and staggered.

Someone shouted in alarm as her knee hit the snow beneath her.

"I'm fine, I'm good," she forced between her teeth, instinctively shoving back to her feet to cover the misstep. Instantly, the world spun as she sank back down again.

A hand caught her arm as Ben's face swam in and out of focus in front of her.

"Whoa, better stay still until Easton gets here to look at you." Ben pulled out his radio. "Hey, man, we've got a problem. River's going AMS on us."

"I don't have altitude sickness," she insisted, but the pain in her head made her words come out a whimper. "It's only a migraine. I'm fine."

"Any signs of HACE?" Easton's voice was a hard snap through the crackling of the radio.

Ben frowned at her before replying. "She says it's a headache, but she went down quick."

"Get her to my tent," he ordered. "Get fluids in her. I'm on my way."

Using Ben as a support, River rose to her feet and staggered in the direction Ben led her. Voices spoke, asking if she was okay, but they blended together in one mass of noise, piercing through her brain. At least Easton's tent was larger than the one she was using and was easier to accommodate both a reclining person and Ben's helping hands. When Ben told her to lie down on Easton's sleeping bag, River didn't fight him. Never had her head hurt so much. The pounding of her blood in her ears grew frighteningly loud, so much so, she could barely hear the opening of the tent's zipper when Easton arrived. She didn't know how far away he'd been, but he must have rushed to get back so quick.

"Whisky girl. You slipped fast on me. Tell me what's wrong." His rumble was quiet and as gentle as his hands on her wrist, taking her pulse.

"I have a headache." River's teeth gritted together, unable to open her eyes to look at him. "It's been building all day, but I didn't say anything. I usually have a high pain tolerance."

"I believe you," Easton said. "Ben, her heart rate is elevated, probably because of the pain. River, do you have any allergies? Any problems with painkillers?"

"I'm in show business. We pop painkillers like popcorn."

"You're from the country, River. Don't pretend you're not as tough as nails. I already know better."

She could hear the kindness in his voice, even though River wasn't about to open her eyes to look for herself.

"Ben, I need something to cover her face. The sun's too bright right now. It's coming right through the tent."

"Here," Ben's voice murmured. "Med kit is right by your foot."

"Thanks. River, I'm going to wrap something around your head. It's not going to feel good, but you'll be glad of it later."

"I'm fine. Do whatever." And then toss her off the mountain, or at least everything from the shoulders up.

Even though they were both talking very quietly, Ben sounded like he was yelling against her eardrum. "What are you thinking, boss? Want me to call Ash to come get her?"

"I'm not going down," River told them as someone gently tied a folded-up bandanna over her eyes. "It's only a headache."

"Maybe, but maybe not." Easton helped draw an extra blanket around her. "Up here, a headache can mean a lot of things."

"Easton, don't you dare kill this project for something stupid."

Despite her arguing with him, Easton's voice remained quiet and soothing. "I'm not going to ruin your film unless I have to. But trust me, River, the moment I have to, I'm not thinking twice. Is everything dark?"

"Yeah, but—"

She clamped down on the rest of her sentence, swallowing her complaint and internalizing the pain. Having something tied around her head only caused the viselike agony to ratchet off the charts. Freedom from the bright sunlight streaming through the tent was nowhere close to being worth it.

River reached to pull the blindfold from her head, but Easton caught her fingers, squeezing in reassurance.

"I'm going to put a water bottle to your lips. Try to keep it down. The last thing you want is to be dehydrated. Ben, give me that small pill bottle."

The rattling of the pills rattled her brains, even though all Ben did was pick them up. "Are you sure? This is some strong stuff. She'll be a zombie."

"I'm sure I'm not letting her get shocky from pain. River, I've got two pills in my hands. I need you to swallow them for me and not throw them up. Can you do that?"

"Will they help?" she joked in a weak, strained voice. "If not, no promises."

"They'll knock you out in five minutes."

"Give me the pills."

Despite her assurance she could keep them down, River almost didn't succeed. She wasn't prone to headaches, but this one was crushing her from the inside out. She felt like she was going to die. She wanted to die, or at least stuff her fingers inside her brain and rip out anything and everything making her head want to explode—oh. *Oh.*

Whatever he'd given her, it *worked.*

If she didn't have a blindfold over her eyes, tied around a rapidly shrinking head, the world around River might have gone blessedly blurry. Instead, it went darker.

"How are you feeling?" Easton asked her softly. "River, can you hear me?"

She would have answered, but her mouth was done moving, her lips more than happy to stay exactly where they were. The conversation around her was becoming detached, muddled, like they were walking backward in a tunnel. River didn't even mind when Easton's fingertips brushed her forehead, checking for fever.

"She's out," Ben decided.

Yes. Yes, she was.

The wind whistled steadily in River's ears. Her first thought was it reminded her of the whistle of the supply trains moving through the pasture back home. Her second thought was the sound didn't weigh like a freight train on her brain.

Whatever Easton had given her, it worked like a charm.

She still felt fuzzy, but when River reached up to touch her temple, she was met with only fabric, not throbbing. Unwinding the bandanna from her head, she blinked in the muted light of early morning. She'd slept the whole night through, and she'd stolen Easton's tent to do it in.

Peering around at the tent felt like sneaking a peek into someone's bedroom. "So this is what it's like to be our fearless leader," River murmured to herself.

The urge to snoop was hard to resist, but a man who helped keep her brain from tripling in size was a man whose things should remain safe from prying eyes. Still, it was fun to imagine what Easton-sized secrets his backpack held.

Other than his love of mountaineering and his general distaste for having cameras on him, River didn't know all that much about Easton Lockett. Except he was gorgeous, and when she'd been in pain, the weight of his hands on her had felt as good as anything could have at the time. Solid. Reassuring.

Rolling over onto her belly, River wriggled toward the tent entrance, intending on taking a peek outside to see what everyone was doing. The tent unzipped as River reached for the pull, leaving her nose-to-stomach with the man himself.

Whatever he'd been doing, Easton had exerted himself enough that his face was flushed, and he was sweating.

Easton gazed down at her, as if finding a woman's nose in his stomach was an everyday occurrence to him.

"Hey," she said, like this wasn't anything out of the ordinary.

The corner of his mouth ticked up on one side as he took her in. "Hey. You look good." Raising an eyebrow at his comment, River had the absolute pleasure of watching Easton blush. "I mean, your color's better. You're not so pale."

Rolling back to her knees, River made room for him to climb inside his tent. "I feel a lot better," she admitted as he sat next to her and pulled off his boots. He knocked the snow off outside the entrance, then set them in the corner, tidily organized, like the rest of his things.

Speaking of looking good, his hair was down, falling to his shoulders. River had never particularly cared one way or another about a man's hair, but his was so long. And shiny. She wanted to run her hands through it.

"I need to grab a fresh shirt," Easton informed her, his voice pitched quiet.

"I can leave," River offered.

With a shake of his head, Easton turned her down. "It's blustering right now. Everyone's tucked in. Might as well stay until it dies down."

Well. If she had to...

"Where did you sleep last night?" River asked, settling cross-legged near the tent's side.

"I bunked up with Ben." Still pitching his voice softer, as if her headache were lingering. His consideration bumped River's already high opinion of this man up a few notches. "I wasn't sure you'd want me in your tent, and you weren't available to ask."

And there it went, even higher. He was dangerously close to being one of the nicest men she'd ever met.

"You didn't stay with Jessie?" River teased.

Easton shook his head. "Something is seriously wrong with him. That guy has the worst apnea I've ever been forced to listen to. He's going to bring an avalanche down on us if we're not careful."

"Bree's planning on dragging him to the doctor when we get back to LA."

"Good. Because that's torture." He paused, then said, "I woke up with the marmot staring at me. I don't know how it got into Ben's tent, but I think it watched me sleep."

River couldn't help her giggle. She watched out of the corner of her eye as he pulled his shirt off and set it to the side. She hadn't intended on peeking. There was so much sheer muscle in the tent with her, it was hard to find a place to look where she couldn't see Easton's broad, triangular back.

A low chuckle rumbled through the tent. "Why am I keeping my back turned if you're going to stare at me?"

"Why am I trying to stare if you're going to keep your back turned?" she replied.

Seeing that same flush reddening the nape of his neck was more than worth it. River grinned, closing her eyes to preserve his dignity. "In my defense, I *was* trying. I'm sorry. I'll keep them squeezed shut."

"Were you?" Easton didn't have to sound so smug.

"It's a man's chest," River reminded him. "Nothing I haven't seen before, in your own house."

"I didn't say you needed to close your eyes."

That sexy rumble was even sexier when it deepened like that. And maybe they were on one of the tallest mountains in North America, but someone had cranked the heat up in this tent a few degrees hotter than a sultry Southern California night.

"I don't know if I'm willing to risk your new love interest's wrath." Opening one eye, River watched the dry replacement shirt settling down over deliciously hard abdominal muscles. With a lusty sigh, River decided playing coy wasn't her style. "You drive me nuts, you know that?"

"At least it's going both ways, sweetheart." He turned, those warm brown eyes sliding over her features. "You really do look better," Easton murmured, repeating his earlier words. "I'm glad. I didn't want to have to take you back down. I know how important this climb is to you."

"It's the film, not the climb. That's just the fun part."

"The Old Man can sense a bullshitter from a kilometer away. If you're not up here for him, he's going to toss you right back off."

"I hate to disappoint his majesty, but I was born with glue on the seat of my pants." River shifted closer, her knees mere inches from his. "Lanes don't get bucked off."

"Your redneck roots are showing."

"And?" She raised her eyes to him in challenge.

Easton lowered his face, mouth near her ear. "And I like it."

What was he doing?

It would be a lie to say that Easton had never flirted with a client before, but that was always after a climb was through and never more than the friendly camaraderie that accompanied the heady accomplishment of summiting.

River was something else.

The morning had started weird. Still half-asleep, Easton had opened his eyes, half hoping prettier ones would meet his. On the side of the sleeping bag where River had been in his dreams, the marmot sat curled up in a ball, watching him with much darker eyes.

Eyes that stared...unblinkingly.

The marmot was going to be a problem. Spending the night with it had crossed some sort of significant barrier, and they now had a new relationship status. Apparently, they were *committed*. The whole situation was more than a little embarrassing and not only for the fact that it was all being caught on film.

He had a suspicion the marmot knew he'd started dreaming about River every night.

Easton had been worried about her, but when he'd unzipped the tent, River had momentarily stolen his breath away. Her hair was loose across her shoulders, and she was blinking up at him as if she'd gotten caught. Easton couldn't help but stare. And when she'd flashed that perfectly innocent, heart-stopping grin at him, Easton knew that, one: he'd definitely caught her up to something. And two: if anyone was in danger of being caught here, it was him.

Falling for River wasn't a bad idea. It was epically bad. He wasn't interested in being some actress's part-time fling on location, and whispering in her ear was exactly what Easton *shouldn't* be doing. Getting drawn in like this, so close all he had to do was inhale and she would be in his arms, was even worse. Easton was starting to lose his ability to say no to the woman in front of him. All she had to do was turn those pale-blue eyes his way and—

Her *eyes*. That was what had happened.

"Your eyes." He could have kicked himself for not being more on top of this.

"What about them?"

"It's your blue eyes," Easton explained. "We're so close to polar north up here, and the elevation has us closer to the sun. The brightness of the light is more than your eyes can handle."

She frowned. "It wasn't a problem on any of my other climbs."

"Your other climbs weren't—"

"Yeah, yeah, weren't the Old Man," she finished for him with a sigh, leaning back on her hands. "Do you realize I was dangerously close to kissing you? And it would have been great, Easton. Fabulous. Now a not-kiss is all you get."

Easton reached for his pack and pulled out a pair of snow goggles with darker tinting than the ones she had brought with her. "I think you'll do better wearing these. Otherwise, the headaches are going to keep coming. A few more, and you won't care about the documentary or anything else. You'll be fighting to get back down as hard as you fought to get up here."

"Don't underestimate my stubbornness."

"Trust me, I wouldn't dare."

Adjusting the goggles to fit her properly, Easton passed them over. And okay. Would he rather have her in one of his shirts? Probably. But he'd take having her in his best—and ridiculously expensive—pair of goggles. As long as she stayed healthy and not in pain.

River giggled as she peered around the tent. "These are dark. I could almost get an actual night's sleep wearing these."

"What's the fun in that?" He watched as she pushed the goggles on the top of her head, like a pair of sunglasses.

"Hey, Easton?"

"Yeah?"

Resting her hand on his arm, River leaned forward and kissed his cheek. "Thank you. For all of this."

For a moment, it was all Easton could do not to wrap his hands around her waist. Instead, he closed his eyes, the thin air doing nothing to cover the lingering scent of her skin. Her hand stayed on his arm, her hair copper silk as he threaded his fingers through it. And maybe he didn't draw her in close. He didn't have to. River was already leaning into him, soft and warm and more tempting than anything he'd ever known.

"We should probably keep this professional," Easton murmured. Not kissing her behind her earlobe, down her neck, and across her shoulder was brutally difficult. Especially when her hands were sliding over his chest, fingers digging into his shoulders.

"Define professional," she challenged him.

"Not this." Slipping his arm around her waist, Easton picked her up, pulling her across his lap. When a tiny noise of appreciation escaped her throat, his willpower plummeted.

"Probably not this either." Her hands traced a path along his stomach, making each muscle contract involuntarily at her touch.

A smack of a hand against the outside of the tent was the only warning they had that Ben's face was about to poke inside the flap.

"Umm, guys, I hate to interrupt…"

"You've got to be kidding me." Easton growled under his breath, letting River slide off his lap.

"Tell me about it," River muttered. "Your timing sucks, Ben."

Ben had the decency to clear his throat, sounding far more apologetic than he looked. "I've got Ash on the line. She's watching the weather, and we might need to stay put instead of heading up. Talk to her. She'll tell you what's going on."

The last thing Easton wanted to do right then was leave this tent and whatever was on the verge of happening between them, but only a fool didn't listen when his people called with weather warnings. Offering River an apologetic look, Easton pulled his boots back on and went to the dining tent. Settling down next to a makeshift supply table they'd formed out of snow, Easton picked up the sat phone. "Hey."

He'd never know what it was that gave him away, but his sister always knew when she'd interrupted him at the worst of times. With that one word, Ash started laughing.

"You can't be serious. Oh man, Graham is going to love this. We've had a bet going since you left. The actress, right?"

He glanced at the corner of the tent where River had joined her people. At his look in her direction, River's eyebrow raised questioningly. Turning back to the radio, he cleared his throat.

"What's got you worried, Ash?"

"There's a cold front coming through from the northwest. They're saying it dumped an extra two feet of powder at Camp

Three on Denali. Came on fast, and everyone there is having a mess of a time digging out. You're not directly in the path, but you'll get some of it. Might want to sit until it passes. Winds are strong. Forty mile an hour gusts."

"Thanks, Ash. We'll hold tight."

"Good. Oh, and, East."

"Yeah?"

"Try not to let the actress eat you alive."

Since she'd kept them from possibly freezing to death in a snowstorm, Easton almost wasn't offended by that.

Almost.

"What's going on?" Bree asked when he hung up with his sister.

"There's a storm on its way," Easton informed his clients, moving to stand in front of them. "Ben will make sure everyone has a radio. Keep it on channel four. There are high winds in this storm, so there's always a slim possibility that the tents will give."

Jessie's eyes went wide, his voice squeaking. "I'm sorry, what was that?"

"Oh," Ben spoke up, cheerful as ever. "I've seen them rip apart like a blood bag in a shark tank. You're screwed when that happens."

"A what?" Bree stared at him. "What's a blood bag?"

"How do you not know what a blood bag is?" Ben asked her.

"How do you *know* what a blood bag is?"

Easton cleared his throat. Loudly. "Yes. Sometimes a well-made tent won't be a match for these kinds of winds. The snow walls we built are solid, but in the time we have before the weather comes through, let's build them up as much as we can. River, don't push yourself."

She opened her mouth, eyes flashing in indignation.

"I know you can pull your own weight. Just don't try to pull anyone else's." Holding up the radio, Easton held each of his team's gazes with a stern look of his own. "Make sure you know how to use this, where the buttons are, everything. We don't know what's coming our way, and you need to be able to make a call in zero visibility. If your tent goes, do not try to get to one of the other tents. Stay put, and not a foot off center. Radio me, and I will come get you."

"I can't decide if that's sexy or scary," Bree murmured to River, who shared a quick smile with the other woman. They weren't taking this seriously enough.

"We're not that high up yet, which might be giving you three a false sense of security. Mount Veil is dangerous, and storms like this are only part of the reason why. You can die as quickly at eleven thousand feet as you can at fifteen or twenty like Denali."

"Aye-aye, captain. We'll fall in line." Jessie had gone back to fiddling with his camera, and Easton wondered if Jessie was doing so because he wasn't worried...or if he was hiding the fact that he was.

Bree started munching on a protein bar, paying attention but completely relaxed. River seemed to be listening, but a tiny smirk played on her face.

"What?"

"It's cute when you're being a worrywart," she told him.

Did anything frighten this woman? Easton respected her nerves of steel, but damn, she made him nervous sometimes.

"You tried, boss," Ben said with a shrug, digging for the rest of the radios.

"Remember," Easton said one last time. "I can find you blind if you stay where you're supposed to be. If not, I can't help you."

Holding River's eyes, he added quietly, "No matter how much I might want to."

Someone had constructed a very nice snow wall around her tent while River had been passed out in Easton's. Still, it never hurt to build it up higher, especially with the ominous clouds gathering in the northwest.

Easton said the storm was supposed to only give them a glancing blow, not a full fist to the face. She wasn't too worried about the storm, but River couldn't shake the feeling of being a sitting duck up there, without any chance to avoid what was headed their way.

As the sky darkened, Easton radioed everyone into their tents, told them to buckle down, and they would wait it out. Try to sleep if they could.

Sleep wasn't anywhere close to River's mind when the storm hit.

The beating of the wind against the fabric of their tents started within minutes, building up to a howl in her ears. She'd tried to put on a brave face for her team, but there was something intrinsically terrifying about knowing the only thing between herself and the raw power of nature was a thin piece of fabric.

If something tore her tent, she'd be toast.

Very cold toast.

Turning down her portable light as low as it would go and still allow her to see, River lay on her back, watching the tent buffeting above her. A wandering mind never wandered in comforting directions, and she'd imagined all sorts of ways they could be buried beneath the results of this storm before River finally shook her head.

"Okay, I need a distraction." Pulling out her radio, she hit the button on the side. "Easton, can you hear me?" Probably not, because she could barely hear herself. "Everything's fine," River added quickly. "I just needed someone to talk to, since it sounds like a wind demon is trying to devour our souls outside."

Static, then Easton's deep rumble. "Over."

"I'm sorry?"

"You have to say over," he explained. "And this isn't half as bad as I thought it would be. We're fine. Try to get some sleep. Over."

Okay. They were fine. Except...well...it still sounded like they were not fine outside.

After a moment, River picked up the radio again. "Do you want to play a radio game?" she asked.

Silence, then Easton's reply. "Do I have to?"

"You don't have to, but it would be awfully embarrassing to play radio charades by myself."

A low chuckle was barely audible above the screaming of the wind. "Fine," Easton gave in. "I spy with my little eyes something—"

"Don't say white," River groaned into the radio. "If you say white, I'm hanging up on you."

"And letting me get some sleep?"

"Please, no one could sleep through this. What do you spy?"

He must have been going to say white, because it took him a moment to switch. "I spy something green."

She had absolutely no idea what was green in his tent. So she guessed. And she guessed some more. And when the normal suggestions ran out, River cast her net wide.

"A bucket," she guessed.

"Nope."

"A marmot?"

There was a long pause before Easton finally murmured into the radio, "It was getting cold."

"You're such a softie." River giggled. "You know it's falling in love with you, right?"

Easton yawned. "Maybe it needed to meet someone who treated it better than the other marmots. It's hard to find the right person these days, especially when internet dating isn't an option in the bush."

"Are online marmot dating sites a thing?"

"I assume so. Are you done guessing?"

River was about to answer when a third voice interrupted them.

"In about thirty seconds, you're going to have me in your tents, smothering you both," Jessie said over the radio. "River, it's a book."

"I said book," River argued.

Easton sounded far too smug. "You didn't say which book."

"*Gone with the Wind*?"

"Nope," he told her. "*Watership Down*."

"Aww. The one with the bunnies?"

Even over the wind, they could hear Jessie yelling in his tent for them to shut up. Grinning, River stayed quiet, at least for a few minutes longer, then she clicked on the radio one last time, pressing it against her cheek.

"Hey, Easton?"

"Yeah?"

"I'm glad you're our guide."

Silence, then her favorite voice in the world rumbled sweetly in her ear. "Me too, River. Me too."

CHAPTER 11

SINCE SHE WAS ALONE IN her tent, no one needed to know River slept with the radio tucked under her arm, tight to her rib cage like a teddy bear.

Somehow Easton's deep voice—so calm and unafraid despite the winds shrieking around them—had allowed River to drift off to sleep. Even with the storm, she slept great. River only started to stir when a loud squawk from the radio startled her upright.

"What? Who—?" Twisting around, her brain tried and failed to keep up.

"Rise and shine." The radio crackled against her breast. "We've got a mountain to climb. Are you coming, or do I need to dig you out?"

River didn't understand what Easton meant until she rolled over and scooted sideways a few inches, reaching for the zipper on her tent. When she unzipped it, she was met with a wall of white.

"I'm good. Don't—"

A mouthful of soft fresh powder kicked into her face midsentence. Easton's warm brown eyes appeared in her view as she blinked snow out of her lashes.

"Good morning." He chuckled at the expression on her face.

"Is it?" River mumbled.

Easton wasn't wearing a jacket, meaning the reflection off the snow must have been heating the site enough she wouldn't need one either. When River drew in a deep breath, her lungs resisted the cold, thinner air. A blast of wind blew the snow past Easton's crouching form and into her tent. How in the world did this man not need a coat?

"Nope. Nope, nope." Wiggling backward, River pulled her jacket around her. "In or out, big guy. It's too early to build a snow cone down my shirt."

"Sorry, time to emerge from your hidey-hole. We're getting an early start today. The snow cones will have to wait for later."

He flicked some snow at her, earning a wrinkled nose and a tongue sticking out.

"You're not half as attractive as you think you are, Easton Lockett," she called after him as the tent flap fell back down. River reached for the zipper pull with her sock-covered toes. "Couldn't even zip...back up...stupid man. Stupid tent. Stupid man-tent." Dropping back to the ground in a dramatic flop, River groaned. "Okay, self, time to get up. You have no choice in the matter. Get up, get moving, and try not to ice ax any men this morning."

"River? You okay in there?" Outside her tent, Ben sounded concerned.

"You count as a man, Benjamin. You're not exempt."

"Okeydokey. Easton said to tell you he's got coffee going."

Okay. So maybe he wasn't quite as terrible as he'd seemed a moment ago. River dressed, then started applying liberal amounts of sunscreen and the heavy-duty moisturizer she had brought for her lips. Finished with her preparations for the day, River put her heavy jacket aside, opting for a windbreaker instead of the thinner long-sleeve shirt Easton had been wearing. Emerging from her tent, River rubbed her arms briskly against the cold air.

"Easton's nuts for not needing a jacket," River told Ben when she saw him. "You are too."

Ben headed over to make the rounds past Bree's and Jessie's tents. "I don't know," he called over his shoulder. "Feels good to me."

True, the sun was heating up the mountainside, but River had spent too many years in the mild temperatures of Los Angeles. It was more than cold enough for her.

As they crawled out of their own tents, River noticed her crew were dragging their feet.

"Why are you all so tired?" River asked them, joining her friends. "I slept like a baby."

Jessie rolled his eyes at her.

"At least someone got some rest." Bree rubbed tired-looking eyes with the back of her hand.

"It's your fault," Jessie told River as they headed to the dining tent.

"What did I do?"

"You and Sasquatch over there kept wanting to *talk*," he grumped. "It was *so* annoying."

Easton was heating up coffee for their breakfast inside the tent, where the heater's fumes could air outside and not make anyone sick. At Jessie's comment, he merely raised an eyebrow.

"Hey, I don't care how many scary eyebrows you waggle at me.

You two need to figure out whatever this is." Jessie made a circle in the air, indicating both River and Easton. "I need my sleep, man."

Ignoring Jessie and his snarking, Easton walked over and handed River a thermos of coffee. "Are you feeling up to another climb?"

Before she could answer, Easton took her elbow, silently asking her to step away from everyone for a private conversation. Since he'd brought her coffee, River was more than happy to sneak away with Easton, even if the sneaking away was a few boot scoots to the left outside the tent's entrance.

"If you aren't, there's no shame in that," Easton added. "It's better to know now than to get in trouble later. We have a solid day ahead of us, and all this powder isn't going to make the traveling any easier."

As she looked around her, River could see what he was talking about. The snow had piled on, leaving their camp mostly buried. She could only imagine what the unfamiliar ground in front of them would be like.

"I'll be fine," River promised, enjoying a sip of the hot liquid.

"Drink up." His voice was gentler than usual. "And if you start to feel off at all or start to get another headache, tell me. We can take breaks if we need to or redistribute the gear."

"Are you saying I can't pull my own weight?"

"I wouldn't dare." Easton took a sip of his own coffee, nodding in greeting to Ben as the other guide went past and into the tent. Then Easton dropped his voice even quieter. "Listen. Yesterday, before the call came in. And earlier, at my place."

She arched an eyebrow. "Outside your torture barn?"

"It's not a torture barn."

"It really seems like a torture barn."

Easton snorted, but she could see amusement in his eyes. "Outside my perfectly normal barn, things got a little..."

River waited for him to finish. Instead, he paused midsentence. "What?" she asked.

"This is where you usually jump in with a clever comment. I've started building in breaks for you, so the conversation flows more freely."

Sticking her tongue out at him for the second time that day didn't make River any more mature, but it sure felt good.

"Things got heated," River finished for him because Easton was still waiting for her. "And they were on the verge of getting a lot more heated."

Easton gazed down at her. "Were they?"

"Weren't they?"

"I want to make sure you and I are on the same page. And if we're not, I won't mind."

That stung more than it should have. "Way to show a lady the love."

Easton turned his head to scan the rest of the campsite. Since all three of their companions were busy eating breakfast, Easton rested a hand on her hip, then slipped an arm around her waist.

"What I'm saying is, if you want me to keep doing things like this, tell me. If you don't, tell me. The last thing I want is to make you uncomfortable."

"Did it ever occur to you that I'm the one making you uncomfortable?" Her fingernails traced down his breastbone.

"Different kind of uncomfortable," Easton rumbled. Could

his voice be any sexier, his mouth warm against her ear? "And all. The. Time."

"You should have kissed me at the barn," River told him.

"Definitely."

Moving closer, she added, "And yesterday."

He nodded in agreement. "Exactly what I've been thinking."

River smirked at him. "Or about three seconds ago, before I smelled breakfast. Too bad, huh?"

This time, his warm laughter stole her breath away. "Terrible." Easton's arm lingered for a moment, strong and solid around her waist. Then he stepped back. "Guess I better work on my timing."

"You really should."

As she ducked back into the dining tent, River winked at him over her shoulder. "Hey, Easton. It would have been an amazing kiss. Just so you know."

This guy was killing her, one sexy chuckle at a time. But when he was serious, it was even worse.

"Trust me," Easton said huskily. "You don't know what you're missing."

If River's headache hadn't responded to the painkillers, Easton would have stayed in place one more day. Acute mountain sickness could strike even lower than where they were at, and even though Easton always made sure to ascend slowly enough for his clients to acclimate to the lower oxygen levels, it was nothing to take lightly. He'd seen his fair share of great climbers taken down unexpectedly. But she wasn't, so he didn't.

In fact, once River had gotten a thermos of coffee in her, she'd been full of energy and raring to go. Still, Easton kept one eye on her as they packed up their gear and started off. The Veil was within a day's hike, but instead of taking them higher in elevation, he decided he wanted to take her somewhere off the direct path. Somewhere worth filming and only slightly higher elevation than their current camp.

He kept telling himself he would have done the same with any other client, but even Easton knew he was lying to himself. River was…different. And until he was certain she was in the clear, Easton wasn't taking her one step higher on this mountain than he had to.

Ben never called him out on his indirect path, seeming content to follow Jessie and Bree and pause when they wanted something from the extra filming supplies Ben had on his pack. Every time the film crew grew distracted, Easton obliged his clients by stopping so they could shoot, which was constantly. Even though he knew it was killing their progress, every pause gave him the opportunity to evaluate River, to make sure she wasn't getting another headache or starting to lag behind in pace. But to her credit, the woman was solid as the rock they were standing on.

She never faltered a step.

The marmot had decided to continue accompanying the expedition, and unlike the rest of them, the fresh snow didn't hinder it. Able to stay on the crust of the snowpack, the marmot scurried along at Easton's side, pausing every so often to gaze at him with shiny, fervent eyes. Its particular suffocating brand of love should have been annoying, but for some reason, the furball was growing on him.

Cuddling up during a storm tended to do that for a guy and his marmot.

Eventually, they reached the location Easton had intended on taking his clients to, but not without Easton finally having to nudge the film crew along. This was one of his favorite locations on the mountain. The glacier beneath them was starting to crack, like candy coating on an ice cream cone. The result was a far more interesting series of vertical ascents on the ice. Beautiful and more challenging.

He'd really wanted River to see it, hopeful she'd enjoy the challenge too.

True to form, River had thrown herself at the climb exuberantly, and between the two of them, they made short work of the ascent. The others...not so much. In the most technical part of the day's climb by far, River's natural abilities not only shone through but resulted in them cresting the top of this rockface far before the others. The chance to sit alone with her was nice, but even the marmot was starting to look bored.

"I should have scheduled an extra week for this." Easton looked down the mountain at Ben, where the other guide waited for Bree and Jessie to scale the section Easton and River had climbed almost half an hour earlier. "Those two want to film every handful of snow they pass."

Her eyes were safely tucked behind his best snow goggles, but her smile was all visible for him to see.

"And yet you're still hanging out with me instead of going down there and pushing them along. Why do I get the feeling you're being overprotective?" River settled in to wait for the rest

of the team, sitting closer to Easton than was technically necessary. "You set the slowest pace we've ever had today."

"Maybe a little." Easton bumped her shoulder companionably.

The air in their lungs was cold, and the wind bit into their
clothes. Still, River's good mood hadn't left. The woman he'd
stopped for on the side of the road had teemed with frustration.
This River was exactly where she wanted to be, and it showed.

Sitting at her side, legs dangling over the edge of the massive
block of ice they were perched on, was exactly where Easton
wanted to be too.

"What's that over there?" River asked, pointing toward the
rest of the glacier sweeping down the mountainside. Like a paint-
ing of an overturned pot of boiling water, the mountainside was
an image frozen: a churning cauldron of blocks of ice bigger than
houses, rolling and tumbling over one another.

"The same thing we're sitting on over here." Easton patted
one gloved hand on the ice beneath them. "All of this is an icefall,
although we're on the far edge...the more stable edge. It's not as
bad as the Khumbu Icefall on Everest. That one scares even me."

"Have you noticed all paths lead to Everest for you?" River
teased.

"It's been in the back of my mind for a long time."

"Now we know what the man bun is hiding." She waggled her
eyebrows comically. "Your ambition is under there."

"Better than a bald spot."

When she giggled, looking guilty, Easton knew she was busted.
"That's why you kept staring at my head, isn't it?"

"I have no idea what you're talking about."

"You thought I was bald."

"Bald guys are hot. And no. I thought maybe you were balding. Bald-*ing*. The 'ing' is the important part." Slender fingers plucked her glove off, touching his hair. "And your hair is very sexy."

Easton took her hand, carefully tugging her glove back on. Then, because she was hip to hip with him and Ben was stuck trying to get Jessie and his gear up the fall instead of him, Easton slipped her hand inside his and stuffed them both inside his jacket pocket for warmth.

The goggles hid her eyes, but there was no hiding the way she leaned into him, her head resting on his shoulder.

He looked down at her, then tugged the end of her braided hair. "Didn't your mother teach you not to judge people by their looks?"

"No. She taught me never to marry a bull rider, unless I wanted to spend my life with a man all beat up from chasing belt buckles. And if a man chased *my* belt buckle, pull a Colt Forty-five on him and see what he's made of."

Easton blinked. "Your mother scares me."

"Says the man everyone is scared of. I don't buy it though. I think you're soft and squishy beneath that overwhelmingly follic-ular display of masculinity."

"I'm not sure if that was a compliment or not."

With another giggle, River bit her lower lip. Never had he wanted a pair of goggles off more. He was dying to see her eyes again, eyes bluer than the glacier they were on. Easton touched his finger to her nose, nudging them down a smidge.

Damn, she took his breath away.

"Have you ever climbed it?"

Lost in her eyes, Easton barely heard—much less comprehended—what she was saying. Especially when her voice grew smoother, richer. He was drowning in her, and there was nothing that could make him come up for air.

"Hmm?"

"Have you ever climbed the icefall?" River repeated.

"Skirting it is safer. Over here, the ice blocks aren't as broken up and unstable. Those tip and crush people."

"I didn't ask if you guided people up it. I asked if you—Easton Lockett—ever climbed the icefall."

"Yeah," he murmured. "Once with Ben. The second time, I soloed."

And if his sister ever found out, Ash would kick his butt from there to Moose Springs.

"Let's climb it." Her whole face lit up at the idea.

"Right now?"

"You and me," River breathed. "Right now."

In that moment, his mind raced, calculating the day it was, the time of year, the supplies they had. Could they? Because damn, he wanted to. Every time he saw the icefall, he wanted to test his skills over there again. But the clients who trusted him to get them safely up to the summit and back down had always been more important.

"You have a movie to make."

"So? Let's make the movie over there."

"Because even expert climbers get hurt trying to cross them. It's probably not one of the best places to encourage visitors to come see." Easton squeezed her hand. "I'm not a superstitious guy, but until this climb is done, let's not have you over there."

"Yeah, you're probably right. The footage we're getting from here will be good enough." After a moment, River looked back up at him. "But someday, let's come back here. You, me, and the marmot. We'll climb it."

There was nothing else he could do but nod, a slow, stupid smile crossing his face.

"Yeah," Easton promised her, meaning it completely. "One day."

They spent the night at the icefall, then woke up the next morning to the toughest climb so far. Easton led them in a straight path up the mountain along the steepest trail they'd encountered. For the first time, they were required to use their ice axes to aid their climb, and it didn't escape River's notice that slipping here could result in sliding down several meters or more if they were unlucky. She was glad Easton had insisted on the spiky crampons strapped to their feet.

The higher they climbed, the clearer the mountain range stretched around them...and below them. They were now seeing the tops of other peaks that had seemed to rise into the sky at lower elevations. The view was breathtaking and disconcerting at the same time, making her heart beat faster.

She'd never experienced anything as exhilarating as this.

The wind had always been a constant above the tree line, but as they approached the campsite Easton had picked out, River found herself growing increasingly distracted by the wind's shrill shrieking. Rising in pitch and volume, it only grew until Easton led them into a protected shelter of rock beneath an overhanging cliff face. The site was level and out of the elements as much as one could be when on the side of a mountain. Buffered from the wind, the noise was still loud, if not unbearable.

"You found us the luxury suite," River called to him.

"What is that?" Bree asked, twisting around.

"It's the wind coming through the Veil. It's above us, about a thousand feet up." Ben pulled out a small bag of foam earplugs from his pack. "Here. They won't be as soft as normal, so don't shove them in too far, but they should help."

He wasn't wrong. The temperature had dropped to ten below, so she made quick work of molding the earplugs to fit inside her ear canals. Easton's eyes followed her movements, and she had the sense he wasn't pleased with her fingers being outside her gloves.

Easton nodded his head toward the peak above them. "When we're above the Veil, it'll be better."

When Easton unshouldered his gear, Ben followed suit, dropping his pack next to Easton's. At a nod from their guide, Ben started to unpack a series of ropes and stakes.

"I haven't been up here since May," Easton informed them, arms crossed over his muscled chest. "I don't know the condition of the line I set through the Veil, so Ben and I are going to go check it. You three are setting up camp, including our tents. We'll be a while."

"Does that mean you're taking us through?" River perked up.

So far, he'd been unwilling to commit to that or to taking them all the way to the summit.

Easton nodded, smiling at her. "Jessie and Bree are getting better by the day. The skill set is there. As long as the conditions in the Veil are passable, I'll take them through."

He'd said Jessie and Bree. River wasn't sure if it was a given she was going too or a given she wasn't. At this point, Easton should know better than to try to leave her behind. "What about me?"

The marmot chirped as it scuttled behind Easton's feet.

"You and the fluffball have to go home. Feel free to fill out a comment card." Easton's teasing look turned more heated as his voice grew huskier. "You've always been ready, River."

Well, if he wanted to put it that way…

"Are you filming this?" Bree muttered to Jessie.

"What do you think?"

The smugness in Jessie's voice made River suddenly realize how close she and Easton were standing. Like there were only two people on this mountain instead of five. At least it was freezing cold so no one would see the flush of heat on her neck and cheeks. Easton didn't seem bothered at all. Instead, he looped an arm around her waist as if it was completely normal to stand with her like that.

"Stay hydrated and stay in camp," he rumbled before glancing at her crew. "No adventures without me, people. This isn't the right site for it."

"I'm not getting a cheerful, 'everything's super safe here, guys' vibe," Jessie drawled.

"It isn't." Easton added, "If we don't radio or return by

morning, call for help. Absolutely no rescue attempts in the Veil. River's in charge. She's the only one who can get you two back down the icefalls if something happens to us."

"What's the likelihood of that?"

"The Veil is a cauldron of pure evil," Ben told them cheerfully. "It's more likely than you think."

Collectively, they cringed. Easton aimed an exasperated look at Ben. "Don't tell them that."

"You told *me* that."

Easton gave River's waist a gentle squeeze before dropping his arm and shouldering his pack. He started to hand her a radio, but before she could take it, Easton tilted it back.

"Under no circumstances, no matter what, are you to go into the Veil after us. I mean it, River. The ground is swiss cheese with crevasses, and visibility is next to zero. If you don't know what you're doing, you'll never come back out again. Promise me."

She didn't promise. Instead, River pushed up her goggles, holding his eyes. "I'm going to be pissed if you get hurt."

The look he gave her didn't make her knees weak…it set her on fire. "The feeling is mutual. I'm on channel four, same as last time. Try not to cause too much trouble while I'm gone."

"Does that sound like me?"

"That sounds *exactly* like you." Easton dropped a quick kiss to her forehead, in front of everyone. Bree was smirking at her as the pair headed out of the camp. River watched as they picked a trail, hiking steadily up the ridge until they disappeared out of sight.

River turned to her crew. "Does it bother anyone else that they left us here, possibly never to be seen again?"

"On a mountainside somewhere below a shrieking banshee of epic proportions? Nah, I'm good." Jessie shrugged. "So, what are we doing first? Filming or setting camp?"

"Setting camp," River replied immediately. "You never know when the weather's going to turn. We need to have shelter."

At this point, they could have set up camp with their eyes closed. Bree stuck close to her side, sharing in the tasks that one of them could have handled alone. Even though they had all been on top of one another since they'd stepped into Alaska, River appreciated her friend's company.

Finally indulging the part of her unable to stop worrying, River turned to Bree. "Do you think they'll be okay?"

"In the cauldron of pure evil?" Bree grinned. "Have you considered they could be headed down the mountain right now just to get rid of us?"

River had to laugh at the mental image. "Watch the whole Veil thing be an elaborate ruse to get a running head start."

They finished setting camp, then went about heating up food at the edge of the dining tent. The marmot must have tried to follow the two guides, but whatever the Veil was had forced it to turn back. Returning to camp, it sat next to Easton's tent, making high-pitched barking noises as it scolded them. Even though Easton had said not to, Bree snuck it a couple of bites of a granola bar.

"If it chokes on a peanut, you're the one giving mouth-to-mouth," River warned her. "It doesn't like me."

"You're direct competition." Tossing another chunk of granola between them, Bree added, "All's fair in love and marmot war."

"Well, we might as well film something," River decided. "Unless you want to rest, Jessie."

"I can't sleep with them out there." Covering his face with an arm, he yawned. "Yeah, let's get this going."

"Do you want a mirror?" Bree asked her.

"Is that a nice way of saying I need a mirror?" River joked.

"You said it, not me. And yes. You really do."

The glass on the miniature compact kept fogging over every time she wiped it clear, so River settled on letting Bree and Jessie poke and prod her into respectability.

"No one expects me to be at my best, right?" Turning to the cameras as they started filming, River put her actress face in place.

"Speak for yourself," Jessie said. "I look great for not being able to feel my feet."

"You can't feel your feet?" Bree's head snapped up, filming forgotten. "Take your boots off. We need to check you for frostbite."

He rolled his eyes. "I don't have frostbite."

"Jessie, we're not kidding around." River aimed her best in-charge look. "Take off your boots."

"No way."

What resulted afterward wasn't River's finest hour, but between her and Bree, they managed to convince Jessie that taking off his boots was more important to his health and happiness than continuing filming. Some tackling and threatening might have been involved.

"See?" he grumped as he pulled his socks back on. "I'm fine."

"I'm worried about how cold your skin felt. I'll ask Easton to check you when he comes back."

Jessie grumbled about that, but when River settled herself

back in front of the camera, she grinned at him. "We never turned off the camera. Do you think all the future viewers could hear your squeaks of resistance?"

"I *didn't* squeak. And I didn't want to shove over a week's worth of stinky feet in your faces."

"It was rancid," Bree agreed. "We still love you, but we'll never look at you the same."

Nodding emphatically, River added, "I've got to go with Bree on this one."

"Enough about me. Focus, ladies. River. You're not a professional climber, but you do have climbing experience. If you were talking to an amateur who wanted to come up here solo, what would you say?"

"I would say they're crazy," River joked. Then she sighed with contentment. "I'd say, I get it. The longer I'm up here, the more I understand. It's like..." Hesitating, River closed her eyes. "At first, you want to see if you can. But the longer you're up here, it's not about if you can. It becomes this primal need to reach the top. I'm supposed to be focusing on the documentary. But when I close my eyes, all I see is the summit."

Turning back to the camera, she exhaled softly. "To be honest, I've never wanted anything this much in my entire life."

"Even Easton?" Bree teased.

Feeling a flush of heat in her cheeks, River still grinned. "Okay, that's getting cut. What about the rest of it? How did I do? We can start over if you want."

"We're good. I've got what I need." Jessie shared a look with Bree, who failed to hide the triumph on her face.

"What?" River didn't understand whatever passed between them, but neither answered.

As they took down the cameras and settled into a game of UniMagP, River tried to pretend that she wasn't keeping the radio glued to her hand. She tried to read when the game was over, but eventually, she gave up and picked up the radio.

"Easton? How about giving a girl a check-in?"

Silence.

"Easton, Ben, if I'm in charge, that makes me in charge of everyone. Give me a progress update. Over."

A crackling static noise made her fingers reflexively tighten on the radio. "Someone's pushy," Ben joked through the radio, his voice nearly lost beneath the roaring of the wind. "We're taking a break right now. Boss man says to tell you someone else came through here and made a mess of his lines. He's been swearing up and down this mountain, but we're almost done fixing the new ones."

Nodding, River said, "Tell *boss man* he'd better get back down here soon."

"Ten-four."

That low chuckle was undoubtedly Easton. He must have been standing right next to Ben. For some reason, hearing his voice helped calm the nerves that had been spiked from knowing they were up there, doing something dangerous without River to keep a watchful eye on him.

Them. Watchful eye on *them*.

When she set the radio down, she saw her coproducer watching her knowingly. "You really do like him, don't you?"

River didn't need to answer Jessie. They both knew she did.

They'd been gone a total of four hours before they got the second call.

Frankly, Easton was surprised she'd lasted so long. River wasn't the type to sit around wondering what was happening. If he hadn't been so close to camp, Easton would have radioed her in a few minutes anyway. His respect for her as a mountaineer and as a woman far outweighed his respect for her patience.

"Easton, Ben, it's River. Over."

"Riverover? Not sure what that means," Easton teased her.

There was a pause, followed by an audible sigh of relief. "You may be the most annoying human being alive. You know that, right?"

"Have you met my best friend?"

"Yes, and I'm increasingly aware of how you and Graham are made for each other. How soon will you be back?"

Easton answered, taking his long, sweet time to do so. "We're coming around the outcrop now. Don't be worried about the blood."

"The *blood*?"

Ben shot him a wolfish grin when Easton didn't answer her. "That was mean."

"She's earned a little teasing. You should hear the crap she's been giving me since we met."

"True," Ben agreed. "But she watches out for you almost as much as you watch out for her. Don't be surprised if she's ready to skin you alive when we get there."

Sure enough, River was waiting for him outside camp, radio

in hand and first aid kit tucked under her arm. Her concern was cute, but the expression on her face was far less cute when she realized he'd been messing with her. Smart man that he was, Ben kept walking, leaving Easton in relative privacy with River.

"Blood? *Really?*" Hmm. It had been a long time since a woman had looked so ticked at him, like she had every right to put him in his place. To be honest, he rather liked it.

Chuckling, Easton wrapped his arm around River's shoulders, hauling her into a big hug. At first, she resisted the hug, a wolverine ready to chew his face off, but Easton had it on good authority that he gave especially good hug.

Even River could only last for so long.

"Uhhh. You're so warm. It's so good, but it's so bad."

"You were worried about me," he teased her.

"Shut up. I wasn't."

"Were too."

She snuck a peek up at him. "Are you sure you're okay? The blood was a joke, right?"

He was absolutely fine. The fact that it mattered to her though…

"I'm perfect." He couldn't feel her cheek through the thick glove he wore, but he liked the pressure of her leaning into his palm.

"Can I kiss you?" River asked softly.

A woman had never asked him that before. Blinking somewhat stupidly, he said nothing.

"Okay, well that answers that."

With the wind biting into their skin, flushing their cheeks rosy, there was no way to tell if he'd embarrassed her or not. But when she took a step backward, her rueful smile said it all.

"You could've kissed me. I wouldn't have minded."

"Nope, you can't grab someone and kiss the crap out of them." With a small huff, River added, "Even if you would look cute dipped in a dramatic embrace, consent is sexy, Easton. Try to keep up with the times."

She wasn't wrong. Knowing she wanted to kiss him only made him want to even more. Easton didn't chase women. He was too large, his presence too overwhelming to too many people. He never wanted anyone to feel uncomfortable around him, especially not a woman half his weight and a foot shorter than him. But if she wanted him, Easton was more than willing to oblige her.

"River, you don't *ever* have to ask me if you can kiss me," he told her, voice lowered and husky with desire. Reaching for her hand, Easton gave her gloved fingers a gentle tug, an open invitation. "Consider this a yes for whatever."

"Hold on there, buddy." Her bright, pretty smile stole his breath away, the way a hard day's climb couldn't. "I'm not offering whatever. Just a kiss."

Leaning down to make his face more accessible, Easton waited. And waited.

"Well, we've overtalked it now. You'll have to wait for the moment again."

With a playful growl, Easton snagged her around the waist. River burst out laughing as he spun her in a circle. Her booted foot hooked behind his knee for balance, her arms grasping his neck. Face-to-face, Easton stopped, holding her up with one arm, his free hand carefully threading into her hair.

"I think we're back in the moment," River whispered, her cold nose brushing his.

"Are you sure?" he rumbled, because her breath was warm on his skin, and he was ready to know if her lips were as soft as they looked.

"So sure. Super-duper sure."

"Extra sure?" Easton started to tease her, but River had already pressed her mouth to his.

It should have started soft, sweet. A first kiss, to see what this was between them. But the moment their lips met, it was like fire and cinnamon, sweet and hot and burning him up from the inside out. Just like she was...perfect.

Absolutely perfect.

CHAPTER 12

NAPS WERE ALMOST AS GOOD as kisses above twelve thousand feet.

Both Easton and Ben were tired from their much longer day. Being used to the altitude didn't mean exertion in lower oxygen didn't get to them. After a quick hot meal, both crashed out in their tents. And if River ended up snuggled next to Easton's side, sleeping beneath the heavy, reassuring weight of his muscled arm, that was purely for logistical reasons. He was warm. She was cold. See? It made total sense.

The marmot threw an absolute fit at being left out in the cold, but River knew there was a perfectly warm dining tent where the marmot was more than welcome. She felt bad about the ousting, but the marmot was getting aggressive in its determination to win Easton as its mate. River refused to get bitten out of jealousy, especially when the fluffy adorable thing had started getting a murderous look in its eyes every time Easton stepped anywhere close to River.

"This is the first time I've woken up in days without a marmot butt in my face," Easton told her when he woke up a few hours later. It was early morning, and River could have stayed asleep a few more hours easily. Well, if the marmot wasn't still crying its heart out at being ousted from the tent.

She yawned. "By the looks I was getting when I zipped up the tent, I may have started a war."

His low rumble was even better with his arms around her. Easton could have started the whole kissing thing again. River was totally on board for that. Instead, he wanted to look at her feet.

It was River's fault, really. Mentioning to Easton about Jessie's feet had triggered a desire in him to poke and prod at all her extremities, which was far less sexy than it could have been, given different circumstances. It was hard to flirt, so they talked instead. Easton was much better at kissing than small talk, but River appreciated his strong hands massaging her feet so pleasantly.

"So you've never seen one of my movies."

Easton pulled River's foot into his lap. "You sound relieved."

"Well, let's say it's nice meeting someone who doesn't connect me to my roles."

"I'm not a big movie guy," Easton admitted, rolling down her sock. "All your toes look good. Can you feel my fingers?"

He squeezed each of her toes one by one. Nodding, River yelped when he ran a fingernail playfully along the underside of her arch, tickling her. "*Hey.*"

"You're ticklish."

"I'm too ticklish. As in don't do it, or risk the consequences. I'm not responsible for any flailing that may or may not occur. I once accidentally tossed a boyfriend who thought it was funny to tickle me headfirst through a desk drawer."

"Ouch."

"I flail," River reminded him because she could see his thumb twitch. "Don't do it."

"You realize it only makes it more tempting, right?"

"You're kind of an adrenaline junkie, aren't you?"

As he turned his attention to her other foot, Easton pulled her other sock off. "I like to think of it as taking well-considered and appropriate risks. If I ever end up going to climb Everest, I'm not going barefoot with my crampons between my teeth."

"Are you actually going to go to Nepal?"

He was quiet for a moment. "I want to. But I'm not sure if it's fair."

"How so?"

"My dad wanted to summit so badly. My mom used to say that Everest was the other woman in his life. All he could do was think of her."

"What did your dad say?"

"He said that when he was with Everest, all he could do was think about my mom."

River sighed playfully. "That sounds like a man. Never knowing what he wants."

"I think he wanted them both." Easton focused on her foot. "Your pinky toe is cold. Can you feel this?" He squeezed her toe.

"Yeah, but not quite as much as the other ones. Am I getting frostbite?"

"Not necessarily, but we'll need to keep an eye on it."

"Are you going to check everyone's feet?" she asked, unable to keep the flirtation out of her voice. "Or only mine?"

"I'm checking everyone but Ben," Easton murmured. "But I probably won't like theirs as much as yours."

"You said probably."

"No, I didn't."

"I heard a probably."

Wrapping his hand around her toes, Easton began to rub her feet in a brisk motion to warm them. "Anyhow, I've been dreaming about Everest since before I was old enough to understand what I was dreaming of," he admitted.

"What does your dad say?"

"I've never brought it up. Didn't seem right to remind him, knowing he can't go with me."

Leaning forward, River gave Easton an impulsive hug. His hug in return was strong and warm and very easy to get lost in. Eventually, he pulled away, if only to tap a finger to her foot.

"How's the toe feel?"

"Nice and toasty. You should charge for your services."

"I thought I already was." Rolling her sock back up her foot, Easton gave her a heated look that she was starting to recognize.

River nudged his forearm with her sock-covered toes, then playfully pressed against his stomach with her heel. Wrapping his hands around her calves, Easton gently tugged her closer until her knees were hooked over his own and their faces were only a few inches apart.

"If you're charging for extra," River said, "I should warn you that this excursion is on a very tight budget."

Sliding his fingers through her hair, Easton shook his head. "Trust me, you couldn't afford this even if you were a big budget film."

"Oh, really? Someone has a high opinion of themselves." River enjoyed it immensely when he drew her in for a long, slow kiss.

"I have a very strong sense of my own self-worth."

There was something about kissing someone on top of a mountain that made it more fun than normal. And since it was Easton she was kissing, by the time she pulled away, River could barely catch her breath.

"Your beard is frosty." She touched a miniature piece of ice clinging beneath his chin. "You have icicles."

"It's a sign of my mountaineering ability. The more icicles, the better guide I am."

"You're such a goofball. No one knows that, do they? They all think you're big and strong and scary. You're actually a total dork."

"And don't you forget it," Easton breathed against her ear, a far better way of tickling her.

A hand slapping against the outside of their tent ended whatever might have happened next. At least this time, Ben didn't stick his head in.

"Hey, sorry to interrupt, but it's that time. The Veil won't climb itself."

Easton climbed to his feet. "It's all right. I need to go check everyone before we leave camp anyway."

"Remember you said probably." As he left her tent, River called after him, "Don't think I won't put your foot fetish in the movie, Easton."

———

The excitement in the air was palpable. They were going through the Veil today.

For once, Easton didn't ask them to break camp. Instead, they were going to climb up to the Veil, go through, then come back down again, retracing their steps. They were high enough on the mountain that pauses to acclimate were necessary. Easton had said if the Veil went well, he'd decide if they would summit. The way to the top was through the Veil, and if they failed to successfully pull it off when more rested, no one was summiting, then coming back down through the Veil when exhausted.

Today was the day to prove to him that River's team had what it took.

Knowing she was getting close to the summit helped River push through the increasingly difficult task of navigating through dangerous terrain. Even with the distraction of Easton in front of her, River found herself looking more and more to the highest point of the peak above them.

Summiting wasn't a hope. Summiting *would* happen.

As they climbed, Easton would turn to check on the progress of the team. Each time his attention turned to her, a sexy smile would curve his lips. A dangerously distracting one that was literally capable of causing a woman to fall to her death.

"You shouldn't do that," she told him once. "It's highly irresponsible. I could report you to your superiors."

"I don't have superiors," Easton reminded her.

"I've met your sister. You definitely have superiors."

"That's still being decided. What am I doing?"

River snorted. "Oh, you *know* what you're doing."

Considering his low, sexy chuckle, Easton did know. Instead of arguing his innocence, he turned back to the climb. When they finally crested the ridge they'd been ascending for the past hour, River stood back to catch her breath.

It didn't work. Not when what was in front of her took her breath away all over again.

"You wanted to know what the Veil was." Easton stopped, gazing above them. "*That* is the Veil."

Even from several hundred feet below, they could all see the billow of snow across the mountainside, funneling out of a steeply sloped canyon cutting through the landscape. The result was an undulating cloud of swirling snow covering the side of the mountain, like a bride's wedding veil blowing in the wind. At first, River didn't understand what she was looking at until she realized the walls of the canyon were made of deep-blue glacier ice. As if someone had stuck a knife in the glacier and dragged it through, the jagged wound had only cut deeper with every year of unceasing winds.

"River," Bree murmured, catching her attention. They were filming her. Of course they were; that was their job. "Tell us what this feels like."

Jaw dropped, River tried and failed to verbalize what she felt upon seeing the Veil for the first time. But she couldn't find the words.

Ben stepped up next to her. "No one has figured out for sure how it formed, but they think it's a matter of aerodynamics. The temperature of the ice inside the canyon is warmer than on the surface of the glacier. Pressure changes, wind speed. All that science crap turned it into a wind tunnel."

"What he's saying is it's a tough climb to get through," Easton added. "The wind's always in your face, and it's ridiculously strong."

"That's why so many people don't try to summit Mount Veil. The safest way to the top is through the passage." A low whistle escaped between Ben's teeth. "You can't see your hand in front of your face, and it cuts like a son of a bitch. I've been through more than most, but she always makes me pause and think: *How bad do I really want this?*"

Glancing over, River saw Easton watching her. "This is usually where people turn back," he told her. "No judgment, no shame in changing your mind."

"I can't make a documentary about *not* climbing a mountain." River turned back to watch the billows of snow gusting down the mountainside below them.

"It's not always about work," Easton reminded her.

"Says the man being paid to go through there."

"I don't have to be paid to climb. I'm lucky enough to get to work my dream job."

Clapping a hand on Easton's shoulder, Ben barked out a laugh. "Buddy, I've seen you stuck on the ground for a climbing season, and you're a nightmare. You should be paying us to let you take us up here."

They approached the Veil at an angle to avoid the worst of the swirling snow. As they reached the opening of the ice canyon, the shrieking of the wind had grown so loud that River couldn't tell she had earplugs in. Easton turned to them, yelling to be heard.

"We're going to have to tether off to this part. We've got a fixed line running through the entire Veil. Clip on and triple-check it. One person on each section of the fixed line. The last thing we want is too much weight on a single section. The stakes could pull free, and it's steep in there."

"Wait." Like Easton, Bree had to raise her voice to be heard. "We should film this."

"No, it's too dangerous." Easton shook his head. "The weather's not going to get any better. Come on. We're going."

Maybe he'd waited until they reached the Veil to give them instructions on how to get through on purpose. Not that River tended to ignore his directions, but she had to admit she listened a lot closer now the ice canyon was in front of them.

The line they'd secured through the Veil started just above where they were gathered. Per Easton's directions, they clipped onto the rope, then headed forward in single file. A properly fixed rope would hold them all, as long as an anchor was set between climbers. A simple enough rule to follow in normal visibility but one that would be more difficult in bad visibility. The climb was not without risk...one of which was an anchor pulling loose from too much weight and everyone on the line falling.

At this steep of an incline, one wrong step could start a fall with little hope of stopping. The idea of a pile of them plummeting down the mountainside made the hair on the back of River's neck stand up.

Easton led them, with River behind, then Jessie and Bree. As usual, Ben took the last position, to make sure someone could help if one of them fell behind.

"Jessie," Bree said when Easton's back was turned. "Give me the handheld."

"No, give it to me." River beckoned him with a quick curl of her fingertips. "I'll have the better shot. Only Easton will be in front of me."

"Here," Jessie muttered to River before he clipped onto the line, pushing the handheld camera into her hands.

River stepped into the path of the headwind. Almost instantly, the visibility went down to next to nothing. Ben hadn't been lying when he called the Veil a wind tunnel. River felt like she was trying to walk into a hurricane, bent over to keep from being blown off her feet.

For the first few steps, she could almost make out Easton's jacket, but despite the reflection off the ice canyon's walls, the flurries of snow spinning through the Veil blocked him from view. Holding the camera up in one hand, River could barely see her fingers.

Turning it on, she fought her way forward a step, trying to keep the handheld secure against her chest with one arm and using the other hand to brace herself on the line. Every time she let go, the swirling snow immediately ruined her sense of direction.

The tug of the carabiner was her only sense of where the fixed line was. For the first time since the climb had started, River's heart started to race, fear pumping adrenaline through her veins. And yes, the few moments of footage she'd gotten were probably going to be amazing. One didn't need clear, bright footage to make a movie. Sometimes the raw, blurry, shakiness of a camera in a terrifying situation was perfect. But the deeper they went into the Veil, the steeper the climb. River needed both of her hands on this: one for the line and one for her ice ax.

Trying to juggle the handheld had been a mistake.

Falling behind put them all at risk, so River kept going, fumbling with the camera. Thick gloves and cold hands didn't mix. All she had to do was turn off the handheld and put it in a side pocket of her now lighter pack.

A simple task...up until she dropped it.

Horrified, River froze in place. So much was on that camera. So many important shots. So much of her documentary they'd never recover. Yes, some had been backed up, but not what was on the memory card inside. They had the other camera, but the handheld couldn't be gone.

"Easton, I dropped my camera!" River yelled, trying to get someone's attention. There was no answer. "Jessie!"

From behind her, there was nothing. It was as if the Veil had swallowed her team whole, and there was no one left but her. Hunkering down, River scraped her glove along the ground, trying to find the handheld. Her fingers met ice and gravel but no camera.

"Okay, River," she said to herself. "Don't freak out. Think through this."

She wanted the camera, and she needed to get it before Jessie reached her section of the line. The ground beneath her was steeply sloped, and the camera had been in her left hand when she dropped it. If it wasn't at her feet, then the most logical explanation was it was on the ground behind her, or it had fallen to her left.

If she left her spot on the line and went backward, River doubted she'd be able to find it again. So she dug into her pocket for the foil wrapper her lunchtime protein bar had come in. Her gloves were too bulky to allow her to twist the wrapper into a knot around the line, so River pulled them off.

Wrapper tied—giving her something to find on her way back—River jerked her gloves back on. Praying the few seconds of exposure to the elements hadn't caused lasting damage to her extremities, River went backward on the rope, counting each step before hunkering down and feeling for the camera. Nothing.

"Okay, stay calm. Go back to where you started." The beating of the wind in her face was getting to her, and she couldn't hear her own voice, the canyon was so loud. Following the line back to the wrapper, River stretched her arm out farther as she searched. Small movements on the rope told her Jessie had clipped onto her section. She was running out of time to find the handheld because everyone else would soon be there.

Ben wasn't as stern as Easton, but she doubted he'd wave and merrily continue on the path with her stuck like a rock in the same place.

"Where are you, where are you?" River muttered, going as far as her tether would let her. Abruptly, her boot nudged something. Not as substantial as a rock but hard enough to feel it, even with limbs numb from the bitter cold. Unfortunately, her boot had knocked the thing out of reach.

There. The camera was *right there*, but no matter how hard she stretched, River couldn't reach it. If she pulled too hard, she'd risk destabilizing the anchors for the line, leaving everyone behind her at risk.

But it was so *close*.

With a noise of frustration, she stretched out one last time, knowing the effort was pointless. Then River took a breath, took a chance, and unclipped her tether from the fixed line.

Freed from her restraint, River took two steps away from the line, memorizing the degrees she would have to turn to get back as she bent down. The camera found her hands, hard plastic filling her gloves. Before moving out of place, River tucked it safely in the pack on her back. Filled with relief, River turned to step back to the line when her foot slipped.

Sometimes a slip was only a slip. Sometimes a slip was the start of a fall.

When River fell, she kept falling.

Crying out in alarm as she slid faster, she reached for her ice ax, pulling it free of her belt. Rolling onto her stomach, she brought the ax down as hard as she could into the ground beneath her. The resultant catch of metal into ice wrenched her arm so badly, she almost let go, her whole body jerking to a sudden stop.

She lay still as a stone, hand clutching the ax, lost somewhere in the icy whiteout that was the Veil. "At least I found the camera," she told herself, trying not to panic. "This is going to be a great story to add. Especially if Easton doesn't kill me."

River shifted her foot, and instantly, the snow beneath her boot gave, crumbling away. Then the snow beneath her calf and knee. She was over a crevasse, one of the carefully avoided pits that

Easton had set the lines to circumvent, with half of her dangling and the other half about to fall too.

This time when River froze, the last thing she was worried about was a documentary.

Emerging from the Veil was always like coming out of the water, half drowned and desperate for that first deep breath of fresh air.

Even after these many trips through, Easton still hadn't gotten used to the way the ice canyon could mess with his senses. Without his father's expertise during Easton's younger years, he would never have developed the skills to navigate the Veil. Now, when he set lines, it was a combination of experience and instinct that guided him.

No one could ever be truly certain what they were standing on in there.

Low, shallow breaths didn't bring the oxygen he needed to his lungs. For the first few minutes, Easton simply stood there, letting his body recover as best it could. Then he unclipped from the line and stepped aside. River was a fast climber, almost as fast as he was. Factoring in her standard pace plus whatever disorientation she must be experiencing, she was going to clip onto his section soon.

For a moment, Easton allowed himself to remember what it was like to kiss her that morning, to rest in his tent with her curled into his side. Easton hadn't ever considered himself a lonely person. Loneliness was impossible when one always had Ash or Graham around. But it had been a long time—too long—since he'd wanted someone else to share his time with. Someone who loved something he loved too. Who lit up at the challenge of a tough ascent and who stuffed her cold nose against his throat, falling asleep without asking if he minded if she joined him.

With every word, sound, or soft pressure from her lips, River continued to blow him away.

Impatient to see her step out of the Veil, to see her reaction when one of the hardest parts of the climb was conquered, Easton shifted on his feet, arms braced over his chest.

River was a strong climber, the strongest in the group and more than capable of getting through the Veil. Like the rest of them, the going was slow, and she'd feel like she'd been buffeted around more than a little, but if she kept her head down and kept trudging through, it would be fine.

Only...it shouldn't have taken her this long.

Easton stood next to the fixed line, watching the minuscule jumps and vibrations indicating someone was moving along it.

"Come on, whisky," he muttered. "Where are you?"

Easton already knew in his gut something had happened, but the first visual of Jessie's jacket made his heart drop down to his feet. With a curse, Easton darted down the line, clipping behind a confused Jessie.

"Did you see River?" he demanded over the wind.

"What? Where's River?" Jessie yelled back.

Snarling in frustration, Easton plunged into the Veil. Going this way was easier in some senses and as difficult—if not more— in others. Instead of the wind driving him backward with every step, making him fight up a steep incline, the wind drove him forward, encouraging a quick and reckless descent that put him at risk for sprained ankles or a broken leg. Not rushing dangerously along the fixed line took all the willpower Easton had.

Yelling her name was pointless, and trying to see her was as pointless. Searching along the line for her, hoping against hope she was sitting in the snow taking a break, Easton moved as fast as he could safely climb.

His carabiner caught on the line, which was strange, but he pulled free, pressing on. He only saw Bree when he was almost on top of her. Bree's steps had slowed as she struggled to get herself through the same winds pushing against Easton's shoulders.

"River," he yelled in her ear so she could hear him. "Have you seen her?" All he got in return was a confused look and shake of Bree's head. Ben had been staying close to Bree, less than the full section of rope that he should have stayed. It didn't fail to reach Easton's attention there were three of them clipped to the same section of the line.

"What's going on?" Ben asked, fighting to be heard over the screaming of the Veil.

"River's unclipped. I couldn't find her tether."

Easton didn't have to hear the curse that escaped Ben's lips: the expression on the other guide's face showed it all.

"Get Bree out of here," Easton barked at the other mountaineer.

River's carabiner must have broken, or she had the terrible misfortune of slipping when unclipping from one section of the line and reclipping to the next. He didn't understand how that could even happen, with the double safety clip system they'd been using.

The path Easton had set was intended for his entirely

right-handed clients to climb with their right hands on the rope to guide them. Only Ben was left-handed, but he would know to stay to the left. River wouldn't cross the line.

He'd checked the carabiners though. He'd checked every single one because he knew how dangerous this part was. Working his way back, searching for any sign of River, something caused the carabiner he'd clipped to the line to catch. It was a little catch, then the carabiner pulled free. Easton wouldn't have noticed it, except...that was twice.

At the same spot.

There was something on his line.

Feeling around the carabiner, Easton found something that shouldn't have been there. Someone had tied something to his line, a place marker.

"Smart girl," he breathed. "I don't know what you're doing but thank you."

Rapidly pulling a longer length of rope from his pack, Easton tied it off to the fixed line. Then, because he didn't only have one life he was in charge of up here, Easton did one of the absolute hardest things he'd ever done in his life.

He did nothing.

If Ben and Bree were still moving at the same pace, they were all still on this stretch of the line. Easton didn't know what he'd find if he found River. But he knew any additional weight would be too much. So he waited, counting slowly in his head, mentally pacing his teammates as they moved through the Veil. As he waited, Easton felt himself grow calm. The gusts beating into his body didn't matter. The windchill didn't matter. The knowledge that all around him was a poorly mapped system of crevasses that would be covered in a thin layer of snow, ready to give beneath their feet. It didn't matter.

All that mattered was River. And somewhere beyond him, River was out there.

The instant Easton's brain told him Bree and Ben were off the line, he started a sweep downhill, plying out the rope behind him as he made increasingly wider arcing passes. Easton knew what was—and wasn't—beneath him, and more than once, his muscles locked down on him when the snow beneath his boot crunched down too far. One wrong step could punch him through into emptiness.

One day, this would make a great story. In hindsight, maybe this whole ascent was one long first date.

Midthought, Easton's blood went cold. There she was, on the ground, not moving.

"*River.*"

With a low snarl of her name, Easton dropped to his knees next to her. She was so still, at first he thought she was hurt. Sharp relief coursed through his veins when she turned and looked at him.

Then he understood what was happening, why her hands were pushing at him. The angle of her body was wrong, as if a sheet of snowpack beneath her had cracked. Her ax had dug in, but it was dug into the snow.

"Go back," she mouthed, but it was too late.

The snowpack beneath them dropped away.

CHAPTER 13

WHEN EASTON FELT THE SNOW give out beneath them both, instinct had him reaching for River as they both fell.

There was a moment when his stomach lurched, unready for the sudden drop. Then a painful jerk as the tie-off line did exactly what it was supposed to do: it caught him in midair. The breath was knocked from his lungs as their momentum slammed them into the side of the crevasse, his shoulder cracking painfully into a wall of ice.

River screamed once as they fell, but she didn't panic. If she had, Easton might have dropped her. His hold around her was tenuous as they hung there, dangling over a crevasse they couldn't see into. The fall had loosened his grip, and Easton could feel her slick waterproof jacket slipping.

"Tie off to the rope," Easton panted. "River, *now*, before I lose you."

River wasn't panicking, but she wasn't listening either. The cracking of ice beneath them was audible over even the wind, signifying there was a long, bad drop below. Fear had frozen her in place, one hand clinging to the rope and one arm gripped around his torso, as if she were holding him.

"River, I need you to listen to me. I have you. Is your carabiner broken?"

"No."

"Let go of me and clip your tether off. I've got you, but I can't hold you for long."

"You'll slip."

She thought she was keeping him on the rope. For a moment, Easton's heart swelled with sheer affection for her. She didn't know he was tied off...how could she? It all happened so fast. As far as River knew, they were both dangling. But with both of their weight on the fixed line, Easton could feel it start to give. The fall must have weakened the integrity of the set stakes.

"River, you have to. On three, you're going to trust me when I tell you to let me go. There's a loop to clip off to right above your head. Do you see it?" She nodded. "Good. I'm tied off, and I'm not going to fall. One. Two. *Three.*"

The click of her carabiner onto the rope was the best sound he'd ever heard.

"Good job," he breathed in her ear. "Do you have your ax?"

"I dropped it in the fall."

"It's okay. I have two. Can you reach my belt?"

River nodded, doing as he asked.

"Now, I'm going to do something you're not going to like, but I need you to climb up the rope first. Crampons into the wall, set the ice ax in but not too deep. Like climbing the waterfall, okay?"

"No big deal," she mumbled.

"Exactly." Easton kept his voice as calm as he could. "Listen to me, River. You climb, okay?"

"What about you?"

"River, just this once, trust me. Start climbing, I'm right behind you. When you get to the top, follow the rope back to the fixed line. Get out, okay? *I'm right behind you.*"

Easton needed her to climb, because she didn't understand the whole fixed line was about to rip loose beneath their weight. When he pulled his second ice ax out of his belt, watching her start upward, Easton didn't apologize.

Locketts never said things they didn't mean.

She looked down at the crack of his ice ax burying into the crevasse wall, then River screamed his name when he unclipped from the rope.

Easton knew what he was good at, and—for lack of a better term—he knew what he was great at. He'd yet to meet a rock he couldn't free-climb, and he'd done his fair share of frozen waterfalls in the recent years. But free soloing a sheer surface of ice required two axes carefully placed in the right spots. Easton had one. He couldn't see higher than where he was currently at. Adrenaline had already robbed his arms of strength.

Even he didn't know if he was capable of ascending in these conditions, but Easton wasn't done. Not anywhere close.

His crampons dug into the surface, giving him purchase, but the wall was slick, the ice harder than he'd realized. The next time, he'd have to place the ax harder or in a better spot.

"Easton!"

"River, *climb*. I'm right behind you."

He hoped. Fear was a part of this lifestyle. Pretending not to be afraid—or being reckless enough not to be afraid—didn't make a mountaineer. Understanding the risks, feeling the fear, but continuing anyway. That was what made a mountaineer. And boy, was Easton scared. Scared for River, scared for the rest of the team if he fell. Scared for himself. Using that fear to drive himself, Easton kept moving, hoping the ax held as he found new grips for crampons and gloved fingers. Then he jerked the ax out of the wall, praying his holds would last for the moment he needed them to, swinging the ax above his head into the ice.

Swing. Move. Grip. Jerk out the ax. Swing. Move. Grip. There was comfort in the familiar pattern. Visibility was terrible, but this could be any other wall, any other climb.

Then he swung and the ax met nothing. Breathing a curse of dismay, he realized his balance was off. Then gloved hands grabbed his shoulders, pulling him forward and back over the edge. He'd made it, and so had River.

She hadn't left him. Still safely tied off, River crouched next to the crevasse. Never would Easton underestimate River's strength, because she grabbed his jacket, dragging him and all Easton's 220 pounds of muscles away from the edge.

Easton didn't know if she was hurt, but they couldn't stay in the Veil any longer. Shoving to his feet, he hauled her up to hers, pushing her to follow the tie-off line back to the fixed line. It was their path out of there. If she could walk, she could climb. But if she stopped walking, he'd get her out of there if he had to carry her.

Traveling through the rest of the Veil was a blur. Her jacket hood in front of him, River's hand refusing to let go of him, as if she feared he'd be lost if she did. Her instincts were sound, because Easton wasn't able to see any better than anyone else in this mess.

"Clip on!" she kept yelling at him, but Easton wasn't going to do that. One slip and a compromised anchor was all it would take to leave her at the bottom of this mountain. One fall today was enough for both of them.

Ignoring River's repeated requests, Easton pushed them on until finally, the brutal winds changed direction, signaling the fixed line had shifted direction. They emerged from the Veil, stumbling and exhausted. River dropped to her knees, either a fall or because her energy had finally run out. Without thinking, Easton hooked her around the waist, staggering several more meters until they were out of the down sweep of wind coming from the summit.

The others had clustered together out of the wind, but upon seeing them, Bree and Jessie started to rush to their sides.

"No, give them space," Ben barked, holding up a hand. "Stay back. They might be hurt."

Which was exactly what Easton was worried about.

"River, are you okay?" His hands pushed at her clothing, checking for wounds from her fall. The ice could cut someone like glass, and the cold could keep them from knowing until it was too late.

There was no saving someone with severe blood loss up here.

Following his own advice, Ben gave them space even as he crouched a few feet away, ready to help if Easton needed him.

She gripped his jacket. "I thought you were going to fall."

"I'm not going anywhere," Easton told her, pulling her into a crushing embrace. He twisted so his body was in between her and the others, safe in the privacy of his arms. If someone was filming her right now, he'd throw that camera right off the cliff.

"What happened?" Holding her closer, Easton closed his eyes, trying to fill his lungs with the air that wouldn't come. "Why did you tie something to the line?"

"I dropped the handheld," River admitted. "I unclipped to get it."

"You unclipped for a *camera*."

"Yes." And she'd almost died in the process.

It didn't matter how far up they were or how cold the rest of him was. Easton's blood burned like fire in his veins.

At Ben's insistence, Easton let the other guide go back into the Veil and resecure the stakes they'd loosened. No one knew how long it would take, but Ben was quick and competent. Within an hour, he was back.

"Only the section you two fell on was loose." Ben offered Easton an apologetic look. "Sorry, man. You must be exhausted, but we don't want to bivouac up here if we don't have to."

No, they definitely didn't want to stay above the Veil without anything other than the gear on their backs.

Rising to his feet, Easton tried very hard not to let his emotions show as he went over to where River sat wedged in between Jessie and Bree. Both looked worried and defensive, but all three had been involved in the utterly brilliant idea of filming the Veil. He'd never been so mad at a client in his life.

"Are you okay?" he asked River quietly.

"Yeah. Easton—"

Cutting her off, Easton lifted his eyes toward the ice canyon. "We need to go back to camp. Sorry, I know it's tough after what happened. The adrenaline dump will make you feel like crap, but staying out here without cover tonight will be worse."

"We should talk about this."

A muscle in his jaw twitched. "I'm going to get everyone back to camp safely. Then we can talk. The good news is the wind will be at our back, but the bad news is it makes the descent more dangerous. Most falls happen on the way back through."

Not adding a pointed "usually" took every ounce of Easton's self-control. The muscle in his jaw twitched again, and only then did he realize his teeth were grinding together.

"Make sure you hydrate," he told all three. Easton turned and walked back to the entrance to the Veil. "Ben, you're on point."

"Sure, East. Whatever you want." Ben hesitated, then added quietly, "You'd tell me if you got banged up in there."

"Banged up but not hurt." Easton spat on the ground. "So mad at her, I can't see straight."

"Unclipping for the camera was a bad call, but any of them would have done it. They're rabid about this movie, man."

In that moment, Easton couldn't have given two craps about their documentary. "Set a strong pace. River might be on the bad side of an adrenaline dump, but she's a fast climber."

Ben nodded, eyes flickering beyond Easton's shoulder. Sure enough, she had followed.

"Umm, I'll go do...the thing."

Snorting at Ben's inability to be subtle if his life depended on it, Easton ignored River.

River was great at many things. Being ignored was not one of those things. She lasted all of three seconds of standing at the corner of his eyeline before stepping directly in front of him. "You really aren't going to talk to me."

"Nope." Not until he knew he wouldn't start yelling.

"Then fine," River snapped. "Because I have some things to say to you, Easton Random-Middle-Name Lockett."

Jaw dropping in sheer astonishment, Easton turned to her, incredulous. "You're mad at *me?*"

"*Yes.*"

River's voice shook as if she were fighting to hold in the emotions she wore etched into her face, clear as day. "What happened today, that's on me. And you were amazing. You saved my life, and I am grateful. I'm so grateful, and I'm so impressed by you. I hate that I put you in harm's way, and I'll never make that mistake again."

The words were right, but beneath them was a silent undertone that made Easton's eyes narrow. "But," he pressed.

"But I am so *angry* with you." Stepping up to him, River raised furious eyes. "You unclipped from the rope too, Easton. You could have fallen. You could have *died.*"

She was stunning on a bad day. On fire, she was all Easton could see, furious or not. And yes, a smarter man would have backed down, but he wasn't a smarter man. No, Easton stood nose to nose with her, unwilling to be railroaded.

"Yeah." A growl escaped his lips. "At least I unclipped for something worth dying for. You did it for a paycheck."

River opened her mouth, then she clamped it shut. "I know, okay? I know it was wrong to go for the camera. But money is *not* what this climb is about for me."

"You want to fight about this?" He stepped back, unwilling to tower over her when they were fighting. "Then we'll have a nice big blowout down at camp. You can scream at me to your heart's content. But until we get back down there, I'm still in charge of what's happening here. Get your gear. We're leaving."

Guilt at pulling rank filled him, but the anger still won out. Easton half expected her to slap him or call him an ass. Instead, River's face went calm, cold, unaffected. The actress face, a blank mask. Never had Easton minded her ability to cover her emotions until that moment, when she used the skill because of him.

"Lead the way," she said calmly. But when he looked into her eyes, Easton wasn't surprised to see that he'd hurt her.

What surprised him the most was that he felt the same damn way.

Easton wasn't a mean person. Still, his words had cut her to the bone.

The absolute last thing River wanted to do was walk back into the Veil, but he was right. They couldn't spend the night without cover, so back into the cauldron they returned. Anxiety kept her hand on the fixed line, and even though her brain knew she couldn't see Easton behind her, River kept turning around to check on him. She was as worried about him getting through as she was the rest of them. Finally, they emerged out of the bottom of the ice canyon and limped to their campsite.

Never before had River been so glad they didn't have to set up camp. All she wanted was to sleep for a month.

Bree met her as she was taking off her gear in her tent. "River? Are you okay? I'm worried about you."

"I'm fine," she said, jerking off her boots and dropping down to her sleeping mat. Bree joined her.

"Jessie's worried too, but you know how he is."

With a small laugh, River said, "He'd rather suck on a lemon than tell me?"

"Something like that."

River stayed quiet for a few moments, but Bree was a patient person. Finally, River sighed. "I should be over there swooning beneath the glory of the man bun, but I'm so mad at him, I can't think straight."

Taking her hand, Bree squeezed it.

"River, I don't know what's going on with you and Easton, but what I do know is there hasn't been a day since we started this climb without cameras on you all the time. Shot after shot, and you know what? He is always there. Just like with Ruby Lou, standing with his arms crossed, frown on his face—"

"We think," River joked half-heartedly. "The beard still fools me."

Bree nodded ruefully. "Yes. We think, but we don't know. But what we do know—or at least Jessie and I know—is for a man who only wanted to be filmed from the knees down, he's in almost every single shot. He won't leave your side, River."

Squeezing her hand again, Bree lay down next to her. "I don't know Easton. But I know the expression on his face when he was trying to find you. He was *terrified*."

Bree let that linger between them before continuing.

"We make movies for a living. We show people excitement and love and romance. We make being afraid exciting and being rescued sexy. But real fear...it's not sexy. It makes you want to curl up in a ball, hide in a tent, and yell at the people you love. Real fear is awful. And you both went through that today."

"You think I love him?" River looked at her friend.

"I think you *something* him. And I know he somethings you too. From what Ben told me, he went full Indiana Jones in there to save you."

River nodded, inhaling a deep breath and feeling like there was never enough oxygen to fill her lungs. Just like Easton. One word, one look, one kiss. One touch of his hand on her skin, and River was laid out, a fish suffocating on the shore. Dying for more. And she'd almost gotten him killed, which was a big, big problem.

Today, Easton Lockett had proved he was willing to die for her.

"For what it's worth," Bree said, "I think he's as upset as you are. I think you should go talk to him."

River climbed to her feet. "For what it's worth," she decided, "I think I should too."

Choosing not to eat with his people, Easton stayed in his tent, brooding over the maps and visualizing the best paths to take up the mountain. The marmot had been waiting for him, clearly upset at being left behind again and giving Easton his second chewing out of the day. He'd thought letting it into his tent would help, but apparently that gave them the privacy for the marmot to express its displeasure.

"I can't take you through the Veil," he told the furball. "It's not safe for you."

A harsh chittering reply told him the marmot strongly disagreed.

"I can't even get them safely through. And I never made any promises to you about summiting."

The marmot bit his boot.

"Oh, that's really mature. Compromise is two-sided you know."

A sniff of disgust was all the marmot would reply.

Distracted by the argument, Easton didn't notice someone approaching his tent until a hand lightly slapped the outside fabric.

"Knock-knock."

He could no sooner refuse her entrance than he could stop the sun from circling the sky. "Come in," Easton grunted. "Watch out. The furball is pissed off."

River had a thermos that smelled of tomato soup in her hand and a look of wanting to make peace on her face. At least the expressionlessness was gone. Easton had never hated anything more than looking at her and her not looking back at him. When the marmot narrowed its eyes at her, he scooped it up and dumped it outside, zipping the tent.

"One lecture at a time," Easton grumbled when she raised an eyebrow.

"You didn't come to dinner," she said by way of explanation.

"Had a protein bar." Even as he said it, he accepted the thermos she offered him. "Thanks."

Easton wasn't hungry in the least, and the protein bar he'd

forced down had tasted like chalk. Still, he kept the thermos in his lap to protect it from the icy ground.

"On a scale of one to ten, how mad are you at me?"

At her question, Easton finally met her eyes. "I'm not sure. But the marmot might be back in the tent tonight."

"And I'm out?" River joked.

"We're still deciding."

"I'm sorry," River said quietly. "I know I screwed up. In the moment, I couldn't let it go."

Easton took a sip of the soup, even though he didn't like tomato soup. She'd made it for him, and that meant something to him. "I know the feeling."

Sitting next to him, River took off her boots, then folded her legs beneath her.

"Did you check your feet?" he asked, rougher than he'd wanted to.

"Yeah. I think I'm getting frostbite on my pinkie toe."

Easton's head snapped up.

"I didn't want to say anything," she admitted, "but I can't feel it anymore."

"Show me." Half expecting her to argue, Easton frowned at her. He didn't understand the smile that came to her face. "What?"

"The beard. It moved the opposite way."

"I have no idea what that means," he grumbled. When Easton checked her toes, her skin was still its normal color. But her littlest toe was numb. Easton unzipped his jacket, then took her foot and put her leg beneath his arm, toes wedged inside his armpit.

She looked at him like he was crazy. "What are you doing?"

"Body heat helps the most to warm you up. So I'm putting your foot in my armpit."

River's eyebrow rose. "And I don't have any say in this matter?"

Frown deepening, Easton cut his head to the side once. "No."

After a moment, she flashed an adorable grin at him. "You totally have a foot fetish."

"I'm trying to save your toe," Easton said, because he wasn't ready to cave yet. "My armpit is the warmest part of my body, so you can either deal with it or complain about it, but either way, you're walking down this mountain with all your body parts still attached."

He hadn't meant to come off as rough as he did. Ashamed at the tone he'd taken, Easton added softly, "Sorry. I shouldn't have said that."

Settling back on her palms, she wiggled her toes. "Is this what being warm feels like? I'd forgotten."

"The Veil is brutal." Easton didn't like thinking about it. "And you were in there a long time."

Too long of a time.

He could have gone easy on her, told her it was okay. Made the peace she clearly wanted. Instead, Easton decided to get real with her. "River? Have you ever seen someone die on a mountain?"

River opened her mouth to say something, possibly to make a joke. Then she pursed her lips and shook her head. "No, I haven't."

Easton had, and it wasn't something he'd ever forget.

"Sometimes you have to leave them," he told her quietly. "When someone is hurt badly enough, there's nothing you can do. The crevasses in the Veil are deep, but the fall might not finish you off."

Looking down at his soup, Easton readjusted her foot in his armpit. "You would have been in a lot of pain, and you would have lain there, knowing I was above you, but there would have been nothing I could do. I would have stayed with you as long as I could, but the Veil's windchill can be the coldest part of the mountain. Eventually, I would have to leave, and you'd die alone. Freezing in an ice tomb, all alone."

Easton raised his eyes to her. "I'm not being dramatic. I'm trying to make you understand. There is nothing on any camera, anywhere, worth that. And I don't know how I'd step off this mountain without you with me. I'm not sure how I'd live with myself," Easton added softly. "Knowing I'd let it happen."

"It's not your job to protect me, Easton. I'm a big girl; I can make my own choices."

His lips curved. "You can make your choices, and I'll make mine. Hate to break it to you, but if you jump, I'm jumping after you. It's the way I'm wired."

"Fine, but all rescue attempts have to be made shirtless with your hair down." She wiggled her toes to try to tickle him. Unable to keep the smile from his face, Easton removed her foot from beneath his arm and cupped her toes within his hands.

"Can you feel my fingers against your toes?" he asked. River nodded. "Even the little one?"

"Not as much as the others," she admitted, "but I can feel it now. I might be hyperaware of it at this point."

"Can you feel my fingernail digging in?"

"I mean...yeah but—ow!"

Easton smirked. "You'll live."

Wrinkling her nose at him, she glared as she pulled on her sock. Somehow in her annoyance at him, she'd become even more beautiful. He was going to marry her if she let him. Also if she didn't kill him first.

"If my toe falls off, I'm blaming your adamantium claws." River huffed, then she sighed and reached her fingers to his cheek, tugging his beard. "You know this is about more than a documentary for me, don't you?"

"I've suspected it was more than only making a point to Hollywood, but you don't talk about it."

She was quiet for a while before answering. "Have you ever spent your life wanting something, but you can't figure out what you're missing? And you try and try, but nothing is ever quite right? That's me. That's been my life. And I feel like whatever it is I'm searching for, I'm going to find it up here. I'm already finding it up here. And I can't quit halfway through. I can't lose half the footage. I can't fail, not when I'm this close."

"This close to what?" Easton asked quietly.

"I don't know. But I'm so close, I can taste it."

He nodded. "Then try to keep those toes on. You'll need them to summit."

The words rolled off his tongue of their own accord, but as soon as he saw her eyes widen, Easton knew he'd get them up this mountain if he had to carry her entire crew on his back. With a squeal of delight, she flung her arms around his neck, then she pulled back, frowning at him.

"This isn't you trying to make up with me, right? We're actually doing this because we earned it."

Easton nipped the finger waggling sternly in his face. "We're doing this because—today aside—*you* earned it. I'm conveniently forgetting you unclipped today in the hope you'll conveniently forget I could have been more diplomatic about being pissed about it."

"Selective memory is better when both parties are involved," River told him. "Can I kiss you?"

At this point, he was never going to figure out what she would say next, so he'd stopped trying. Instead, Easton said, "Already told you. You never have to ask."

She was all fire, but when he put his hands on her, pulling her close, River was sweet and rich on his tongue. He wanted her, so much more than he'd ever wanted a woman. The sheer idea of drawing someone into his arms, pulling her onto his lap and relishing the feel of her legs tightening around his waist on a climb was so unprofessional. Before her, he'd never been tempted. He'd never had a partner he literally couldn't resist, but she was it.

River was his drink of choice, and Easton didn't have the willpower to say no.

This time, she didn't ask permission before resting her gloved hand on his face and kissing him again. Then she peeled off those gloves, and bare, chilled fingers found his jawline.

"You'll get frostbite," he warned, turning his face to press small kisses to the tips of those slender fingers.

"I need a moment. I'm getting to know your beard."

Easton sighed. "It's only facial hair."

"Oh no, it's an entity all its own." Fingernails running through his beard, she tightened her hands into his hair, kissing him like she hadn't taken a bad fall today. Like they both hadn't almost died. She was strong, made for this kind of life, and her ability not only to exist but to thrive in his environment—one so brutal—only skyrocketed his attraction to her.

Then her knees dug into his waist, her teeth nipping at his lower lip.

"You're killing me here, sweetheart. If you keep doing that, I'm never getting off this mountain in one piece."

"Would that be so bad? I kind of love it here." A soft laugh escaped her, the fire in her eyes changing to a deeper, better kind of flame.

Yeah. Him too. And as he wrapped her in his arms, it was only getting better.

CHAPTER 14

THE NEXT MORNING, THE MARMOT broke up with Easton. Its little marmot bags were packed. It was moving on. Sometimes, love wasn't enough, not when you deserved better. And clearly, the marmot knew it deserved better.

Getting relocated out of the tent for River must have been the straw that broke the love story's back.

Never had River witnessed anything as funny as Easton standing there, getting chirped and barked at, until the marmot had bit the side of his boot in dismissal while he apologized to its furry backside. Ben tried to be supportive, telling Easton it would be okay, but it was all River could do not to laugh hysterically as the marmot headed back down the mountain, toward the tree line and someone who would meet its needs. Bree and Jessie didn't even try to cover their sheer glee.

And did they get the marmot leaving him on camera? Every single minute of it.

After being dumped and left high and dry on the mountainside, an embarrassed Easton ordered them to break camp, then head back through the Veil, this time with the added burden of the extra weight on their backs. Above the geological feature was nothing but a steep ascent of ice and snow, with the occasional exposed outcrop to break up the landscape. They made camp beneath one of those outcrops, which did little to keep the steady—if quieter—wind off their tents.

Yes, the view was amazing, and yes, they were getting great shots. But River was ready to get to the top already. The summit hung tantalizingly above their heads, but Easton was insisting they stay at camp for another day to get used to the altitude.

It was the relentless cold as much as the man bun that encouraged River to ditch her tent. River wasn't the move-in-with-a-guy-on-the-first-mountain type of woman, but she was willing to make exceptions.

The man was so *warm*.

"I thought you wanted to keep things professional on your worksite," Easton murmured as River wriggled closer to him. She hadn't bothered to hide from everyone that she had no intention of sleeping cold and alone when a perfectly furry mountaineer was handy in the tent next to hers.

"I didn't want Ben making googly eyes at Bree and annoying her," River replied with a yawn. "She told me she's not interested in romantic encounters with someone who hasn't bathed in over a week."

Easton's lips curved against her ear. "But you are?"

"Mmm. I'm considering it."

His hand was warm despite the cold, thin air, and his body was even warmer. The sheer amount of heat this man radiated made her want to plaster herself all over him. And maybe she wasn't at her best, but the way he was looking at her made River want to plaster herself all over him for far less practical reasons.

Easton brushed his thumb over her side in wordless question, a small, welcome touch that she pressed into. Taking her response as the consent it was, he ran his hand along her side, then up her back in a slow, soothing motion that made her instinctively arch into him. Then he rested his palm on her hip, anchoring her in place as he shifted.

The sleeping pad was soft against her shoulder blades, the ground beneath it freezing cold. But when she wrapped her arm around Easton's neck, drawing him down to her, it was the warmest she'd been since she'd stuffed her toes in his armpit and admitted whatever this was, it was important enough not to let it slip away.

Brushing his lips against hers, River could tell he was being careful, his weight propped up on one elbow so he didn't squish her.

"We can't get naked up here," she reminded him. "I'm not having my nipples pop off from frostbite."

"They wouldn't actually pop off," Easton replied. "They'd more turn black and sort of slough off."

Gagging at the image, she asked, "Is this really your version of sexy talk?"

A warm chuckle rumbled through his chest, vibrating against River's fingertips. "You started it."

Somehow her hand had found its way from his neck, down his muscled chest, and was lingering on granite-hard stomach muscles.

"I need your exercise regimen," she murmured.

"I shiver. A lot. It burns a ton of calories."

"Maybe I can help with that?" Smiling, River ran her fingers up his arm, feeling his bicep contract despite the layers of fabric between them.

Easton's gaze dropped to her lips.

As River bit her lower lip, watching Easton watch her, there was something raw, something powerful in how she felt. She didn't know what she wanted, but she knew why she wanted it. Something was missing in her life, some fundamental part of herself that she'd lost or maybe never had to begin with. And only up here, with the bitter winds on her face and reflected in the heated gaze of a stranger who already knew her too well, did River feel like she was close.

Whatever it was that she needed so badly, it was right beneath her fingertips.

She'd paused, overwhelmed by the emotions coursing through her.

"Are you changing your mind?" Easton asked. "Because that's okay."

Could that low, soft rumble be any sexier? River's mind was constantly changing, but not about this. Not about him.

"This would be easier without fifteen thousand pounds of fleece and puffy jackets between us," she decided.

"Hmm...I like a challenge."

"Oh really?" She giggled as he pressed his cold nose to her neck, what little of it was still accessible. Then River burst out snickering as Easton started making playful noises against her throat.

"I'm glad you didn't murder me in your torture barn," River decided.

Easton's eyes crinkled with humor. "I'm glad *you* didn't murder *me* when I picked up a hitchhiker."

"I wasn't hitchhiking—" River started to protest, indignation making her wrinkle her nose at him. Easton took her face in his hands and kissed her. A long, slow kiss that made the wind and the cold and the effort of this climb disappear into white fluffy clouds shaped like unicorns.

With a contented sigh, she snuggled in. "If this were a commercial, I'd have bubble heart emojis floating over my head."

Easton's beard twitched on one side. "My thought process. Point A." He touched his thumb to her breastbone. "Point B." Then to her lower lip. "Point C." This time it was a chaste, soft kiss.

"Your thought process." Easton placed his thumb back to her breastbone. "Point A. Point—let's go over here. And over here. And what's over there?"

As he teased her, Easton drew random patterns back and forth over her torso, fingers tickling into sensitive parts. Dissolving into giggles, River wrapped her arms around his neck, pulling him back in. Easton was more than willing to indulge her.

At some point, she needed to try to sleep, but River was lost, tangled up in his arms, coming completely undone.

"River! Easton!"

Even in their tent, River could hear Jessie yelling. She'd never seen Easton move so fast as he hoisted himself to his feet and jerked his boots and jacket on. River was still scrambling to catch up when Easton unzipped the tent. Face as white as the snow around them, Jessie rushed over, breathless from his sprint through the thick powder.

"Breathe slower," Easton instructed, putting a hand to Jessie's shoulder to steady him. Ben hustled over as River finished getting on her gloves. "What happened?"

"Bree...we were filming out on that outcrop...she slipped..."

"How far did she fall?" Ben demanded as alarm filled River.

"I'm not sure, but I think she's hurt. I told her not to move, that I'd get help."

When Easton told River to stay at camp, he should have known she'd ignore him. One of her people was hurt; she wasn't going to stand around and wait. Instead, she stayed hot on his heels as Easton followed Jessie away from camp. To River's horror, he led them straight to an outcropping beyond the area Easton had said was safe to film.

"What the hell were you two doing over here?" With a snarl, Easton scaled down the rock. "There's a reason I didn't want us on this path. It's too steep. You have to stay tethered to each other."

Jessie didn't answer, face strained as he descended behind Ben and River. She caught a flash of a brightly colored snow jacket on the ground, then the rest of Bree curled up in a ball. River's heart leapt into her throat at the sight of her friend not moving. Despite how fast Easton and River were climbing, Ben reached her first.

"Hey there," Ben said as he swept the snow off her nose and mouth, her eyes blinking away the powder in them.

"Well, that was interesting," Bree managed to pant. "I think I learned to fly."

"I think you learned the opposite." River took Ben's position by Bree's head, supporting her neck as they worked to clear her. "What were you thinking coming all this way out here?"

"We got up and wanted to get some shots," she wheezed. "Knew Easton had us on a tight schedule, so we went out here alone. We should have said something."

Yes, they absolutely should have said something to someone. But River wasn't going to kick her while she was down and clearly in pain.

"Hey, Bree," Ben said as he checked her neck for injury. "In case you were wondering, I'm still waiting for you to ask me out on a date." He flashed Bree a flirtatious look to distract her.

"Hey, Ben, you're probably going to be waiting for a while," Bree quipped back, but her face was ashen. When they were sure it was safe for her to move, Bree sat up slowly, hunched sideways and arm tight against her side.

"I think I banged my ribs up." Bree leaned into River's shoulder.

"Don't be too tough," River told her, wrapping her arm around Bree's waist to support her upright. "If it hurts, tell us."

"It hurts." Closing her eyes, Bree drew in a hard breath.

"I've got her, River."

Ben might not have been Bree's type, but she sure had a hold on him. Even at the elevation and the exertion of fighting through the powdery snow, Ben still bent over and took over for River. Careful not to put pressure on Bree's rib cage, he lifted her into his arms, carrying her back to their camp. It was a long trek, but Ben was strong. Still, despite how gentle he was being, Bree yelped as he laid her down on a blanket in the dining tent.

"East, my pack." But Easton already had it, having antici- pated what Ben would be asking for. Easton pulled a small metal tank out of his pack and a hose attachment. He placed the face mask of the hose over Bree's mouth and nose.

"She needs oxygen," Easton explained to River. "It'll help her warm up."

As Easton and River wrapped every spare sleeping bag around Bree, Jessie hovered, an expression of worry on his face. "Is she going to be okay?"

"We won't know for a while." Ben frowned, eyeing Jessie. "Why don't you sit down, man? You're looking wobbly."

Jessie ignored him, visibly shaking as he pulled Bree into a hug.

"Be careful of her ribs," Ben admonished gently, sharing a look with Easton.

Bree pulled the oxygen away from her mouth, turning to River. "What happened to my camera?"

"It's gone," Jessie told her. "When you fell, it did too. Unlike you, it didn't stop."

River's heart instantly sank. But as upset as she was at losing the camera, it was better to lose a camera than her friend. Bree must not have felt the same. She let out a string of curses, only pausing when she needed to take a breath of oxygen.

"The tripod too?" Bree asked.

At his reluctant nod, Bree unleashed a second round of curses more creative than the first.

"Well, you're not dying," Ben murmured in appreciation before catching her eye. "Bree, Easton and I need to check you for injuries. Do you want River to stay with you? If not, we're too crowded in here."

She tried to be patient and not interrupt Ben and Easton, but the best River could do was pace outside the dining tent, listening for any scrap of info drifting her way. Shaken from the accident, Jessie joined her.

"How's Bree?" he asked.

"I don't know." River shook her head. "I'm still waiting for them to come out and tell me."

When they'd started all this, River had never truly considered what would happen if things went wrong. Now, with the Old Man's summit looming over her, reminding her of her smallness, her insignificance in comparison, River felt her heart shrinking in her chest.

Jessie and Bree were her responsibility.

Closing her eyes, River tried to take a deep, steadying breath. She couldn't stay there any longer, so River walked to the edge of camp, staring out into the panoramic scenery and for once not appreciating the view.

A heavy arm wrapped across River's collarbone, drawing her back into a strong form.

"I dated this guy before coming here," River murmured. "He told me that I was driven to the point of recklessness. Both professionally and in my own personal life."

"What did you tell him?"

"To kiss my ass. I am who I am, and I wasn't going to apologize or change for anyone."

Warm breath against her temple was the only thing warm about her anymore. "Sounds like he didn't get you at all."

River rested her chin on his arm. "For a long time, I didn't think anyone got me. But Bree and Jessie have been the closest. I never thought twice before pitching this project to them. And they never thought twice before saying yes. I barely got the words out before they agreed to be a part of it. And now..."

Trailing off, River swallowed hard.

"Things happen on climbs," Easton told her, voice quiet as the wind died down to a whisper. As if the Old Man himself were listening. "You can't plan it, and you can't avoid it. You can only survive it."

"Which is why we brought you." Turning her head, she looked up at him. "So far, you haven't let any of us eat it, no matter what we've thrown at you."

"And you won't now, not if I can help it," he told her firmly. "Which is why I need your help."

"Uh-oh." River dug the heel of her palm into her tight neck muscles. "As reassuring voices go, that one isn't making the grade."

Dropping his arm to wrap around her waist, Easton drew her in closer to him. "I'm calling the climb as over, River. Jessie's a midlevel climber at best, and he's spooked from this. Bree's accident got in his head. That happens sometimes. Not his fault. He did his best, but Jessie's climb is done. He needs off this mountain."

There wasn't anything River could do to argue that.

"And Bree?"

"Ben thinks two broken ribs. Maybe more. She's tough, but

that kind of pain up here…" Grimacing, he glanced at Bree's tent, where Ben was still tending to her. "You're going to need to talk to her. She's insisting on summiting and won't listen to us. She doesn't want to let you down."

"You think she'll listen to me?" River wasn't so sure.

"I think those two are as loyal to you as they are to this film. Jessie's going to go where we point him for now, but Bree's determined to go up. If she falls and one of those ribs punctures a lung, she'll be in trouble."

When Easton hugged her waist tighter, River accepted his silent offer of comfort. Allowing herself to rest her weight against his, River closed her eyes. She wouldn't say it, because no movie would ever be worth more than her friends were to her. But to come so far, with the summit so close she could almost taste it…

"I'm sorry. I know how important this was to you."

River turned in his arms, shaking her head. "Not as important as they are. I'll talk to Bree."

The soft pressure of his mouth to her own was exactly what River needed. Then she followed Easton back to the others.

As soon as River ducked into the tent, Bree let out a sigh of relief. "Good, you're here. River, talk to them. These two are convinced we have to go back down. Tell them I'm fine. A couple of bruised ribs—"

"They're probably broken," Ben spoke up, earning himself an annoyed expression from Bree.

"A couple of bruised ribs never stopped me before," Bree continued, ignoring him. "I've had worse on a climbing wall."

Settling down at Bree's side, River took her hand. "It's not only your ribs, Bree. Jessie's exhausted. It's not safe for him to keep going."

Exhausted was nicer than saying it the other way: his nerves were shot. Jessie shot her a grateful look, and River nodded with an understanding smile.

"We were close, okay?" River said. "We got enough footage, and it'll be good enough."

Bree didn't answer for a long time. "Then it's done."

Heart in her throat, River nodded. "Yeah. It's done. We tried."

"No." Bree shook her head. "One of us can get up there. You, River. You've been outclimbing everyone this whole trip. You look like you could run circles around the rest of us. There's absolutely no reason you shouldn't summit."

"There's two great reasons, you and Jessie." River added softly, "And, Bree, I'm tired too."

"But you don't really want to go down. If you tell me, right here, right now, that you want to go down, I'll shut up. But don't lie to me, River. You know I'll believe you, so don't lie."

River opened her mouth...then she shut it again. Outside the tent, the summit hung above them. A visceral need to reach the top had her even now. Saying she didn't want to summit would be an untruth of epic proportions.

Bree knew River's silence for exactly what it was. "I'll go down with Jessie if you go up. And you take the handheld. Otherwise, I'm staying right here, and when I feel better, I'm crawling up there myself."

River wouldn't look at Easton, because she could already feel his eyes boring into the back of her head. This was not what he wanted. This was not why he'd asked her to come talk to Bree. But right now, this wasn't about him or her. It was about all of them.

Finally, River nodded. "I'll summit. But you and Jessie are leaving."

Squeezing her hand, Bree finally relaxed back on the bedding, sucking in a deep breath of oxygen.

"Deal."

CHAPTER 15

RIVER WAS GOING TO SUMMIT.

There was no fighting her when that stubborn look was in her eyes. Which meant Easton's options were limited to knocking her over the head and dragging her forcibly down the mountain or abandoning her to do it alone. Asking Ben to descend alone with both Bree and Jessie wasn't even a possibility. It would take both of them to help the pair through the Veil.

Ben joined him, the other guide looking as worried as Easton had ever seen him. "Do you think she means it?" he asked.

"Which one?" Easton kicked the snow. There was nothing else to kick.

"Both of them." Ben grimaced. "Bree needs off this mountain. We have to break camp and move. Can you talk to River?"

"River made her decision. She's going to stick with it."

"I mean, you and her have been a thing this whole trip. You can't..." Ben drifted off, waggling his eyebrows.

"You think I can seduce her into not summiting?"

"You could try." A quick grin, because Ben never stayed down for long. "Take your hair down. Bree says River has a thing for your hair. Flex your biceps, quote some poetry. Work your magic, man."

To Easton's knowledge, he'd never actually successfully worked his magic. But he supposed he could try. Easton didn't have the ability to drag River down against her will. If there was anything the Old Man stole without remorse, it was one's strength, one's speed, and one's ability to convince fiery redheads to give up.

"I'm not sure she has any quit in her." If he didn't respect her so much, he'd be furious with her for agreeing. "I'll try to talk to her, but I don't think it's going to do any good."

River had started to break down Easton's tent when he returned. "I think we need to abandon the dining tent," she told him. "Bree can't carry any weight, and Jessie looks exhausted. He should have as little as possible. We can fit two in your tent and two in Ben's."

"River..."

With no other choice, Easton did it. He pulled out his hair tie, and he let his hair fall down his shoulders.

Now, for the record, none of them had showered since stepping foot on the mountain, which did not make for a good hair day. But River paused midsentence, staring at him.

"You really do go in slow motion," she mumbled. "Can you do that again?"

"If you'll go back down with me, I'll do a strip tease for you every time we stop to hydrate."

River laughed, a soft, breathy sound that he loved. It had only been a couple of hours since they'd curled up in his tent, tangled together. Too bad they weren't still there, acclimating for a summit instead of trying to get an injured climber off the mountain.

After a moment, River turned back to her task. "The weather is as good as it's going to be," River told him. "You need to leave. I'll summit tomorrow, and then come back down after you."

"River, you don't know the way." Hunkering down next to her, Easton took her hand, silently asking her to pause in her work to focus on him. "The only safe way up is along the southeastern spine, and it's a sheer drop on both sides. You need to be with me."

"I'll be careful."

"And it'll take so long, you won't have time to get up and get back down before the windchill gets to you. River, I don't have the right to tell you what to do. But if you go up there alone, years of experience tells me you're putting yourself at far too much risk." Taking her face in his hands, Easton drew her dark protective goggles away so he could see into those blue eyes. Then he kissed her. "I don't want to lose you, River. Give me a reason why I can let you do this."

"Do you remember that day when we were riding? When you said that up here, you could be yourself? With no one watching?"

Easton nodded.

"I don't know who I am, Easton. I know who I want to be and who I've tried to be. I know who I'm going to be if I head down right now. Going back is the right thing to do. It's the responsible thing to do, because I know how dangerous it is to keep going alone." River turned her face to the mountain range and to the clouds clinging to the frozen peaks around them. "But what if this is it? What if this is my only chance? I've spent all these years trying to find myself, always feeling like the real person under my skin wanted out. What if I go back down, back to my life, and I never really know who I could have become? I don't want to be..."

"Trapped."

He understood. At the top of Mount Veil was where he'd found himself too. And as hard as it was, as much as this went against his better judgment, Easton knew he'd fight for her to have the same life-changing experience.

River wiped at her eyes quickly, voice choked. "Yeah. I'm being selfish, but I can't help thinking if I don't do this, it'll never happen."

Closing his eyes, Easton inhaled a deep breath. Then he nodded. "Okay, we'll do this."

"We? Easton, they need you—"

"I know. And when I'm done helping evacuate Bree and Jessie, I'm coming back to you. Stay here in camp so I know you're safe. I'll get them down and come back up again."

The worry in her eyes warmed him, but the sheer relief he felt when she nodded in agreement took his breath away. "Is that too much elevation change for you?" River asked. "This isn't worth it if you get hurt."

"I'll be okay. I'm used to this mountain." Which might have been an overestimation of his abilities, but she didn't need to know that. "I'll radio Ash to come get us below the Veil. It's the highest her helicopter can safely fly."

"Hey, Easton?"

"Yeah?"

"You look really good with your hair down. Definitely keep walking around with your locks flowing in the breeze like this."

Rolling his eyes at her, Easton still exhaled a breath. "You're exhausting," he decided. "I like it."

"I know. It's part of my charm."

Decision made, Easton made short work of breaking down the rest of the camp they were taking with them while Ben finished taping Bree's ribs to stabilize them. River hugged Jessie goodbye.

"I'm sorry," he muttered, but River shook her head.

"Don't be. Just get down safe, okay?" Adding a limping Bree into the group hug, River held them both for a long moment. "I'll get the best footage ever. I promise."

"Of course you will." Bree's faith in River was impossible to deny. "I'm glad SH is going with you. I still think he should stay, but I'm glad he's not totally bailing on you."

River nodded. "Me too. I don't think Easton would know how to bail on someone if his life depended on it."

The compliment would have meant a lot more if that wasn't exactly what Easton was doing. Easton strode over to her, and in front of the rest of the group, he took River's face in his hands.

"Keep that radio on you," he said in a rough, low voice. "I'll call when I get to the pickup site and start back up. You can't leave, River. Promise me. Don't go anywhere you can't keep your hand on the tent. The weather isn't calling for a storm, but the wind is picking up. If visibility goes down too far, you could get lost. Promise me, or I can't leave you here."

"I promise." River wrapped her hand behind his neck, going up on her tiptoes as much as her crampons would allow. "You can trust me, Easton."

Resting his forehead to hers, Easton inhaled another deep

breath. Then he kissed her, a quick, hard kiss. "I'm coming back, River. I'm *not* leaving you up here."

Her smile was the breath in his lungs. "It never once occurred to me you would."

Grown women weren't scared of the dark. Or the not quite dark of being on a mountaintop near the North Pole.

But like a tree falling in the woods, if no one was there to witness River being a scaredy cat, it wasn't actually happening, right?

"People make vampire movies out of situations like this," River decided as she sat in her tent, staring out a tiny hole she'd unzipped in the flap.

Opening the flap fully wasn't happening. With night came the cold, and this cold was beyond any she'd experienced so far.

"I'd rather have a nice warm werewolf if something was going to show up. Or an abominable snowperson. Those can be sexy. I'm sure somewhere out there is a ripped snowperson, waiting to find true love."

Talking to oneself wasn't a bad sign. River had told herself that every conversation she'd had since her team had disappeared out of sight.

Being alone on the mountain was...surreal. Even though it was technically day, the wind picked up, like Easton had predicted. As she stayed in camp, super-duper alone, River tried to decide what was scarier: being in the wilderness and not knowing what was out there or being in the wilderness and knowing *nothing* was out there.

Nothing at all.

"Maybe one vampire would be okay," she murmured to herself.

Zipping up the opening in the tent, River bundled up as best she could, keeping the radio tucked close to her. Taking out the handheld camera, she settled into as comfortable a position as she could find.

"This is River. I'm on my handheld because, well, things didn't go as planned up here. A small accident happened."

River made a face into the camera. "Small is a relative term, because it scared the crap out of all of us. Even Easton looked strained around the eyes. Bree and Jessie were filming outside camp, and she got hurt. I really love Bree. We're friends, you know? We've worked on three movies together, and when you spend that much time with someone…"

River drifted off, gathering her thoughts. "Anyway, I'm really glad Easton and Ben were here. I can't imagine being up here with anyone else. Except, well, I'm not up here with Easton anymore. I'm by myself. Bree and I decided that I should summit and finish the film. Easton needed to help Ben get everyone back down, so we agreed I'd stay here. It's quiet. It's so quiet."

Holding the camera steady was difficult, especially when her hands shook from the cold. So River set it between her knees, pointing at her face. The angle was terrible, but she didn't care.

"You know what I keep thinking up here? I don't miss back home in LA. I miss my *home* back in Wyoming. I miss the sound of my father's voice. I miss my mother's arms hugging me. I miss the smell of the ranch in the mornings, the dew on the grass, and the breeze coming across the pastures. I miss my grandmother's hands. I even miss my sisters."

River made a face at the camera. "I bet my sisters never thought I'd say that, but I do. I miss you. I miss having people who matter within arm's reach. It used to be suffocating, but now...now I just want to be suffocated."

Closing her eyes, River tried to gather herself.

"Okay, enough of that. Easton said he'd be back tomorrow. I don't know if sleep will actually happen, but I'm going to close my eyes and think about what it's going to feel like making it to the top of this mountain. People have done it before. I will too."

Setting down the camera, River curled up on her mat, holding the radio tucked tightly to her chest, whispering to herself.

"I will too."

As trips down the mountain went, this one couldn't have gone fast enough.

After putting in a call to Ash—and hearing several times that she told him so—Ash had agreed to pick them up. Twelve thousand feet of elevation was about as high as she could safely land, and they knew of a spot to touch down there.

Easton had never been so glad he'd trusted his gut on anything as he was about calling the climb on these two. Jessie was done, both physically and mentally. The oxygen had helped Bree, and she was faring relatively well, but her pace was so slow, Easton was having trouble staying patient with her shuffling steps.

River needed him up there, not going the other way at a crawl.

Ben and Bree had bonded as they descended—now that Bree wasn't focused on her filming. He spent the better part of his time helping her traverse the terrain, making jokes and telling wild stories to make Bree laugh. The pair's spirits were high, but some of that might have been the painkillers they kept feeding her. High as a kite, she kept mentioning the stories she'd have to tell once she got back home.

Getting them both through the Veil was a challenge. The only positive was there wasn't a client unclipping from the line and going off course on him.

"Are you okay?" Ben asked on their two-thousandth break to catch a breath. A break Easton knew was necessary but drove him crazy.

"Not really," Easton told his friend. "I hate that I left her up there."

"River's tough, man. She can handle it."

Yes, but that didn't mean he shouldn't be up there too so they could handle it together. Easton had forced himself to accept they couldn't set a tougher pace, but his skin crawled with the need to get moving, to get back up and get to River. She'd never soloed a climb before, and the mountain did strange things to someone when they weren't used to being alone.

Knowing her, something would happen that would give her a perfectly logical reason to leave the safety of the tent, or worse, the camp. He'd mentally berated himself the entire descent, switching off with Ben as they kept a helping arm around Bree's waist. As they descended, Easton found himself missing the furball. Bad breakup or not, at least the marmot understood him. It would have been chafing at the pace too.

The weather was good, so they pushed past their previous

campsite and kept going to the spot Easton had prearranged for Ash to meet them. As soon as they reached the flat outcropping— flat enough to safely land a helicopter—Easton and Ben worked to set up a temporary camp.

As he did, Easton watched the cloud cover get thicker around the mountainside.

When the call came in, Ash sounded worried. "Easton, your people are going to have to hang tight. At these temps, I can't fly through all that soup without icing up."

"Call the park department to come get us."

"I already did," Ashtyn told him. "They're up to their eyeballs in a mess. You're lucky. Denali's been taking the brunt of the bad weather. Give me a few hours for this to clear out, and I'll be there. It's time to get you all off this mountain."

When Easton didn't answer, Ash's answering silence spoke volumes. Finally, she groaned. "Seriously? It's the actress, isn't it?"

"We'll talk about it when I get home. River's still up there. We're summiting, then coming back."

Ash had a few less than complimentary things to say about Easton's judgment where River was concerned, then she hung up on him, leaving Easton with no one on the other line to argue with. Instead, he turned on Ben, who made the mistake of approaching him right then.

"I'm surrounded by stubborn women," Easton decided.

Ben scratched the back of his neck. "Umm...yeah. Sure, boss. Is one of them coming to get us?"

"Ash's rotors will ice up. We have to wait." At the expression on Ben's face, Easton pointed a finger at him. "Make a rotor joke about my sister, and I will literally throw you off this mountain."

Clearly amused, Ben stepped back to give Easton room. "Wouldn't dream of it. Hey, relax. We're good here. Bree's passed out in a painkiller coma, and Jessie's getting some sleep."

Finally, something that might help. Easton turned to Ben. "Do you have this handled?"

"Good as gold."

Heartened at the positive news, Easton shouldered his pack.

"Wait. You're not headed back up there right now, are you?" Ben shouldn't have asked, because it was clear that was exactly what Easton was doing. "Are you sure that's smart?"

"I left a client alone." At the most dangerous place on the mountain besides the summit.

"Yeah, and she'll stay there, safe and sound, while you get some rest. East, you're not thinking clearly."

Easton frowned. "I feel fine."

A slight smile touched Ben's lips. "No, man. About River. You're rushing back up there like she needs you to save her or something. She doesn't. That woman is tough as nails, or you never would have trusted her to stay alone. What she *can't* do is carry you down if you get yourself hurt going back up when you're too tired to make the climb."

A low growl pulled from Easton's throat. As much as he hated to admit it, Ben was right.

The other guide held his hands up, because Easton maybe growled a second time with a few choice words added in the mix.

"I didn't say you *couldn't* make the climb," Ben clarified.

"Just that you shouldn't. I don't doubt your capability any more than I doubt River's ability to handle herself up there."

"You're a pain in my ass, Ben."

Clapping him on the back, the other guide barked out a laugh. "Yeah, I know. But you love me. Give me the radio. I'll break it to her and save you some face."

No way that was going to happen. When Easton called her, it took a moment for River to answer. He experienced a moment of gut-wrenching nervousness in that pause, his brain going to the very worst things he could imagine. Her injured in the snow... or bopping about without a care in the world, climbing the mountain like a Dall sheep.

"Hello?"

The elephant crushing his chest finally allowed Easton to breathe. "River, it's me."

"It's about time. I was starting to think you'd forgotten about me."

The sleepy sound of her voice caused a tension Easton didn't realize he was holding to release. He knew that tone, even though he'd only been lucky enough to be present when her eyes were opening from slumber a couple of times.

"Did I wake you?" he asked quietly.

"Yeah, but it's good you called." He could almost see her turn over onto her side, pulling the sleeping bag around her shoulders. "I've been worried about you. How is everyone?"

"We made it down safe." At a snail's pace. "And Bree's doing better." Mostly. "Are you okay if I stay down here for a couple of hours and rest up for the trip back?"

She hummed, as if considering it. "As long as you all aren't having a party without me."

Chuckling, Easton cradled the radio in the crook of his arm. "I'd never do that to you."

"Over."

"What?"

"You'd never do that, over."

Damn, he liked this woman. "Get some rest. Stay warm and eat something. I'll see you soon. Over and out."

"Bye, Easton."

The softness in her tone dragged at him, like slender fingers gripping at his heart. He didn't want to be down here when she was up there. It was wrong, and not because she couldn't handle it. Because *he* couldn't handle it.

"So, River, huh?" Ben gave him a knowing look.

Easton sat and stared at the ground between his feet, saying nothing. Apparently so.

———

He never slept. There was no question that he wouldn't sleep, but Easton did lie still and silent on his side of the tent. And the exact minute four hours had passed—the amount of time Easton had decided he would have forced another guide to wait before ascending—Easton rolled to his feet.

"Radio her that I'm starting up there. And radio me when Ash picks you up."

Bumping a fist to Easton's, Ben yawned and nodded. "Will do, boss."

For the first time all season, Easton was alone. Nothing stood in his way, nothing affected his decisions, no one slowed him down. By the time he passed through the Veil, Easton was still going strong.

He should have timed it, because he might have made it back up there in record time. All Easton could focus on was putting one foot in front of the other and getting back to her.

River was waiting for him outside her tent, watching the path she knew he'd take to get there. And because she was who she was, River was standing one extra step away from the tent, just to tease him. A stunningly beautiful smile spread on her face as she flapped her hand, showing him the dramatic dangerousness of being a couple of inches away from where he'd asked her to stay.

"Don't worry," River joked as Easton strode over to her. "I didn't pee once when you were gone. Safety first."

It took every bit of self-control he had to not crush her painfully tight against his chest.

"I'm never leaving you again."

She wrapped her arm around his neck, drawing his face down to hers, giggling as she said, "You are so much better than a vampire."

Yeah, he'd never understand her. That was fine. She was in his arms, which was all that mattered. When he kissed her, the fiery redhead who'd carved her way into his heart, Easton knew summiting with River would be worth every ounce of effort it had taken them to get that far.

They would do this together.

CHAPTER 16

"GOOD MORNING," RIVER WHISPERED AGAINST Easton's shoulder.

Warm brown eyes blinked open, his voice husky with sleep. "I half expected to wake up with the handheld on me."

She couldn't resist teasing him even as she snuggled in. "Once we're outside the tent, all bets are off."

The snuggling was a given. At this far below zero, River would have snuggled with him even if he was a less sexy than Hagrid version of himself or smelled like Oscar the Grouch on a bad trash can day. But he wasn't, and he didn't, which meant the snuggling was more than satisfactory.

Especially when Easton's version involved long, slow kisses, murmured compliments against her skin, and promises that he'd take his hair down from the bun as slowly and as often as she wanted.

Okay, maybe that last one was wishful thinking on her part, but a woman could dream.

The snuggling was great, but talking with Easton was even better. Curled up together in their tent, River basked in the comfort of his presence, the sound of Easton's voice lulling her into a sense of peace. Funny how all it took was Easton to turn an isolated campsite into one of the most romantic experiences of her life.

At some point, she'd like to know what it felt like to cuddle with this man without fifteen layers of puffy jacket fabric between them. Memories of a certain shower had been etched into her brain. In between talking and those soft, slow kisses that promised so much more, they did manage to sleep a bit. And in waking, River knew from the brightening light outside the tent that it was time to do what they'd come all this way for.

It was time to summit Mount Veil.

"You've got that look." He playfully tugged at the braid she'd secured her hair in.

"What look?"

Easton rolled, drawing her across his chest as he relaxed back into the sleeping pad. "The look that says I need to be worried." A contented expression had crossed his face, as if he had no concerns in the world.

"Oh, you definitely need to be worried. It's summit day."

"Most people are fighting to get used to the air at this point." He added teasingly, "Are you sure you didn't down a tank of oxygen while you were up here?"

"And risk the wrath of my guide?" River winked at him. "Don't worry. I behaved. Mostly, I interviewed myself and tried not to worry about everyone else to the point of insanity. How are Bree and Jessie? Are they going to be all right?"

"Ash contacted me and said they're okay. Beat up and exhausted, but they'll be fine. She's annoyingly responsible like that."

"Annoyingly responsible sounds like a family trait." River

sat up, resting her palms on his stomach. "Are you up for this? Because I'm ready to climb this thing."

Wrapping his hands around her waist, Easton sat up using only his abdominal muscles, holding her in place on his lap. "Where you go, I'm following."

"Summit or bust?" she asked, breathless with anticipation.

"Summit or bust." Then he kissed her, a long, slow kiss that left her cold toes curling.

At this rate, they weren't going anywhere.

"We should do this at the bottom of the mountain," she told him after regretfully pulling away. "Or closer to the bottom of the mountain." Another kiss had her murmuring, "Or maybe back here after we summit."

Easton nipped her earlobe. "Are you sure you want to get to the top?"

"Definitely." Giggling, she escaped his hold. They put on their boots, then River grabbed his hand. "Come on. We need to get going. I want to summit. I turn thirty today."

"It's your birthday? Why didn't you say anything?"

"Why? Would you have gone out and gotten me a present?" River grinned at him. "Because all I see is snow and snow."

"And rocks too," Easton murmured against her ear, hugging her. "Happy birthday."

River leaned into him, enjoying the heat radiating from his body. "I used to be terrified of turning thirty. I thought it would signal the official death of my career. I'd mourn, but I'm too busy doing the most awesome thing I've ever done in my life."

"Peeing in negative degree windchill?"

River pressed her nose into the scruff on his throat. "Hmm. That too. Hey, Easton? Let's go climb a mountain."

"I'll race you to the top."

As they got ready for the day's climb, Easton double-checked and triple-checked all the supplies she had packed, including making sure her carabiners were in good shape, her radio was tucked in her pack, and her transmitter was turned on.

"You're being a worrywart," River told him as he tossed her a protein bar.

After a considering look, he pulled out a second one and slipped it into River's pocket.

"We're burning calories like crazy up here," Easton explained. "Try to eat as much as you can."

River narrowed her eyes at him, even as she ripped open a bar and began to chew. "If I'm doubling up, so are you."

Easton tucked a second protein bar in his own pocket without protest. "Are you always this bossy?"

"Are you?" River countered, arching an eyebrow at him before putting on her goggles.

"Only about things that matter," he told her, moving in closer.

"Don't you bust out the sexy low rumble on me." River took a large bite of her protein bar, jaw protesting as she chewed the cold-hardened meal. "I'm completely immune."

She wasn't immune in the least, but he didn't need to know that.

"I have never had a client hold up this well to the climb," Easton complimented her. "You might have missed your calling."

"Oh, trust me, I nailed my calling. This is the best of both worlds. Mountain documentaries may be my thing. I'll travel the world, climbing my way through the glass ceiling."

"If you need someone to hold your beer while you're busy kicking professional ass, let me know."

"I might even let you buy me a drink when I'm done taking names."

"How do you think you came by the beer in the first place?" Easton rumbled.

"I bought it myself and bought you one too. But you can get the next round."

Another one of those rare, broad smiles met her statement. After a moment of comfortable silence, Easton glanced at her, still working on the rope tying them together.

"You could do this, you know," he said quietly. "You're skilled enough. With some more experience, you could climb anything."

From someone like him, who made a living climbing monsters, the validation meant more than River could articulate. Instead, she went up on her tiptoes to kiss his cheek. "Maybe you'll have to pencil me in for your next adventure."

"You always have a place with me," Easton said quietly, holding her eyes. Then he cleared his throat, tugging on the rope between them. "We're ready. You want to lead?"

His offer took her by surprise. Every single step of this adventure, Easton had been in the lead.

"I thought it was dangerous."

"It is." Nodding in agreement, Easton stepped closer, slipping his fingers inside the tether on her belt. Tugging that too, even though he'd already checked it. "But you've proven more than capable of handling yourself up here."

River couldn't help but tease him. "Says the man terrified to leave me alone. I don't need rescuing, Easton. Except, you know…"

"That one time I rescued you?" No amount of beard could hide his smile.

"As far as I'm concerned, that never happened. What happens in the cauldron of evil stays in the cauldron of evil."

"Really? Because I was hoping my ability not to let you plummet to your death would add to my appeal."

"You literally could put a cereal box over your head, draw googly eyes on it, and you'd still have more than anyone's fair share of appeal."

Standing a little closer never hurt anyone. Camaraderie and all that. It certainly had nothing to do with the way he was looking at her…like hot chocolate on a cold winter's day. Or a particularly good steak.

Who knew a man clipping an extra carabiner to her belt would be akin to getting roses? It was either tease him or propose. At the moment, both seemed equally good options.

"It's hard to kiss a man with a beard. You have to go spelunking to find his mouth."

A warm chuckle was all the response she received, but his finger tucked into her jacket pocket, tugging her closer, increasing the angle she had to tilt her head back.

"Man buns are tough too. You never know what's beneath them. Is the bun actually an intricate comb-over?"

A corner of his lip twitched beneath the beard.

"Short guys are my thing really. Less neck strain in sexy situations."

"Anything else I should know about you?"

"I'm completely, utterly full of crap."

Strong gloved hands cradling her already-tilted face. Bearded kisses were quickly becoming River's favorite.

"You're perfect," Easton decided. "And you're definitely full of crap. It's my favorite part about you."

It was summit day. They had to stop this, no matter how much River was enjoying making out with him.

"We technically have a very tight schedule to adhere to," she reminded him.

"Mm-hmm," Easton agreed. "You're the one leading, so this is all on you."

"You really trust me enough to take the lead?"

"I'm guessing you'd be playing leap frog all day if I didn't. But we stay tied. Absolutely no untying. And you let me film. Even you need all your hands and focus up there."

"You're filming this?"

Easton rested his forehead to hers in a brief gesture of solidarity. "After everything you've done to get here? There's no way I'm letting you summit without filming it for you."

This time, she didn't go up on her toes, and she didn't pull his head down to hers. Overwhelmed with emotion at his understanding, at his consideration, at all the other warm, perfect parts of this sweet man, River could only stand there, holding on to his arms, breathing in how perfect this moment was. He waited for her, quiet and patient, giving River the moment she needed to compose herself. Then he pressed a soft kiss to her temple and stepped back.

Gesturing toward the summit waiting for them, Easton lifted the handheld camera and flipped it on. "Lead the way. I'm right behind you."

Which was how, at fourteen thousand feet, River fell head over heels in love without once touching the ground.

Taking the camera might not have been the best idea Easton had ever had.

The problem wasn't climbing while filming, although he quickly learned to respect what Jessie and Bree had been doing since the very start of the trip. A helmet-mounted video camera would have been much easier than keeping his arm in a lifted position so much of the day, but even that wasn't too big of a deal.

No, the problem wasn't the camera. The problem was filming River's back—and subsequent backside—as they scaled the last thousand feet of elevation. It wasn't a huge amount of ground, but the climb was technically difficult and only got tougher with every step.

"Let me see." River held out her hand for the camera when they paused to take a break halfway up.

"You're not going to like it."

"Why won't I like it?"

He handed it over to her, predicting the expression on her face about to come his way. Sure enough, after a few moments of replaying what he'd filmed, River's eyes narrowed.

"Why is there only film of my ass on here?"

"Because technically, that's what I saw when I was climbing." Sticking to innocence seemed the safest approach. "Why? Was that wrong?"

Rolling her eyes at him, River stood with the camera instead of resting, turning in a circle to take in the vista. Despite the difficulty of their trek so far, River was all but bouncing on her heels in sheer excitement.

She might not have been a professional climber, but River was pretty darn close.

"All right, Easton. This is our final interview before the climb. Do you have anything you want to say to all the people watching us at some indeterminate point in the future?"

Maybe he could have thought of something if she hadn't flashed him the prettiest smile, a strand of her auburn hair blowing across her eyes.

Easton wasn't a big talker, but he wasn't used to being absolutely tongue-tied around a woman. She was just so beautiful. Easton had never met a woman more determined, bullheaded, and maddeningly reckless in his life.

He'd never wanted someone more.

"Nope."

Laughing, River handed the camera back to him. Then she knelt, her hands scooping up a double handful of snow. He knelt too, setting the camera next to him so it wouldn't get damaged by her intentions, watching as River deliberately formed a massive snowball. Two more joined the first in a pile at her hip, with a fourth balanced and waiting on the palm of her hand. They were at the top of the world, one wrong breath from death, and she wanted to have a snowball fight.

"I'm going to do this," River promised him. "You've never been snowballed like I'm about to snowball you."

"That sounds like a threat."

"Oh, it's totally a threat. Are you ready for me?"

He hadn't been ready for her in the least, not since he pulled over on the side of the road. But like back then, try as he might, he simply couldn't help himself.

"Bring it," Easton told her, because he knew that was exactly what she planned on doing.

The first snowball was lobbed in his direction, a warning shot. The next two were a direct frontal assault. The fourth was intended to force him into action instead of sitting there, by way of gloved fingers bopping the snowball against his nose.

"That was cold," he murmured.

"You're absolutely no fun, are you?" She frowned, nose wrinkling. Then a gust of wind across the mountainside stirred up a spray of snow all on its own, making that cute nose wrinkle become an even cuter sneeze.

"Are you done torturing me?" he asked.

"Depends. Are you going to stand there like a grumpy lump all day?"

Easton flicked a bit of snow in her face to hear her giggle. Scrubbing at her nose to rid it of the snowflakes, she blinked, then found herself with a forehead, mouth, and nose full of the stuff. Unlike her weapons of choice, his snowball had been packed loosely, barely surviving him lobbing it in her direction.

He'd do about anything for her, but Easton had a professional reputation to maintain.

"I'm not grumpy." Easton scooped up a second handful of snow. "I'm considering the stakes. They're going to kick me out of the league of mountain guides if I knock you off here with a snowball. So it's either make you happy…" He loosely packed another snowball. "Or risk professional humiliation."

"A little professional humiliation never hurt anyone." River's grin was full of mischief.

She reminded him of a wolf. Dangerous, smart, willing, and more than able to flash her fangs when she needed. But like a wolf with their mate, she wanted him to play with her. This time, she tried to duck his snowball and failed.

"Wolves mate for life, River."

"That was the most random sentence I've ever heard." Spitting snow from her mouth, she blinked the flakes from her eyes and dropped down to her knees next to him.

Smiling slightly, Easton settled back on the snow. There, now they were at a better height. Her head slightly taller than his. Taking her face in his hands, he allowed himself a moment to enjoy this. Having her here, with him in his favorite place in the world.

"River?"

"Hmm?"

"Even lone wolves mate for life. I want you happy. If you want to play, I'm game."

How could he not be? After all, those sweet, snow-chilled lips were pressed to his. And Easton had never, ever wanted something as much as he wanted this.

Wrapping his arms around her, Easton tugged River into his form. The thick layers of jackets between them couldn't hide the tension in his muscles, his body responding to her proximity. Her lips were cold, but the passion growing between them made him feel as if they were on fire.

"I can't breathe," she whispered.

"It's the lower oxygen up here."

She gripped his arm, pulling him closer. "No. I can't breathe when you're next to me."

Breathless or not, River pulled his face to her own.

A brief rest was all they had time to take, so eventually, they extracted from each other's arms. The last part of the climb was the most technically challenging. And yes, her steps were slower than they were lower on the climb, but River's determination to keep going never dropped, her eyes never leaving the prize of the summit above them.

That final pinnacle of rock and ice was tantalizingly close. Each careful step, each secured handhold brought them nearer. Until finally, with one more hoist of their bodies up the last few feet of the spine they were traversing, there was nothing left in front of them. A bit of ground covered in snow and ice, with one solitary granite boulder the size of a small car capping the summit.

"Be careful," Easton called ahead in warning. "It's weathering away on the north side."

River didn't answer, but as she took those last few steps, she stayed away from the northern edge of the summit. Then she turned, and the expression on her face was one of utter shock.

"Easton," River breathed. "*Look.*"

He was looking. And it wasn't at the stunning vista around them. All these years, he'd led others up this mountain. So many trips, but this was the one he'd never forget.

For Easton, watching River stand on the top of the world, realizing she had accomplished the near impossible, was better than anything.

The reward for her effort was a view so beyond any she could have experienced so far, knowing the mountains she'd climbed. Mount Veil was beneath them now, a sea of ice and snow, of dark rock speckling otherwise pristine white. From here, the glaciers they'd climbed had become frozen rivers cutting wide swathes down through the mountainside, like drips from an ice cream cone. And farther below was the tree line, where they'd taken their first steps into this adventure. The cloud cover hung around them, clinging to peaks on other mountains, climbs yet to be taken, challenges yet to be met.

When River pushed up her goggles and started to cry, Easton understood completely. Setting the camera down, because he couldn't hold her and film her at the same time, Easton angled it toward the summit and joined her. She'd gone through a lot to get here, more than most. Anyone else would have given up long ago, but not her.

He'd never thought any summit would top his first on Mount Veil. But Easton had never summited with River before. He'd never had someone else's emotions so deeply tied to his own. Her joy, her pain, her determination…all cumulating in this final moment of triumph. It was a long way down, but right now, all that mattered was that they had made it there together.

No, summiting with River was so much better than it would ever be on his own.

"Was it worth it?" he asked her quietly.

Nodding, it was clear River was beyond words. Slipping an arm around her waist, Easton stood there, letting her fall apart.

"I don't even know why I'm blubbering like an idiot."

"Because there is nothing like this feeling. And there is no way to describe it that comes close to being enough. No book, no movie, documentary. It just...is."

"This is your life," River whispered.

"This is your life too, whisky." Tightening his hold on her, Easton braced his legs apart in case the wind gusted unexpectedly. "When you're at the top of the world, everything feels smaller. Your priorities shift. If you're anything like me, you'll spend the rest of your life chasing this feeling."

"Is that so bad?" she asked softly.

A lifetime of this...a lifetime of this with her...no. The idea wasn't bad at all.

"Easton? If I told you I loved you, would you run screaming down the mountain?"

"You barely know me." Even now, even here, he couldn't imagine being lucky enough to have this woman's heart.

She turned in his arm, raising those glorious eyes to his. "So?"

The top of the world was no place to play games. And it was not the place to announce to the world how he felt. So it was with entire seriousness that Easton whispered in her ear, words for her and no one else. And when he was done saying what needed to be said, he went back to the camera, lifting it and pointing it at her.

"Okay, River. Right now, you're standing thousands of feet above Moose Springs. You've seen everything there is to this place. You've argued with our mayor, eaten from our best restaurant, flown in a helicopter, snuggled with a lovelorn marmot, survived the Veil, and you know firsthand how terrifying it is to sleep in avalanche country with Jessie snoring."

Even though he felt like an idiot saying it, Easton had heard Jessie and Bree enough to know exactly what he should say. "Tell us why someone should come to Moose Springs."

For a long time, River couldn't say a word. Then she finally whispered into the wind.

"Because it's where I found you."

—————————

The climb down was slower than the climb up. River wasn't sure why until she looked at her mountaineering watch. The wind had picked up, and even though the direction wasn't buffeting them, the temperature sensor on her watch read that with the windchill, the temperature dropped from negative five degrees to negative fifteen degrees.

"How close are we to camp?" River called ahead.

"Not far. Another hour if we keep up the pace."

He didn't say she had fallen off the pace he tried to set, but River knew Easton kept having to wait for her. He'd taken the lead, and she was more than happy to let him. Being able to summit first had been one part of an absolutely amazing experience, but now they were headed back down, she could feel the adrenaline dump coming.

"I'm slowing you down," she told him on one of their many breaks.

"We're fine," he promised her. "Keep putting one foot in front of the other."

Easton gave her a reassuring pat on the shoulder and then turned, heading back down.

River never did see what caused Easton to fall. She just knew he was upright one moment, then on the ground the next.

When River had fallen in the Veil, the whole thing had happened faster than she could blink. But when Easton fell, taking her with him, everything went in slow motion. He yelled in warning before his weight and momentum snapped the line at her belt. She watched her boots come out from under her as she was knocked off her feet. Easton reaching for his ax, trying to slow their fall as, tied together, they slid down the mountain. Glimpsing her boots outlined against the summit, she realized she was falling headfirst.

A cry escaped her throat before she realized they'd slammed to a stop. The impact was so abrupt, it knocked the wind out of her. All River could do was lie there and gasp like a fish out of water, chest rising and falling rapidly as she fought to get the thin mountain air to fill her lungs.

"That was exciting." River rolled to her knees, making sure her crampons were dug tight into the ice. "When you decide to take a tumble, you do it with style, huh?"

He didn't answer. Silent and unmoving, Easton lay there in the snow, facedown where he'd come to a stop.

"Easton?"

Scrambling to his side, River fought to roll him over.

Unconscious, Easton was heavy and his body difficult to shift. Finally, she got him onto his back. A cut above his eye bled less than it should have for as deep as it was. She shook him, hard.

"Okay, big guy, this is not the time to go down. Easton, come on. Wake up."

Easton groaned, stirring beneath her hands.

"Are you okay?" he demanded roughly, rolling over to try to get up to his knees. The fact that he promptly threw up was a bad sign.

River wrapped her arms around him, supporting him as he emptied his stomach.

"I'm fine," she promised. "Try not to move. I think you hit your head." Touching his forehead resulted in her pulling back gloved fingers stained with blood.

"Are you okay?" Easton repeated, voice slurring. He tried to push himself upright, reaching for her, but his eyes were unfocused. Hushing him, River ran her hands over Easton's sides, looking for more injuries. When he asked her a third time if she was okay, she knew he was in trouble.

"I think you have a concussion."

Worse still, she didn't know if he'd hurt his neck. Unsure of what to do, River sat back, looking at how far they'd fallen off course. She knew where the path back to camp was, but she didn't know what was between where she was and where they needed to be. They'd already fallen into one crevasse. River wasn't interested in going into another. The weight leaning against her grew heavy enough she had a hard time staying sitting upright.

"Easton, are you still with me?"

He mumbled something, but she couldn't hear what he said

over the rising cry of the wind. Seated like this on the frozen ground, the cold was quickly settling into her bones, and the weather was only getting worse. Easton was in no shape to climb, but they didn't have a choice.

Somehow River was going to have to get him off the mountain all on her own.

CHAPTER 17

"BEN, IT'S RIVER. IF YOU can hear me, please answer."

She waited with the radio by her ear for a reply, but nothing came. "Ben, I have a big, Easton-sized problem up here."

Radio silence had a whole new meaning when she was stuck up here with what she guessed was two hundred and a million pounds of semiconscious beard and man bun. She knew the satellite phone was in Easton's pack, which had taken a beating in the fall. He kept drifting in and out, making conversations about proper rescue attempts impossible.

"Sorry for the breach of privacy, but you're not available for consultation." She dug through his pack until she found the sat phone. He'd programmed several numbers in, and among them was his sister's name. River went straight to that one first.

"Hey, any time you want to get back down here, I won't mind," Ash said by way of greeting. "Your clients are both being a pain in the ass."

"Ash, it's River. I've got a problem. Easton hit his head, and he's got a bad concussion."

Ash let out a string of curses so expressive, River was forced to cut her off. "Trust me, I feel the same way. Listen, I'm sorry to interrupt, but I need to talk to Ben. I don't know what to do."

"I'm here," Ben said. He must have taken the phone from Ash. "What happened?" After River explained, she could hear the concern in his voice. "Do you know if he has any other injuries?"

"He's not bleeding from anywhere but his forehead from what I can tell. His clothes aren't ripped. I don't want to take anything off him to look. The weather's getting cold up here."

"How cold?"

River checked her watch. "My watch is stuck on negative fifteen, but it feels colder than that."

Ben inhaled a tight breath. "Easton has a portable temperature sensor in his supplies. Check that. It factors in windchill."

"Does it matter?" River asked as she dug through his things, looking for the sensor. "There's nothing we can do about the weather."

When Ben didn't answer, River ignored what that silence might mean. Instead, she found the sensor. "Okay, it says negative thirty-four degrees."

Having never been in temperature anywhere close to that cold, River wondered why she didn't feel panicked. Ben's voice stayed calm.

"River. If you can't wake Easton up, you need to leave him."

"What?" There was no way she could have heard Ben right.

"Listen to me. He's too heavy for you, and those temperatures are too dangerous for you to stay outside in. Leave Easton, get to the tent, and then get warmed up as best you can. When you feel strong enough, take him something to wrap around him. But do not stay out with him."

For a long time, River sat there. "I'm sorry, are you saying I need to let Easton freeze out here?"

"Where are you at?"

When River explained the fall to him, including where they had landed, Ben's voice grew deeper, gruff with emotion.

"Give yourself an hour for him to snap out of it, and if he doesn't, leave him. We'll get up there as quick as we can to help."

In the background, River could hear a steady stream of curses. Ash was clearly not handling this well.

"River, he loves you," Ben said quietly. "A man like Easton isn't going to want the woman he loves to get hurt, not if he can help it. This is a reality for us mountaineers. Take shelter. I'll meet you as soon as I can safely get to elevation. Ash's helicopter won't go that high, so I'll need to get someone with a bigger bird to help."

This was her fault. As she looked down at the man in the snow, his beard still, his eyes closed, she knew that if he died, it was 100 percent her fault.

How many nights ago had they stood in the Tourist Trap, with Easton gazing down at her, telling her he wouldn't be able to leave her up here? River had thought she understood what he meant, but now...now she got it. If you couldn't leave someone behind... if you had to, but you couldn't.

Or if you wouldn't.

Sucking in a shallow lungful of frozen air, River steeled her spine and her shaking hands. "Ben, I'm bringing him down with me. Tell Ash I'm not leaving her brother up here. Either you'll have two Popsicles or no Popsicles, but I'm not leaving him."

"River—"

"Don't even think about it." Using the voice that made the roughest of roughnecks pause, River added, "Would he leave me?"

Silence, then Ben exhaled a hard breath. "You know he wouldn't."

"Exactly. So what's plan B?"

Ben explained plan B twice to make sure when River hung up the sat phone, she knew what she needed to do. She just didn't know how in the world she was going to pull it off.

"Remember when you and Ben said it was a bad idea to bivouac up here?" she told the semiconscious Easton, earning a slurred mumble in response. "I completely agree. And if I'm not bivouacking, you definitely aren't. So try to wake up, because you are not a small man."

Ben had said if he couldn't walk and she wouldn't leave, then the best thing to do was try to drag him. Semiconscious had turned to unconscious, which made tying her climbing rope around his torso and beneath his arms harder. With a determined grunt to get them going, River started to pull.

"You know," she wheezed as she walked. "There should be a limit on weight up here. No guides over a hundred pounds."

Dropping down to her knees in the snow, River gasped for breath. "No guides allowed to pass out either."

Then she stood and started to pull again.

"You are so lucky I'm a cowgirl," she told him. "You are so, so lucky you're probably hot beneath the beard. And if you hadn't had the fluffy white towels, you and I would never have been in this situation."

Even as she spoke, River knew it wasn't true. The day she had met Easton Lockett, she'd known instinctively that the man in the truck who wanted to help her was different. What they had was so different from anything she'd experienced, and River wasn't ready to lose him, not yet.

"Falling down the mountainside was so easy." She said when his boot caught on the ice. "Why is this so freaking *hard*?"

Finally, the campsite came into view. "Easton, I don't care how heavy you are. You and I are going to get to our tent. We are going to get warm. And safe. And we're going to get back down tomorrow. Because I'm not freezing on a mountaintop thousands of miles from home with a man who doesn't even know my real name."

"What's your real name?" a masculine voice rasped.

"Now you wake up?" River could have kicked him if she weren't so glad to see those warm brown eyes blinking up at her, finally able to focus on her. "How many fingers am I holding up?"

"You're not holding up any," Easton replied.

"Good. You're fine." She dropped back to the snow, too tired to move even the short distance between where they were and the tent.

"What happened?"

"You fell then decided to take a nap. It's getting ridiculously cold, and I had to get you down before you turned into a Popsicle."

Blinking in surprise, Easton looked at her. "You carried me?"

"It was more like a dog mushing situation."

Easton sat up, wincing as he touched his forehead. "Must've knocked my head on something."

Tougher than most, Easton staggered to his feet. He turned, waiting for her.

"Go. I'm right behind you."

"I'm pretty sure I used that line on you." Despite his wobbly legs, Easton bent down and took her arm, helping her up.

Together they crossed the remaining distance to the tent, climbing inside. Easton sat down, pressing a hand to his head. "How long was I in and out?"

"Hours." She crawled to him, then lay down.

"River."

"I know." Even as she said it, River didn't know what she was insisting she knew.

"River, don't fall asleep."

Why would he ask her to do something so cruel? Hadn't she saved his bacon? "You must have a brain bleed. A guy without a brain bleed would be giving me thank-you kisses instead of bugging me to stay awake."

"Take slow, steady breaths for me, River."

Even though he was injured, River couldn't fight Easton as he put a mask over her face, opening the second small portable oxygen tank they had. Within moments, her head cleared, when she hadn't even realized how fuzzy everything had gotten. As focused as she was on getting him to camp and getting into the tent, River hadn't noticed she hadn't taken her boots off. She wasn't on the sleeping pad either. Instead of the extra layer of protection from the frozen ground, she was lying next to the side of the tent.

Hooking an arm beneath her, Easton muscled her over to the sleeping pad. One more breath of the oxygen and River pushed at the mask.

"Your turn."

He didn't fight her, instead taking several long, slow breaths of his own. Then Easton closed the tank, setting it aside.

"How cold is it?" Easton asked.

"The last I knew, it was negative thirty-four." It hadn't occurred to her to check the sensor since talking to Ben.

"It's too cold to be out there. We have to stay here."

"After lugging your solid self from halfway down the summit, I'm not going anywhere."

"It shouldn't have dropped this low," Easton told her as they lay together, body heat no longer heating the air between them. "Not for another couple of weeks."

"It's not your fault," River promised him, pressing her face to his armpit in an attempt to find somewhere warmer. "Stupid climate change. Tell me why I dragged us up here again."

"Not exactly what you planned, was it?" Nuzzling his face to the crook in her neck, Easton's strong arms squeezed her tighter. "Remember, this is a really great story we're going to tell everyone about how we met."

"I thought we met on the side of the road."

"That story doesn't paint either of us in the best of lights."

"I'm going to tell everyone you thought I was a hooker," River teased him.

"That day was the best day of my life." Easton's rumbling voice was like soothing fingertips across her soul. "I didn't even know it."

"You're not actually hitting on me right now."

"If not now, then when?"

Then he kissed her, because if they were going to have to wait in the freezing cold, they might as well make the most of it.

The night took its toll. One look at his client, and Easton knew immediately River's trip was over.

The amount of energy she had expended getting him to camp had depleted what was left of her reserves. The cold had taken what they didn't have to spare. She'd stayed awake with him all night, but she was having a hard time remaining that way. Even when the sound of the rescue helicopter's blades whipping through the air finally cut through the soft cry of the wind, she barely stirred.

In this location, there was nowhere to safely land, so Ben radioed to Easton to come to them if he could.

"Come on," he murmured, gathering her up to his chest. "Let's get out of here."

"What's happening?" she mumbled.

"I'm getting you home."

"About time you earn your keep. Don't forget my camera." No. Anything but that. "Or the marmot."

Even now, she made him laugh.

She probably could have walked, but it was easier for Easton to simply scoop her up into his arms, carrying River toward the National Park Service helicopter hovering beyond camp. Ben was with them, the first one to climb down the ladder to help. "Bad string of luck," he said. "We'll get them all up next time."

"Thanks for coming back," Easton replied with a grunt.

"Not gonna leave you behind a second time, boss." Ben took River from Easton's hold. "Not if I can help it."

As he watched Ben hook River up to a harness, lifting her

to safety, Easton knew he had made the right choice helping her summit. Some things were worth fighting for.

And for him, River had always been worth the risk.

CHAPTER 18

THE NURSING STAFF AT THE Moose Springs Medical Clinic couldn't have kept Easton away from River if they'd tried. And boy, were they trying.

"I need to see her."

"Ms. Lane is still resting." Duncan, Easton's nurse, paused in his work to make a tick mark on the hospital room's white board, the way he did every time Easton asked. "Which is what you should be doing."

Duncan hit Easton with a look that he was sure normally worked well on other patients. But no matter how good Duncan was at his job, Easton had no intention of sitting there, waiting for people who didn't know her to decide if it was okay for her to have visitors.

"Listen to him, Son." From the recliner in the corner of the room, Joshua never once looked up from his magazine.

"I don't want River to wake up alone." Easton pushed aside one of the many blankets they'd used to warm him up, frowning at the IV in his hand.

"Why do they always pair me with the difficult patients?"

Duncan grabbed the IV fluid bag attached to Easton's bed. "You're going to spurt everywhere if you pull that out."

This time, Duncan's look was enough to make Easton pause... at least until the other man hung his fluids on a mobile IV stand.

"I didn't tell you this." Duncan talked as he worked to get a blanket wrapped around Easton's shoulders. "She's going to be fine, but Ms. Lane's being treated for exhaustion and frostbite on her foot."

Easton grimaced. "How bad of frostbite?"

"Let's hope you don't have a foot fetish. You, in contrast, needed some fluids, some warming up, and—for the hundredth time—some *rest*. Which you won't get worrying about her, so we're going over to her room. You're a lucky guy, but even lucky guys can crack their skulls open if they collapse in a hospital hallway. Unless you want to see what a second concussion on top of a first can do, then you'll start listening to me."

"Her friends are with my sister," Easton said, tired of repeating himself. "Which means she's all alone."

Solitude was something Easton had been lucky enough not to experience. When the National Park Service airlifted River and Easton to the small building that served as the Moose Springs hospital, not only had Easton's family been waiting for him, but Graham and Zoey had been there too. Despite his reluctance at being separated from River, he'd understood the physicians' need to evaluate them both. And even if he hadn't, Ash and Joshua would have personally dragged him into imaging, where they ran test after test on him to make sure he wasn't bleeding internally—cranial or otherwise—from his fall.

Duncan disappeared into the hallway outside his room, then returned, pushing a wheelchair.

"Nope." No way. Never in a million years.

"Wheelchair or nothing."

"I think he's got you there, Son."

"Dad, you're really not helping."

The magazine lowered enough for Joshua to aim a smug look at him. "It sucks being in love, doesn't it?"

Refusing to respond to that, Easton dropped down in the wheelchair.

"She really dragged you down a mountainside?" Duncan whistled in appreciation as they left the room. "I can barely push you down the hall."

Annoyed beyond belief, Easton said lightly. "I'm happy to walk."

"Not worth my job." Turning at the end of the hallway, Duncan paused at the first room on the right. "Okay, lover boy. Here she is."

Duncan pushed Easton inside the hospital room, then closed the door to give them privacy.

The lights had been turned down low, leaving only the soft illumination of the machines monitoring River's vitals and one strip of lighting behind the hospital bed. Without layers of thick protective clothing, River looked so small in the hospital bed that had felt so confining to Easton. Since River's back was turned to him, Easton rolled to the far side of the hospital bed so he could see her face.

Easton ran a thumb gently over her arm, grateful to be able to touch her again.

"That tickles." With a sleepy noise, she leaned into his hand.

He'd missed her voice so much in the few hours they'd been separated. He'd missed the feel of her beneath his hands even more. The tight band of pressure squeezing his heart into his feet finally loosened now that he could see her for himself.

River opened one heavy-lidded eye.

"What's wrong? You have Easton face." Both eyes popped open as she took him in. "And why are you in a wheelchair?"

Easton twisted in his wheelchair and grabbed a regular chair from behind him. He shifted from the wheelchair to the other chair, then he draped his arm around her waist, the way he had when they slept on the mountain.

"I hate to disappoint you," he murmured, "but I was born with Easton face. Ash tried to scrape it off a few times, but it kind of stuck."

She snuggled up to him as well as the IV in her hand would allow. "So that's why you covered it with a beard."

"I'm actually very attractive," he promised her. "It's not fair to the other men."

"I bet it isn't." Her fingertips touched his arm. "Tell me what's wrong."

Running his hand over her hair, Easton gave in and slid his arm beneath her head. He couldn't help himself. He needed to hold her. "I'm fine. I just wanted to see you."

"I'm okay." River buried her nose against the inside of his elbow. "Are Jessie and Bree—"

"They'll live. Bree had two broken ribs. They treated Jessie for dehydration and sent everyone home to rest at my place a couple of hours ago. Right now, everyone's worried about you."

"I'm definitely feeling less than spectacular," she admitted. "The Old Man tried to take us down, didn't he?"

Easton brushed a strand of hair away from her eyes. "The Old Man has nothing on you. River, did they talk to you about your toe?"

A flash of pain crossed her features. "I was kind of hoping that part would magically go away. Maybe we can talk about something else?"

"At least it isn't your nipples."

Her snicker was a balm to his soul. Since they'd come this far and she had her fingers wrapped around his heart and his wrist, Easton allowed himself a question he'd wanted the answer to since they'd left the mountain.

"River? What's your real name?"

Her words were soft, almost inaudible. "What makes you think River Lane isn't my real name?"

Easton's voice softened too. "Only a hunch. Or maybe I remember you saying you didn't want to die on the top of a mountain, thousands of miles from home with a man who didn't even know your name."

Those perfect blue eyes wouldn't look at him. At least they wouldn't look until he rested his chin on the edge of the guard rail, face inches from her own.

"Jamie Danielle. My last name really is Lane. My daddy calls me JD, like a boy. He always wanted a son, but he ended up with four daughters instead."

"Poor guy was overrun."

"Tell me about it," River agreed. "I haven't seen him or my

mother in two years. I used to be so busy, I just couldn't find the time. Now I have the time…"

"And you're afraid to tell him why," Easton finished for her.

River sighed. "They always supported me. Never complained, always said they were proud to have a daughter who worked as hard as I did to make something of myself. I didn't know how to tell them I failed. Kind of like this documentary."

"You think you failed?"

"I couldn't film Moose Springs so I made a documentary about why someone *shouldn't* climb Mount Veil. I pretty much sucked at this entire project, start to finish."

Pressing his lips to the inside of her wrist this time, Easton couldn't help but disagree. "You showed the truth of what being here and being on the Old Man is like. It's up to whoever watches to decide if they're willing to take the risk." When she didn't look convinced, Easton added quietly, "What happened up there was real, River. You can plan all you want, but when the mountain decides it's going to win, there's nothing you can do but fight to survive. You fought for both of us. You saved my life, and I'm grateful for it."

A slight smile curved her lips. "I owed you."

"No, but I'm thinking I might owe you when you get out of here. Buy you dinner at the very least."

"I'll take you up on that. Did you lose anything?" She held up her hands and wiggled her fingers at him. "All ten fingers and toes accounted for?"

Easton shook his head. "The only thing I lost was my pride. Scoot over."

"There's not enough room," River protested.

"Nah, it's fine."

"You're a beast-sized person. There's definitely no room."

Even as she argued playfully with him, River moved over, making a spot for Easton. And yes, there really wasn't room, but that didn't matter, not when he turned on his side, drawing her in flush to his body. She snuggled in, pressing her face to his neck.

"So this is what it's like." At her askance look, Easton explained, "Holding you without fifteen feet of jackets between us." The IVs weren't ideal for cuddling, and his pulled at his hand when he moved wrong, but being able to feel the soft skin of her arm along his was worth it.

River grinned at him. At least he assumed she grinned at him, because he could feel her lips curving against the skin of his throat. But like Easton, she seemed far too happy to be close to actually look up at him.

She felt good. Far better than a guy like him deserved.

"So, Jamie, huh?" He tried her name to see how it fit.

River sighed dramatically. "No, please don't. I'm legally changed to River now, for better or for worse. I've married myself into this personality."

Easton didn't care what he called her, as long as she was tucked in his arms like this.

"What's a girl got to do to get a 'we survived, yay' kiss?"

Easton nuzzled her neck, pressing a soft kiss to her pulse point. "Like that?"

"Not quite."

"There?" Another kiss to her earlobe, then behind her ear.

"Hmm, that's better. But not yet."

Settling in, Easton tangled his hand in her hair, gazing into her eyes. She was so beautiful, even more so when she pulled him to her. Drawing her deep into his arms, Easton rolled so the weight of his body didn't press down upon her. Lost in her, Easton didn't realize they had company until a delicate female cough at the doorway was followed by a deeper, masculine snort.

"I take it this isn't a good time?" Graham asked cheekily.

Graham and Zoey stood inside the doorway, twin expressions of curiosity on their faces.

When Easton groaned, his best friend chuckled. "We're getting you back for all those times you interrupted us, buddy. Hey, Zoey, East has a girlfriend."

"I know," Zoey played along. "And she's really pretty. Maybe too pretty for him. Do we know what he looks like under the beard?"

Graham flopped down in Easton's wheelchair, making himself comfortable. "The real questions is, does *she* know what he looks like under the beard?"

"Would you two get out?" Easton glared at them. "We're fine—"

"Clearly," Graham spoke up, grinning broadly.

"—so please leave us alone. River needs rest."

"Do I?" River arched an eyebrow.

"Is that what they're calling it these days?" Zoey's eyes sparkled behind her glasses.

"There's three of them now." Easton grunted, dropping his head back onto the stiff hospital pillow. "It was bad enough when it was only him."

River needed rest, but as she smiled at the playful banter, it occurred to Easton that there was something she needed more than rest. Sometimes family was the one you were born into. Sometimes family was the people you kept close, the people who mattered. Keeping her tucked to his chest, he turned to the family he had chosen.

"Want to hear about our first date?" he asked them. "A marmot fell in love with me."

For a man who needed the people he cared about to be safe and happy, River's soft laugh against his neck was everything.

———

River really didn't want to lose her pinky toe. So far, the process of saving it hadn't been pleasant.

The first step had been rewarming her partially frozen toe, during which River had been blissfully asleep. The next part was a series of wraps, topical creams, and cleaning off dying skin that River refused to watch. It was enough knowing what was happening. She didn't need to see it. The physician in charge of her case promised the increasing pain of the process was a good sign. The more nerve endings and blood flow restored to her toes, the better.

Easton had offered to stay with her, but some things a person didn't want witnesses to.

River's nurse was cleaning her foot when a voice spoke up from the door. "That's disgusting."

River had been staring intently at the wall, but she turned her head.

Bree stepped into the room, giving her a once-over. "You look terrible."

River waited for Bree to cross the room, hugging her. "Tell me how you really feel."

"I feel like you're going to break my already broken ribs. Don't squeeze so hard."

"How are you? How's Jessie?"

Pulling a stool to the side of River's bed, Bree watched River's foot in fascination. "Better than you. Your toe is—"

"Nope, nope, nope. Do not tell me. I don't want to know."

Bree chuckled. "Trust me, I should be taking stock footage on this. It's a hundred times worse than the torture barn."

"Nothing is worse than the torture barn," River disagreed, relaxing back against her pillows. The nurse finished with her foot, rewrapped it, and gave her a dose of painkillers in a small cup before leaving. Despite being in a significant amount of pain from the procedure, River set the cup aside.

"I'd be popping those and chasing them with hard liquor if I were you," Bree said. "That looked like it hurt."

"It's weird, but I like the pain. If I can feel it, I know my foot is going to be fine. Hey, how's Easton? I think he's been putting on the tough guy front for me."

"Oh, that man is a nightmare. It's not a front; he's really that tough. His sister is worse. Since Easton's been busy driving the hospital staff up the wall over you, she decided to 'take charge' of us." Bree made air quotes with her fingers. "I have never felt so micromanaged in my life. If she hadn't rescued me off a mountain or kept stuffing us full of scrambled eggs and coffee, I might hate her."

"You love her."

"Probably." Bree made a playful face. "The Locketts are lovable people. Strange, pushy, and occasionally off-putting, but lovable."

There was something River couldn't quite put her finger on about Bree. Her friend sounded relaxed, but so much time with her had taught River the tension in Bree's shoulders was too tight. Her fingernails kept drumming against the railing of the hospital bed. Bree was determinedly not looking at anything but River, when she normally watched everything around her.

"What's wrong?" she asked.

"Who says anything's wrong?"

River narrowed her eyes. "Literally every part of you but your lips."

"I have your phone," Bree said randomly. "I should probably give it to you, but I really don't want to. The last thing you need right now is the stress of dealing with everyone."

River frowned, sitting up higher. "Define everyone."

Bree sighed. "Someone at the hospital leaked the story."

"How do you know it was someone at the hospital?"

"There's a picture of you in a hospital bed on every entertainment website and TV show right now." Picking up the remote control connected to her bed, Bree turned on the television. "Someone caught a picture of you and Easton kissing."

She increased the volume, then went to the most popular entertainment and celebrity gossip station. Two women sat perched on stools in a studio with an oversized picture of...yep. That was a grainy photo of River and Easton, on her hospital bed, entwined and kissing right between the two television hosts.

The host on the left spoke brightly. "While River has been unavailable for comment, sources close to the actress say she's in good spirits despite her ordeal. More to come soon. Rill, can you imagine being stuck on a mountain in the freezing cold? I can't even leave the house if it dips into the seventies—"

As they began to talk about sweater weather, Bree paused the screen.

"The internet is worse," she said. "It's everywhere. You need to get someone on this. Your agent and your publicist, maybe? Someone will have to put out a statement."

"Will they?" Sighing, River leaned her head back against her pillow. "Bree, do you remember what it was like to not have anyone care about all this crap? What we eat, what we wear, what we make faces at because it's stupid?"

Crossing her legs beneath her, Bree winced, then changed positions. "No one ever cares what Jessie and I do. River, do you mind if I speak honestly with you?"

"It would be preferable to lying to me and letting me bop along clueless to the truth."

"When we first got here, and even when we got to Mount Veil, you were playing a part." Bree shrugged. "Like every other movie we've made together, you were acting. The scenery was different, and the drama on set was far scarier—"

"Except for the torture barn."

"Yes, that was horrifying. Anyway, you were playing the role of actress number one, director and coproducer number two. At times, it didn't feel like a documentary. It felt like you were going through the motions."

River tried hard not to be insulted by that. "I care about this project, Bree."

"I know, but it's like muscle memory. You're so used to going through the motions, you didn't know how *not* to do so. But when we started to climb, you stopped playing a part. You were you. The footage we got then was better than anything I've ever filmed before."

"What does this have to do with anything?"

"We've been keeping this documentary close to the cuff. No one knew we were up here. But that picture of you and him...it's getting attention. People didn't even know you and Sweeny had broken up. And now you're with some sexy Alaskan hunk in a hospital bed? This could drum up the kind of publicity that would really help the documentary be a success."

River couldn't see her own face, but she must have not looked happy.

Bree set the remote down next to River's hand. "Or not. It was just an idea. Either way, someone is going to have to say or do something. Jessie's talking to the hospital staff on how to manage things, but I think you need some backup."

Bree handed River her cell phone.

"Why?" But River already knew the answer.

"Because the paparazzi love a great story. And there's a shit ton of them outside."

CHAPTER 19

"I'M GOING TO KILL THEM."

"You can't kill them, buddy. With that many cameras, someone would catch us, and you know what would happen then. I'm too pretty for jail. It wouldn't go well for me."

Easton was not in the mood for Graham's sense of humor right then.

When it was decided that all Easton really needed was rest, they'd discharged him and sent him home to rest in his own bed. He hadn't liked leaving River at the hospital, but she'd been sleeping too, and they'd convinced him to go home. Graham had offered to drive with him back to the hospital the following morning, only to find a swarm of camera crews and equipment vans clustered outside the tiny hospital's front entrance.

If Easton had known what he'd be leaving her to face alone, he never would have left.

"How long have they been here?" he asked with a snarl as Jonah strode over, his deputy at his heels. Easton was standing on the far side of the parking lot, fuming, because so far, Graham hadn't let him closer. It wasn't only River everyone was shouting about to the poor doctors and nurses coming in and out on their shift change. Easton's name was being shouted too.

"I think they all took the same plane," Jonah informed them. "They showed up about an hour ago. A few of them got on her floor before security pushed them back out, but no one was ready for this level of attention."

"Security" consisted of two very hassled young men who up until that point were used to spending their time playing cards in a small room off the main entrance.

"I've called for another squad car for backup," Jonah continued. "The only one nearby is Fish and Game, but Garcia's partner said they would help."

Someone turned their head, and that was all it took. Like an ocean wave crashing around him, suddenly he was surrounded by the paparazzi, lights and microphones in his face. Unfamiliar voices yelled questions at him, each louder than the last.

"Easton Lockett. Can you tell us how River is doing?"

"Easton, are you and River Lane in a romantic relationship?"

"What about Sweeny, Easton? Is he concerned about how much time you and River spent together?"

Easton didn't even know who that was.

"Is it true you saved her life on the mountain, Easton?"

"She saved mine," Easton said. He never should have said anything, because the roar of questions that followed his words was overwhelming. Lights flashed, blinding him no matter which way he turned. Graham kept his body shoved in front of Easton, protective and loyal to the end, but neither of them were wired for this kind of thing.

Everyone get back." Jonah and his deputy's efforts were utterly ineffective, except for being extra bodies between him and the cameras. "Come on now. Give the man some room."

"Get that out of my face," Graham said when a boom swung dangerously close to his forehead.

"Graham? Jessie said we need to get Easton inside."

Zoey was the last person they needed in the middle of this mess. Someone was going to trample her and not even realize it. Easton reached for her and only got more reporters in his face.

"Hey!" Ash suddenly appeared in the midst of the craziness. "Hey, morons! If you want to hear anything, shut up and *listen*."

God bless his sister and her naturally inherent ability to intimidate everyone with an inborn sense of self-survival. He hadn't even known she was there. He'd been too focused on the camera crews.

"River's going to be fine. When she's ready to tell you more, she'll tell you more. Easton doesn't have to say anything unless he wants to." Ash turned to him, her turquoise-colored hair nearly white in the flashing lights. "East. Do you want to tell them what it was like up there?"

"Not really—" he started to say when they erupted in questions all over again.

Ash had missed her calling as a drill sergeant, because her bellow for silence shut them all up, wide eyed and startled.

"I'm his sister, and I'll tell you what it's like. It's cold, it sucks, and they're lucky they're not dead. You're in Alaska, children, so keep a solid swinging distance between you and us. I have no problem destroying every camera here. Now let my brother through."

The group hesitated enough for her to narrow her eyes.

"LET. HIM. THROUGH."

Never had a press of paparazzi parted so fast.

Easton wasn't oblivious to the fact that his friends and family had formed a wall around him, using their bodies to shield him from the camera. Zoey at most came up to his sternum, but she'd grabbed hold of his arm in a protective way, glaring a death glare at everyone they passed. They reached the door and pushed through the remaining reporters and their microphones, the group tumbling into the hospital entranceway.

"Well, that was interesting," Graham declared, looking back through the sliding glass doors to the still flashing cameras. "Is that what she goes through every day?"

"Nope." Jessie's face was a familiar relief. "This is what it's like when something interesting happens. On a normal day, they try to catch her with her hair and makeup all a mess or looking pregnant. For some reason, everyone keeps trying to make her pregnant."

Waving them away from the still-curious eyes outside, Jessie snorted. "It's like a pack of starving dogs out there, isn't it? But hey, what can you do? Work is work."

"East," Graham murmured. "You're growling."

Maybe. But not at Jessie per se, just in his former client's general direction. Jessie shot him an amused look. "Man, you really have it bad, don't you? Well, get used to it. This is her life. People want to know what she's up to."

Easton found River in her room, sitting up with the controller in her hand. The television was on mute, but it was obvious what she was watching. Already film of Easton pushing his way into the hospital played on repeat.

"Welcome to the insanity," she quipped, sounding embarrassed. "Feel free to run screaming."

Since the railing was dropped, Easton sat on the edge of her bed. "Jessie says that people want to know what's happening to you."

"They also want to have a commentary about it too. Look on the bright side. The more of a fuss they cause, the more buzz they're building about the town. Maybe the tourism board will pay us after all."

Easton took her face in his hand, stealing the controller away from her fingers. "You need to rest. The last thing you need is to be worrying about all this."

"I'm not." She hesitated.

Tilting his head to catch her eye, Easton stroked his thumb down her cheek. "You sure?"

"I'm not worried. I just feel bad about them coming here. The town's going to be upset."

"The town can deal," Easton said firmly. "Graham's the mayor. He can handle those idiots. They're his payback for not giving you your filming permits."

"Oh, he'll *hate* it."

She wrapped her arms around him, pulling Easton down to her. Careful not to crowd her, he settled in to steal those giggling lips.

"We need to talk," he told her before things grew too heated.

"Four words that are never a good sign. Do we have to? I'm liking the not talking."

Easton squeezed her hand before pressing a kiss to the inside of her wrist. "Me too. For the sake of more of the same, what's it going to take to make all those people go away?"

"Honestly?" Pursing her lips, River thought a moment. "I

probably need to make a statement to the press. Preferably from right here. If they get the good stuff, I have a better shot of being left alone long enough to get back home."

"If that's what you want, I'm not going to argue," he told her. "But I hate the idea of letting those vultures anywhere near you."

"The protective growl is cute." She kissed him again. "You should do that more often. And this more often."

It was impossible not to. Settling back in, Easton was more than happy to distract her until suddenly River pulled away, a horrified expression on her face. "I'm going on camera. In front of the world. Minus a toe."

"Technically, you still have the toe," he reminded her. "And I'm fine with locking the doors so no one ever bothers us again."

"If only it were that easy." She ran a worried hand over her hair. "If I look half as rough as Bree said I do, they'll never leave."

He had no idea what she was talking about. But then again, his face was currently buried more interesting places, trying to remind her how much more fun it was to stay distracted.

"Hey, Easton? Do you know anyone who's good with makeup?"

"Hmm?"

"Like *really* good with makeup?"

As a matter of fact, yes, he did.

"What do you think?" Zoey held up a compact mirror for River to see her reflection. "Good enough?"

"I think you're a godsend."

Zoey smiled at her. "My job wasn't hard. Are you sure you don't want me to make you look less put together? I mean, you are in the hospital right now. Even I'm having a hard time believing you and Easton went through what you did."

"Thanks." Returning her smile, River squeezed Zoey's hand. "I appreciate that, but I need to look my best. If I'm all messed up, it'll only make everyone more interested. Trust me, the town does not want them sticking around."

"How bad was it up there?"

"Most of it was amazing. A few times, when things were going wrong, I was scared. But it's hard to be too worried with Easton there."

"He's a really good guy." Zoey glanced at her shyly. "Did he tell you he found me when I was lost in the woods? I was on an ATV trip that went sideways, and I ended up getting stuck out in a storm. I was scared to death, then I turned around, and this massive Sasquatch-looking guy was there. He got me back home safe. I've had a pretty big soft spot for him ever since."

Totally understanding, River nodded. "Yeah, Easton's kind of got that whole sexy mountain man thing going on. I was a sucker from the moment we met."

"I feel the same way about Graham." Zoey's entire face lit up at the mention of the diner owner's name. "The people here have been really good to me, but Graham and Easton are the best guys I've ever met."

"Are you sure? Because I kind of wanted to punch Graham within thirty seconds of first meeting him. If he's sucked you into a cultlike situation, please let me know. I'm happy to rescue you."

With a sweet laugh, Zoey tucked her makeup supplies back in a bag. "Trust me, he drives me crazy plenty. It wouldn't be any fun if he didn't. But I'm kind of ridiculously in love with the big lug, so I ignore his more irritating habits. Okay, you're all set. How do you want me to handle everyone out there?"

With a grimace, River sat up straighter in her bed, ignoring the pain in her toe as she pulled her blanket over her foot to cover it from view. "Open the floodgates. Trust me, they'll find me."

And find her they did. Stuffed together so tight in the tiny hospital room, everyone's personal bubbles had officially been popped by the time River started her interview. To her credit, Zoey stubbornly stayed at River's side, although the poor woman was uncomfortably squished between the hospital bed and a cameraman's shoulder.

"Wow, this is a lot of attention," River joked. "I should have fallen off a mountain earlier in my career."

A murmur of laughter rippled through the camera crews.

"River, how are you doing?" someone asked.

"I have some frostbite on my foot. It's not pretty, which is why no one gets to see it. Other than that, I'm fine. I need to rest up awhile, and then they'll send me home."

Another reporter held out a microphone in her direction. "River, what happened on the mountain?"

"You'll have to see my documentary to know that." She flashed the same pleasant expression she had practiced for years in her mirror. "As my first job behind the camera, I've both appreciated the opportunity and deeply enjoyed experiencing all the wonderful things Moose Springs, Alaska, has to offer. I think the Alaskan Tourism Board will be pleased with the end result of our documentary. As for the actual details of the film, you all know the drill about how nondisclosure agreements work. None of us can talk about what happened, legally."

"River, can you tell us about Easton Lockett? Are you and he in a romantic relationship? What about Sweeny?"

"Sweeny and I are friends, and we still enjoy each other's company."

Actually, she couldn't stand him, but she knew better than to ever tell the paparazzi the truth of the relationship. Instead, she pushed ahead.

"Easton is the guide who got us up and safely back down the mountain. But like the rest of us, Easton's signed a nondisclosure agreement. Everything we've been doing here in Moose Springs has been a part of filming, so we really can't talk about any of it. You ladies and gentlemen know how much trouble we'll all get in if we spill the beans."

"River," a familiar entertainment report asked. "What *can* you say?"

She hesitated, then finally looked into the cameras. "Easton saved my life, and I saved his. That's the kind of shared experience that leaves two people connected. I'm grateful for everything he has done, and I ask for everyone to please respect his privacy. He didn't ask for this, and he didn't sign on for cameras shoved in his face. He's a man who did his job. That's all I'm going to say for now. Thanks, everyone."

They continued to ask questions, but River smiled brightly, shaking her head. Eventually, they started to filter out, having been given all she was willing to share.

"How did I do?" River asked Zoey, who looked a bit wide about the eyes.

"Better than I would have. They're pushy, aren't they?"

"It's part of the life. But soon, if I can keep getting producing gigs instead of being in front of the camera, they'll forget all about me."

Brushing her bangs away from her eyes, Zoey adjusted her glasses up on her nose. "Do you want me to go get Easton?"

Yes. Absolutely. But as she watched the remainder of the paparazzi lingering in the hallway, ignoring the staff's requests to leave, she knew that he'd hated one camera in his face. This...it was too much to ask of him.

"I'm okay. He's probably going to want to steer clear from these guys for a while."

There was no point in dragging him deeper into her world. They both knew she'd be leaving his soon anyway.

When River decided to talk to the press without him there at her side, Easton respected her decision. He didn't like it, but he respected it.

He also couldn't stand waiting in a private room down the hall, door closed, knowing she was being surrounded fifty feet away from him. Pacing the room didn't help, and neither did sitting still. The result was standing up and sitting down at irregular intervals, trying and failing to be patient as River went through her interrogation session down the hall.

Graham had made himself comfortable, stretched out on a

clean hospital bed with one foot kicked up on the rail. Right arm folded behind his head and left making liberal use of the remote control, Graham was not the supportive, calming presence he claimed to be.

If Easton had to hear his best friend crunch through one more mouthful of ice chips, he wasn't going to be responsible for his actions.

"She's fine, man. River's a tough cookie. Besides, if she needs anything, Zoey will let us know."

They'd planted Graham's fiancée in the room, not that it helped Easton feel more comfortable at all. "What's she going to be able to do if they crowd her too much?"

Graham seemed utterly unconcerned. "Zo will handle it."

Easton dropped back down into his seat. "Aren't you worried about her too?"

"Nope." Graham scooped up another handful of ice chips, crunching them so loudly, Easton couldn't believe his teeth didn't hurt. "Zoey has something neither of us are equipped with: perspective. She'll know if we're needed."

"Where did you get those anyway?" Easton grumped.

"Some nice nurse got them for me. Duncan, I think his name was?"

The door opened, a nose and a pair of glasses popping inside the crack. "She got through the interview fine," Zoey promised, slipping in the door and closing it behind her. "But there's still paparazzi out there, so she said to tell you to hide out for a while longer. They'll clear out soon enough."

Graham hooked an arm around Zoey's waist, pulling her

giggling into the bed with him. The pair were officially the last thing Easton could handle. He pushed to his feet.

"I'm not staying in here anymore."

"Okeydokey. Have fun, buddy."

Easton could still hear Graham chuckling as he left the room, whispering to Zoey. "Five bucks he hits someone."

"Graham, that's not funny."

"It's a little funny…"

"Tell Duncan not to give Graham anything else," Easton said as he went past the nurses' station. "He's a pain in the ass."

Muscles strung tight with strangers-induced tension, Easton strode down the hallway. Sure enough, there were stragglers in the hallway outside her room, trying and failing to look innocent as they lingered. When the closest cameraman noticed him, his face brightened with renewed zeal.

"Easton," he said, sticking a camera in his face. "What can you tell us about—"

Easton didn't give the guy a chance to finish the question. One hand on the camera, he pushed it down, staring at the cameraman.

He didn't say anything. He didn't do anything. He just stared.

With a cleared throat, the cameraman stepped aside, giving Easton access to River's room. "Sorry, man."

Easton closed her door behind him, then pulled the privacy blinds. He grabbed the room's recliner and dragged it in front of the door, wedging it beneath the handle.

"Wow. I thought you were going to eat that guy."

Easton didn't reply to her teasing tone.

"Come here." When he didn't move, she flapped her hands at him. "Come on. Sit over here with me."

"You look pretty," he muttered, dropping down to sit on the edge of her bed.

"That almost sounded like a compliment. It's hard to tell, though, because your beard is glaring at me."

"Don't let it get to your head. I'm still mad you let all of them in here and kicked me out."

"Then I suppose I'll have to make it up to you."

Hmm. That was a lot better idea than anything Easton had been considering. A hand pressed against his chest, stopping him from leaning down and kissing her.

"Easton, we need to talk." Her voice was quiet and too serious. "They're releasing me tomorrow. The doctor came in before the press briefing. I guess I'm keeping my toe after all."

The toe was great news, but Easton's heart squeezed down so tight, he wondered if it was possible to feel it ripping in half. He knew what she was going to say, and he didn't want to hear any of this.

"Our original plane flight was scheduled for tonight. Bree and Jessie are going to leave on it, but I rescheduled mine for tomorrow."

And just like that, what was left of his hope crumbled like dust. Sitting back in his seat, Easton tried not to look as devastated as he felt. "You're leaving tomorrow."

River had never sounded so sad. "Would you rather me stay and drag this out?" she whispered. "String you along until we both hate each other? Ruin the last couple of weeks?"

Yes. But...no. Hell, he didn't know. Everything was moving so fast. Ripping a bandage off a wound might hurt less, but his heart was telling him to slap that sucker back on. In the end, Easton didn't reply. There was nothing he could say.

"The way I see it, we can leave things where they're at. What happened on the mountain can stay on the mountain." River offered him a sad look. "Easton, I love it here, because you're here. But my life—my career—it's not in Moose Springs."

"Do I get another option?" he asked quietly.

"The other option is what happened on the mountain doesn't stay on the mountain. But that's going to be short, messy, and complicated. I won't ruin us, Easton. Tomorrow, I'm getting on that plane, no matter how much I wish I weren't."

"River, every single minute I've spent with you has been messy and complicated. I wouldn't trade any of it. Not for anything. Whatever this is, let's see it to the end. Even if that's only twenty-four hours from now."

"Summit or bust?" she asked, slender fingers tugging at his hair, drawing him back to her.

"Summit or bust," he breathed against her lips.

CHAPTER 20

SINCE THEY WERE RELEASING HER tomorrow, River had one more night in the hospital room. It seriously sucked.

At least she was wearing her normal clothes again.

River's back was to the door, and the constant footsteps in the hall caused her to stop paying attention to unexpected noises. Which might have been why River was completely unprepared to turn her head and find a border collie in a three-piece suit in her room, a thornless long stem rose held carefully in between his teeth.

At first, River stared. This was no normal canine outfit. Someone had gone to a lot of effort to tailor the suit for the adorable, floppy-eared dog. Not only was it tailored, it was also pinstriped, with matching bow tie and pocket square.

A fedora had been secured between those ears, tilted jauntily.

"Hey there," she cooed, earning herself a vigorously wagging tail. Only when River scooted off the bed to kneel next to him did she realize the dog had a thick film over his eyes, indicating his blindness. "Puppy, who lost you?"

"I didn't *lose* him." Graham Barnett's voice spoke up right next to her, making River jump. "Like I would ever lose my best friend. Jake, can you believe that?"

Jake—the well-dressed border collie—barked in mutual offended agreement, accidentally dropping the rose. He sniffed the ground, then picked it back up again, the flowered end closer to his teeth and the long stem drooping out the other side of his mouth. It was officially the cutest thing River had ever seen, and she'd seen Easton cuddle a marmot.

"Graham, where are—?" River started to say, then she noticed the baby monitor tucked into the breast pocket of Jake's suit. "Oh. Very sneaky, Overwatch."

"Jake has been asked to escort you to an evening of wonder and romance, courtesy of someone who has never successfully pulled off either," Graham informed her cheerfully. "Jake, give the nice lady her flower."

A wet nose snuffed her hands, then Jake set the slightly slobbered-on rose in her fingers. Unable to contain her sheer delight, River spent a solid minute ignoring the man on the monitor in favor of telling Jake how perfect he was, petting those floppy ears, and taking multiple selfies.

"Wow, and I thought Zoey had it bad. Jake, you're such a ladies' man. Now, if you don't mind changing, we're on a deadline here. Jake, give the lady some privacy."

"I'm wearing clothes," River said as the border collie politely turned around and sat with his back to her. "For a disembodied event organizer, you're dropping the ball here."

"Hey, I'm doing this blind. Can't a guy catch a break?"

"Give me that." Ash's voice came over the line, sounding

annoyed. "He always has to make everything about himself. River, come outside, okay? Head to the back parking lot, and you'll see where to go."

River put on her shoes, careful not to tie them too tight over her still bandaged toes, and dutifully took Jake's leash. She kept the rose in her free hand, trying to sneak both past the curious eyes of the nursing station. The entire trip through the hospital, River had the feeling Zoey was lurking in the background, but she could never quite catch her, not even when she ducked an extra corner or two.

Easton's truck was parked in the back of the hospital, on the very far side of the parking lot, where the woods butted up to the asphalt. Someone had set an empty pizza box in the back of the truck, with a much neater handwriting than River's own.

"Don't stop," she read, chuckling at the arrow pointing to the trail hidden behind the truck's bulk. "No film crews allowed. Private event."

Graham's voice came back over Jake's monitor. "This is where you're on your own. Please leave the handsome devil on your left in the bed of the truck and continue on the trail."

"Okay, now whose getting led into the woods by a crazy person?" she joked, scratching Jake beneath the chin. "Thanks for the escort, Jake."

"He says you're welcome. Oh, and, River?"

"Yes, Graham?"

"Thanks for taking care of my buddy out there." In a kind voice, Graham added, "I hope you have a nice evening."

Okay, so maybe Zoey was right, and Graham wasn't *all* bad.

Leaving Jake was tough, because who really wanted to leave a dog in a fedora? But River did as directed, tying Jake safe and sound in the bed of the truck with the duo of puppet masters still hiding in the cab, sneakily watching her through the side mirrors.

Following the indicated trail, River had to squeeze through closely grown branches. The trail stayed tight for the first several yards, then it opened up as the trees grew higher and farther apart. Even though they were so close to the hospital, River felt like she was back in the bush again.

It was harder to know where the natural trail was anymore, but someone had already taken care of that. Every few yards, a glow stick was suspended from a branch at face height, showing her the way. She followed the glow sticks around a corner and then stopped in her tracks.

River's breath caught in her throat.

Of all the impromptu picnics or surprise dates in her lifetime, this was by far her favorite. The campsite Easton had picked was perfect. A tiny fire had been built and carefully circled with rocks in the center of a small clearing, the crackling of the burning wood almost lost beneath the softly babbling brook skirting the edge of the camp. River didn't recognize the tent in front of her, but the man waiting for her was burned into her soul.

The first time River had seen him, Easton had been wearing a dark T-shirt and worn blue jeans. Maybe he knew how good that particular combination looked on him, because he'd never looked as gorgeous as he did right then, biceps flexing with dangerous appeal just from his hands being stuffed into his pockets. Even from this far away, River could tell he was going both shoulders on her. And it worked too, because she wanted to be pressed against that tall, strong body, those arms around her.

"What's all this for?" she asked, inhaling the deep, luxurious scent of evergreens and cedar wood.

Easton cleared his throat uncomfortably. "I'm not all that great with this stuff. Thought about taking you out for a nice meal, but you've been kicked out of pretty much everywhere in town."

"Har har," River said, rolling her eyes at him. "I'm only technically not allowed back at the resort."

"I didn't want to share you." This time, Easton's voice was stronger, surer. "I know they all want to see you, but I want you the most."

River closed the distance between them, and only then did she realize his beard had been trimmed down neatly, leaving his smile visible to see. Reaching up to brush her fingertips along his jaw, she knew she didn't want to share him either. And in a couple of hours, she was going to have to give him up completely.

"You're very handsome, Easton Lockett. I know why the reporter gave you such a hard time. You probably broke her heart."

Those kind brown eyes gazed down at her, the usual warmth replaced with a heat that River could feel down to her toes.

"Was the walk too rough?" he asked in a low voice, hands finding her hips.

She shook her head, because she would have hopped on one foot to get to him, to have this night with him. "No, it was perfect," she promised, unable to keep her palms from sliding up his chest.

"Are you hungry?"

"Definitely." At first, she misunderstood, reaching for him

and drawing him down to her. Easton bent his head willingly, his arm wrapping around her waist and lifting her up on her good toes. When they pulled away to catch their breath, he smiled against her lips.

"I meant actual food," he told her. "Come on."

River let him draw her to the campfire, where their dinner waited. Upon seeing what he'd prepared, River slipped her hand into his, delighted.

"You ordered pizza. Pepperoni and pineapple. I can't believe you remembered that."

Easton's fingers threaded with hers. "Not much I'm going to forget about you, sweetheart."

They ate their pizza cuddled together by the fire. Because he was Easton, he made sure to put the pizza box in a bear-proof trash can back at the hospital, leaving her a couple of minutes of solitude to soak up the crackling fire as she relaxed in front of the tent. It wasn't the same one they'd left on the mountain—that would have to stay there until it was safe to go back next season and retrieve it. But the tent was nice and smelled fresh and clean when she slipped inside.

The handheld had gone with Bree and Jessie, but River didn't need a video camera to remember tonight. The little pillow he'd brought for them because she'd never loved sleeping without one on the mountain. The simple tin cup to share the bottle of Fireball whisky he'd set next to the sleeping bag. A collapsible sink in the corner of the tent to make her laugh. She'd remember it all.

When Easton ducked back in the tent, River was seated on the sleeping bag with the bottle open.

"What's the risk of furry animals interrupting us, deep

crevasses swallowing us, or freezing cold weather taking us by surprise?" She poured him a shot into the tin cup.

"The cold front passed, or I wouldn't have you out here," he murmured, running a thumb over the top of her injured foot as he sat next to her on the bedding.

"Don't want to lose any more digits?" She waggled her fingers at him playfully. His hand slid up her leg, briefly squeezing her knee before he accepted the drink.

"Trust me, the only interruptions we're getting are the ones we decide for ourselves." Easton swallowed the liquor, then slipped his arm around her, drawing her down to lie with him. "River, this doesn't have to be anything. No pressure. But we started out beneath the stars and I thought..."

He drifted off.

"I know," River whispered. "It's a good thought. You should keep thinking it because I'm thinking it too."

"I don't want to say goodbye," he told her. "But since we have to..."

"Might as well make it good?" River gazed at him, chest rising and falling as she breathed deeply, drinking in the air and Alaska and *him*. He murmured his agreement, eyes drifting.

"I'm up here," she teased him, even though she didn't mind one bit. She wanted to see that smile again.

"You're everywhere," Easton rumbled softly, dipping his mouth to her ear. "You've completely taken me over."

River knew exactly what he meant, but she didn't have the right to say it, not when she was the one leaving. Instead, she whispered she loved him, pulling him to her. The alcohol lingered on her tongue, sweetness and fire as his hands traced a different fire over her skin.

"Are you sure?" River asked Easton, because she had absolutely no doubts. And when he repeated what he'd said on the summit of Mount Veil again, voice rough with unapologetic emotion, that was all the answer River needed.

As he reached for her in the firelight, River closed her eyes and let him sweep her away.

CHAPTER 21

GETTING ON THE PLANE IN Anchorage was the hardest thing River had ever done in her life. Even harder than the day she stuffed her things into her car and moved to LA.

The airport in Alaska wasn't LAX. Anchorage was small, busy but cozy. Filled with the smells of cinnamon rolls and hot dogs, the low murmur of people talking, the scent of cortado coffee, and vacations of a lifetime. LAX was simply noise. Once, she had loved this. The bustle and the energy had been a drug to her younger self. A part of her still did love it, but River had seen the other side now.

Coming home didn't feel like home. It hadn't for a long time.

The plane ride hadn't been horribly long, but with every mile it took her away from Moose Springs, her heart had fought her. And she'd made the right decision...that town was Easton's home, not hers. But she missed him terribly.

As she made her way toward baggage claim, River was so lost in thought about the man she'd left behind, she forgot that her face had been on the television a lot more recently. She should have worn a hat of some sort, or maybe a hoodie, if she hadn't wanted to be recognized.

"Excuse me. Are you River Lane?"

Darn it. River turned to give a polite wave to the woman who had said her name, but she found herself looking down at a child instead. The young girl in front of her had pigtails and the shiest, sweetest look on her face. Behind her, the girl's mother stood with her phone, videoing her. Instead of giving an excuse or asking that the camera be turned off, River knelt so she was face-to-face with the child.

"Hello," she said, smiling encouragingly. "What's your name?"

"Jacie."

"Jacie wants to be an actress," her hovering mother supplied.

"Do you?" Did she? Or did Jacie's mother want her to be an actress? The child seemed so shy. But she was also beautiful like her mother. River tugged the ear of Jacie's toy moose. "I like your moose. I saw some in Alaska."

The child's wide, toothy beam was the first thing to make River feel better since she'd gotten up that morning and gotten on her plane. "I want to be a moose."

"Well, Jacie, I want you to know that you are amazing. You're smart and you're strong, and you can be anything. An actress, an adventurer, a cowgirl. Anything you want."

"Even a moose?"

"Even a moose." River shared a chuckle with the girl's mother.

Without warning, Jacie hugged her. Until that moment, River hadn't realized how badly she needed a hug. While the mother took pictures and they both thanked her, River used every single trick in the book to hold it together. Then she walked calmly to the bathroom, locked the stall door behind her, and burst into tears.

When someone asked if she was okay through the stall divider, River mumbled, "I'm fine. Bad breakup."

"Oh, I've been there." The stranger in the next stall told her over the sound of tinkling. "Have yourself a good cry and then go drink them away. I've never met a person who wasn't two shots of tequila away from a bad memory. In fact..." A bottle appeared under the door. "Here. Start now."

Startled, River scooted away from the uninvited hand in her stall. "Oh. Umm, I couldn't."

The bottle waggled at her. "It's no bother, I have plenty. Drink him away, darling."

When one is faced with the option of drinking the bathroom tequila or not drinking the bathroom tequila, one...well... shouldn't. But screw it. She'd survived Mount Veil. She'd survived leaving Easton. She could survive anything.

As always, the freeways in LA were packed, so River had plenty of time to miss her mountain man as her rideshare driver drove her to the studio in Hollywood where her friends were already editing their documentary. When she reached the studio, River knocked before sticking her head in the door.

"Am I interrupting?" she asked playfully.

Only one of the two figures inside turned around from their laptops, but when Bree jumped up, coming over to her, Jessie at least pulled off his headset and waved his hand absently.

Bree hugged her tight. "River, there you are. Jessie and I had a bet on whether you would actually leave."

"How are you feeling?" River asked, fighting through the sadness Bree's comment caused.

"My ribs are still sore, but I'm tough."

"That you are. How's the whiner?"

"The whiner is currently busy editing your cluster of a documentary." Jessie swiveled around in his seat. "Okay, we lost a lot of footage when we lost the second camera, but we had enough backed up that it isn't too bad. The best stuff was on the handheld anyway. Check this out. It's only an early mock-up, but I think it has potential."

River sat in Bree's vacated chair, taking Jessie's headset as she watched his laptop.

At first, it was exactly what she'd wanted. Exactly what she'd expected from two people as amazing at their jobs as they were. But the longer she watched, the more River started to shift uncomfortably in her seat. Her jaw clenched as she finally hit pause.

"No." Absolutely not.

Bree looked at her. "What's wrong with it?"

"You keep showing us together." River shook her head. "The focus of this is all wrong."

Bree and Jessie shared a look.

"Listen, River, we need to talk. When we were up there, we kind of..." Jessie hesitated, searching for the right word. "Documented."

"Of course you documented. That's what you do on a documentary, as you love to remind me."

"Yes," Jessie agreed. "But we documented *everything*."

Bree put a hand to her ribs, wincing as she leaned into the back of River's seat. "Show her what we were looking at earlier."

At Bree's suggestion, Jessie twisted around and clicked on

his keyboard, pulling up a new file. The computer screen was large enough that there was no pretending what she was looking at wasn't her and Easton, sitting hip to hip at camp, his hand cupping her cheek as he kissed her. The handheld camera filming the moment bobbled slightly, then zoomed in on River taking his hand and tugging Easton to his feet, leading him toward the tent.

"Why are you showing me this?" she asked quietly.

It was beyond cruel.

"Because we thought we were going up there to film about Moose Springs. But every shot, every scene, there's this stuff." Jessie pulled up another file, snow blindingly white as they stood high on the southern face of Mount Veil. Easton's arm around her waist as she took in the vista. Then another file, with River yelling at him for putting himself at risk in the Veil and Easton growling right back.

"It's you and him." Jessie shrugged. "Everywhere, every scene. This is a real-life love story, River."

She shook her head in a curt gesture. "Love stories have happy endings. I hate to break it to you, but I'm here, and he's back in Moose Springs. Whatever you're trying to spin this as, it isn't real. And the Alaskan Tourism Board won't care that he and I had a fling. They care about bringing more visitors to Moose Springs."

"Actually, it's the most real you've ever been. Look at him, watching you do your interview. He can't take his eyes off you. And you fronted the bill on this. Your only contracts right now are with us. No one's successfully made a film about Moose Springs. Maybe you're one more."

"And the alternate option is?" River really didn't like where this was going.

"We turn this into the indie film it deserves to be." Jessie rarely sounded this calm when discussing his work, which meant he was trying to sell her on what he wanted. By the look of excitement on Bree's face, River knew he wasn't the only one.

Bree leaned forward and clicked to another file, labeled "summit." Easton had placed the camera down and joined her on the very peak of the mountain.

"What did he say?" Bree pressed. "Up on the summit? We can't get the audio."

River's fingers flexed at her side. "I can't tell you. I don't think it would be right."

"But, River—"

"No." Closing her eyes, River tried to compose herself. "Okay, you're right. It was real. And now it's gone. It's done. What Easton and I had was one of the best things I've ever known in my life, and I won't let you make this into some sort of sideshow. I can't do this to him. Let's stick to the original plan."

Jessie wasn't ready to give up the fight. "You realize the kind of film we're looking at here could be huge, right? We could turn this over to the tourism board and cash a measly paycheck, or we could turn it into the documentary it deserves to be. This could turn your career around, River."

"The answer is no. Trust me, if Easton were here, he'd agree with me."

As she left the studio, River knew that whatever they'd had, it was going to stay on that mountain. She cared about him way too much to exploit him, even if it didn't get them anywhere professionally.

And if it tanked her filming career before it even started? Well, that was a risk River was willing to take.

The problem with being in a small town was everyone knew when you'd gotten your heart broken. When he found out they'd even started a thread about him in the town chat room, labeling sad Easton sightings, he seriously considered going back out and finding the marmot. It understood his pain.

For a man as private as Easton, being the topic of interest particularly sucked.

It didn't help that everywhere he went had been touched by her in some fashion. His house. Places around town. He couldn't even turn on the highway without seeing her walking down it, suitcase of rocks in hand, those brilliant blue eyes challenging him for stopping to help. Even his favorite coffee shop had been ruined.

He couldn't remember how she'd ordered her coffee that day they'd done the gear check. He'd gone for a cup after failing to successfully return to his routine without her. For some reason, Easton was so upset by his inability to recall the proper combination, he almost crushed the offending drink in his hand. Instead, he sat on a bench outside, looking at the park where she'd handed him the worst coffee he'd ever tasted.

Damn, he missed her.

"May I join you?"

Easton's jaw twitched, but he kept his tone controlled. It wasn't Tasha's fault his heart was thousands of miles away. "I'm not commenting on the climb, Tasha. Or on River."

He didn't need to, not with her face plastered on every television station he turned to. More than a few regional papers had reached out for interviews, but Easton had nothing to say to any of them. There *was* nothing to say. It was done. She was gone.

End of story.

Tasha sat next to him, her pen and notepad in her purse. Once, he'd enjoyed her presence. Now, it reminded him that the one he wanted, the right one, wasn't there.

"Do you want to talk about it?" Tasha asked quietly, taking a sip of her coffee. "Off the record?"

He snorted. "What's the angle?"

"We're still friends, Easton," she reminded him. "I'm capable of caring and listening without a recorder in my hands."

Sighing, he leaned forward, elbows on his knees. "There's nothing to talk about."

She waited, and when Easton didn't continue, Tasha nodded. "You know, I thought I loved you once. I even thought you might have loved me. But then I saw you and River together after we talked last time, and I knew what we had wasn't even close. It was nothing compared to the way you looked at her. And I'm okay with that. I'm just worried about you." Taking his hand, Tasha squeezed it. "You look like someone hit you with a truck."

He felt it too.

"It doesn't matter," Easton finally said. "River left because her life isn't here. She was only here to film a documentary that I screwed up for her. It was my job to keep her safe, to get her to the summit and back down again. Instead, they lost half their footage, and all three of them ended up in the hospital. She never did complete the climb down. I'm not real sure how to make that up to her."

Tasha nodded. "Easton...you don't run a diner for a living—"

"Thank goodness. Thirty minutes of that was more than enough for me."

She smiled. "You don't run a diner. You don't write articles for a paper. You climb mountains. The tallest, most dangerous mountains. And just because your record is so good doesn't mean that there won't be climbs that go wrong."

When he started to interject, Tasha squeezed his hand again. "The difference is, you're in love with your client. As someone whose been lucky enough to get close to you, I know how deeply you care about the people you love. It was never me, but it is River. If you're trying to find some way to process losing her, beating yourself up over a tough climb isn't it. You did your job. The rest of it...got messy."

Taking a final sip of her coffee, she added, "Sometimes messy is the best part. Sometimes it's worth it. You always were for me. I'm betting you were for River too."

When Easton didn't answer, Tasha left him to drink his coffee alone, but her words stayed with him. The climbing season was over, meaning Easton should have been focused on scheduling his off-season work. Guided alpine climbs were his bread and butter, but teaching people to climb these mountains, even indoor climbing, was what Easton excelled at. He could have helped Ash or bothered Graham at the diner. Instead, he stayed in the woods the rest of the day, taking refuge from prying eyes as he tracked the local wildlife to practice his skills. He wandered into town on foot and eventually found himself at Rick's, on a stool toward the end of the bar.

As Easton sat nursing a beer in between his hands at the pool hall, he didn't look at the mirror behind Rick's shoulder. He wasn't interested in seeing the loss in his eyes or the fact that he could use a shower and some fresh clothes.

"You know, most guys your size nurse getting their guts ripped out in the solitude of their own homes. You're scaring off all Rick's customers with your death face."

Easton didn't look up at Graham's voice. "My death face?"

Ash dropped down in the seat on his other side. "That's his clever way of saying you look terrible. Whew, you're ripe smelling. Rick, how many has he had?"

The pool hall owner tilted his head toward the fridge, where he kept the supply of bottled beer. "I haven't been counting. He's so big and takes so long to drink them, he might as well be drinking water."

"Two whole sentences in a row. See that, East? Even Rick here is worried about you."

Easton refused to rise to Graham's baiting.

"I think it's time we switch to hard liquor," a third voice decided. Easton had never been as close with Jackson Shaw as Graham, but they'd spent enough time together socially that he wasn't surprised by Jax's presence.

Finally looking up from his beer, Easton frowned at them. "What is this, an intervention?"

"Figured you could do with a reminder you aren't alone, buddy." Graham clamped a hand down on Easton's shoulder as Jake pressed tight to Easton's leg. "L, the first round is on you."

"Of course," a feminine voice said kindly.

When Easton turned in his seat, he saw Lana standing behind him. Lana gave him a sad look, then she hugged him, all but disappearing in his arms when he hugged her back.

"I'm so sorry, Easton." Lana's arms tightened around him. "If there's anything I can do, tell me."

There was nothing anyone could do to fill the gaping wound in his chest where his heart used to be. But Easton was a pack animal and always had been. He took comfort from having the people who mattered surrounding him.

The only problem was his mate was gone, and...well...wolves mated for life.

"A real drink would be good," he told her. "Fireball whisky."

Because even if he was going to drink, he might as well lose himself in River the only way he had left.

The rest of the night passed in a blur of shots and voices. He drank until he was numb, and then he drank more. Finally, when it was determined he'd had enough, Easton and his empty bottle of Fireball parted ways.

"We keep sayin' goodbye, whisky," he told her softly, wondering if somewhere she was drinking him away more successfully than he was her.

Well and truly drunk, it took Rick and Graham both to pour him into the passenger seat of Graham's truck while Ash, Zoey, and Jax hopped in the back seat. Lana pressed a kiss to his cheek before closing the door, standing back with her arm around Rick's waist. Another day, he'd be embarrassed at being three sheets to the wind in front of them, but...well...he was far too drunk to care.

"You okay up there?" Ash asked him from her seat behind his, idly tugging on the seat belt they'd strapped around him.

"Nope." He closed his eyes against the spinning of the world. "Wish she coulda been more like Z-Bear. Or the marmot. The marmot was all in. Shoulda been a marmot."

"Does anyone understand the marmot stuff?" Ash asked.

"River said what happened on the mountain stayed on the mountain, especially the marmot stuff." When Graham groaned, Zoey asked, "What?"

"You said the 'R' word," Graham reminded her.

"S'okay, Z-Bear." At some point, Easton had started calling Zoey that, but he couldn't remember why.

Settling Jake on her lap in the back seat, Zoey corrected him, "I didn't stay for Graham."

Graham made a playful, wounded noise as he started the truck. "You're damaging my masculine pride here, Z-Bear," he teased.

"Hush, only Easton's allowed to call me that. And I didn't. I stayed for me, because this was where my heart was. You have to follow your heart if you want to find happiness. Graham being here was the icing on the cake."

"Or the icing on the cinnamon roll. I know the way to your heart, Zo." They shared a smile through the rearview mirror.

"Aww." Jax almost managed to sound like he meant it. "You two are adorable. Disgusting but adorable."

"Why are you in here again?" Ash drawled to the third person in the back seat. Having gone shot for shot with Easton most of the night, Jax was almost as drunk as Easton was. He assumed anyway. With all the spinning, it was hard to tell.

Jackson leaned his arms on the front seat between Graham's shoulder and Easton's slumping face. "Because he's too heavy for even you fabulous females to carry back in the house. East deserves better than being dragged through the dirt by the arms."

"Whisky dragged me. By my arms." Sighing, he slumped in his seat. "She was so pretty."

"Sorry, buddy." Graham gave him a sympathetic pat on the head. "When you fall in love with that kind of woman, she's going to be a pain in the ass to get over."

"I get it. Some women are worth the torment." Jax turned to Ash, giving her a puppy dog look and earning the most brutal of eye rolls.

"The answer will always be no, Jax," Ash said. "Especially when you're drunk."

When they pulled up to Easton's house, Graham killed the engine. Apparently, the party wasn't finished yet, because they all followed suit when Easton opened the passenger door.

He stumbled out, with Ash scooting after him. She ducked under his arm. "Oof, you're not lighter than you look."

"I can walk."

"Are you sure about that?"

So many of them, their voices were starting to merge together in one lump of annoyingness.

"What the hell?" he grumped as he tried to get his balance. "You poisoned me."

"No, we got you roaring drunk." Graham took him from Ash. "Which helps, trust me. River ripped your guts out, but when you're throwing them up tomorrow morning, you won't feel it so bad. And if you do, we'll do this again."

"You're encouraging me to become an alcoholic."

Even Easton knew he was slurring so badly, they couldn't understand him. But Ash squeezed him into a hug because she might not be able to understand him, but she always understood him.

Graham helped him into the house, dropping Easton down on a couch River had slept on.

"She liked my towels," Easton told them woefully. "I don't know why, but she really liked my towels."

"I know, buddy. I know." And because he wasn't a good responsible friend but a best friend who threw caution to the wind, Graham plopped down on the opposite side of the couch with a fresh six-pack of beers. He handed Easton one.

"I kicked everyone else out, and Zoey's watching some show in the bedroom with Jake." Graham twisted the cap off his bottle. "You want to talk about her?"

"No." Because talking meant acknowledging she was never coming back.

"You want to tell me about the marmot?"

"Okay."

It'd been a long night. Easton didn't remember what he'd said or done, but he knew he was grateful for the nice bush he was throwing up into, situated so conveniently off the front porch. He didn't even know how he'd ended up on the porch. The last thing he remembered was walking into Rick's.

"Never should've drank that much."

"Nah, probably not. Rick and Lana brought your truck home for you after they closed last night." Graham pushed an oversized water bottle at him. "Here. Drink something better for you."

"Why are you still here?" Easton asked miserably.

"Making sure good intentions don't turn into vomit aspiration. Plus, what kind of friend would I be if I wasn't here to help you greet the sun? How do you feel?"

"Like I know better than to drink until my liver explodes."

Graham folded his arms behind his head. "You know what your problem is? You always do what you should. You're a rule follower. If there's a sign that says to go left, you're going to go left, even if you know you should go right."

Aiming a glare his way did nothing to curb the smirk on Graham's face.

"Listen, man. I'm not judging here. You play by the rules because you like to do what's right. You're a good person, better than I am."

Easton took a long drink from the water bottle, paused, then drained the rest. "Agreed."

"Aww, that wasn't nice. True but not nice. But after watching you eat your heart out over her, what I'm wondering is, River... What is she worth to you? Really worth?" Graham's voice quieted, his tone serious. "There's a woman sleeping in your room right now who I would die for. I wouldn't even think twice. Zoey's it, man. She's the one. So who's River? Is she the woman we're going to drink off the next couple of months? Or is she more? Because if she's more..."

"Then what?"

"Then what are you *doing* here? If Zoey was back serving tables at her truck stop in Chicago, you can bet my ass would be sitting in her section, drinking coffee until my bladder gave out. Because that's where the love of my life was."

"You're saying I what? Hop on a plane and fly to Los Angeles? What am I going to do there? It's not me."

"You can live without her, East. I'm just saying, if you don't have to, then don't. I don't know River very well, but if you love her, put on your big boy pants and do something about it."

"That was the worst pep talk ever," Easton grumped.

Graham offered, "I could go get another six-pack."

"Hard pass."

Eventually, Graham had to open the diner. He offered to take Easton with him, but Easton chose instead to stay where he was. Easton didn't know what he wanted or what to do, but he knew the Tourist Trap only held strangers, not answers.

Staring at the phone in his hand, he tried to decide if he should call her. The break had been clean, like ripping a bandage off a wound. Maybe that was what River needed from him? Or maybe she was sitting somewhere, thousands of miles away, wondering why he never bothered to text or call.

When a car rolled up his drive, Easton frowned. He recognized the sticker on the windshield identifying it as a rental car, but he wasn't expecting anyone. Definitely not expecting Jessie to park and get out of the car, laptop in hand.

Rising to his feet, Easton met his previous client in the driveway. Jessie gave him a rueful look. "Wow, you've looked better."

"Long night," he grunted as they shook hands, then Jessie pulled him in for a brief hug.

"River took up all your time when we were here. I never got a chance to thank you for getting me off that mountain."

Easton blinked, not at all expecting the hug or the comment.

Jessie added, "I figured you'd be here, smelling like booze. Damn, you had it bad for her. It's almost embarrassing, man."

Easton snorted. "You flew all this way to tell me that?"

"Nope. I came here to show you something." Jessie walked over to the porch and sat, opening his laptop. "This is all our hard work. It's not done. We still have a lot to do, but I think you can tell what we're getting at here. There are two versions of this. One is the Moose Springs focused story, which is good. River's great at what she does, and Bree's audio was phenomenal. The tourism board will love it."

"But?"

"But this is better."

Then Jessie turned the laptop Easton's way. He sat down and watched. Maybe he shouldn't have. With every scene, Jessie reached deeper into his chest, finding the remaining shreds of his heart to pull out with brutally effective fingertips.

Still, he had to smile. Watching River and Bree hook arms and laugh together at how horrifying his barn was. Watching Jessie up in a tree, yelling shrilly because of a bear. Ben's constant grin, no matter how hard the day's climb. Even watching the marmot shuffling off after saying goodbye to Easton, turning back to look longingly over its furry shoulder every few feet to overly dramatic breakup music. River whispering into the camera, alone on the mountaintop, about how much she cared about her friends.

Despite losing so much of their footage on the mountainside, what they had put together was...powerful. It might have been the best film he'd ever seen.

"This town is going to be overrun," he finally said with a grunt.

"Not necessarily. This isn't the film River approved. It's the better one, but River told us no. She's determined to preserve your privacy, and she won't let us edit this in a way that showcases what really happened on that mountain."

"Looks to me like you did it anyway."

Jessie shrugged. "River's footing the bill. She'll get final say on what gets put out there. But you need to know, this is the kind of thing that doesn't just happen. This is...special. And if it's received the way I think it will be received, she'll be the new rock star of the industry. We all will. Careers are cemented by this kind of film. "She won't do anything to sacrifice your privacy or destroy your trust." Jessie looked seriously at Easton. "This is up to you."

For a long time, Easton sat there, thinking about it. Then finally, he nodded. "If this is what will help her, and if River agrees to it, then do it."

"Are you sure?" Jessie seemed to need stronger confirmation. "She's not wrong that pulling this trigger could affect your life. The media will find you, no matter where you are."

"I've got a nice big backyard to go hide in if people get too annoying," Easton reminded him, jutting his chin toward the mountains beyond.

"True," Jessie admitted.

They sat quietly for a few moments, then Jessie exhaled a tight breath. "When I went through the Veil, I came out a different man. And not for the better. It's not fun to get a good look at yourself and realize you aren't half as brave as you want to be."

Taking a sip of his water, Easton grunted. "It's not about being brave. Either it's in your blood or it isn't."

"It's in hers. I've known River a long time, and this was the happiest I've ever seen her. This was the life she was meant to have. Too bad she got sucked into being the next biggest film producer in the industry." Jessie stood, laptop still open in his hands. "It's a tough life."

Maybe. Or maybe a life didn't have to be one thing or another. "Hey, Jessie. Where in LA is she?"

"River? I figured she would have told you." Jessie shook his head. "She decided it was time to move back home. She'll still fly out for work when she gets her next job, but our girl's in Wyoming now."

"Why?"

"When you lose the love of your life, what else do you do? You go home." Jessie waggled the laptop at Easton, where it had paused on them at the summit. "Hey, out of sheer curiosity, what did you say to her up there?"

He didn't have to answer him, but Easton was done fighting this. Heading for his truck, Easton replied over his shoulder, "I told her I'd love her with every last breath I take."

"Cool." Jessie nodded, satisfied. "Can I add that in subtitles?"

Easton climbed in his truck. "No."

"Are you sure?"

He slammed the door shut, then rolled down his window with the manual crank, saying to Jessie, "Never been so sure of anything in my life."

Riding a horse was like riding a bike. Only riding a bike didn't make every muscle in River's body hurt after only four hours.

At her family's ranch, it wasn't unusual to spend all day in the saddle, it was expected. If River still had a tailbone or skin left on her inner knees by the time she managed to get done with her day's work, it would be a miracle. They'd named her horse Ticktock, claiming it was only a matter of time before the dun gelding decided to toss her in the dirt, but other than a few sidesteps and one pointed snort of annoyance, Ticktock had behaved himself.

As for River, the only thing close to climbing was riding. Even if she couldn't sit down tonight, she was exactly where she wanted to be.

A whistle pulled her attention. Her father's foreman pointed toward the circular drive in front of the barn, bringing all the ranch hands' eyes to where he was looking. Her father turned his roan mare toward the road, causing Ticktock to sidestep as the foreman trotted up to them.

"That's one big son of a bitch. Boss, you expecting company?"

In a group of men this tough, it took someone special to make them all sit up straighter. Settling her mount before twisting in the saddle, River saw the person who had caught their attention. She felt her jaw loosen in shock.

"You're kidding me."

Preston Lane—her father—raised an eyebrow. "You know him, honey?"

"That's Easton."

Her father chuckled. "Well, boys, I guess that's an Easton."

"What the hell is an Easton?" the foreman asked.

Her father shook his head. "You'll have to ask JD. She's the one he's here for, not me."

Leaving them to their teasing, River turned Ticktock and trotted to the fence Easton was leaning on. Heart in her throat as she reined in, River couldn't help reaching out her hand for his to make sure he was real. Large, callused fingers closed around hers.

"You're in Wyoming."

Those kind brown eyes gazed up at her.

"*You're* in Wyoming," Easton said in his quiet rumble. "Didn't make sense to be anywhere else."

The bag slung over his shoulder wasn't enough to pack an entire life in, but it was big enough to pack a week's worth of clothes and a heart bigger than the man in front of her. His courage for showing up there left her breath caught in her lungs.

She'd missed him so much.

"I earn most of my money guiding climbs in the summer back home." He cleared his throat. "Can't leave my dad alone at Christmas. As for the rest of it, I figured wherever you were at seemed a whole lot better than missing you alone."

River's face hurt from the smile splitting it. "Christmas in Moose Springs?"

"It gets interesting." His beard flashed her a quick grin.

"Will they want me there?"

"*I* want you there. And if you make that movie the way it deserves instead of for the Alaskan Tourism Board, they'll like you a whole lot more."

"The Old Man's about to become a lot more popular. People are going to want to find their own adventure up there. Maybe even fall in love with their own mountain man. Think you can handle it?"

"As long as they know I'm spoken for."

"The marmot?" River teased.

"I figured I'd see how this went first, ma'am."

They shared a smile, and in that moment, River knew she'd found her home. Wyoming, Alaska, it didn't matter. Home was where Easton was.

"Ma'am me like you mean it, big guy. Kiss me too, since you came all this way."

With a sigh of relief, he ducked the fence. It occurred to her that he hadn't been sure of his welcome, but Easton would always be welcome in River's life. Always. Leaning down off the side of Ticktock, River pressed her lips to his.

And up until the damn horse tossed her off and stepped on Easton's foot, breaking two of his toes, it was the best kiss ever.

No one made a movie very quickly. By the time River's documentary was finished, simple as it was, they'd agreed to a new routine. Summers and Christmas in Moose Springs with his family. Winters and Thanksgiving in Wyoming with hers. Trips to LA as she negotiated her next film. Utah and Toronto to promote the documentary, with a few overseas excursions in the mix.

No matter where they went, no matter what they did, they always found something worth climbing. And in the rare places they couldn't, they had all they needed in each other, with River climbing into his arms.

Easton had never been happier.

Her father had found Easton a horse that would fit him, but the mare tended to give him disappointed looks every time he saddled her up. So he trailered Chance down to Wyoming instead. The mountains around the ranch weren't his own, but the local ranchers quickly learned how skilled of a tracker Easton was. Soon, he was the first one they called when they needed a stray tracked or a mountain lion run off from the herd. And when the work on the ranch was done, Easton and River would slip away together, heading up the mountains as high as they could go without taxing their mounts.

"So, what do you think?" River asked him randomly as they settled in on a rock ledge together. Ticktock and Chance were tied off a hundred feet below, along with both their boots.

This time, River had remembered her chalk and climbing shoes.

"What do I think about you?"

She should already know. He'd spent all morning and half the night before showing her that she was the perfect woman for him, that she was everything he'd never known he wanted and absolutely all he would ever need.

"About here. Wyoming." Her eyes sparkled as she shot him a grin. "And yes, about me too."

Easton wrapped his arm around her shoulders, pulling her into him. "I think they're all down there watching your movie. We should probably join them."

"I'm not sure I have the ability to sit through two hours of them teasing us for acting like lovesick teenagers on a mountaintop."

True. Besides, he didn't need to watch them falling in love. He'd been there. Every single moment with her was etched in his heart, and he'd never forget it. But there were more mountains to climb together, more adventures to be had. Easton had never been the type to dwell on the past. They had their whole lives ahead of them.

"Easton? They finalized the schedule of my next film." Jessie had been right; they were clamoring for River to produce now. She had more job offers than she could possibly take. "I'm supposed to wrap up filming by April. In May...how would you feel about not taking a group up the Old Man and going with me to Nepal instead?"

Desire burned in his veins. Looking at her, knowing she knew him the way no one else ever would, Easton had never been so glad he'd pulled over to ask a woman if she needed a ride. "You want to climb Everest?"

"I want both of us to climb Everest. I think we can do it."

He had always been a man of few words. But as the sun dipped below the mountaintop, bathing them in soft reds and pale gold, Easton took her hand in his, squeezing it tight.

Together they could do anything.

ACKNOWLEDGMENTS

Sometimes a book is the book of your heart. The one you don't just want to write but *have* to write. *Enjoy the View* is that book for me.

I love the outdoors, and I love Alaska, so a mountain climbing story set outside Moose Springs was a dream project. Easton, in all his man-bunned glory. River, determined to find her best, happiest self. I pored over this book, fretted over this book, cried a few times, and definitely wrung my hands over it. It was the story I wanted to tell, but it was such a troublemaker! In the end, I'm so proud of these two characters and their love story.

When I was twenty, I threw all my stuff into the back of my car and moved to Los Angeles. Was it easy? No. Was it a little crazy? Yes. But it was the start of a life I have loved and would never have seen coming. I like that River and I have similar backgrounds, and I wanted her to find her happily ever after so badly. I wanted her to keep searching until her dreams came true. And when she finally sits on the mountainside with Easton, hand in hand and at peace, it gives me a sense of peace, too.

You don't always know where you'll end up in life. All that matters is that you're next to the right person for the journey.

Thank you to Cat Clyne, Mary Altman, and Christa Désir for your incredible editing. You three made this story come alive in a way I never could have alone. Cat, thank you for not minding every time I said "let me tweak one more thing!" and for letting me go full in on the marmot scenes. Thank you for wanting these stories...you changed my life in all the best ways.

Thank you to my agent, Sara Megibow, for everything you do. Also for the idea of the marmot in the first place...you're a genius. Thank you to Stefani Sloma, Sarah Otterness, and the entire Sourcebooks Casablanca team for all your hard work, every single day. Thank you for embracing my quirky little town of Moose Springs and letting me have so much fun writing happily ever afters for the people there.

To my critique partners, C.R. and Christina, thank you for putting up with all the revisions on this manuscript. Laurel, thank you for being a constant, incredible support for these stories. Leigh, as always, thank you for your friendship and your awesome attention to detail. Also, thank you to Chuck Heh for the climbing info. (Any and all mistakes are mine.) Endless gratitude to my Golden Heart sisters for being there through thick and thin. You are a daily joy in my life.

Thank you to my wonderful family for supporting me through the adventure of Moose Springs, especially to my husband, Kenney. Thank you for your love, your hugs, and your endless enthusiasm. These books are only here because of you. Everyday I know I'm next to the right person for the journey.

Last but never least... God, thanks for letting me be a writer. It's the best job ever.

Kyle, this one was for you. I love you, kid.

ABOUT THE AUTHOR

Geologist and lifelong science nerd Sarah Morgenthaler is a passionate supporter of chocolate chip cookies, geeking out over rocks, and playing with her rescue pit bull, Sammy. When not writing contemporary romance and romantic comedy set in far-off places, Sarah can be found traveling with her husband, hiking national parks, and enjoying her own happily ever after. Sarah is the author of the Moose Springs, Alaska, series, including the *Publishers Weekly* starred novel *The Tourist Attraction.*

BOYFRIEND MATERIAL

Wanted: One (fake) boyfriend, practically perfect in every way.

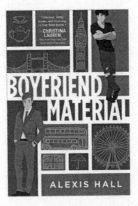

Luc O'Donnell is tangentially—and reluctantly—famous. Now he's back in the public eye, and one compromising photo is enough to ruin everything. To clean up his image, Luc has to find a nice, normal relationship...and Oliver Blackwood is as nice and normal as they come. In other words: perfect boyfriend material. Unfortunately, apart from being gay, single, and really, really in need of a date for a big event, Luc and Oliver have nothing in common. So they strike a deal to be publicity-friendly (fake) boyfriends until the dust has settled. Then they can go their separate ways and pretend it never happened.

But the thing about fake dating is that it can feel a lot like real dating. And that's when you get used to someone. Start falling for them. Don't ever want to let them go.

"I LOVE THIS BOOK."

—Christina Lauren, *New York Times* and *USA TODAY* bestselling author

For more info about Sourcebooks's books and authors, visit:
sourcebooks.com

MOOSE SPRINGS, ALASKA

Welcome to Moose Springs, Alaska, a small town with a big heart, and the only world-class resort where black bears hang out to look at *you*.

Sarah Morgenthaler

The Tourist Attraction

There's a line carved into the dirt between the tiny town of Moose Springs, Alaska, and the luxury resort up the mountain. Until tourist Zoey Caldwell came to town, Graham Barnett knew better than to cross it. But when Graham and Zoey's worlds collide, not even the neighborhood moose can hold them back...

Mistletoe and Mr. Right

She's Rick Harding's dream girl. Unfortunately, socialite Lana Montgomery has angered locals with her good intentions. When a rare (and spiteful) white moose starts destroying the holiday decorations every night, Lana, Rick, and all of Moose Springs must work together to save Christmas, the town...and each other.

Enjoy the View

Hollywood starlet River Lane is struggling to remake herself as a documentary filmmaker. When mountaineer and staunch Moose Springs local Easton Lockett takes River and her film crew into the wild...what could possibly go wrong?

"A unique voice and a grumptastic hero! I'm sold."

—*Sarina Bowen, USA Today* bestselling author

For more info about Sourcebooks's books and authors, visit:

sourcebooks.com

THE KISSING GAME

"I bet you a kiss you can't resist me."
Game on.

Rena Jackson has worked her tail off to open her own hair salon, and she's almost ready to quit her job at the local bar. Rena's also a diehard romantic, and she's had her eye on bar regular Axel Heller for a while. He's got that tall, brooding, and handsome thing going on big-time. Problem is, he's got that buttoned-up ice-man thing going as well. With Valentine's Day just around the corner, Rena's about ready to give up on Axel and find her own Mr. Right. But Axel has a plan of his own when he makes one crazy, desperate play to get her attention…

"Sexy, sweet, and thoroughly satisfying."

—Lauren Layne, *New York Times* bestselling author

For more info about Sourcebooks's
books and authors, visit:

sourcebooks.com

BAD BACHELOR

Everybody's talking about the hot new app reviewing New York's most eligible bachelors. But why focus on prince charming when you can read the latest dirt on the lowest-ranked "Bad Bachelors"—NYC's most notorious bad boys?

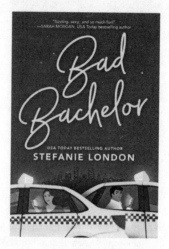

If one more person mentions the Bad Bachelors app to Reed McMahon, someone's gonna get hurt. A PR whiz, Reed is known as an "image fixer," but his womanizing ways have caught up with him. What he needs is a PR miracle of his own.

When Reed strolls into Darcy Greer's workplace offering to help save the struggling library, she isn't buying it. The prickly Brooklynite knows Reed is exactly the kind of guy she should avoid. But the library does need his help… As she reluctantly works with Reed, she realizes there's more to the man than his reputation. Maybe, just maybe, Bad Bachelor #1 is THE one for her.

"Original, witty, and sexy. My #1 romance read of the year!"

—Jennifer Blackwood, *USA Today* bestselling author